MELISSA TEREZE

First Edition April 2020
Published by GPC Publishing
Copyright © 2020 Melissa Tereze
ISBN: 9798629111610

Cover Design: Melissa Tereze
Editor: Charlie Knight

Find out more at: www.melissaterezeauthor.com
Follow me on Twitter: @MelissaTereze
Follow me on Instagram: @melissatereze_author

All rights reserved. This book is for your personal enjoyment only. This book or any portion thereof may not be reproduced or used in any manner without the express permission of the author.

This is a work of fiction. All characters & happenings in this publication are fictitious and any resemblance to real persons (living or dead), locales or events is purely coincidental.

ALSO BY MELISSA TEREZE

ANOTHER LOVE SERIES
THE ARRANGEMENT (BOOK ONE)
THE CALL (BOOK TWO)

THE ASHFORTH SERIES
PLAYING FOR HER HEART (BOOK ONE)
HOLDING HER HEART (BOOK TWO)

OTHER NOVELS
AT FIRST GLANCE

ALWAYS ALLIE

MRS MIDDLETON

BREAKING ROUTINE

IN HER ARMS

FOREVER YOURS

THE HEAT OF SUMMER

FORGET ME NOT

MORE THAN A FEELING

WHERE WE BELONG: LOVE RETURNS

NAKED

CO-WRITES
TEACH ME (WITH JOURDYN KELLY)

TITLES UNDER L.M CROFT (EROTICA)

Pieces of Me

You have the power to say, "This is not how my story will end."

;

CHAPTER ONE

Lydia's gaze settled on the horizon, her car coming to a stop in a parking space close to the railing edging the river. A vast expanse of murky brown water met a clouded sky, the pier quieter than Lydia had anticipated this evening. Quiet was precisely what she needed.

She allowed her head to fall back against the leather interior of her Jaguar. With the way she felt tonight, she wondered if she could afford this model anymore. She'd purchased it before she decided that she hated her boss. Her *new* boss.

Bree Stevens was a complete bitch. If it wasn't for the fact that the job was Lydia's dream position as marketing consultant, she would have walked away from *Strive* a month ago. Bree was everything Lydia loathed in a person. Her naturally aggressive tone meant that Lydia often didn't know where she stood with Bree, the sly smirk she permanently sported only confusing her further.

For someone in management, Bree couldn't manage a piss-up in a brewery. That woman held zero managerial skills, roaring around the office and expecting people to pay attention. Lydia was *so* over working under Bree that she had even turned down her usual Friday office drinks invitation. Lydia wanted her bed, nothing more.

She considered calling her best friend, Sophie, but her brain didn't hold the capacity for anymore drama tonight. Soph had spent the week complaining about her boyfriend not paying enough attention to her, but Lydia would give anything for some companionship of late. Even a one-night stand was potentially in the cards. Desperate times called for desperate measures.

"A one-night stand is only possible if you leave the house," Lydia mumbled to herself.

As the weeks passed, staying in was becoming more common than she would like. Truth be told, she spent ninety percent of her life inside her own head. At 33, she knew she really needed to get out more.

Lydia's hands-free shocked her, slim fingers instantly finding the call button on the steering wheel. "Yes?"

"Christ! You sound how I feel."

"Soph, hey."

"Another bad day with bitch-tits?"

"I don't know if it could get any worse."

"I've told you what to do! Super glue her arse to the office chair."

"Very mature."

"Eh, it's Friday. Maturity goes out of the window."

"Did you call for a particular reason?" Lydia's gaze fell to a woman standing at the railings. Nothing seemed right about her. Lydia's heart thundered. "Just...I was planning to head home."

"Will there be wine?"

"While I lie in the bath and contemplate my life, yes." Lydia focused on the body art of the woman by the river. Then the woman shuddered; she wasn't wearing a coat. "Crazy."

"What is?"

"Oh, nothing. Just at the river people-watching."

"So rock and roll."

"It's just been a shitty week, Soph."

"No, I know. I get that," Soph sighed. "Give me a ring tomorrow. We could do lunch."

Lydia watched the woman at the railings bend down and place what looked like her phone on the concrete. "Lunch sounds like a plan."

Something felt off. Lydia felt an unease growing inside her that she couldn't name. And then it dawned on her. The woman had one foot settled on a lower horizontal bar and...

Sheer panic tore through Lydia. "Oh, fuck! I have to go."

"Lyd?"

"Call you later." Lydia cut the call and sprung from her car, leaving her valuables on the passenger seat. Her long, black hair whipped around her face, the wind strengthening as darkness fell over the river like a blanket. The woman climbing over the railings shook, her back now to Lydia. Lydia approached carefully, aware that she should keep a respectable distance. "H-hi, excuse me. I think you dropped your phone."

"Don't need it." The woman's voice trembled. "Code is nine one nine eight. Wipe it and give it to someone else."

"I'm Lydia," she said. "Do you think maybe you could come back over this side of the railing and we can talk?"

"Nope."

"Can I at least get your name?"

"Ryann."

Lydia was thankful to get the tiniest piece of information. "Beautiful name."

"Look, I kinda have something I need to do."

Lydia shuffled closer, her heels not helping with her desire to be inconspicuous.

"Don't come any closer." Ryann glanced over her shoulder, Lydia catching her eyes for the first time.

"H-hi," she said again. Lydia didn't have anything else to offer. As she focused on Ryann, Lydia saw pain. Apprehension. While

Ryann had remarkably beautiful deep brown eyes, they shone with hurt. Ryann blinked slowly, her body appearing weak, and in the dim light Lydia realized her eyes were the colour of a fine Scotch whiskey. Intense, yet sad.

Lydia studied the intricate black and grey rose tattoo covering Ryann's entire shoulder, finishing low on her upper arm and wrapping around her tricep. The shading gave off a realistic feel, as though Lydia could reach out and stroke the petals. She followed Ryann's neckline, impressed by the mandala tattoo enveloping her throat, ending where her undercut finished up the back of her head.

This woman was intriguing.

When Lydia realised she was about to lose Ryann's attention, she started to panic. "I've just had a really shitty week at work."

Ryann looked out into the distance. "Me, too."

"You have an arsehole boss, too?"

"I am my boss," Ryann said with a scoff. "*Was* my boss."

"Did you maybe want to talk about it?"

Ryann fell silent.

"It seems like we could both use a friend tonight." Lydia reached the railings and looked down but immediately wished she hadn't. Her stomach lurched when she was met with a sheer drop. "Ryann, I'd really like you to come back over this side. If you sli—"

"I won't slip. I won't fall. When I step off here, I'll be perfectly fine in doing so."

Lydia didn't believe that for a moment. Ryann didn't appear to be certain of anything—least of all throwing herself into the river; she looked scared. Terrified. Lydia really needed to talk her down. She needed to believe she could.

"I really don't want you to do that." Lydia's voice broke, shocking both her and Ryann. She didn't know this woman; she had no reason for the emotion lodged in her throat. As Lydia glanced around, she realised Ryann was drawing in a crowd. "Ryann..."

"You should get out of here. It's Friday night. Be with your friends." Ryann held a rigid posture, her shoulder muscles flexed and tense.

"I don't want to do that. Unless you're planning on joining me."

"Me?" Ryann laughed, side-glancing Lydia's way. "Trust me, you don't want that."

"Why?"

Ryann squeezed her eyes shut, her entire body trembling. "The mood changes when I'm around lately."

"Perhaps other people are the issue. A new circle of friends never hurt anyone."

Ryann gripped the railings behind her tighter, frowning when she continued to stare at Lydia. She knew something had hit a nerve with Ryann, but she didn't appear angry. That could only be a bonus in this god-awful situation.

"I like to keep my circle small," Lydia explained. "I have no time for other people's drama. It's all about self-care. I mean, what use is it having people in your life if they don't enrich it in any way?"

"You're right."

Lydia's eyebrow rose. Was she getting through? "And if you do this tonight, I won't know if you should have been in my circle or not. Although to be honest, I already know you would be. You seem kinda cool."

"I'm not," Ryann stated, matter-of-factly. "I used to be. Once upon a time."

"And then you involved yourself with the wrong people. Happens to the best of us, Ry."

Ry? Lydia could have kicked herself. This woman had an effect on her she couldn't quite put her finger on. An effect she was willing to explore. Ryann—in terms of friendship—could be right up her street.

"I have a bottle of wine and a crate of beer back at home.

Before you go, I'd really love to share a drink with you. To get to know you."

Ryann suddenly turned around on the weatherworn, concrete ledge. Lydia's heart jumped into her throat. One wrong move and this cold, dark conversation would have been for nothing.

"Y-you're crying," Ryann said, studying every inch of Lydia's face. "Why?"

"Fear...of you doing something I really don't want you to do."

"You could have gone home, but you didn't," Ryann whimpered.

"No. I couldn't." Lydia noted the sheen of sweat on the skin of Ryann's chest.

"You have kind eyes..."

"I also have a kind heart. So, why don't you come over here and I'll help you through whatever you're dealing with tonight?"

"C-could you help me over?" Ryann asked, lowering her eyes to the floor when she spotted the growing crowd. "P-please?"

Lydia stepped closer, gripping Ryann's shirt and dragging her off the ledge and over the railings. They both fell to the ground with a thud, Ryann lying flat on her back and sobbing. Lydia sat back on her knees beside Ryann, taking one of her frozen hands. She reached for Ryann's phone on the floor and handed it over. "You want to get out of here?"

Ryann nodded slowly, shielding her face with her hands. "I want to get away from this lot. I'm sure one of them has called the police."

"Come on," Lydia said, helping her up. Both stood on shaky legs. "You can come back to mine and get warm before you decide what's next. Maybe we could go to the hospital?"

Ryann shoved her hands in the pockets of her jeans, unable to meet Lydia's eyes. "I could really go for that beer you mentioned."

Lydia decided not to push. Ryann needed a moment, that was clear from how her body shook. She needed someone to talk to, and a coat. Lydia could provide both. "I already have them chilling in the fridge."

The journey was quiet. Ryann felt like a fool and as the seconds passed, she suspected Lydia was beginning to regret her offer of a warm home. Ryann understood; she could be anyone. They may have talked briefly, but Lydia couldn't possibly know Ryann or what she was capable of.

They stopped outside a large detached house, a good twenty minutes from the city. Edwardian, perhaps Victorian, Ryann surmised; her grandparents had lived in something similar. Lydia didn't look like the type of woman who would live in something so old style, and she would be surprised if the interior matched the exterior. It surely wouldn't have the original features—not many did anymore. The engine cut out, Ryann's heart now situated in her throat.

Lydia twisted in her seat to face Ryann. "You okay?"

"Embarrassed."

"Don't be." Lydia offered Ryann an honest smile.

"Look, I understand that I scared you, but you don't need to invite me in. I can take the bus back."

"With no coat?"

"I'll be fine." Ryann wished everything was fine. The truth...it really wasn't. Her life was quickly crumbling around her. But it wasn't Lydia's problem.

"I don't really want to let you go home alone."

Home.

She didn't have one anymore.

"I'll be perfectly fine."

"Are we going to ignore the fact that thirty minutes ago you tried to jump into the river?"

"This isn't your problem. I'm very grateful for you talking me down, it was foolish, but you've done enough."

"Ryann—"

"Please, go and enjoy your Friday night." Ryann placed her hand on the passenger door handle. "I've taken up far too much of your time. I'm honestly not worth it."

"But, the beer—"

"It's probably not a good idea for me to drink alcohol."

"Tea? I make terrible tea, but I'll try to whip up something you won't choke on."

Lydia's beaming smile lit up her Jaguar, and for a moment, Ryann's life. This shouldn't have been her evening; Lydia was too kind.

Ryann wrinkled her nose. "You really don't mind?"

"I'd actually appreciate the company."

Ryann chose to take Lydia up on her kind gesture. All she'd wanted lately was someone she could talk to. Someone who would give Ryann the slightest glimmer of hope. Life had run smoothly until a year ago. If only she hadn't...Ryann forced herself not to go there. "Okay."

Within seconds, Lydia had closed the front door, kicked her shoes off, and slung her bag over the bannister. Ryann took in the décor; it *was* original. She was taken aback. The parquet flooring throughout the hallway had been kept in fantastic condition, and the ceiling architecture was impressive. Cornices edging the hall were accompanied by ceiling roses with striking lighting sitting in the middle. Many homes had the next best thing when it came to Victorian and Edwardian interior—usually plasterboard or polystyrene—but this was definitely the real thing.

"Great place." Ryann stood behind the front door, still not sure she felt welcome.

"Thanks. It's a lot to maintain but it's been passed down over the years."

"So, you living here with your folks?"

"Oh, no. They buggered off to Spain two years ago. Dad was made redundant. He took his pay-out, Mum retired, and they bought a place out there. I hate being here alone but I'm grateful to have a place without a mortgage."

"Wow."

"Dad just expects me to pay the bills and keep this place as fresh as I can."

"Your parents sound great."

"They really are." Lydia took a few steps further down the hallway, flicking a light on. "Wanna join me in the kitchen?"

Ryann bit her lip. "Sure, okay."

"Tea or coffee?" Lydia yelled from the next room.

"Well, since you didn't really sell the tea before, I'll go for the coffee."

"That's a wise decision. Have a seat." Lydia pulled out a stool at the breakfast bar, offering it to Ryann. "Can I get you anything else? Something to eat or a hoodie? I could probably stretch to both."

"You've done enough, trust me."

"Well, I usually order in on a Friday, so…"

Ryann focused on the countertop. Granite and gleaming. She didn't have any cash with her. She hadn't thought she would need it.

"I normally go for the Chinese option," Lydia continued, "but if you prefer something else…"

"Coffee will be fine."

Ryann should leave. She could get back to her shop—for the final time—and retrieve her wallet. They wouldn't be changing the locks until tomorrow.

"Do you think maybe you should see someone, Ryann? Talk?"

Ryann frowned. "I'm talking to you."

"I meant someone qualified. A professional. Perhaps the mental health team?"

"Oh, no."

"Because what you did before is worrying behaviour. I know it's none of my business, but I don't like the idea of you leaving here tonight without support."

"Lydia..."

"No, you're right. Just tell me to mind my own business. This, it's a downfall. Helping people."

"I wouldn't say it was a downfall." Ryann caught Lydia's kind eyes again. Grey, and intriguing. As she sat at the breakfast bar, Ryann was surprisingly thankful. Tonight, at the river, Ryann felt as though it was the only way to end the trouble she was facing. But now, sitting in a warm home with a wonderful, caring person offering support, life didn't seem so daunting. "There aren't many people out there who would invite a total stranger into their home."

"You don't strike me as the kind who would tie me up in the cellar."

"No." Ryann smiled faintly, running her fingers through her brown hair. "Maybe I'll have dinner with you but then I really should go."

"Where?"

"Home," Ryann lied.

"And you'll be okay?" Lydia's eyes held an apprehension. Worry. Understandable but unnecessary.

Ryann rubbed at her eyebrow; she couldn't believe someone actually cared. She'd gone from depressed to disbelief for the same situation in a short space of time.

Ryann's chest tingled. This was a stark contrast to how her day had begun.

"Ryann?"

"I'll be okay. Tomorrow is a new day."

"About earlier..."

"You want to know why, I guess?"

"I don't want you to tell me anything you don't wish to say, but a little insight would be appreciated."

"Everything is just getting on top of me lately. My personal life, my business...everything is falling apart."

"I'm sorry to hear that."

"When I woke up this morning, I'd had enough. It's just been one thing after another. I'm tired of people taking the piss. Of constantly being fucked over. I thought I had quite a good life, you know. I thought nothing would ever lead me to standing on a ledge at the river."

She inhaled a shaky breath, willing herself not to cry.

"Everything just feels like it's too much. I don't believe I have the strength this time around. I never should have come home from Australia. If I'd never met her, never run home to set up a life with her, I wouldn't be in this position."

"Who?"

"My ex-girlfriend."

Ryann glanced up. Though Lydia's eyes were sympathetic, this was too much for one person to take on. A person who didn't know Ryann. Lydia didn't need to know any of this.

"Sorry, I overshared."

"I asked."

This woman—this angel—didn't need a running commentary of Ryann's life troubles. Just a cup of coffee and company was good enough. It was certainly more than she'd bargained for when she woke up this morning at the shop. Her business. At one time, her pride and joy. Dark Angel would soon become exactly what it said on the sign above the door. Dark...and derelict.

"So," Ryann exhaled. "I don't have any cash on me for dinner, but I could bring it by tomorrow. I didn't think I'd need my wallet when I left this morning."

"Dinner is on me. Call it a thank you for not doing something terrible tonight."

Ryann quirked an eyebrow. "Shouldn't I be the one thanking you?"

"Nope. You've saved me countless sleepless nights."

"I'm sorry," Ryann offered. "It can't have been pleasant seeing that. It was selfish of me."

"I wouldn't say it was selfish. A cry for help, maybe…but not selfish." Lydia paused. "And you're safe now. You have someone you can talk to. Just…I was there. That's the main thing."

"Thank you." Ryann leaned forward, placing her heavily tattooed hand over Lydia's. "For being there. For caring. Just…it means more than you know."

Ryann pulled her hand back as soon as she was done. Lydia didn't appear to be uncomfortable, but none of this evening could be considered normal. The last thing Ryann needed was to scare off the new friend she'd made. The woman who saved her life.

CHAPTER TWO

As much as it hurt her to think it, Lydia was having a surprisingly good evening. Three hours on from returning home, Ryann was visibly relaxed. Lydia couldn't be sure Ryann was okay—the woman had planned to end her life today—but she was currently safe. That had to mean something. Lydia could be considered crazy for bringing Ryann into her home, but she was good. Genuine.

When Ryann leaned forward, her tattooed body captivating as she took a spring roll, Lydia could only watch the scene play out in front of her. Friday night didn't often involve her sitting around at home—Soph made sure of that—but Lydia set her phone to silent the moment she sat down with Ryann for dinner.

If Soph knew Lydia had a woman here, her best friend would hammer down her door. Lydia didn't need that; it wasn't *that* kind of night. And Ryann most definitely didn't need a crazy best friend here. She needed quiet. Time to reflect on today. A moment to recharge. Lydia hoped Ryann could do that here. Her safety mattered a lot.

"You said you came back from Australia?"

Ryann chewed slowly, nodding.

"What was it like?"

"Incredible." Ryann wiped her mouth with a napkin. "Totally different way of life. Everything just seems to slow down a little. At least, for me it did."

"How long have you been home?"

"Oh, a few years now." Regret poured from Ryann's dark expressive eyes.

"You ever think about going back?"

"All the time."

Lydia was captured by the sadness Ryann exuded. As much as she wanted to offer a hug, a hand, Lydia didn't believe it was what Ryann wanted. "But?"

"It was a different life. A different time. I had all kinds of options before I left for Australia last time."

"Yeah. I don't suppose it's easy to just up and leave for the other side of the world."

"I wish it was."

"Maybe in the future." Lydia would say anything to reassure Ryann tonight. If it meant she didn't leave here and step in front of a bus, Lydia would tell Ryann anything. "Can I get you anything else?"

"No, thank you."

"So, where is home?"

"Other side of town. There's a bus that runs from here. I think the last one is at nine."

"I can take you home." Lydia knew Ryann would decline her suggestion, but she still felt it appropriate to offer.

"Thanks, but I think I'll take a walk first. Clear my head."

Lydia's face fell. Was she making a massive mistake not keeping Ryann here? *I can't keep someone against their will.*

"Could I use your bathroom before I leave? At least you'll have a few hours left to yourself before the night ends."

"Of course, yeah. Straight up the stairs, second door on your left."

Lydia had a plan. Highly frowned upon, but a plan, nonetheless.

Ryann disappeared—leaving her phone on the coffee table. In the hours she'd been at Lydia's place, it hadn't chimed once. That wasn't necessarily unusual, but if Ryann had left anyone a note, they hadn't found it yet.

Lydia swiftly unlocked the handset, stopped by the passcode. Then she remembered their conversation at the river. Nine one nine eight. She tried the combination, a mixture of emotions travelling the expanse of her body as a screen of apps appeared in the background, a little boy the wallpaper of choice. Lydia didn't have time to wonder who he was; the toilet flushed upstairs.

Lydia pulled up Ryann's messages. There had to be a common theme, a familiar name throughout. The list held too many options, so she switched to Ryann's recent contacts on her call list. She had multiple calls to someone named Sam. *That could be the ex. Not necessarily a good choice.* The idea was quickly dismissed when another number showed below—listed as 'Bitch.' Lydia quickly lifted her own phone and snapped a picture of Sam's number. She didn't have time to add it to her contacts since Ryann was descending the stairs. Tonight may have been the first time she'd ever been thankful for creaking stairs.

Ryann appeared as Lydia locked and placed her phone down. "Okay, so I'm going to head off."

"You really have to go?"

Ryann offered a weak smile. "I do."

"And I can't drop you off?"

"Lydia, I really appreciate everything you've done. You saved my life tonight, but it's time for me to go and figure out my own mess. You have a beautiful home *and* a beautiful heart, but I have things to do. Stuff to figure out."

"Right." Lydia lowered her eyes.

"Please don't think I'm not grateful; I really am."

"No, I know."

"And if you're around tomorrow, I'd like to bring by what I owe you for dinn—"

"You don't need to do that."

"I don't like owing people." Ryann slid her phone into her back pocket, heading for the door. "I'll just post it through if you're out."

"Could I at least get your number? You know, to keep in touch?"

Ryann's forehead creased. "You really meant that?"

"What?"

"When you said you could be a friend?"

"Well, yeah." Did Ryann truly believe that Lydia had lied to get her off that ledge?

"Then that would be really great."

They exchanged numbers and Ryann promised to text Lydia when she was home. But then something caught Ryann's attention on her screen, the slightest of smiles curling on her lips.

"Is everything okay?"

"Yeah." Ryann turned her phone towards Lydia, her eyes bright. Lydia couldn't help but notice just how gorgeous they were when Ryann smiled genuinely. "My cousin's kid. Luca."

"He's very cute. How old is he?"

"Turned one a few weeks ago."

"You're close to him. I can tell."

"He's great. So are his mums. Sam found the love of her life for the second time around a few years ago. They really are great parents." Ryann spoke with such love about them, it was clear she was involved with her family. That had to be something positive in all of this. "And there was me, willing to never see him again."

"Well, any time you feel as though you're outnumbered in life, pull up a picture of him. He'll remind you that everything isn't a lost cause."

"Yeah, you're right."

"Promise me you'll text me when you get home."

"I promise."

"And if you need to talk, you'll reach out?"

"Yeah. I, uh...I'll make some calls on Monday. You know, if I feel as though I need some support."

"I think that's a good idea."

"I know this is probably a bit weird, and you can say no, but is there any chance of a hug?" Ryann shifted on the balls of her feet, but Lydia dragged her into a hug.

It felt right. Comfortable. Ryann was a good hugger. The kind you need when something really shitty happened. She smelled pretty good, too. Okay, she smelled gorgeous.

"Let me get you a coat. I'll just get it off you when I see you next." Lydia pulled out of their embrace reluctantly. Ryann had strong arms. Strong but gentle.

"No, I'm really okay."

Lydia frowned. She knew what Ryann was trying to say. "I'm not going to see you again, am I?"

"I swear, I'm not leaving here to do something stupid."

"That isn't even what I was talking about." Lydia's shoulders sagged, the weight of her day finally getting the better of her. "That's okay. But please, seek help. I'd ask you to come here if you felt that way again, but I know you'll walk out of here and I won't see you again. I just...I'm glad you're still around, okay?"

"And I'm glad *you* were the one who came to those railings tonight."

"Yeah, no problem."

"Next time, I want to hear all about your shitty boss, okay?"

"N-next time?" Lydia's heart thumped a little harder.

"Friends?" Ryann quirked an eyebrow.

"Friends."

Ryann gave a small wave as she disappeared down Lydia's steps and into the cool air. Spring was approaching, but Lydia felt winter deep in her bones as she remained on the doorstep. She had a sinking feeling in her belly, one that she knew wouldn't lessen any ing. If she didn't have this place to open up every morning, Ryann wouldn't know what to do with herself. She'd spent the last week sleeping here—her home with her ex-girlfriend no longer an option—but now she would lose the studio tomorrow.

If Ryann knew she could keep her head above water and continue paying for the shop, she would. But it wasn't feasible right now. Not with a huge debt behind her. The last several months' worth of payments on it hadn't been made—something Jen used to take care of—so the keys would be handed over in the morning. She hadn't even known that bailiffs worked Saturdays, but apparently, they did.

Especially when they wanted to take the one last thing you have left.

Ryann knew it wasn't their fault. They simply had a job to do. That didn't make losing her livelihood any easier. And through no fault of her own. It really stung. Deep down in the pit of her stomach, it hurt more than she could ever admit.

A car suddenly screeched to a halt in front of her. A familiar, brand spanking new white Range Rover Sport. Ryann's heart tumbled into her stomach. Why was Sam here? She should be at home with her wife and kid. The driver door swung open with aggression, Sam's face soaked with tears as her eyes trained on Ryann.

"S-Sam? Is everything okay?" Ryann shot to her feet. "Did something happen to Luca? Luciana?"

"Is everything okay?" Sam cried. "Are you really asking me that?"

"Huh?"

"What would Luca have done without you? What would *we* have done without you?"

How the hell did Sam know about tonight? This wasn't good. There was a reason she didn't call her today. Sam didn't need this. Nobody did.

"Ry? Is it true?" Sam approached, stopping directly in front of Ryann. "Did you try to take your own life tonight?"

"Who told you that?"

"Someone who I would class as an angel."

"Sam, I'm okay. Please don't upset yourself."

"I called Jen. She didn't know where you were. Here was the only other place I could think of to come to."

"You called Jen?" Ryann's eyebrow rose. "Why?"

"Because she's your partner. One day, your wife."

"No. She's not."

"What the hell is going on?" Even in Sam's hysterical state, she still looked immaculate. Ryann would be lying if she said she wasn't jealous of her cousin's lifestyle. Still, she was happy for her. "Ryann?"

"Everything is a mess, Sam. And by everything...I mean literally *everything*."

"When Auntie Marian left, I promised myself I would see that you were okay. And I thought you were. I just...I thought everything was okay."

Ryann smiled weakly. "Me, too."

"Did something happen with you and Jen?"

"We're not together anymore."

"What? Why?"

"I don't even know where to begin." Ryann shrugged. "And to be honest, I don't really want to. Not tonight, anyway."

"No. We're going to deal with this now."

"Sam, seriously...not tonight."

"Okay, so if you're not together anymore...where are you staying?"

"I've been staying here. At the shop."

Sam scoffed. "You can't stay here. You need a home."

"I won't be staying here tonight, don't worry." Ryann held back the emotion welling in her throat. There was no use crying. It was too late. "I lost it, Sam."

"Lost what?"

"The shop." Sam's face fell. "We're not all business savvy like you, apparently."

"How the hell did you lose it?" Sam looked at Ryann incredulously. Sam wouldn't understand. She was so on top of her business that she couldn't possibly come to terms with how this happened.

"Oh, this wasn't on me. This was all Jen. She's been taking out loans in my name and the business's name for God knows how long. The debt...I can't even bring myself to think about it. And then to top it all off, I walked into the house last week to find her wrapped up in bed with another woman. The same woman I caught her with last year but then I fucking stupidly took her back!"

"No." Sam shook her head. "No. This can't be true."

"You're calling me a liar?"

"No, I just...why didn't you come to me?"

"For what?" Ryann frowned.

"For help."

"Because there's no way you can help. I lost the business. I lost my fiancée. I lost everything. And I'm pretty sure I'm close to losing my mind. Although, judging by this evening...it's already gone."

"Come on." Sam motioned towards the car. "You're coming home with me."

Ryann held up her hand. "Oh, no I'm not. You're going home to your pregnant wife and I'm going to figure this out myself."

Sam laughed. "Yeah, that's not going to work for me. There is *no way* I'm leaving you alone so you can do something stupid."

"I won't. I promised someone I wouldn't."

"Lydia? The woman who saved your life tonight?"

"How do you know about Lydia?"

"Why do you think I'm here?" Sam cocked her head, smiling weakly.

"Okay, I don't know what's going on, but I want answers. Did she contact you? How did she do that? She doesn't know who you are; I only talked about you and Luca briefly."

"She was worried. And I'm glad she called me."

"She called you?" Ryann paced. How dare Lydia call Sam. This was all totally fucked up and backward. "Some fucking friend she was."

"Oh, no. You don't get to blame her for any of this. If she hadn't been at the river, I'd be sitting at home none the wiser. I'd be...I'd be planning your funeral."

"Sam. Go home. I'm fine."

"Ryann."

"No. Just stop. You have your own life to deal with. Luca needs you at home. So does Luciana. Why do you think I didn't call you today before I went to the river? You don't need this bullshit in your life. Because that's what it is. Fucking bullshit. Jen fucked me over once again and that's my own fault for taking her back. She told me everything I wanted to hear last year, and I fell for it!"

"I didn't know." Sam lowered her eyes, toying with her car key. "I didn't even know you'd had issues. I thought you were both completely in love."

"Yeah, so did I. Seems it was one-sided. But I learned my lesson and now I have to figure out how the hell I'm supposed to move forward."

"Let me help you."

"How exactly can you help me, Sam? I've just lost my business and my home. You know, since I was stupid enough to allow Jen to sign the tenancy agreement in her name. Now, she's fucking another woman in the bed I bought us."

"God, I could rip her head off." Sam growled. It was almost funny.

"Calm down, Wonder Woman. This isn't your fight."

"I'll buy the business back."

Now Ryann laughed from deep within her belly. "What?"

"I'll buy the business back as soon as it goes to auction. No problem. Then we will work something out."

"Nope."

"Why?" Sam frowned, her dark hair whipping in the wind. "It makes sense."

"No. It's completely crazy and not happening."

"Okay, and what else do you propose we do?"

"*We* don't do anything. *You* don't do anything. I'll go to the job centre on Monday morning. I'll take whatever is on offer. Maybe I could call around. I've helped enough artists over the years; I'm sure one of them will have my back."

"You're the best around here."

"The UK is a big place, Sam. I'll find something." Ryann was over this conversation. She wouldn't be the reason Luciana was home alone. "Stop worrying about me and go home to your wife."

"Stop using Luciana as a way to get rid of me. She's fine. She's in bed watching complete shit on the TV."

"And you should be with her." Ryann nodded as she fixed her coat around her. She'd taken what she could from the shop, her tattoo gun and her inks, and her coat was the last thing she grabbed on the way out. She certainly needed it tonight. The wind chill was already seeping through her layers. "So, I'm going to go now. I can't look at this place any longer."

"Ry, wait!"

Ryann took Sam's hands. "Go home, Sam. I love you like a sister and I appreciate everything you bring to my life, but please... go home."

"And where are you going to stay?"

"With a friend. I've already confirmed it," Ryann lied.

"I'll drop you off."

"She's only in town. It's a five-minute walk. I'll be there before you're even nearly home."

"I don't like this, Ryann."

"Yeah, well..." Ryann was finally admitting defeat, glancing up at the dimmed sign above her shop. It would probably be ripped down by the end of the weekend. Once the local kids got wind of its repossession, they'd go to town on the place. It was inevitable. "I'm sure everything will work out in time."

"You should really go and see Lydia when you're feeling up to it."

"Why?"

"Because she's beside herself with worry."

"No, I can't trust her. She shouldn't have called you. She must have gone through my phone to get your details and that's really not okay."

"Yeah, and neither is threatening to jump into the river."

"It wasn't a threat." Ryann shook her head. "If she hadn't been there, it would have happened."

"And what's so special about Lydia that it stopped you?"

Ryann smiled for the first time since she'd left Lydia's place. "Her eyes. She had kind eyes."

Lydia had nothing but kindness seeping from every pore. Her eyes. Her smile. Her voice. She could have been a really good friend, but she'd betrayed Ryann's trust tonight. Trust that was already teetering on a knife-edge. It would take some time to get over that.

"But it doesn't matter. She has her own life. I don't even know her."

"Doesn't mean you couldn't get to know her."

"I don't even know what that means..."

"It means you should go and visit her. Perhaps take her a gift for everything she did for you."

"Oh, yeah, I'll just grab the cash for that gift off the money tree in the back garden of my non-existent home." Ryann laughed, shaking her head.

"How much do you need?"

"I don't need anything," Ryann countered. "But I think babysitting is going to be off the table for a while. I don't know what job I'm going to end up doing, so I should expect to have no free weekends for a while."

"Please, come home with me."

"I can't. But thank you for the offer." Ryann needed to leave. Where she was going, she didn't know, but Sam and her eyes, her pained voice, they were breaking her heart. "Goodnight, Sam. Give Luca a kiss from me, okay?"

"You don't have anywhere to go, do you?" Tears fell down Sam's face freely. "You're going to sleep on the street."

"Don't be ridiculous." Ryann didn't know how she was keeping her composure. Her mother would hit the roof if she saw the condition her daughter's life was in. But yes, on the street was exactly where she would be sleeping tonight. And probably would be until further notice.

"You do realise you're about as good at lying as I am. Which is terrible. You don't even have any clothes, Ry."

"I have everything I need." Ryann lifted her backpack from against the wall, her tattoo gun safely inside. She did have some clothes inside the shop, but she didn't have the energy to carry them around with her. Everything else remained at her old place with Jen. "I'll call you through the week, okay?"

"You're honestly going to walk away from me? When I'm offering you a place to stay…you're going to walk away?"

"I am, yes." Ryann leaned in, kissing her cousin's cheek. "Because you can't solve everyone's problems, Sam. And I know how much you want to; you're amazing like that. But I'm going to be okay. If I leave the city, I'll call you and let you know."

"You'll…call me? And you're going to let me know?" Sam sneered. "Really? That's it?"

"Yes, I will. Sounds kinda shitty, I know…but leaving could be good for me."

"What? So, you can spend your life on the streets in a different city?"

Ryann sighed. Sam wouldn't buy her lies, so Ryann would be

honest instead. "Look, it'll only be for a while. I'll find my way. I always do."

Sam's jaw clenched. "You won't sleep on the street. I'll be cold in the ground before I let *any* of my family sleep on the street. Get in the fucking car, Ryann. Before I drag you inside it!"

"Sam—"

"NOW!" Sam pinched the bridge of her nose, sighing. "Please, get in the car. I really need you to GET IN THE CAR!"

"Why are you yelling at me? This is why I didn't ask for any help. I don't need it."

"Maybe not, but you're getting it regardless. God, you're so fucking stubborn sometimes."

"Wonder who I get that from." Ryann smirked, slinging her rucksack over her shoulder.

"That's not even funny. In other circumstances, maybe. Tonight? Not at all."

"When Mum left, did you promise to take over that role, too?"

"So fucking help me GOD!" Sam gritted her teeth and it was at that point that Ryann admitted defeat.

"Fine. But it's only for the night. I'm gone in the morning."

CHAPTER THREE

Lydia flung back the blanket covering her legs, the wood burning fire now too warm since the midday sun chose to shine through the window. Saturday usually included nursing a hangover, one that often spilled over into Sunday. Not this Saturday, though. Lydia's routine was all over the place.

She had Ryann to thank for that. Ryann, the woman who hadn't called. Lydia wasn't sure why she expected contact; she was surely the last person on Ryann's mind.

With perfect timing, Lydia's phone started to ring on the mantelpiece. She shot up, almost tripping over the coffee table. "Hello?"

"Finally!" Soph's voice filtered through the earpiece. "You were supposed to call me back."

Soph had repeatedly tried to call Lydia last night; Lydia needed a moment alone, though. Once Ryann left and Lydia contacted her cousin, she didn't have the strength for any more conversation. Bed with a glass of wine was where it all ended. Or so Lydia thought. Ryann remained firmly at the front of her mind.

Lydia rubbed her forehead. She would desperately welcome company today. "Can you come over? If you're in any fit state…"

"Lyd, is everything okay?"

"Yeah. It's just been a crazy night. Bring chocolate."

"You got your period? That's what this is about?"

"Just bring the damn chocolate." Lydia cut the call, needing a few more minutes before Soph arrived, demanding the answers to everything.

She looked out the bay window in her living room; the sky was bright. Her mood should have lifted just watching the white clouds move with ease against the blue, but nothing elevated the dark veil she felt shrouded by. A sadness she needed to boot before Monday morning. Lydia couldn't go into work feeling like this; Bree would sense it and ultimately prey on it.

She considered calling Ryann's cousin, the phone still gripped in her hand. But what would she possibly say? Lydia may have been there when she was needed most, but Ryann was from another world.

While Lydia spent most days in heels and suits, her fingernails immaculately manicured and refreshed every couple of weeks, Ryann appeared to live for her tattoos and buzz-cuts. That wasn't the personality Lydia would usually attract, whether that be in terms of friendship or something more, but Lydia *did* feel an attraction. A connection, at least. In what capacity, she didn't know, but it wouldn't ever matter. Ryann was in Lydia's life *and* heart for unrelated reasons. Reasons she wasn't willing to turn into something more. She wanted Ryann to be okay and happy, nothing more. It was foolish to contemplate even a friendship.

The doorbell rang out, breaking Lydia from her troubles momentarily. Soph would have a million things to say about last night's events, that much she was sure of. Lydia braced herself, pulling her hoodie around her body in an attempt to protect herself as she opened the front door.

"Hey, come in."

"Where the hell have you been?" Soph's shrill voice pierced Lydia's ears.

"I've been here."

"And what the hell was that after work last night? You *never* cut your best friend's calls. You've moved down three places on my Christmas list for that!"

"I'm devastated."

Soph flopped down on the couch, stealing Lydia's blanket in the process. She watched her best friend intently, her eyebrow raised as Lydia's eyes landed on her.

"Don't give me that look."

"Well, if you told me what's going on, I wouldn't have to."

"Last night at the river..." Lydia sat in the bay window, pulling her long, black hair up into a bun. She needed some space while she discussed this with Soph. "Someone tried to jump."

"Stupid bastard."

Lydia didn't know why she thought Soph would understand. Her best friend was one of those people who believed suicide was selfish and inconvenient. The kind who would complain about being stuck on a train if somebody was on the line. Soph was like a sister to Lydia, but they held opposite views on many things.

Soph threw up her hands, scoffing. "I don't know *what* would possess someone to do something so stupid."

"Well, at least I don't have to worry about you since you seem to have the perfect life."

"Oh, I don't. I have a boyfriend who doesn't know I exist lately."

"The horror." Lydia rolled her eyes. She was truly sick to death of hearing about David. He worked his arse off to give Soph anything she wanted. "Hasn't he just booked the Maldives for June?"

"So?"

Lydia exhaled. She was fighting a losing battle. "Never mind."

"Anyway, back to the idiot at the river..."

"You know what, we don't need to talk about it. It doesn't

matter." It wasn't down to Lydia to defend Ryann and her behaviour, but she would. "How's David, anyway?"

"Working again."

"I'm sure you can find something to keep you busy," Lydia said. "You usually do."

"Let's go into town. I could do with a wardrobe overhaul."

"Not today. You should go ahead and treat yourself, though." And Soph would. She often did. "I don't plan to leave the house today."

"Um, why?" Soph cocked her head, her platinum blonde hair falling down the front of one shoulder.

Lydia had no desire to sit down and explain how what happened last night affected her. She'd tried and failed the moment Soph arrived. "Just tired. It's been a long week."

"Tired? You didn't even go out last night."

Lydia got to her feet, the kitchen her destination. She needed to keep busy; perhaps she could spend the day baking.

Soph followed behind her, the air palpable with Soph's desperate need to open her mouth. Lydia felt it. She knew her best friend too well.

"We should go out tonight. Cocktails. Clubs. Dancing. We can even go to one of those gay bars you like."

"Soph, I really don't feel like it."

"What the hell have you done with my best friend?" Soph's hand dramatically landed on her hip. "It's the weekend. Live a little."

Live a little. If only Ryann would live a little. Maybe then she would see that not everything was bad. Live a little... It was an interesting phrase. Wasn't Lydia already doing exactly that? Living. Breathing. Appreciating every moment she spent on this earth.

"Can I call you later? I'll see how I feel throughout the day. I could probably do with tidying around and doing some laundry."

"God, you sound like my mother."

"Soph..."

"I know, I know. You're miserable because you haven't had a shag in a while."

Lydia frowned. "What?"

"Oh, come on. First Friday night is a no-go...and now Saturday, too?"

"Last night was difficult for me," Lydia said, her voice low. "I didn't expect I'd have to save someone's life, but I did and now I'm a bit...I don't know. I just need some time alone, I think."

"What do you mean, you saved someone's life?"

"T-the woman at the river. The one I was telling you about before...her."

"How exactly did you save her life?"

"Well, I talked her off the ledge. Maybe it isn't considered saving someone's life, but I managed to stop her from doing something she shouldn't. You know, I offered a shoulder."

"We should call the paper. Tell them all about it. You'll be a local hero."

Lydia turned her back, flicking the kettle on. She hadn't expected understanding or a heart-to-heart with Soph, but she also didn't think *that* would be the response. "No, thanks."

"People should know what you did. That woman would be dead if it wasn't for you."

"Why do you care? She's probably an inconvenience to you because I wasn't available to listen to you on the phone all night."

"It doesn't matter what she is to me, Lydia. She's going to be okay because of what you did. Alright, you won't ever see her again, but she'll remember you and see it in the paper."

"I was hoping she may have called by now..."

"Why would she call?" Soph asked.

"Well, I brought her back here. She really needed someone to just be with her. God, it was heartbreaking watching her climb over that railing."

"Y-you brought her here? Are you fucking stupid?"

Lydia frowned. Why *wouldn't* she bring Ryann back home with her? What else was she supposed to do? "So, I was supposed to leave her on the street?"

"Well, yeah."

Really? Soph wanted Lydia to be a cold, heartless bitch? Lydia shouldn't be surprised. She thought her best friend would offer more understanding. More support. No such luck.

This was typical Soph, it always would be. But Lydia wasn't taking it anymore. Soph couldn't get away with her attitude for much longer. Lydia seethed, and her body tensed as her fist came down hard against the kitchen counter.

"You know, the world doesn't revolve around you and your little pink bubble, Soph. There are people out there with real issues. Terrible things happening in their lives. But you? You just think it's the end of the world because David hasn't shagged you in a few days."

Soph's eyes widened. "Excuse me?"

"Be as shocked as you like." Lydia shrugged, pouring hot water into her cup. And then she froze. "And thanks! You've just burnt my fucking coffee!"

"I'm nowhere near you."

"No, but I forgot to put the milk in first because you're having a fit about who I bring into my home. Now it's burnt." Lydia turned; she was sure Soph would soon see the steam coming from her ears. "If you have nothing nice or supportive to say, you can piss off home."

"What the hell is wrong with you?"

Lydia gripped the edge of the countertop. If she just breathed, all of this would die down. Soph would be supportive and the last ten minutes wouldn't have happened. "You haven't even asked me if I'm okay."

"Why wouldn't you be okay?"

And that was the final straw. Soph was incapable of giving a single crap about Lydia unless it included herself. As Lydia climbed from her bed this morning, all she wanted was a hug. Something safe and warm. She'd spent the entire night going over every scenario in her head. What if she hadn't convinced Ryann to climb back over? Would Lydia have jumped in to try to save her? Her head was in a complete scramble; nothing felt right.

"No, you're right. I'm fine." Lydia took her cup from the counter, pouring it into the sink. Her coffee was a lost cause, along with this day. "I need to go and shower. You can see yourself out, can't you?"

"Y-you asked me to come over..."

"And now I'm asking you to leave, Soph. I mean, you didn't even bring chocolate like I asked you to." Lydia shouldn't be surprised; Soph often arrived with a complaint and nothing else. "I just want a day alone. Sorry you came *all the way* from down the road. I'll see you next weekend."

Lydia didn't look back as she left the kitchen. Instead, she rushed up the stairs, slamming the bathroom door shut behind her.

Ryann climbed from the crisp, white, Egyptian cotton she'd been enveloped by all night. The temperature must have dropped significantly through the night; she could see the dampness around the grounds of Sam's home as the day began outside. The sun beamed high in the sky, but goosebumps prickled Ryann's skin as she opened the bedroom door. The house was quiet. Far too quiet for a place that a one year old resided in.

Last night had ended far more positively than she'd thought it could, but she knew Sam would be waiting in the wings, desperate to get her claws into Ryann's mind. In all honesty, she felt brighter this morning. She didn't feel as though she had no place to turn. Ryann had no intention of allowing Sam to help financially—that was still a given—but a warm bed was a welcome change from the antiseptic smell of the studio. A smell she was going to miss.

Ryann landed in the hallway, the sound of the TV playing low in the open space. It could have been coming from the kitchen or the living room. Sam's house was so big that the acoustics played tricks on the ears. She glanced down her body where Sam's wife's clothes were covering her. Grey sweatpants and a white racerback with 'sounds gay, I'm in' emblazoned on the front.

"Ryann, is that you?"

"Y-yeah." Ryann cleared the sleep from her throat, yawning as she pulled her hair up and out of her face. The buzz-cut to the right side of her head needed a trim. She could now pinch the hair with her index finger and thumb; it was too long.

"I'm in here if you want to join me."

"Oh, Luce." Ryann smiled. "Sorry, I didn't think anyone was home."

"Couldn't be arsed moving yet." Luciana shrugged. "Fresh coffee in the pot. Bring it through when you've made it. I want to smell it."

"Um…"

"I've had my one cup for today," Luciana explained. "Sam will murder me if I even think about another."

"That's actually a thing? No coffee when you're pregnant?"

"Seems like bullshit to me, but yes, it's a thing."

"Wow. Shitty existence if coffee isn't involved."

Luciana laughed, changing her position on the couch. "Amen."

Ryann chose to forego the coffee; it was better not to tease Luciana with it. She was already in the way just by being here. She sat in the seat facing Luciana, running her hands up and down her thighs. "So, uh…"

"What happened last night, Ry?"

Ryann lowered her eyes. Although she hadn't known Luciana for that long, they still got on and had become quite close since

Luca was born. She didn't want to add any stress to Luciana's life. Especially while she was five months pregnant. "Nothing. It doesn't matter. I'm okay now."

"You know, I could put you in touch with my therapist." Both allowed Luciana's words to hang in the air for a few seconds.

Ryann didn't need a therapist. She needed a partner who didn't take her for everything she had. Her business included. Ryann appreciated Luciana's offer, her suggestion, but she just needed to get herself back on track.

"I think I'll be okay. Just had a moment, that's all."

"Well, it was some moment, kid." Luciana shook her head. "Sam slept outside your room last night."

Ryann's eyes widened. "She what?"

"Mmhmm. She was worried you'd leave in the middle of the night. She's taken it pretty hard."

"I am sorry, Luce. For bringing this to your door. I told Sam I didn't need to come back here last night, but she wouldn't listen."

"I'm glad she wouldn't. We need you to be safe."

"I will be. Just...I have stuff I need to do. Things to finalise."

"What things?"

"I need to go back to the house for a start. Get my belongings."

"Jen was really cheating?" Luciana sat forward, her attention firmly on Ryann. "Sam said it's happened before."

"Last year. I found a message on her phone and when I asked her about it, I expected her to lie. Or that she'd tell me I'd got it completely wrong. She admitted everything and we worked it out. I thought that because she'd been honest, everything would be okay in the end. You know?

"But then I got a final notice letter a few weeks ago. I'm not usually home around the time the mail comes so Jen was just hiding anything else that had come through the door. Getting rid of them, whatever. Luce, she's taken out tens of thousands in loans. In my name. The business. It's a lot. I don't know what she's been doing with it or how she managed to borrow so much, but it's all there in black and white. She always dealt with the accounts, but now that I've looked...she was having them deposited into the joint account and then transferring it straight over to her own personal account."

"Why would she do that?"

"I don't know. Maybe her other woman needed money. I really have no clue."

"This other woman…"

"Is living in my house. Watching my TV. Fucking *my* fiancée."

"Ry, I'm so sorry."

"I was at first, too. But then I realised that I now know exactly the person she is. Better late than never, right?"

"Right."

"Where's Luca?"

"Susan has him today. A party at the neighbour's or something."

Ryann sighed. "Convenient."

"No. The truth. Sam will be home soon and then you two can sit down and figure out whatever it is you need to do. Sam knows I'm okay with whatever decisions she makes. Just…let her help, Ryann."

"I really can't do that."

"Oh, come on." Luciana climbed to her feet, her belly more noticeable since Ryann was here last weekend. "We both know Sam has more money than sense. And, you know she wants to help. Give her the satisfaction of doing so or I'll never hear the end of it."

"I don't know." Ryann and Luciana found themselves in the kitchen, Sam's car rumbling up the gravel drive. "Oh, God. She's back."

"Fucking hell, Ry. She's not that scary."

"I've seen how you bow down to your wife. You know exactly how scary she is." Ryann winked, a genuine smile forming on her lips.

The front door swung open, and Sam stood in the doorway in all her pristine business glory. Ryann gulped, backing up and taking a seat on the kitchen stool. Sam cocked her head, smiling. "Good to see you in the land of the living."

"Hey..."

Sam's heels clicked against the hardwood floor, her dark hair flowing behind her as she strode into the kitchen. "Get dressed. We have things to talk about."

Ryann sat outside Sam's home at the outdoor furniture. The lawn a deep green, it looked as though each blade of grass had been individually planted. Luxury *and* typical Sam. This was a place of beauty, the lake Sam and Luciana were married on perfectly still, the surface a mirror, as the sun began to fade behind the trees. If there was anywhere in the world Ryann could be today, it was this place. Something about it left her soul feeling complete. Relaxed. In love with nature and everything around her.

There was no air pollution from the cars in the city, no blaring car horns or emergency sirens. Just the sound of the birds, the whoosh of the breeze, the crinkle of the trees. Idyllic. Incredible. Inspiring.

Ryann took a moment to think about the past twenty-four hours. She couldn't quite comprehend how Lydia had changed everything for her, and though she was slightly angry that Lydia called Sam, deep down she was appreciative.

She could stay mad at her new friend and refuse Sam's help, or she could admit that she was in trouble. It wouldn't be easy accepting help, but perhaps Luciana was right. Sam did have a lot of money. She also felt strongly about family and supporting one another. While Ryann didn't want to believe for one second that she needed this...she did. She needed a lifeline. Something to kick start her again. Someone to tell her that all was not lost.

Sam was that person.

Ryann sighed, nodding to herself and wiping her hands down her thighs. She would accept whatever Sam threw at her. Nothing would be permanent; Ryann would soon be in a position where she could repay Sam. She knew she would be. She *had* to be.

"Before you say anything," Sam said, appearing behind Ryann, "I have some things I want to say first."

"Okay."

Sam took a seat beside her cousin, crossing her legs and relaxing back against the back of the chair. Her business suit still appeared immaculate; Ryann wondered if Sam ever did any work. "I understand that you don't want any help; nobody wants to have to ask for it. There were times when I struggled before I opened the business, and if it wasn't for the people who *did* offer to help me, I wouldn't be where I am now, Ryann. Just answer me some things. Do you feel suicidal or was this a cry for help? Is your financial situation getting on top of you or is it something more?"

"It's the finances," Ryann admitted. "I'd never felt suicidal before, Sam. Even when Mum left, I didn't feel like this. You know how close we were, and I didn't feel like this. I just...I didn't know what to do. I couldn't see a way out. She's really fucked me over, Sam. It seemed less painful to stop existing altogether. I wanted to stop thinking, to stop feeling."

"Do you need to speak to someone? I can find you a therapist if it's what you need."

"I don't think I need a therapist, but I don't know. What I did last night wasn't normal."

Sam shook her head. "No, it wasn't. But, not having a penny in the bank can make you feel that way. When you feel as though you have nowhere to turn, your mind will play games with you."

"Yeah, my mind was definitely playing games." Ryann had never felt so unsure, but now that she had opened up and explained what was happening, it didn't feel so daunting. Of course, she still had nothing...well, nothing but the love of her family. Sam was the only one she had left around here. "I feel better this morning. I just needed to tell someone what was going on. That life wasn't as perfect as I thought it was." Sam toyed with an envelope in her hand. Ryann focused on it as it appeared between them and frowned. "Is everything okay?"

"You know Lindsay and Cheryl bought a bigger place, don't you?"

"Yeah. Lindsay mentioned it the last time she came into the shop. She was passing through; Cheryl was having her hair done."

"Right...so my apartment in the city is free. It has been for weeks. And it's now yours." Sam handed over the envelope. It weighed more than Ryann expected—clearly a set of keys. "I was planning to put it on the market. I didn't think it would be needed anymore."

"Sam, I don—"

"We will sort out the paperwork another time. Luca has been a pain in the arse this week with his routine, and I honestly don't have the patience for paperwork."

Ryann blinked repeatedly. What was happening? Sam was giving her an apartment in one of the best buildings in the city? This couldn't possibly be right.

Ryann glanced around, expecting to find a film crew laughing behind their cameras. Sam was generous, she always had been, but this? "Sam, I—"

Sam placed her hand over Ryann's, shaking her head. "We don't need to discuss this. It doesn't require anything of the kind. This morning, I put a thousand in your personal account. Does Jen have access to it?"

"No." Ryann continued to frown. The moment Sam stopped explaining everything, Ryann would break down.

"Good, okay. Inside the envelope is the keys to the apartment. The codes for the main door and everything else you need to know is in there, too."

Ryann slipped her finger under the lip of the envelope, forcing it open and glancing inside. "Sam, are you sure about this?"

"That place is sitting empty and you don't have anywhere to live at the moment, so why don't you take it over?"

"I don't think I can afford somewhere like that."

"There is no mortgage on it, Ryann. It was paid outright when I bought the place. It's sitting there, going to waste."

"Sam, this is a really big thing you're doing. I don't know if I can accept it."

Ryann swallowed hard. Sam was incredible.

"And the thousand…you don't need to do that."

"Too late. It's in your account. It should see you over the weekend."

Ryann squared her shoulders, realising that accepting help wasn't the worst thing in the world. At least not until she was steady again. "I'll go to the job centre first thing Monday morning. I'll pay you back as soon as I'm sorted out. I promise you."

"Not interested in you paying me back, Ry. I'm interested in your health and wellbeing. So long as you promise me that you won't even look at Jen again, and that you'll find yourself someone worthy, you've already paid me back."

Ryann threw her arms around Sam, holding her cousin as close as she possibly could. She spied Luciana in the window, rubbing her belly and smiling. Ryann smiled back. This family truly was one of the greatest gifts she had. Reconnecting with Sam had been the most beneficial thing in her life since she returned from Australia.

"There are some other bits in the envelope, but you can sit down with it all later once you're at the apartment. With a beer or whatever."

Ryann wiped away the tear that had escaped from her eye and settled on her jawline. "Sam, I don't know how to even thank you for this."

"Well, more nights with Luca would be greatly appreciated."

Sam smirked, squeezing Ryann's hand. "I'm sure I'll find something for you to do."

"And I will be here in a shot when you do. Seriously, thank you so much."

"Your mum helped me out when I was at university. I'm just paying it forward."

CHAPTER FOUR

Ryann stopped outside the house she once shared with Jen. The last few years didn't make any sense anymore. Ryann could have lived with the knowledge that she'd been cheated on repeatedly during their entire relationship—at least that's how it felt—but she couldn't ever forgive Jen for the debt. The loans. The lies. Now she had only hatred for the woman she'd once loved.

She hadn't quite decided what she would do about the fraud just yet, but Jen would get her comeuppance; people like her always did. Nobody got away with something like that forever and Ryann would make sure of it.

So, here she was. Standing outside what was her home, planning to collect her clothes and whatever else she could fit into a taxi. Sam had given her a reason to hope in the form of an apartment, so she no longer had a reason to sneak back here. Jen and her new squeeze could do as they wanted. Ryann was well and truly out from this moment on.

She took her keys from her leather jacket, opening the front door quietly. Jen probably wouldn't be home; she wasn't usually during the day. *Probably out spending money that belongs to me.* Ryann moved into the living room—everything was as it should be. Clean and tidy. Her sixty-inch TV was sitting on the oak stand in the corner of the long living room.

And then she heard it.

Jen was home.

This time, Ryann wouldn't leave. She had every right to be here. While the woman upstairs was ruining Ryann's life, she believed she had more than every right to collect her things.

Ryann flew up the stairs, taking them two at a time. The sound of sex came from behind the bedroom door. Unfortunately, Ryann was about to interrupt her ex-girlfriend's impending orgasm. She snuck into the spare room, grabbed her hold-all, and swung the bedroom door open.

"Don't mind me, ladies." She found Jen's girlfriend on all fours, her mouth hanging open with shock. "Just need to pick up a few things."

"Ryann! What the fuck!" Jen scrambled under the covers, her face reddening by the second.

"Oh, as you were. Don't stop on my account. You've been fucking each other senseless behind my back for a long time. May as well do it in front of me now." Ryann opened the wardrobe and started to neatly fold her shirts into piles on the floor. "Sorry, am I in the way?" She wrinkled her nose, noting the anger on her ex-girlfriend's face. "Did you want me to hand you a better toy? I mean, that one was always shit."

"Ryann!"

"Mm?" Ryann focused on the wardrobe, holding back the laughter desperate to erupt from her belly. This was more fun than she thought it would be. Jen's face was certainly a picture. Her girlfriend, well...she looked like she wanted the ceiling to fall through. "That should do me for the time being, but I will be back."

"I'm changing the fucking locks!" Jen spat.

"You do that and I'll kick the door in. Simple."

"And I'll have you arrested for criminal damage!"

"You will? Then I'll go one better, and have you arrested for fraud, you fucking bitch!" Ryann noted that anger in her own voice, how her fist was clenched at her side. She should leave. Before she smashed this entire house up, she should really leave. Ryann made a beeline for the door before turning back to face Jen and her girlfriend fully. "Enjoy my sloppy seconds. She's a shit shag, anyway!"

Ryann bound down the stairs with her hold-all, slamming the front door behind her. Jen would really change the locks? Ryann would truly love to see the outcome of that. As much as it pained her to see Jen in bed with another woman, she felt some satisfaction in interrupting them. After all, who wants to have their orgasm quashed by the woman you've just cheated on? Cock blocking at its finest.

Ryann grinned, hailing a Hackney cab as it rolled down the road with its orange light switched on, signalling it was available to take a fare. "Bryant Tower, thank you." Ryann sat back, hugging her hold-all close to her chest.

As the taxi sped away, she didn't look back. She had no reason to, Jen was her past. Now, she was looking directly ahead at her future. One that wouldn't be possible without Lydia.

Lydia. She smiled. *I really should stop by and see her.*

Ryann stood at the window, overlooking the river she almost gave her life to. This view was impressive. There was a reason Bryant Tower had the best apartments in the city—the view alone could vouch for that. Now almost six years old, they had slightly lowered in price, but not much. There still weren't many who could afford to live in such a building.

The huge expanse of open space shone brightly, the floor-to-ceiling windows offering an absurd amount of light. Ryann knew the wood flooring was expensive since it didn't crack and creak as she walked across it.

This apartment had once been close to resembling a bachelorette pad, Sam having little interest in its decoration, black and chrome the predominant feature. But Lindsay and Cheryl had overhauled the place once they moved in, and now it felt warmer. Pastels and soft tones made the sometimes cold space much homelier.

If Lindsay could fit in here, so can I.

Mostly occupied by footballers or other VIPs visiting the city, Ryann felt totally out of place. She didn't have a posh car sitting in her designated parking space, but she didn't care. Sam had truly changed her outlook this morning when she handed her the keys to this place. It hadn't even occurred to her to enquire about its availability.

Ryann wouldn't have anyway; she wasn't that kind of person. She didn't need charity, and she wouldn't usually accept it, but Sam was family and she was more than appreciative for the help. The help she shouldn't even need.

When Ryann arrived at the apartment, she had found a letter addressed to her sitting on the huge kitchen island. She hadn't opened it yet; she couldn't bring herself to do so. But this view made it hard to worry. So, she slipped the lip open and removed the lined paper from inside. Sam's handwriting stared directly back at her.

Ryann,

I never thought I would be in a position where I could help someone I love. Family. I also never thought I would receive a call from a complete stranger, telling me that my cousin and my son's best friend had tried to take her own life. I still don't know how I feel about it. I'm processing.

While I don't yet know where we go with that knowledge, I plan to help you financially. As your mother did for me when I was setting out in life. You do so much for me, my family, and now it's time to return that. It's not something that needs to be discussed again, it never happened. I've done it; accept it and move on from this stage of your life.

You have so much love inside, so much to give, don't let this blip prevent the world from seeing that. Don't let Jen's actions take away your spirit. Don't leave us. We need you in our lives more than you think.

We're getting your business back.

All my love, support, and gratitude.

Sam

Ryann's tears fell to the paper in her hands, blurring the ink. Sam had completely changed everything for her; she owed her the world and more. It didn't matter to Ryann that Sam was a multi-millionaire—she just saw Sam as her cousin. The money didn't define Sam, it never had, but knowing that she was willing to help Ryann out, to get her back on her feet, was overwhelming.

While Ryann had spent her time recently thinking about Lydia, more so than she should be, it was Sam who had changed everything. No, that wasn't true. Lydia was the reason she was alive. But Sam was right. Ryann did have a lot of love to give. She had so much that she could burst at times.

Maybe it was time to give that love to someone who wanted it and appreciated it. Ryann didn't know. She didn't want to be alone, but it always came back as the best scenario for her. However, she felt that she had something she needed to do.

She had to visit Lydia. Thank her for encouraging Ryann to take a second shot at life.

Ryann lifted her phone from the kitchen island, her cheeks still damp with tears. It was Saturday evening so Lydia was probably out on the town. She seemed like that kind of person. Someone who lived life to the fullest. She texted anyway.

R: Hey...

Ryann didn't expect anything back soon. So long as she got the chance to thank the woman who talked her down, that was good enough for her. If it happened tomorrow, so be it.

L: Hi...
R: I was wondering if I could drop by?
L: Yeah, I guess that would be okay.

Ryann paused, her thumbs stilling as she contemplated her next message. Lydia didn't appear to be bothered whether she showed up or not, but Ryann had to do this. She had to thank Lydia. She'd drop to her knees if necessary.

R: I won't stay long.
L: That's okay. When should I expect you?
R: An hour?
L: An hour works for me.
R: See you then...

Ryann locked her phone, placing it on the kitchen island before eyeing her hold-all. She had to unpack what she'd grabbed from the house earlier. Everything would fall into place within the next few weeks when she could make the apartment her own, and since she didn't have much right now, it wouldn't take long to hang up the few items of clothing she'd packed in her holdall. Once she was showered, Lydia was next on the agenda.

Lydia jumped, the doorbell almost sending her glass of wine to the floor. Ryann had been in touch, but it hadn't been a simple 'thanks I'll see you around.' No, Ryann wanted to see her. Now, Lydia wondered what she could possibly want. The doorbell rang again; this time Lydia should really answer it.

She steeled herself, blowing out a deep, calming breath as she opened the door. But it wasn't Ryann. "Soph, what are you doing here?"

"Thought I'd bring you that chocolate you asked for earlier."

"O-oh, I—"

Ryann appeared at the end of the path, stopping at the open gate, and Lydia fell silent. This wasn't supposed to happen. Soph and Ryann couldn't meet yet. The moment her best friend got wind of who this woman was, Ryann would leave. Soph would open her mouth and say something cruel, and that would be it.

Lydia's heart tumbled into her stomach; she didn't know how to remedy this situation. But she couldn't leave Ryann standing on the street.

"Ryann, hi." Lydia suddenly found her voice, flustered in the process. A heat quickly crept up her neck that she hadn't expected.

Soph frowned, turning around. "Oh, wow. I mean, hi."

Ryann smiled. "Hi."

"You have a date?" Soph whispered yelled. "Why didn't you say? It's about time you had a gorgeous woman in your bed. And holy shit, you picked an absolute beauty."

Soph pulled Lydia into a hug, gripping Lydia's body tightly. Lydia couldn't meet Ryann's eyes; the embarrassment was too much at the moment.

"I'm just going to leave." Soph grinned, backing away. "If you don't want her…I do."

Lydia laughed. "You're not even gay." Okay, she'd squealed that louder than she should have.

"Oh, I think I could be."

Lydia finally looked at Ryann. She wore a shy smile and an outfit that complemented her entirely. And she was beautiful. "Ryann, come in and go through. I seem to have a mad woman on my step."

"At least I know you're not talking about me for a change." Ryann stepped past Soph, slipping inside Lydia's home. "I'll just wait in the kitchen. Nice to meet you," Ryann said, her eyes switching to Soph.

Soph's eyes brightened. "Yeah, you too." Ryann disappeared, leading Soph to a prolonged whistle. "Well, you bagged yourself something special, Lyd."

"She's not my date."

"Did you see the arse on her?" Soph's brow rose. "Good Lord!"

"Okay, you need to leave now." Lydia shook her head, taking the chocolate from Soph's hands and choosing to dismiss her best friend's observation. Ryann wasn't here for Lydia to check her out, but now that Lydia's sexual orientation was out of the bag…what would it mean? "I'll call you, okay?" Soph nodded, waving over her shoulder as she left.

Ryann probably thinks I want to sleep with her. No, Lydia couldn't think that way. Ryann *did* look an absolute vision tonight, though. Lydia now wondered why.

She closed the door, aware that she'd left Ryann waiting too long, and went through to the kitchen. Ryann stood at the kitchen island, her back to Lydia. Ripped, black skinny jeans clung to her legs, her arse sculpted in the tight denim. Lydia watched Ryann slide her leather jacket off, her shoulders exposed in the black, oversized tank top she wore. The sides dropped significantly, Ryann's black bra visible and the olive skin of the sides of her stomach showing. The Ryann in her house tonight wasn't the woman who'd tried to end it all.

Lydia needed to focus. "Hi."

Ryann turned. Lydia hadn't noticed the flowers in her possession upon arrival. "Hey. Sorry to interrupt your evening."

"You haven't."

"You're sure? Your friend was here…"

Lydia shrugged. "Unannounced."

Ryann's smile grew wide, her pearly whites showing. "Here. These are for you."

Lydia took the arrangement of flowers, bringing the rose petals to her nose. Soft, pink, beautiful. "They're gorgeous," Lydia exhaled. "Thank you."

"This is nothing. It was just a small start to me repaying you for what you did last night. And I know I'll be repaying you for the rest of my life."

"That really isn't necessary, Ryann."

"Please. It is."

Lydia chewed her lip, brushing past Ryann as she looked for a vase. "I'll just put these in some water." Ryann's perfume soothed Lydia, and she inhaled deeply. She felt Ryann's eyes on her, following each move she made. It was intense but Lydia couldn't explain why.

"Have you eaten?"

"N-no." Lydia continued to focus on the task at hand, filling a vase with water and standing the flowers inside. She would arrange them properly later when she had some semblance of calm. "Have you?"

"Not yet. I hoped maybe I could buy *you* dinner tonight?"

"D-dinner?" Lydia spun, gripping the counter and steadying herself as Ryann's whiskey-coloured eyes pierced through her. Flowers...dinner. What was this?

"Yeah. Whatever you fancy. Unless you had things to do."

Lydia stared.

"So, what do you say? You must have some menus to choose from."

Ah! Takeaway. How stupid of Lydia to assume Ryann was asking her *out* to dinner. At a restaurant. Idiot.

"Yep. Loads. Sounds good." Lydia internally winced; what was wrong with her?

"Hey, is everything okay?" Ryann asked. "Just...you seem different. I can go if that would be better for you. I just wanted to thank you, is all. But if this is uncomfortable, I can totally leave."

Lydia composed herself. This was ridiculous. "No. Stay."

CHAPTER FIVE

Laughter filled Lydia's huge living room, Ryann almost choking on her beef biryani as Lydia described her new boss. She sounded like absolute hell on earth; her attitude needed taking down a notch or two. While they'd laughed about the situation Lydia found herself in recently, Ryann also saw the fury in Lydia's grey eyes. Anger and disappointment. Lydia explained how much she loved her job—prior to her new boss setting up in her office—but now it had been tainted. Lydia didn't hold enthusiasm for the woman like she did her position.

Ryann lifted her beer from the oak coffee table, swishing it in her mouth before attempting to speak. Tonight, she had let Lydia take the lead with conversation, not wanting to bring down the mood with her explanation for the episode at the river. She would bare all, Lydia deserved that at least, but not yet. The vibe between them was good, and Lydia was a joy to be around. Ryann wanted that to continue for as long as possible.

She eyed Lydia. "So, your friend..."

"Mouth almighty?" An eyebrow rose.

"I'm assuming that's not her birth name, but whatever works for you."

"Soph. We've been best friends since the end of primary school. I love her, but she's hard work."

"You really need to pick fewer problematic friends, Lydia."

"Huh?"

"Well, you say she's hard work…and then there is me." Ryann laughed. "I'm hardly one of the bright and cheery ones, am I?"

"Do you have a heart?"

"Last time I checked, yep. Although, I'm thinking of trading it in for a colder one. Seems women don't want someone with a good heart."

"How do you mean?" Lydia watched Ryann expectantly. Ryann had just told herself she wouldn't do this yet, but maybe it would feel good to bitch about Jen with someone who didn't know her. Lydia was more likely to be on her side, anyway.

"Just…my ex."

"Ah. Yes. The ex." Lydia stabbed her fork into an onion bhaji. Ryann suspected she didn't usually eat her Indian how she currently was—with cutlery—but neither really felt overly comfortable around one another yet.

To lighten the mood, Ryann tore into her peshwari naan and scooped her curry up with it, dripping it down her chin in the process.

"Real classy."

Ryann poked out her tongue, reaching what she could on her chin before taking the napkin beside her. "Eh. I know you're dying to do the same."

Lydia's eyes flickered to her plate. "Actually, I am. I just wasn't sure it was appropriate."

"We're all friends here, aren't we?"

"Well, I hope so…"

Lydia dropped her fork to her plate, mirroring Ryann's movements.

"Your friend. She embarrassed you before, didn't she?"

"Soph is always finding ways to embarrass me. It's nothing

new. I'm sorry if she was out of line, though. The whole date thing."

Ryann shrugged. "I've been accused of dating worse people."

Lydia's face flushed as Ryann expected it would. How hadn't Lydia landed on her gaydar already? She had to hear it from someone else; Ryann was way off her game.

"Sorry."

"It doesn't change anything, does it?" Lydia asked, swigging her own beer. "Me being gay, too."

Ryann sat back, her plate in her lap. "Why on earth would it change anything?"

"I don't know. I just...I don't want you to think I asked you back here last night because I'm into you. It wasn't like that. I just needed you to be safe. Warm."

Ryann's heart swelled in her chest. Lydia wasn't what she expected as she stood at the river, not at all, but she was more than happy it was who was there.

"That wasn't what I thought," Ryann said, placing her plate down on the table. She sat forward, resting her elbows on her knees. "The same as I didn't come back here because I'm into you."

"That's a good way of looking at it."

"Right?"

"I would like us to be friends, though."

Ryann smiled. "You became my friend the moment you talked me down."

Yes, she'd momentarily hated Lydia when Sam turned up outside her shop, but that was quickly quashed when Ryann realised just how much her life meant to Lydia. At least it meant something to someone. Yesterday, Ryann thought she was invisible to the world; she genuinely believed she could throw herself into the water and nobody would bat an eyelid. How wrong she'd been.

"I did hate you for a while last night, though..."

"Why?" Lydia sat up straight, confused.

Ryann cleared her throat. "Because you called Sam."

"I'm sorry. I don't regret it, but I am sorry for going through your phone. I didn't know what else I was supposed to do. You told me you were going home, but that didn't mean you actually would. Then you texted me to tell me you had gotten home okay and I instantly felt awful. I should have told you I'd taken Sam's number...but I am okay with the fact that I'd called her."

"I lied."

"About?"

"Going home. I...didn't have a home."

"What?" Lydia's forehead creased. "So, where did you stay last night? You could have stayed here; I wouldn't have minded."

"I ended up staying with Sam, but only because you called her. I was supposed to be on the street last night. I would have been okay, but it was nice sleeping in a bed for the first time in over a week."

"You've been sleeping on the street for a week?"

Tears filled Lydia's eyes. Ryann was taken aback. She didn't know why, but Lydia clearly felt for her from the moment they met; this emotion from another woman was new for Ryann.

Jen hadn't looked back once when Ryann told her she was leaving, but here was Lydia crying for Ryann and the situation she was in. Ryann really had wasted time on her relationship with Jen. Deep down, she already knew that, but Lydia's overwhelming support and emotion was confirming it once again. In some ways, it was a lot to take in. In others, it was nice to know that someone not obligated by family cared for her, had Ryann's best interests and wellbeing at heart.

"No, I was sleeping at my shop."

"That's still not right."

"Well, when your ex cheats on you in your own bed...you kinda have no option but to take the next best thing. Luckily, I had a comfortable couch in the shop."

"She cheated but you're the one living elsewhere. Something about that seems completely messed up."

"I chose to leave. It was the best thing for me. It wasn't the first time she'd done it, so once I found out it was still going on…I had to leave. I couldn't stand the thought of being in the same house with her. And it wasn't just the cheating. Other stuff has happened."

Ryann took a breath and then spilled, telling Lydia everything. From the moment she met Jen out in Australia, down to the second she realised she couldn't keep her business. Lydia was understandably horrified, but it really didn't matter anymore. Sam had thrown her a lifeline; Jen and her behaviour was in the past. A past Ryann never wanted to relive.

"So, what now?" Lydia asked. "I have a spare room here that you're more than welcome to. You can help me repaint the other living room to make up for the rent."

"I appreciate that, but I have a place to live now."

Lydia narrowed her eyes. Of course she didn't believe Ryann. She'd just admitted to almost sleeping on the street last night.

"I swear to God, I do have somewhere to live. Because you called Sam, I told her everything, and she's offered me her empty apartment in the city. Her sister, Lindsay, was living there but she's just moved into a house with her girlfriend."

"You're sure?"

"I'm sure. And, it's kinda swanky so I'd struggle to turn down Sam's offer, however great it would be living here with you."

Ryann froze. Was that a slight flirtation she had just partaken in? She hoped not. Ryann shouldn't react that way to a woman she'd only just met.

"Damn. I thought I was getting a decorating job for free then." Lydia swatted the coffee table jokingly. "Ah, well."

"Oh, I'm more than happy to help you with that. It's the least I can do." It was true. Ryann owed a lot to Lydia.

"No, it's fine. Dad's friend is a decorator. I'll get him in when I have the time."

"Oh, come on. It could be fun."

Lydia laughed. "What's fun about decorating?"

"Well, if you add a few beers into it and a takeout when it's done…tonnes."

"You know, I think I'll take you up on that offer. You seem kinda creative."

Ryann smirked. "Whatever gave you that impression?"

"Well, you certainly picked impressive tattoos." Lydia's eyes trailed Ryann's bare shoulders, something about the action catching Ryann off guard.

"Thanks."

"Where do you go for them?"

Ryann's chest ached. The thought of losing her shop was more heartbreaking than actually losing her girlfriend. "Dark Angel."

"Oh, that's the one next to my local."

"You mean the pub? You can smell that place from five streets away." Ryann could smell the stale alcohol inside her shop during the summer months.

"So?"

"Just…you don't seem like the kind they serve in there."

Lydia cocked her head. "You mean the office job and fancy shoes?"

"I don't like to judge, but yeah."

"If I showed up at the office wearing jeans, my boss would hit the roof."

"Stuck up bitch."

"She is," Lydia laughed, "but I'm used to it. When I'm not working, I'm usually in my pyjamas."

"You're not seeing anyone?" If Lydia was, they didn't live together. Ryann missed having someone by her side. Then she realized what she'd just said. "Sorry, that's none of my business."

Ryann couldn't pinpoint where that question had come from.

She could shrug it off, play along as though it was just a general question...but inside she *really* wanted to know if Lydia was single.

"The dating scene isn't what it used to be. There hasn't been anyone significant since my ex."

"Together long?"

Okay, less of the relationship questions, Ryann.

Lydia shrugged. "Few years."

Ryann wanted to ask what happened. She shouldn't, but Lydia made her feel extremely at ease.

"Niamh was ready to settle down. She was a few years older than me so once she reached thirty, she decided it was time to have kids. I just wasn't ready."

"So, it was a mutual split?"

"Pretty much, yeah. We kept in touch for a while, hung out, but once she met someone, she didn't really contact me anymore."

Ryann offered a sympathetic smile. "I'm sorry."

"It was probably for the best. I needed to move on from her. I realised I wasn't doing that while we were still meeting up for lunch and making plans together."

"No, I suppose not."

"You'll see why I'm single once you get back into the scene."

Ryann laughed. "No plans for that any time soon."

"Still...when you're ready."

Ryann sighed, sinking down into Lydia's duck-egg-blue couch. "I'm not sure I ever want another woman in my life again."

Lydia propped her elbows on the coffee table, resting her head in her hand. "Don't say that. We all have someone out there for us."

"Maybe. I don't know."

"I'm really sorry she hurt you. We're not all like that, though. I promise you."

For the second time in just twenty-four hours, Lydia's beaming smile brightened Ryann's existence. It was warm. Inviting. Special. When Lydia smiled, a single dimple appeared. Cute was the only way Ryann could describe the woman currently staring at her.

"Anyway," Ryann exhaled, wiping her hands down her jeans. "You got any tats?"

Lydia chewed her lip. "Just one. An angel on my shoulder. I prefer piercings. They're not as permanent."

"You don't have any piercings." Ryann studied Lydia; she had an old scar beneath her bottom lip, but nothing else other than her earlobes pierced. "You can't wear them at the office?"

Lydia coughed, taking her beer. "I do have a piercing."

Ryann frowned.

And then she knew. "O-oh."

Lydia suddenly blushed but Ryann was impressed. She had a few herself, but none as intimate as Lydia's appeared to be. She couldn't be sure, but Ryann assumed that was the reason Lydia's cheeks resembled a Royal Mail post box.

"Did it hurt?"

"I don't know if I'd say it hurt. The pain was…different."

"I mean, I have my nipple pierced, but I did that myself after a few whiskeys so I can't remember the pain."

"You pierce?" Lydia's eyebrows shot up with surprise.

"Y-yeah."

"You work at Dark Angel, don't you?" Lydia made her way to the couch, getting comfortable beside Ryann.

"I *owned* Dark Angel." Ryann held back the emotion in her throat, swilling it away with beer. "I lost it this week."

"O-oh, I'm sorry."

"It's okay. I'm beginning to come to terms with it."

Lydia took Ryann's hand, her touch soft and tender as it coursed through Ryann's entire body. This sensation was new, *different* to what she'd felt around other women. Ryann wanted to put it down to gratitude, the undeniable urge to repay Lydia in some way, but she would be lying to herself.

Lydia *did* mean something to Ryann. Something more than she deemed acceptable.

"You've really had a bad time, haven't you?"

"Lately, yes. It wasn't always this way. Sam has been a saviour by allowing me to stay at the apartment. I really don't know what I would have done without her."

"I wouldn't have seen you on the street, Ryann. You know you're always welcome here."

Ryann's eyes found Lydia's. "Why?"

As much as she appreciated all of this, she really was intrigued. Ryann wasn't the type to just pick up friends left, right and centre, so Lydia's attention felt uncertain. She also didn't understand this attraction she was experiencing, attraction that wasn't *friendly* as she'd tried to pass it off as.

"You know nothing about me but you're willing to have me in your life."

"I like you. You're exactly the type of person I need in *my* life."

"Huh?"

"You're...different," Lydia explained. "I'm used to being cooped up in here with Soph. And while I love her to death, we're not on the same wavelength anymore. She constantly bitches about her boyfriend and you know, he's actually really great. He does everything for her, but she still finds a reason to complain. And like I told you at the river...I no longer have the patience for other people's drama."

"But you've taken on my drama."

"Not quite." Lydia leaned forward, taking her bottle of beer followed by Ryann's. As she handed it over, Lydia leaned in and pressed a kiss to Ryann's cheek. "Your issues are genuine. Don't ever feel like a burden or that I don't want to help you. You're really sweet, and I want to be your friend."

Ryann's mouth fell open slightly. Not only had Lydia accommodated her once again this evening, but now she was receiving a kiss, too? Ryann wouldn't say no to a gorgeous woman in her company, especially not Lydia, but all of this was overwhelming.

A simple kiss on the cheek had sparked something inside Ryann. Something she wasn't entirely sure she was ready to explore.

This is stupid. I don't even know her.

"T-thanks."

CHAPTER SIX

The week had been up and down, but now Lydia was sitting at her desk on a Friday morning, tiredness evident in the way her shoulders slumped. Bree had passed by several times; the best Lydia could offer was a simple smile. Fake, one she could barely muster, but manageable given the circumstances.

Lydia focused on the template sitting on her screen. The colours merged into one as her eyes blurred, burning in a desperate attempt to remain open. Lydia hadn't slept fully all week. It had been a week since she'd met Ryann.

Though Ryann was now safe, Lydia felt compelled to ensure it stayed that way. Ryann was something special, a breath of fresh air in Lydia's life. Lydia realised that when she spent the entire week alone, contemplating calling Ryann every day. She missed her.

This is ridiculous. You've done your bit. Let her be.

Lydia rubbed at her temples. This week, as far as she was concerned, was a write-off. Bree would soon get tetchy. She'd only yelled twice today; that couldn't possibly be all the office was in for. Friday was the end of the working week, but Lydia knew better than to expect Bree to be chirpy.

Gareth, one of the lads on her team, brought her coffee. He'd been here over a year and knew Lydia was a lesbian but insisted on invading her personal space at any given opportunity. His flirting game was terrible, and Lydia had told him as much a few months ago on a night out.

"Busy week?" Gareth's chestnut hair flopped over one side of his head. It was a nineties haircut, no doubt about it.

"Yup. Kinda."

"You're not coming for drinks tonight...again."

Lydia looked directly at him. "Nope."

"Everything okay?"

Lydia didn't have the patience for Gareth and small talk today. It was nice that he was concerned, but they weren't friends. "Everything is fine. Thanks."

"Because you seem kinda distant tod—"

"Miss Nelson!"

Lydia froze. Bree's tone really would be the final straw today. Gareth slowly retreated back to his desk, leaving a vast space between Lydia and her boss.

"Can I see you?"

Lydia pondered saying no. It really would feel good to say no and walk right out the door. Jo, Lydia's previous boss, had been more of a friend than a superior. Pastries and posh coffee waited every morning, along with Jo's beaming smile. Jo had respect for her team; Lydia wasn't sure Bree knew the meaning of the word.

"Well?" Bree's hand sat on her hip.

"Sure." Lydia puffed out her cheeks, exhaling dramatically.

She was ushered inside Bree's office, a chill in the air as the door swung closed. Bree's tall figure had at one time been intimidating, her deep red hair styled immaculately to perfection, but now Lydia just felt sorry for her boss. It took a lot for Lydia to dislike a person, but Bree made it easy. Too easy.

"What's going on?"

Lydia stared at her boss' back as Bree asked the question. She preferred to converse with someone to their face but evidently that wouldn't be happening today. Call her stupid, but it was the manners Lydia had been raised with.

"Nothing is going on."

"I'm not satisfied with your work."

Lydia frowned. Her work was perfectly good. "Okay. What work?"

"The social media campaign?" Bree's eyebrow rose as she finally turned and looked at Lydia. "It's not good enough. When Pete calls, and he will, should I direct the call to you?"

"Social media?" Lydia repeated. "I wasn't assigned to any social media campaign."

"Are you calling me a liar?"

Yes. "I'm saying something must have got mixed up along the way." Surely that response would satisfy Bree. It wasn't a yes, but it wasn't a no. Lydia wouldn't allow the blame to fall on her, so it was the best Bree could have.

"I don't *get* projects mixed up."

You also don't know how to communicate with another human being.

Lydia cleared her throat. "But someone, somewhere has mixed it up."

"Do I need to give someone else your position? Because I know a number of staff who would fall to their knees for your salary."

Lydia had been lucky to keep the salary she received when Bree joined the company. The daughter of Walter Quinn, owner, Bree planned to overhaul the place once she got her hands on it. What she hadn't anticipated was the pay freeze stated in long-term employees' contracts. A win for Lydia; Bree, not so much.

Walter passed away a year ago, but he'd handed the reins to Jo Carmichael many years before. The company wouldn't be where it was now without Jo, and in some ways Lydia, but Bree wouldn't believe that. From the moment Jo left, Bree was determined to lead staff to believe the opposite. That the company was having difficulties. Threatening pay-cuts wasn't anything new with Bree, and Lydia knew that was exactly where this was going.

She chose to call Bree's bluff. "If you don't believe the work I'm doing is up to par, I can step aside."

The woman herself had confessed how good Lydia was at her job just a few weeks ago. She was drunk at the time, but Bree had said it regardless. She had a habit of being two different people inside and outside the office.

When they were off the clock, Bree wanted to be everybody's best friend. Overly friendly. But the moment she stepped into the office, the power went to her head. Power she didn't need to feel. Nobody was threatening her with their own agenda. The staff at the company just wanted to hit the targets set and work in a happy environment.

"Just let me know where you want me instead. I'll take whatever project you have for me."

Bree narrowed her eyes.

She just stared.

"Okay?" Lydia pressed.

"You know, I'll take a look at the campaign again. See if we can't work together on it. Make it perfect between us."

Lydia shrugged. "Sure, but I'm not actually working on any campaign at the moment, so I honestly do not know what you're talking about."

"Like I said," Bree paused, holding up her hand to signal the conversation was over, "I'll work it out."

Bree knew she was in the wrong; Lydia could see it in her uncaring eyes. Bree wouldn't admit to the error—nor would she apologise to Lydia—so Lydia chose to nod, smile, and walk away. "Okay, great."

Lydia spied her phone lighting up on her desk as she moved back into the open plan space, all eyes landing on her as her heels dug into the unnecessarily thick-piled carpet. She would break an ankle one day. With any luck, it would be one day soon.

"What did she say?" Gareth asked, sidling back up to Lydia. "She didn't look happy. Did you do something wrong?"

"Do I look like I did something wrong?"

"Well, I don't know. Hard to read you sometimes."

Lydia smiled sarcastically. "Then stop trying to read me. She got something wrong, as usual. Then she turned it around as though nothing had happened. Just your average day, Gareth. Go back to your desk."

Lydia fell down into her swivel chair, brushing her raven hair from her face. She eyed the clock; just another two hours to go.

Her phone lit up again. A text message. From Ryann.

R: Hope work has treated you well this week. And your boss has stayed off your back.

Lydia smiled at her screen. Ryann was thinking about her. It was sweet.

L: Just had a close call. Nothing I couldn't handle.

R: You've got it. Don't worry.

L: Any plans this weekend?

Lydia wasn't quite sure why she'd asked Ryann that question, but it was out there now. She couldn't take it back even if she wanted to.

R: Booked a removal van. Going back to the house to take everything.

L: Everything?

R: Anything I paid for. Which was basically everything.

L: I thought Sam's apartment was kitted out with everything you needed?

R: It is. That doesn't mean I'm giving Jen the satisfaction of keeping all my things. The removal company will drop it all off at a charity for those in need of furniture.

L: That's incredibly sweet of you.

Lydia relaxed back in her seat, Ryann warming her heart with each message they exchanged. Just a simple message had taken all Lydia's issues off her mind, something she hadn't imagined possible today. Ryann had stuff going on, so for her to take a few minutes to check in with Lydia meant a lot.

R: I'm just doing my bit. Enjoy the rest of your afternoon.

L: Thank you for checking in. I hope you've had a good week. Talk later?

Talk later? Maybe that was too much. Lydia was really taking a liking to Ryann, but she should slowly back away and allow Ryann the space she needed to think over the events of the weekend. She would always be there if Ryann needed to talk, but Lydia felt as though she was becoming too attached.

R: Yeah, I'd love to.

Well, this wasn't going to plan.

Ryann slouched back on the couch, the huge TV on the wall showing a repeat of the midweek football matches. Her team had already been shown, but Ryann liked to keep up with the rest of the table. See what her side had to contend with.

It had been a long season, one that she was ready to see the back of. The boys in blue could regroup over the summer and work much harder than they had been over the last few months. The only possibility left was the quarter-final of the cup, if the team managed to make it out of the last sixteen.

A knock at the door pulled her eyes from the screen. Nobody she knew had access to this building. Only Sam and Lindsay. Ryann rushed to the door and opened it. Sam was on the other side, dressed in her usual business suit and looking fantastic.

"How are you settling in?"

Ryann stepped aside, inviting Sam out of the corridor. "Really good."

"And it's spotless, I'm impressed." Sam nodded, taking in the apartment she once lived in.

Ryann knew this apartment had been a difficult time in Sam's life, but she was now home with her wife and kid...another on the way.

"I haven't heard from you this week."

Ryann cleared her throat. "Sorry."

"I thought you may have been in touch…"

"I took your advice and visited Lydia." Ryann pulled two cups from the shelf, powering up the fancy coffee machine. "Want coffee?"

Ryann fell silent for a moment, chewing her bottom lip. Sam didn't know that it had been almost a week ago that she'd visited Lydia, but Ryann had been laying low. She didn't want to get in Lydia's way. A text message here and there wasn't too much, not in Ryann's mind, but showing up or arranging to meet one another could be considered odd.

At the back of Ryann's mind, there was an attraction to the woman who saved her life. An attraction she wouldn't divulge to Sam. Lydia's kiss to Ryann's cheek had played on her mind—ridiculous but true. This was why she should remain single. If she could leave one relationship and contemplate another so soon, she had issues to work through.

Shouldn't she be heartbroken after leaving Jen? Shouldn't Ryann be crying into her pillow each night, wishing things could have been different? Ryann wanted to believe that *that* should be her reaction...but she couldn't. Though they'd worked through their issues in the past, Ryann never felt as though Jen was all in. In turn, Ryann refused to give every last piece of herself to Jen.

"I'd love coffee." Ryann felt Sam's eyes burning through her. "So...Lydia?"

"I went over there with some flowers and bought her dinner."

Sam's eyebrow rose.

"What?"

"Nothing." Sam pursed her lips, something clearly playing on her mind. "And how was Lydia?"

"Not looking forward to work. She has a bitchy boss. One I don't think I like the sound of."

"Good thing you don't have to concern yourself with her work life then, huh?" Sam pulled herself up onto a stool, relaxing back and crossing her legs. "You know, since she's just an acquaintance."

"Oh, yeah. Of course."

"Unless there was something more?"

"You've lost me." Ryann placed a coffee down in front of her cousin, her brow knitted. *Not now, Sam. Please, not now.*

"She saved your life. Then she offered you dinner. And now you're returning the favour...flowers and all."

"Um, correct me if I'm wrong, but you told me to take her a gift."

"I did."

"So, what's the problem?"

"No problem. Just don't get yourself too attached. You've just been through a break-up, amongst other things."

"You think I want to sleep with her?" Ryann couldn't contain the laugh she felt working its way to the surface. Even if Ryann *was* attracted to Lydia, she had no intentions of sleeping with her. "Christ, Sam. That's not me."

Of all the things in the world to be said, Ryann hadn't expected that. She didn't do quick lays. She didn't entertain one-night stands. Ryann was very much a long-term relationship kinda girl. She always would be.

"No, I know." Sam waved off Ryann's response. "All I'm saying, is that I don't want you to get yourself into something that wouldn't ever happen."

"And now you think I *couldn't* bed her if I wanted to?" Ryann was giving herself whiplash with the back and forth in her own mind. Sam had completely thrown her with this conversation.

Could she bed Lydia if she wanted to? Ryann chose not to think about that possibility.

Sam held up her hand, trying her coffee. "I have no doubt that you could bed *any* woman in this city. You're gorgeous. But don't let this turn into something that may not work out for you. I know you probably feel indebted to Lydia in some way and that's understandable, but she's just a friend, right?"

"The last time I checked, yeah."

"Then that is fine."

Ryann wouldn't reveal the information sitting on the tip of her tongue. Sam didn't need to know that she planned to help Lydia decorate some of the spare rooms in her home. But even if she did make Sam aware of that, it didn't change Ryann and Lydia's relationship. Ryann wasn't ready to settle down with anyone yet.

For the foreseeable, love was the last thing on her mind. Or so Ryann was trying to tell herself. She *did* have to concentrate on herself. Her wellbeing. She hadn't forgotten that she'd almost ended everything just last week, and as much as she loved Lydia for helping her, something more simply wasn't possible.

Lydia didn't need a woman in her life who didn't know which direction her future would take. Ryann was also positive that Lydia wouldn't entertain the idea.

"S-she's gay." The words spewed from Ryann's mouth unexpectedly.

Too late. She couldn't take them back now.

"Lydia?" Sam's forehead rose. "Interesting."

"No, it's not like that." Ryan shook her head. "God, why do lesbians just assume everyone wants a shag at the mention of a friend's sexuality?"

"I wasn't assuming anything, but it does change things, don't you think?"

"No, I don't. Lydia was amazing last Friday night. If it wasn't for her, I wouldn't be here. That doesn't mean I'm going to climb into bed with her as way of thanks...or to repay her."

Sam smirked. "But if she did want you to hop into her bed?"

"She doesn't."

"Oh, so you've already discussed not sleeping with one another? I'd have *loved* to be a fly on the wall for *that* conversation."

"She was worried," Ryann explained. "She didn't want me to think that she'd offered me her time because she knew I was gay. Her friend kinda outed her to me on the doorstep and it was playing on her mind. It was sweet of her to explain, but she really didn't need to. We just hung out and had dinner together. It was nice having a friend, Sam. You know I don't take well to new people, but Lydia really is great."

"I'm happy she's in your life. And, I want to meet her."

"Why?"

"To thank her for keeping you around. For calling me. I'd like to actually meet her, rather than do it over the phone again."

"I'm sure she doesn't mind if you don't meet her. She's busy with work anyway."

"Mmm." Sam sipped her coffee, nodding slowly.

"What does 'mmm' mean?"

"You don't want me to meet her. Why is that?" Sam wore a crooked, suspicious smile. One that Ryann wouldn't entertain. *If* something ever happened with Lydia, and that was a very big *if*, Ryann would explain in her own time.

For the moment, Ryann was done with this. There was nothing going on between them. If Sam felt she really needed to meet Lydia, Ryann wouldn't stop her, she just wasn't sure it was needed.

"You know what, never mind. You have her number, I'm sure you can arrange a day and time that suits you both."

"Yep. Exactly what I was thinking."

Ryann finally joined Sam at the counter, satisfied that the Lydia conversation was over. Now she had so much to thank her cousin for, she just didn't know where to begin. "Y-you said we were getting the business back. How?"

"I called this morning. It's going to auction next week."

"Sam, no." Ryann couldn't allow Sam to do something like this. She'd done more than enough.

"I'm considering offering them above the asking price, so it doesn't go to auction. Your tattoo studio is situated in an ideal area of the city. It could go wrong for me on the day. Repossessed properties usually sell lower than what an asking price would be, up to thirty percent sometimes, so if I go in with a higher offer, they should swing it my way. Chances are, I probably know the company selling it off anyway. I'll send them a nice Christmas hamper."

"Sam, you can't do this. You have a kid on the way."

"I'm not sure what that has to do with anything. I'm investing in property. One that you will reside in. That's all."

"And how often do you 'invest' in property?"

"When my family needs me to," Sam said, placing her coffee cup down. "And I'm having the papers drawn up for this place. It'll soon be yours."

"No, I'm renting it from you."

"Rent won't be required." Sam slid off her stool, her heels clicking against the expensive wood flooring. "Get yourself set up here. If I manage to get the studio back without the need for an auction, I'll call you."

Ryann watched Sam head for the door. "That's it? You drop all of that on me and now you're just going to leave?"

"Ry, I have a business to run." Sam winked. "I can't sit around drinking coffee with you all afternoon."

"B-bu—"

"Oh, and I've made my lawyer aware of Jen's behaviour. She's ready to go as soon as you are."

"With what?"

"Calling the police. Fraud."

Ryann ran her fingers through her hair. She really needed a cut. "Right, yeah."

"You *are* going to take it further, right?"

"Of course. Just...you're throwing all kinds of information at me this afternoon and I don't know which way is up."

Sam nodded, opening the door. "You probably want to wait a while before you check your bank account then. Call me when you want to come over for dinner."

The door closed, leaving Ryann startled in the middle of the kitchen. What was Sam talking about? Her bank account? This day had been too much. She needed to lie down.

CHAPTER SEVEN

Lydia flopped down on the couch, her pink and blue check pyjama bottoms riding up her leg as she pulled a blanket across her. Friday was over, dinner had been eaten and cleared away, and now she planned to lie on the couch until her eyes no longer wished to remain open. Bree hadn't bothered to come by to apologise after their run-in, only showing up at Lydia's desk to demand an early start on Monday. As much as Lydia wanted to turn down her request—there was no reason to start early—she didn't have the energy to argue.

Now, lying here, she contemplated calling Jo. It was no secret that Jo wanted Lydia with her at the new agency she was slowly building, but Lydia needed stability. A steady income. Jo couldn't provide that when she walked away, and perhaps she still couldn't, but Lydia was close to taking whatever she could get. Bree would survive without her. Or so Bree would say. *I don't want a job I hate.* Lydia sighed; why couldn't life be simpler?

With the remote control in her hand, her body curled up and snuggly, Lydia surfed the channels. Friday night meant zero TV opportunities unless you wanted to watch one of the soaps that aired daily at the same time each night. Lydia didn't have the patience for soap operas. She'd never understood how people discussed them at work as though it was real life. Friday also didn't usually end with her being home, but here she was for the second Friday in a row…sober and with no plans.

With the TV muted, Lydia turned onto her back and lifted her phone from the coffee table. Soph hadn't been in touch since Saturday when Ryann showed up on the doorstep. As much as she wanted someone to talk to, Lydia would wait for Soph to contact her. She worked long hours through the week.

The doorbell sounded, causing Lydia to frown. Tonight was supposed to be just her and her thoughts. Her blanket. She may be thirty-three, but she enjoyed the small comforts. Whoever was interrupting her, it wasn't appreciated. Not at all. Lydia climbed from the couch, sighing as she reached the door.

When she opened it, she was met with deep, dark eyes. Eyes she had thought about all week. "Hi."

"I'm so sorry for just showing up, but I needed someone to talk to."

Lydia smiled. She may have been unhappy that someone had called, but not Ryann. She'd never be mad if Ryann showed up, even unannounced. "Come in. Is everything okay?"

"We're definitely friends, right?"

"Of course. Come in here." She dragged Ryann into the living room, closing the door behind her. "What's going on?"

"Sam," Ryann exhaled deeply, running her fingers through her dark hair. "She's gone too far."

Lydia wasn't sure what that meant. Ryann was visibly distressed, perhaps annoyed, but she'd chosen Lydia to confide in so the least she could do was listen. "Sam?"

"She showed up today," Ryann started, "just to check in, or so I thought. She just…she went way too far this time, Lydia."

Lydia wasn't sure she could ever tire from hearing Ryann say her name. As it slid from her lips, it sounded sincere. As though it meant a lot. Lydia forced herself to focus. "Okay, but why?"

"You know I lost my business."

"Because of your bitch of an ex, yes." Lydia couldn't quite pinpoint where that anger had come from, but Ryann was staring, frowning. "Sorry."

"Oh, don't be. It's kinda nice to know that someone else thinks the same as me."

"I just hate what she did to you. But, you're not here to discuss that. You're here because you seem quite annoyed."

"I am." Ryann paced in front of the fire. "I'm so annoyed with her. She just...God, she's crazy."

"She didn't sound crazy when I called her a few nights ago."

"Sam..." Ryann paused. "She's a multimillionaire. The place I'm staying—Bryant Tower? She built it."

"Wait! Hold on..." Lydia needed a moment to process. "You're living in Bryant Tower? And your cousin built it?"

"Correct."

"That's impressive."

"First, she told me she was getting my business back, then she told me I didn't need to pay rent on the place...she's *giving* it to me. And then, today...I checked my account and she's put twenty grand in it!"

"Kinda wish I had a cousin like that." Lydia smiled weakly. "I don't know what the problem is."

"Everything. It's all a problem."

"She's family. She wants to help."

"But it's too much. Far too much. Surely you see that, too. And now she won't answer my calls."

Lydia understood Ryann's predicament to an extent, but shouldn't she be happy her family were willing to help? Not many had the opportunity to begin again. Lydia certainly wouldn't turn her nose up at twenty thousand in her bank account. If she had that, she wouldn't be in her piss-poor job.

"Sorry." Ryann stopped pacing, glancing at the blanket on the couch. "I'm interrupting your evening."

"Yeah, because I was really busy."

"You know what I mean. I'll go. You've done enough for me already."

Lydia grew confused. "What exactly was it that you *wanted* me to do this time?"

"Just...be an ear. A shoulder. Whatever."

"Then sit your arse down and get comfy."

Lydia added another log to the fire, satisfied that it would keep the temperature just right. At the opposite end of the couch, Ryann was removing the leather jacket Lydia was becoming accustomed to. It just fit Ryann so well. Her body and her personality.

Lydia faced Ryann, offering her a small smile. "I can understand why you're mad with Sam."

"I probably sound ungrateful, but it's far too much, what she's doing for me."

"Agreed. It probably is."

Ryann narrowed her eyes. "I feel like there is a *but* coming..."

"But she cares about you and she wants to help you. I saw how hurt you were on Saturday night when you spoke about your tattoo studio. Sam is throwing you a lifeline here, and I think you would be a fool not to accept it."

"You know, it's not even the studio. It's the money in my account. The free apartment."

"To be honest, it's nice to see someone who has more than enough offering to help another person out. A lot of people wouldn't, Ryann. Sam is clearly one of the good ones."

"She is. I know that." Ryann fell silent, focusing on her hands in her lap. Contemplative, Lydia decided to sit down slowly and wait for Ryann to realise that what her cousin was doing was good. Nobody *wanted* to ask for help, least of all Ryann, but this would enable her to get back on her feet.

"You know, this would be one almighty fuck you to your ex, don't you think? Getting yourself back together. Accepting help from Sam which Jen doesn't need to know about. Right now, she probably thinks she's won. But if you accept this, it would change everything."

Ryann's lip twitched, the slight signs of a smile present. "Jen wouldn't like this."

"Which?"

"Me sitting here with you. Someone who speaks sense and has a heart of gold."

Lydia's heart swelled in her chest. "O-oh."

"She also wouldn't like knowing that it all worked out okay for me. I saw the look in her eyes when I caught her again. She didn't give a shit. But you know, neither do I. Not anymore."

"No?"

"No, because by losing her...I somehow gained you. A friend for life. And in my opinion, *that* is worth more than anything else."

A friend for life. Lydia wished to be something other than a friend; God knows Ryann brightened her miserable life from the moment they met.

But this wasn't about Lydia's feelings. This was about Ryann, and being sure she was okay.

"That means a lot," Lydia exhaled, pulling her knees up to her chest. "I just hope you will consider Sam's offer." Time would tell, Lydia knew that, but Ryann needed the help right now. It didn't mean she was weak or that she would take whatever she could get; Lydia truly saw the anguish in Ryann's eyes as she contemplated what Sam had done. This wouldn't be taken lightly. "Have you spoken to your ex at all?"

"No. And she doesn't know about the removal van I have showing up tomorrow."

"What if she's changed the locks?"

"She knows what will happen if she has." Ryann sat forward, torment evident in her body language. "But you've been great *again*, so thank you."

"Any time."

"I should go. Let you get on with the rest of your night."

"I was trying to find something half decent on the TV. No luck."

"Friday. Shockingly bad." Ryann smiled. "I'll see myself out, okay?"

"You don't have to go, you know."

"I have a date with a hot bath, and I should probably call Sam, too. Thank her for being amazing instead of yelling at her via voicemail."

"I'm sure she would appreciate that," Lydia said. "Did you want a lift home?"

"No, the bus is fine."

Lydia nodded. Ryann was in a much better place, meaning Lydia was satisfied that she could be trusted to head home alone. *Bryant Tower.* Lydia couldn't believe just how well Ryann had landed on her feet. She was thrilled for her friend, of course she was, but Bryant Tower was where the people with money lived. A lot of money. A place she could only imagine visiting. Lydia's Jaguar was nothing compared to the Ferraris and the Maseratis locked away behind the huge gates of the complex. Nothing whatsoever.

"I'll see you when I see you, okay?"

Ryann brought Lydia back from her daydream. Perhaps Ryann would invite her over one day. Give her a tour of the place. She imagined Sam's apartment was impressive; nothing was mediocre in that building. Lydia had seen the photographs online. She'd also seen the price tag.

Lydia's eyes suddenly fell to Ryann's arse as she turned and walked into the hall. It was impressive. Perfectly rounded. *Stop!*

Lydia shot to her feet, following Ryann. "Did you, uh…" she shook her head.

Ryann frowned, her hand placed on the back of the door. "Did I what?"

"Did you want to grab a drink next Friday night?" Lydia's

heart plunged into her stomach. Ryann would surely turn down her offer. "I'm sure you're busy and that's fi—"

"Did you just ask me out for a drink only to take it back not even a second later?"

"No, I just..." Why did Lydia feel so anxious? "Would you?"

"I'd love to." Ryann's smile flashed, the atmosphere between them suddenly shifting. Lydia couldn't quite put her finger on why, but everything seemed to relax. To calm. "Wait, don't you usually go out with work on Friday?"

"Yeah, usually."

"And why won't you be doing that next week?"

Lydia felt a blush creep up her neck, working its way to her cheeks quickly. "Honestly, I'd rather spend time with you than the people I see all day."

Lydia caught the slight smirk Ryann was suppressing. Did she sound desperate?

"It's just a drink...as friends."

"Of course, yeah." Ryann waved off the stuttering mess Lydia was becoming. "Just friends."

"I'm not trying to get you into bed or anything like that."

Ryann nodded slowly. "Same here."

As Ryann confirmed Lydia's intentions along with her own, Lydia suddenly felt disappointed. This wasn't supposed to play out like this. She didn't know Ryann, and she certainly wasn't her type. Lydia had never looked at someone like Ryann twice. What changed? Why did she feel as though she wanted to ask Ryann over more often? And why the hell had she suggested drinks?

Lydia cleared her throat. "You'll miss your bus."

"R-right, yeah. See you." Ryann shot out the door, closing it behind her. Lydia could only imagine what Ryann must think of her, a dithering mess who couldn't manage a friendship with a beautiful woman. *This is all going to go horribly wrong.*

Lydia peered out of the side of the blinds in her living room. Forty minutes ago, she received a call from Ryann's cousin, Sam. As nice as she sounded, Lydia wasn't sure why Sam had asked for her address. Now, Lydia's heart slammed against her ribcage. A pristine white Range Rover was sitting on the street outside her house. If Sam wanted to meet with Lydia, she wasn't doing a very good job of it. The car, and its driver, had remained unmoving for fifteen minutes.

But then the door opened, and Lydia's eyebrows rose with surprise. Sam was a vision. *And married.* Lydia reminded herself. Long, dark hair wisped around in the breeze, and an impeccable black, designer suit covered a tall slender body. Lydia immediately noticed the resemblance Sam had to Ryann. *Okay, she's going to be lovely. Just open the door.*

Lydia steeled herself as the sound of heels pounded up her garden path to the front door. The doorbell jolted her, but Lydia remained calm on the outside. Inside, her stomach lurched. Her hand nervously found the door handle and Lydia pulled it open. "H-hi."

"Lydia?"

Lydia's smile beamed. "That's me."

"I'm so sorry I kept you waiting. Unexpected business call."

"Oh, that's okay. No plans." Lydia moved aside, offering Sam access to her home. "Is everything okay? Nothing happened to Ryann, did it?"

"Ryann is...fine." Sam eyed Lydia, studying her. She, too, had a piercing gaze. One that mirrored Ryann's in every way possible. "Why wouldn't she be?"

"No reason. I guess I'm just still worrying about her."

"That's sweet but I'm not here about Ryann. Well, I am, but she's okay. You two are out for drinks on Friday, right?"

Lydia frowned. "Y-yeah. She told you?"

"It came up, yes."

Lydia ushered Sam through to the kitchen, flicking the kettle on as she motioned towards the dining table. "Sorry, I only have instant at the moment. Would you like one?"

Sam smiled. "Instant is great."

"Okay, well...have a seat." Lydia's nerves dissipated slightly. Sam's presence was less terrifying than she imagined it would be. As she focused on the two cups sitting on the counter, Lydia's mind wandered. *Why would Ryann tell Sam about my invitation for drinks?* "So, you wanted to see me?"

"I wanted to thank you." Sam crossed her legs as she took a seat at the dining table. "What you did, Lydia—"

"Was only what anyone else would have done."

"Oh, I don't know about that."

"When I saw her at the railings, I thought it was a bit odd. She wasn't wearing a coat. She didn't seem to have anything with her other than her phone. And then she climbed over. She absolutely terrified me, but I knew I had to go and speak to her. If one conversation was the difference between life and death, I couldn't not."

"I don't think I can ever truly repay you." Sam's voice cracked, surprising Lydia. Sam didn't appear to be an emotional woman. "Ryann doesn't have anyone else around here. Just me and my wife. And our son."

"She spoke very highly of Luca. You and your wife, too."

"Yet she didn't feel as though she could come to me for help." Sam sighed, clearly upset with Ryann's lack of reaching out.

"Yeah. It's something she's still struggling with."

Sam frowned, apparently waiting for an explanation from Lydia.

"She came over last night. You'd been to her place and surprised her with...well, you know."

"Ah, the money."

"I'm not sure I've ever seen anyone looking so terrified and confused."

"Ryann doesn't like to rely on people. We're similar in that way. But she needed it and I was able to offer my help. She will get over it all soon enough."

"I told her she would be a fool to turn down your offer."

"You know," Sam said, sitting forward and smiling, "for someone who Ryann has only known for five minutes, she certainly takes notice of everything and anything you say."

"I-I don't…" Lydia paused, her brows drew together. "I mean, I'm sure she would have taken advice from anyone she could have."

Lydia noted the smirk playing on Sam's full, pink lips.

"I just want to be a friend. A support when she needs it. I really like Ryann and want us to keep in touch."

"You've definitely been what she needed. And drinks on Friday. That'll be nice."

Something in Sam's tone had Lydia eyeing her suspiciously. Inwardly, at least. Lydia wasn't sure she could ever stare Sam down. This woman knew exactly how to work the room and exactly how to hold a conversation on her terms.

"If Ryann doesn't cancel, it'll be lovely."

"Why would she cancel?"

Lydia laughed. "Oh, come on. I don't think I'm really Ryann's scene. Her usual type of friend."

"Ryann has very few friends. She's always been that way. Me, too."

"You're *very* similar, huh?" Lydia leaned against the counter, folding her arms across her chest. It was clear to her that Sam and Ryann had a close relationship, so knowing that Ryann would sooner end her life than ask for help made this all the more painful. "You look like her, too."

"Minus the impressive body art." Sam sipped her coffee, watching Lydia over the rim of the cup. Sam was sweet, but when she looked you straight in the eye…terrifying. "Don't you think?"

"T-think what?"

"That her body art is impressive?"

"Oh." Lydia cleared her throat. "Yeah."

The body art. Lydia had never felt a pull towards women who had extensive tattoos, but Ryann was an exception. Had she thought about them? Wondered how they may look beneath her clothes? Briefly, yes. Briefly, because if she thought about them too much, it would only leave her wanting more.

"Is she actually covered in them?"

"Mmhmm." Sam smiled fully, her eyes sparkling against the kitchen spotlights. "Very much so."

"Well...that's nice."

"She's great," Sam said. "Really great."

"She is." She wasn't sure what Sam was trying to get at with this conversation.

"I just hope she finds someone who deserves her. Ryann is... every woman's dream."

"How so?" Lydia shouldn't ask, it wasn't her place to do so, but she found herself enquiring, nonetheless.

"She has so much to give. When she's in love, it's something beautiful. At least, I thought it was with Jen. What a bitch she turned out to be." Sam's anger for Ryann's ex was more than noticeable. Those deep, soft eyes turned dark and stormy. "She's great with kids. Absolutely loves them. She's just a stunning person."

"She said she wasn't interested in a relationship." The words left Lydia's mouth far too easily, causing Sam's eyebrow to raise. "We were talking a few nights ago and she said she had no plans to fall in love again."

"Christ, she sounds like me a few years ago." Sam rolled her eyes playfully, laughing as she shook her head. "Ryann will fall in love again. She's too good to remain single. She just needs to find herself the right kind of person. Someone kind and trustworthy. Someone who can show her that they're fully there for her."

Someone like me. Lydia's heart rate picked up at that mere thought. Was that what Sam was trying to say? Lydia didn't believe so. She couldn't possibly.

And then a sadness settled in Lydia. Ryann wasn't her type. *She* wasn't Ryann's type.

"I hope she can find someone like that when she's ready."

Sam climbed to her feet, her heels clicking against the stone kitchen floor. "I think she's going to be perfectly fine. I have a feeling she won't have to look far."

"W-wha—?"

"I should head back to the office. I promised Luciana I wouldn't be late tonight."

Lydia followed Sam out of the kitchen and towards the front door. She wanted to know what Sam was implying, but her own thoughts prevented her from doing so. Sam had flicked a switch inside Lydia, one that she really didn't want to play around with.

"If there is *anything* I can ever do for you, don't think twice about asking, Lydia." Sam embraced her. "Thank you for everything you've done for Ryann. I won't ever forget it."

CHAPTER EIGHT

Ryann slowly approached the front of Sam's home. She'd arranged to meet with Luciana while Sam finished up her business for the day at the office, but an instant unease settled deeper with each step she took. An unease that had only grown as the day progressed. The reason for that feeling: Lydia.

Ryann had tried to recall the moment when she knew she was attracted to the woman who had saved her life, but the last few weeks had been a blur. It could have been Lydia's wonderful personality, it could have been the slight kiss, but it didn't matter. What mattered was the fact that she felt the attraction at all. Surely it could only be a bad thing.

Given the circumstances around how they met, nothing positive could come from feeling this way. Ryann believed it could be because Lydia had been so welcoming, but it felt like something more. Something real. As she woke this morning, she felt a weight pressing down on her. It shouldn't be that way towards someone she was attracted to. She should feel good, right?

This is ridiculous. Ryann shoved her hands in her pockets, blowing out a deep breath as she took the steps up the decking. Luciana was waiting at the door; this was going to be interesting.

"Have I done something to offend you?" Luciana asked, frowning.

"What? Why would you think that?"

"Because I thought for a moment that you were going to run back down the path and cancel on me."

Ryann smiled weakly. "Just...have a lot on my mind."

"Come in. You can tell me all about it." Ryann felt herself being dragged through the door, Luciana closing and locking it behind them both. "What's going on? You don't look too good."

Ryann scoffed. "Thanks. Just because *you* have fat ankles, don't take it out on me."

"I do?" Luciana frowned as she looked down at her legs. "Sam said they were fine. I fucking knew she was lying."

"She's your wife. She's *supposed* to lie."

"Sam looked gorgeous when she was pregnant with Luca. I just look like a whale."

"You don't. I'm playing with you." Ryann hugged Luciana, shedding her coat as she moved through the house. "You're both gorgeous. Always have been, always will be."

"And this is the reason why I took an instant liking to you at our wedding. You're good for my ego."

"Whatever works for you." Ryann flopped down on the couch, rubbing at her face. "I need help."

"You want me to call my therapist?"

"Not *that* kind of help."

Luciana sat beside Ryann, looking at her expectantly. "O...kay."

"It's about Lydia," Ryann said. "She's great. She's brilliant. But...I don't know."

"You don't know what?"

"Luce, I think I'm into her." Ryann sat forward, placing her head in her hands. Her emotions had been all over the place today, but right now she was close to breaking down. Not because of how she felt for Lydia, but because it could never be. "And I really can't be into her."

"And, why not?"

"It wouldn't be right. Surely you understand that?"

Luciana offered Ryann a small, sympathetic smile. "You know how I feel about love, Ry. We have to take what we can get while we can get it. Nobody knows the reasons why we fall in love with particular people. If you want my honest opinion, I think you should explore the possibility."

"The possibility of what? Me and Lydia?"

"Yes."

Ryann's brows rose. "Have you seen her? She's gorgeous and has some fancy job in marketing."

"So?"

"So, I'm just some tattooed fuck up who wouldn't know the difference between River Island and Chanel."

"I'm not sure what designer labels has to do with any of this, but that's a poor excuse."

Ryann sighed. Luciana couldn't possibly understand. She may have been an escort at one time, Sam being the reason for her quitting that career, but it had been high-end. Classy. Expensive.

"You know what, it doesn't matter. It's ridiculous that I'm even thinking of Lydia as something more than a friend."

"Again, why?"

"Because..." Ryann paused. "Because it just is."

Ryann was aware of the fact that she probably sounded crazy. None of it made sense in her own head, either. Lydia had been there, helped her through the darkest moment of her life; wasn't that good enough? Couldn't she just get on with her life and stop thinking about the woman who was close to blowing her idea of remaining single right out of the water?

"Look," Luciana started, "you've had a really shitty time lately, Ry. The worst. Jen completely knocked you for six, me and Sam both know that. But that doesn't mean that you should tar every woman with the same brush."

"Oh, I'm not. Lydia is *nothing* like Jen. Nothing whatsoever." It would be ridiculous to even consider Lydia and Jen to be similar. They were poles apart. Universes away from one another. This dilemma had nothing to do with who Lydia was as a person but everything to do with Ryann and what she believed. How she felt.

"Then you should consider it," Luciana pressed. "She's clearly doing something right if you're thinking about her as more than a friend."

"She asked me to go for a drink on Friday night with her..."

"Yeah. Sam told me."

"But then she makes little comments about how it's only as friends. I don't know how to take that. The same way she told me she didn't invite me back to her place the night we met at the river because she was into me."

"That doesn't mean anything." Luciana took Ryann's hand, squeezing it tight. "Lydia is probably feeling the same way you are. She's probably worried she may overstep and then you'll both go around in circles forever and never truly know how either one of you feel."

Ryann shrugged. "Maybe it's best that way."

"If you want to forever wonder what could have been, then yeah...sure."

"I'm not sure I'm in the right place for a relationship yet, Luce."

"And that's fine. Nobody said you had to be. We've only just found out that you're no longer engaged to Jen. We're the last people who are going to tell you something we think you want to hear for the sake of it. If you need time, you need time. Lydia will be there when it all feels right for *you*. Not for anybody else."

"I just don't want her to think that I'm rebounding. It's really not like that."

"How does she make you feel?"

Ryann froze. Was it the right time to tell Luciana this? To bear all and hope for the best? Ryann couldn't be sure, but Luciana was here and very much willing to listen...to support her.

"Happy." Ryann smiled. "When I'm at her place, she makes me feel happy. Happier than I have been in some time. I don't know, she just...she has this kindness about her that I've never really come across before in a woman. Like, she would do anything for anyone. In this day and age, it takes a special person to be like that. Everyone is so self-absorbed and egocentric, but not Lydia. I mean, she listened to me and helped me through things, even though she was dealing with her own shit at work. That meant a lot, Luce.

"And it's not even just the fact that she was there for me, though it does play a big part. She's really sweet. Her smile. Her caring eyes. How she speaks to me. Jen always had a harsh tone, you know? When I asked for something, it was as though I was putting her out or interrupting her. But Lydia just holds conversation with me, no judgement. I've never felt like I was pissing her off by being there.

"And she has her own place. Okay, her parents own it, but they live in Spain. She doesn't come across as the type who would be in it for a free ride. Not like Jen turned out, anyway. She has her own money, her own car, her own life. She seems like someone who knows what she wants. Maybe that's the kind of woman I need in my life. Someone who would be equal. Someone who would love me as much as I love her. Someone who *isn't* self-centred."

Ryann wrung her hands, finally finding Luciana's eyes after burning a hole through the coffee table with her stare.

"Sounds to me like you already know the answer to this issue you seem to have."

"Do I?"

"I could be wrong, but it seems to me like you know how you feel about Lydia. And it doesn't matter if it feels wrong at the moment. You've had a shock recently, but in time it will all come together. That is…if you *want* it to."

"And that's the problem. I don't know what I want," Ryann breathed out. "Everything in my life just feels too complicated at the minute."

Ryann realised she was blowing this way out of proportion. Lydia likely didn't feel a thing for her. Who wanted someone who could come so close to ending everything? Lydia certainly didn't come across as a woman who wanted other people's drama. She'd even said as much during their first encounter.

"You know what, I'm getting way ahead of myself here." Ryann laughed. "Lydia is in no way shape or form attracted to me. I don't know what I'm worrying about."

"You're sure about that?"

"Yep. Pretty sure. She hasn't once hinted that she was remotely interested."

"Right."

"Right." Ryann nodded. "So, this is all a waste of time."

"But you'll be going for drinks on Friday?"

"Sure. Why not?"

"I just don't want to see you upsetting yourself, Ry. And I know things are looking up in other aspects of your life, but what about Jen? Have you washed your hands of her and that's it? Is she likely to show up in your life again?"

"Oh, I don't think so. I hope not, anyway." Ryann ran her hands down her thighs, blowing out a deep breath. "She's involved with someone else. Good riddance."

"Please, for your own sake, don't get involved with her again."

"No plans to, Luce." Ryann got to her feet, taking her jacket from the back of the couch. "You mind if I sit out by the lake for a while?"

"Nope, not at all."

Lydia gasped as Ryann's hands trailed down her stomach softly, carefully. Considering this woman was hot in every way imaginable, Lydia hadn't anticipated just how gentle Ryann would be. She wouldn't complain; her hands were on Lydia and that was what mattered. Slender fingers tweaked Lydia's nipple, Ryann growling how beautiful Lydia was in her ear as her hips rolled against her. Hot, steamy, sweaty. Nobody had ever touched Lydia in all the right ways, but Ryann was quickly becoming her favourite encounter. One she wouldn't ever forget about.

The moments leading up to this—the sexual tension between them—had been worth it. Lydia's arousal rolled through her, Ryann's partially covered body and bare, strong shoulders doing everything imaginable for Lydia and how she was feeling. Wanted. Needed. The only one in Ryann's world.

Ryann's fingertips brushed against Lydia's swollen clit, a low moan rumbling in both their throats as Ryann's hand moved lower. To Lydia's entrance. To exactly where she needed the woman on top of her to be. Ryann pushed two fingers deep inside, the palm of her hand pressing against Lydia's clit...

Lydia shot upright in bed. Her body throbbed, her heart slammed harder than she ever thought possible, but her room was dark, and she was alone in bed. "Fuck."

Lydia rubbed her eyes, squinting as she glanced at the clock on her nightstand. Four in the morning. She only had another two hours before she needed to get up and ready for work, but Ryann and her dream had Lydia feeling all over the place. Where the dream had come from, she didn't know, but she was disappointed in some way to no longer be in it.

Dream Ryann had felt so real. So raw. Lydia didn't believe it was possible to dream so vividly, but it had just happened, and she didn't know how to react. Ryann was her friend, not her lover. As much as she'd thought about her, her body, this was a new development. One she couldn't possibly come to terms with so early in the morning.

And who would she turn to when the time came to discuss this? Not Ryann. Also, not Soph. Neither of them would help matters. Soph would only play on it...encourage this stupid behaviour. And as for Ryann, Lydia couldn't possibly bring up her sex dream in conversation. Why would she? *How* would she?

With her head a jumbled mess, Lydia lay back down and calmed her breathing. She couldn't dissect the dream right now. She had work to go to in a few hours. But she *would* delve deeper when she had the chance to. She would think about the relationship she had with Ryann and decide her next move.

Would it be a good idea to lessen the time they spent together? Probably. Did Lydia want to do that? No. Not in a million years.

CHAPTER NINE

Lydia focused on the pile of clothes in the middle of her bed. She had no idea where to go with her choices tonight, but she wanted to look good. Not for Ryann—or so she told herself—but because it would be the first time in a while that she hadn't gone out with work or Soph. Tonight, she would enjoy herself more than she had in as many months as she could remember.

Ryann had been in touch, suggesting that they meet in Lydia's local next to her tattoo studio. That only led Lydia to feel more attracted to Ryann. She hadn't suggested some high-end cocktail bar. She hadn't thought about a swanky restaurant. No, it was the local pub. One that Ryann knew Lydia loved…but one that Lydia knew Ryann wasn't fond of.

Casual. That would be the theme of tonight. Going to the pub meant that Ryann wasn't expecting Lydia to show up in a little black dress with heels. She could opt for a nice pair of jeans and a blouse. She felt much more comfortable that way; the barmaid wouldn't question whether Lydia was lost.

She took the dark-wash skinny jeans sitting on top of the pile, a few rips evident but nothing too skin-baring. A sheer white blouse was already hanging on the back of her door, but she needed an opinion. Soph would be here in the next few minutes, and Lydia really needed help. Would a sheer blouse be too much for drinks with a friend? Usually, she wouldn't believe so, it was something she often wore, but with Ryann? She didn't know.

I'm overthinking this far too much.

Lydia dropped down onto the edge of her bed, clinging to the jeans in her hands. Ryann wouldn't care what she looked like. It was only a few beers and a chat. Friends, as Lydia had so bluntly put it last week, multiple times. And why did she care so much? Lydia hadn't ever been the kind of person to care what other people thought of her. Seemed Ryann had the opposite effect on her. An effect that, as this week wore on, became concerning.

The doorbell rang.

Lydia rushed down the stairs and tugged the door open in a split second. She didn't have time to sit around discussing any of what this was, she just needed Soph's opinion on her choice of clothing. Soph would give her so much more than that though; that much was clear when Lydia looked her best friend in the eyes.

"You're panicking," Soph stated as she stepped past Lydia. "Why the hell are you panicking?"

Lydia snorted. "I'm not."

"Okay, tell that to your trembling hands and your hoarse voice."

"Soph."

Soph turned around to face her best friend. "Mm?"

"Help."

"That's what I'm here for. Where do you need me?"

"Bedroom. Now."

Soph belly laughed. "Never thought I'd hear those words coming from you. I'm not sure David would appreciate it."

"Har-har!" Lydia pulled her best friend up the stairs, rushing into her bedroom in a frenzy. "Look, I have everything I own on my bed and no idea what to do with it."

"Well, it's going to need hanging back up, that's for sure. But what's wrong with the jeans in your hands?"

"Nothing. I just don't know what look to go for."

"Correct me if I'm wrong, but this is drinks with a friend, isn't it?" Soph's eyes trailed Lydia's face. "Unless this isn't what you originally told me it was."

"No, it is. Ryann is just my friend."

"Then why don't you go in what you're wearing already?"

Lydia looked down her body. She had a pair of old washed-out jeans on, Converse that had seen better days, and a T-shirt which read "badass" across the chest.

"I wouldn't even go to the shop in this."

"Lydia," Soph said, taking her best friend's hand and guiding her towards the bed. "What's really going on here?"

"Nothing. Why?" Lydia's brows drew together, Soph could see right through her.

Should she come clean and explain how she'd felt as the week progressed? Lydia hadn't even told her best friend who Ryann was. While Soph had ogled her on the doorstep some two weeks ago, Ryann was also the same woman Soph had berated for threatening to jump into the river.

"You go on dates all the time. This isn't even a date, or so you claim anyway, so I don't understand why you look like you're about to throw up. What is this woman to you, Lyd?"

"She's not anything to me." Lydia lowered her eyes. "In some way, I'd like her to be. But it wouldn't work. It couldn't happen. It's a waste of time feeling this way."

"Feeling what way?"

"Like I should have asked her on a date," Lydia explained. "She's just this incredible combination of chaos, art and intrigue. I-I don't know. I mean, I don't *know* her. Not really. But I want to. I want to know so much more."

"This is the same woman who was here the other week, right? The one with the incredible arse?"

"Yes, thank you for that." Lydia rolled her eyes. She didn't need to be reminded how great Ryann or her backside looked. She could remember it perfectly well without Soph's input. "It was the same woman. Her name is Ryann."

"She's kinda hot and mysterious. I can see why you're feeling a little flushed."

"Soph, not now." Lydia placed her head in her hands, desperately wishing she hadn't asked Ryann to go for a drink with her. "I'm sitting here getting worked up about nothing at all."

"How do you work that one out?"

"Ryann isn't interested in me. I just...I helped her when she needed someone, and I should let her get on with her life."

"Helped her how?" Soph asked, twisting her body and facing Lydia fully.

"S-she was the woman at the river."

Silence.

Soph just stared. Right through Lydia.

"You've fallen for the woman who was going to end her life? Fucking hell, Lyd. You certainly do pick them."

"I haven't *fallen* for anyone. I just...I want to get to know her more, and not as friends like she believes." Lydia told herself last week that she should step back. Then, when it got to Wednesday of this week and Ryann hadn't been in touch, she told herself the same thing again. She had no plans to even follow through with drinks tonight; she didn't think Ryann would contact her, but she had and Lydia found herself unable to say no at the last minute. "You saw her. She's not my type."

"She's not, but that doesn't mean you couldn't date her."

"Come on, Soph. She's a tattoo artist who probably does all kinds of cool stuff I wouldn't dream of doing."

"Like what?"

Lydia lifted a shoulder, focusing on the jeans still in her hands. "I don't know."

"Exactly. You're trying to talk yourself out of something that, at the moment, is nothing other than a drink. You said she thinks it's just friends."

"It *is* just friends."

"Then meet her. See how it goes. Read the situation and go from there."

"I'm happy having her as a friend," Lydia said, nodding. "But I'm worried that the more time I spend with her, the more likely it is that I'm going to pin her against the nearest wall."

"I told you we needed to find someone you could spend the night with." Soph stood up, rummaging through Lydia's mountain of clothes. "Casual. That's what you want. Nothing that screams 'take me to bed.'"

"I don't think I have anything that screams that. I really need to sort myself out."

"This is how it's going to go," Soph started. "Tonight, you will have drinks with Ryann and her gorgeous arse. Then, you will come home and go to bed. Alone. Tomorrow, I will be over at midday and we will get you on some dating sites."

Lydia didn't understand. Why would she date someone else when it was Ryann she had her eye on? Had Soph listened to a single word she'd said?

"O...kay."

"Okay, good."

Lydia frowned. "That's it?"

"Well, yeah."

"And you're not going to tell me how stupid I am for finding the woman whose life I saved attractive?"

"No. And about the other week...I'm sorry." Soph had a sincerity in her eyes that Lydia hadn't come across for quite some time. Perhaps her best friend was beginning to realise that her life was pretty damn good. "I just...I've been complaining about everything lately. When you kicked me out, I understood why."

"I just wanted you to ask me if I was okay, Soph. Instead, you complained that Ryann was stupid for doing what she did."

"Well, she is." Lydia opened her mouth to admonish her best friend, but Soph held up her hand. Clearly, she wasn't finished. "Because if she *had* gone through with it, she wouldn't be lucky to have someone like you in her life…however it all works out."

"Truthfully, do you think I'm making a mistake?"

"Depends what you want out of this relationship with Ryann. Do you just want to be friends? I mean, can you live with that if she turns you down? Or do you want a full-blown relationship where you settle down with this woman, no other outcome?"

"I could live with her friendship," Lydia said, taking her lip between her teeth. She wouldn't go to the pub tonight and expect anything, but even if she could just show Ryann that she was interested, it would be a job well done considering the shitty week she'd just had. "I don't really want that, but I wouldn't back off completely."

"Maybe you could speak to her?"

"About what?"

"About how you feel. Communication is important, Lydia."

Lydia held back the laugh in her throat. Had Soph really just said that to her? The woman who came around to bitch about her boyfriend instead of discussing it with him? "Right. I don't think it's quite the time for that."

"Because?"

"Because Ryann doesn't even know I'm into her. I can't exactly sit down and just lay it all out on the table. Not yet. It's far too soon."

"Okay, I can see your point." Soph took some hangers from the bed and started to hang up Lydia's clothes. "The blouse on the back of the door is perfect by the way. Throw on some heels with those jeans and you'll have her in your bed way sooner than you think."

"You've honestly lost the plot." Lydia laughed as she shook her head and disappeared towards the bathroom. "But I wouldn't have you any other way."

Ryann turned her wrist towards her. Lydia was due any moment now. On the way here, Ryann called Sam's wife, Luciana, needing a slight pep talk. Ryann's issue was that Lydia was her friend. And that's how it should remain. She couldn't bear the thought of ever hurting her. And allowing her thoughts to run away with themselves would cause exactly that.

Ryann wasn't in a place where a relationship was possible, and thankfully, she recognised it. Lydia had been there when she had nobody. Maybe that was why Ryann felt so compelled to allow something more to grow between them. She'd toyed with that idea all day, but both she and Luciana had dismissed that during their call.

Ryann wasn't stupid. She knew the difference between attraction and obligation. Lydia wouldn't ever expect her to want something more for the sake of it; that woman was well aware of herself and what she wanted in life. Ryann couldn't possibly be it, so she pushed all thoughts of the attractive side of Lydia to the back of her mind, choosing to focus only on the friendship between them. If she could keep it that way for the rest of the night, everything would go to plan.

Ryann waited outside the pub, Dark Angel in blackout next door. She'd been pleasantly surprised when she arrived here to find the sign she assumed would be destroyed was still sitting in its rightful place. She didn't know what the outcome of her business would be yet, but Sam was working on the purchase. If anyone could pull something back from the brink, it was her cousin. She'd done it many times over the years both within her business *and* her personal life.

As Ryann peered through the window, a smile crept across her mouth. She loved this place. The space was perfect for what she wanted, multiple rooms off the main area with a grungy, graffiti vibe. Complaints from her customers were few and far between. *I have to get this place back.*

"Thinking about standing me up and sneaking in there?" A soft, recognisable voice filtered through the still night air.

Ryann's smile grew.

She turned, truly taken aback by Lydia. "O-oh, wow." Those words weren't meant to leave Ryann's lips. She knew that even as they worked their way to the surface, unable to stop them. Lydia looked like an absolute vision, but Ryann struggled to keep her eyes above Lydia's chest. The blouse Lydia wore—complimenting her cleavage in every way imaginable—really was going to be an issue tonight. She cleared her throat. "What I mean is...Hi, it's great to see you."

"You, too." Lydia cocked her head towards the pub entrance. "Do you need a few more minutes? I can wait for you inside."

"No, I'm good." Ryann wasn't allowing Lydia to walk inside the pub without her. Whether they were only friends or not, she would happily let the public believe Lydia was all hers. She stretched out her arm, opening the door for Lydia. "Come on then."

Ryann couldn't prevent her eyes from travelling south. Lydia in tight jeans was an image sent from the heavens.

"What are you having?" Lydia glanced back over her shoulder. She paused and Ryann knew she had been caught. "Were you just checking me out?"

"Me? No." Ryann scoffed, removing the image of Lydia's lace bra from her mind. It was certainly visible through the fabric of her blouse. "I'll just have a pint, thanks."

"Mm."

Fuck! Maybe just one or two drinks was best tonight. Ryann didn't want to put herself in any positions she would come to regret. If she was drunk, Lydia looking the way she did would surely tip her over the edge. She would lay bare how she felt, and it would all go tits up from there. Ryann needed Lydia; she was a wonderful person.

"So, how was your week?" Ryann slid up next to Lydia at the bar, offering her a smile when the barmaid set two pints down in front of them. "The boss?"

"Fine. Usual. I'm considering calling my old boss. Just to see if there's anything available with her."

"You've really had enough, huh?" Ryann sipped her pint, licking the froth from her top lip as they left the bar, finding a seat towards the back of the pub. "Have you tried talking to her?"

"To Bree? I may as well talk to myself."

"Sorry you're not enjoying it." Ryann placed her pint down, taking a seat facing Lydia. She wasn't sure it was the greatest idea since she had an uninterrupted view of her chest from where she was sitting, but sitting next to Lydia wouldn't be much better either. "Could you not take some time off?"

"No, I need to be doing my job. I hate sitting around."

"Me, too."

"I see the shop is still closed…"

Ryann ran her finger down the moisture gathering on her glass, her eyes focused on the amber liquid. "I'm just waiting for Sam to work her magic. But, you know, if she can't get it back for me, it's not the end of the world."

"I don't think she will come away without the shop for you. She seems…headstrong."

"You've met?" Ryann frowned. Sam had conveniently chosen to keep that little piece of information to herself this week.

"Yeah, she came by a few days ago. She called me first, of course."

"Right." Ryann nodded, sipping her pint. She made a mental note to give Sam a call the next time she had the opportunity to do so. "Talk about much?"

"Mainly you."

"I'm not sure if that's a good or a bad thing."

"Good. Only good."

Ryann studied Lydia's eyes. Bright and inviting. Sincere and trustworthy. She didn't know many people who had eyes she could get lost in, but Lydia's appeared to have that ability. She appeared to have many abilities when it came to Ryann. If Lydia wasn't saving Ryann's life, she was stealing her sleep.

Ryann had chosen to step back this week, not because she wanted to move away from Lydia, but to sort through her thoughts. The day they met at the river, she hadn't anticipated the impact Lydia would have on her life, nor did she expect to feel something more for her. As Sam sat joking with her over a coffee last week, teasing her about Lydia, Ryann hadn't thought much of it. But since their last encounter, Ryann *had* missed her friend. *Can you really be her friend?*

"How did the removal go?"

"Hilarious," Ryann laughed. "You should have seen Jen's face when I started dismantling things."

"What did you leave her with?"

Ryann wrinkled her nose. "The bed. I didn't want *anyone* to have that after the goings on in it."

"I'd say I feel sorry for her, but it's hard to have empathy for someone who not only threw away a relationship with you, but also ruined your life."

Ryann remained silent. Lydia always said all the right things, but her tone tonight seemed more honest than ever before. The world truly was upside down this evening.

"I hope she gets everything she deserves," Lydia spat.

"Hey..." Ryann's hand worked its way to Lydia's, settling over her smooth skin. "Don't be angry. She's not worth it. And I'm *completely* over her."

Over her? Ryann didn't know why she had just said that. Lydia hadn't asked.

Lydia sat back against the worn, maroon leather bench,

crossing her legs and narrowing her eyes as she said, "Good to know."

Ryann's seat had moved as the evening wore on. Within a couple hours, she was sitting shoulder-to-shoulder with Lydia, her warm body touching the skin of her arm. Ryann felt comfortable there. Lydia really was hilarious; the more she drank, the looser her tongue became but Ryann didn't see the issue. Lydia hadn't been hurtful towards or about anyone, the only ears likely to be burning tonight were Bree's.

Lydia had talked at length about her childhood, Ryann absorbing every shred of information she possibly could. In all honesty, Ryann could listen to her talk all day long. Lydia was an only child like Ryann, but their childhoods had been significantly different.

While Lydia took herself outside and engaged with the world, Ryann chose not to. She felt different, as though she couldn't fit in. If she wasn't concerned about how she looked, she was terrified that she would get into conversation with someone and sound stupid for not knowing what to say. As the years passed, she no longer cared for small talk with irrelevant people in her life. It was only her family that she felt connected to.

Coming out had been easy for them both, something neither took for granted. Their hometowns were more welcoming than most, but they both knew of people who couldn't bring themselves to be their authentic selves. Ryann chose to lend an ear, volunteering at a local LGBTQIA+ centre in her early twenties, and Lydia opted for media campaigns to light the way. They may have appeared polar opposites in their appearance, but inside...they got one another.

"Remind me to show you my medals." Lydia leaned in, her lips close to Ryann's ear.

"Medals?" Ryann tried to ignore the hairs on the back of her neck as they stood on end. If she focused on the conversation, everything would be okay.

"I was an Irish dancer."

Ryann's eyes widened. "No. Way."

"I was." Lydia nodded, gulping her beer. "For a good ten years."

"Why did you stop?" Ryann would be lying if she said she wouldn't love to see Lydia prancing around onstage. Or was it jigging?

"Boobs." Lydia wiggled her chest, her boobs doing the talking for her. As much as Ryann didn't want to focus on the exposed skin before her, Lydia was making it hard. "Double D's and jigging do not go well together."

Ryann cleared her throat, exhaling a long breath. "Right."

A laugh rumbled in Lydia's throat.

She leaned in painfully close.

"Do I make you nervous?"

"I, uh…" Ryann scratched the back of her neck. "No. Why would you make me nervous?"

"I don't know, but occasionally tonight, you've looked terrified."

"I have?" At least Lydia didn't recognise Ryann's body language as arousal. Maybe she needed to work on her facial expressions if she was passing it off as terror. She didn't want to frighten the ladies away. Or, one lady in particular. "Sorry about that."

As Ryann was about to swiftly change the topic of conversation, the DJ called Lydia's name. "Oo, that's me." She shot up from her seat, swaying as she made her way to the man with the microphone.

Ryann changed the position of her seating, her eyes firmly on Lydia as a familiar and favourite song of Ryann's started to play. *Okay, could she be any more perfect?*

Lydia's eyes softened when they landed on Ryann. Bringing the microphone up to her lips, Lydia belted out her very own rendition of Bon Jovi's *Bed of Roses*, her voice raspy and intense. In this moment, Lydia Nelson was exuding sex. Her blouse fitted perfectly, four buttons from the top undone. People wolf-whistled, something Ryann hated but could completely understand tonight.

A hint of jealousy rolled through her as Lydia's eyes landed on another woman. She smiled and winked at the busty blonde, sending Ryann's body sinking deeper into her seat. What she wouldn't give for Lydia to look at her that way.

But then Lydia's eyes landed back on Ryann.

Piercing her.

Holding her in place.

Momentarily stopping her breathing.

Every word Lydia sang, Ryann felt deep in her belly. Tugging and pulling. As Lydia continued to sing, Ryann wanted to stand up, move closer, and kiss her. She didn't care who was around. She didn't care if it was wrong. Ryann's lips ached for the woman serenading her.

She had to do something to change this; she couldn't make a move on a woman who considered her a friend. Someone she could confide in when her job was getting her down. As much as Ryann wanted to put herself and her feelings first, Lydia deserved somebody who could guarantee more *up* days rather than *down*. And that's what Ryann couldn't provide right now: guaranteed happiness.

Ryann made a beeline for the bar, ordering fresh drinks and glancing at Lydia once or twice. Enamoured by the woman hitting every note and still watching her, all she could do was smile and watch on. Lydia really was a blessing in her life. Ryann would be forever thankful for her.

As the song came to an end, Ryann watched Lydia walk her way. She seemed embarrassed, perhaps? She really had no reason to be, her voice was great.

"H-hi," Lydia said, her eyes trained on the bar counter. "Isn't it my round?"

"After the voice I just heard, you're never paying for another drink again."

"It wasn't that good."

"Nope. It was better than good." Ryann beamed. "And my favourite song of all time, too."

"Sure it was."

"Oh, it was." Ryann handed over a drink, surprised when Lydia scanned the bar. "What's up? Did you want something different?"

"Marg, can I get some shots?"

"Usual?" the barmaid asked, receiving a nod from Lydia. "No can do, love. Don't have any Tia Maria left."

"You're joking?"

"Sorry, love. I'll keep a bottle back next weekend for you."

"Well, there goes that idea." Lydia sighed, taking Ryann's hand and dragging her back to their table. "Have you ever tried a baby Guinness?"

"I don't believe I have, no."

Lydia checked her watch. "How do you feel about getting out of here soon? It's only ten-thirty."

"Sure. Where did you have in mind?"

"My place..."

Ryann's blood travelled south. Everything within her screamed to turn down Lydia's invitation. "Sounds great."

Lydia's smile beamed impossibly wide. "Yeah?"

I'm going to live to regret this. Ryann shrugged. "Sure. Why not."

CHAPTER TEN

Lydia fell through her front door, laughing as Ryann almost toppled over her in the porch. The air had hit them once they left the pub, and now they felt as though they'd been drinking all night. Okay, they had drunk more than Lydia anticipated, but this really had been the perfect night. Ryann was absolutely the company she needed when she was at the pub. She wouldn't tell Soph that, though. It would only lead to one miserable face, and Soph assuming things that weren't true. She'd even pondered not telling Soph that Ryann had come back with her. Lydia would never hear the end of it—something that would only leave her craving more as Soph pestered her about it all.

"Oh, my God. That taxi driver seriously needs to clean his cab." Ryann heaved dramatically, gripping Lydia's shoulder for support as she kicked off her boots. "I swear, the seats were stained."

"Please, don't. I paid a lot to feel drunk tonight. I don't need to throw it up and waste it."

"So..." Ryann leaned back against the wall in the hall, her hands now in the front pockets of her jeans. "About those Guinness thingies?"

"Oh, you'll love them. Come on, in the kitchen."

"Can I use your bathroom first?"

"Sure. You know where it is. I'll get what we need and wait for you in here, okay?" Lydia turned to walk away, stopped by Ryann's hand on her wrist. "W-what's up?"

"I've had an amazing night with you."

"Yeah?"

"The best I can remember." Ryann smiled, releasing Lydia from her grip as she bounded up the stairs.

The best she can remember. Lydia tried to suppress the smile she was wearing. It was no use thinking of what could be. Ryann told her last weekend that she couldn't imagine dating again. Lydia wouldn't be the woman to change that decision; she wasn't *that* worthy. As much as she would like to believe she could be someone's everything, she was also realistic. Ryann, in all her tattooed, sexy glory, would never choose someone like her.

Lydia chose to curb her thoughts for the time being, moving into the kitchen and gathering the drinks she required. Thankful that she'd replenished her stock, she took a bottle of Baileys and a bottle of Tia Maria from the cupboard. Setting out several shot glasses on the kitchen island, Lydia grabbed a teaspoon from the top drawer and cracked the lids on the alcohol.

Her mind wandered back to the pub. What the hell had made her sing to Ryann? That was a moment of stupidity, Lydia owned up to that, but Ryann had looked at her exactly the way she had looked at Ryann. It may have only been for a split second, but Lydia saw it. She couldn't ever forget it. If that was all she ever got from the woman currently upstairs, she would savour the moment forever.

When Ryann looked at her with those deep, dark eyes...life faded away around her. Her shitty job meant nothing, her terrible taste in past women disintegrated, and life as a whole was fantastic. When Ryann held her gaze, it was something to keep forever.

Ryann entered the kitchen, but Lydia found herself unable to meet her eyes.

And then Ryann cleared her throat.

"Oh, hey." Lydia shook herself from her thoughts.

"You good?"

Lydia's eyebrow rose. "Me? Amazing."

"Yeah. You are," Ryann exhaled, closing the distance and joining Lydia at the counter. "So, do these shots actually taste of Guinness?"

"No. They just look like it."

"Thank God." Ryann pulled a face. It only melted Lydia's heart further.

Lydia prepared their concoction, explaining to Ryann how it came together. It was imperative that a teaspoon was used, giving the shot of Tia Maria a head as the Baileys poured over the back of the spoon. "You have to get this bit right."

"Yes, ma'am." Ryann nodded.

Lydia noted how Ryann watched her hands. Every move. Tonight, Lydia wanted to move those hands to places that didn't involve serving up shots. Tonight, she wanted them touching Ryann *and* her body.

Lydia suddenly dropped the spoon, sending it clattering to the surface.

"Well, this is a good start." Ryann laughed. "Need a hand, butter fingers?"

Lydia closed her eyes momentarily. "No, thank you. I've got it."

"Then I shall step away and let the master work her magic."

Yes, you really should. Lydia lifted the spoon again, finishing several shots for them both. Ryann couldn't stay much longer; Lydia had to think up a reason for her need to be alone. She could sneak upstairs and call Soph, but did she really want to do that? Ryann deserved more than someone who would call their friend to ask for an emergency date phone call. Besides, considering this wasn't a date, the idea seemed a little far-fetched.

"H-here." Lydia steadied her voice. "Try this one."

Ryann gripped the shot glass, bringing it to her lips and watching Lydia over the rim. Everything within her body ignited. She'd never felt this intensity before. Ryann and her unspoken words did everything to her body. Just one look, and Lydia could melt.

Ryann knocked it back, setting the glass on the counter as she licked her lips. "Okay, that's good."

"R-right?" Lydia helped herself to one.

"Can I have another?"

Lydia found Ryann back at her side again, their bodies closer than they had been since they sat with one another in the pub. "Help yourself."

Ryann took another shot, followed by Lydia. This time, Lydia was too busy focusing on Ryann's tongue as it popped out between her lips, now dribbling a little of her own drink down the side of her mouth in her spellbound state.

As she swallowed the coffee cream liqueur, Lydia's knees trembled when Ryann reached out, using the pad of her thumb to remove the residue from the side of Lydia's lip. Ryann slipped her thumb into her mouth, releasing it with a pop and stepping closer before Lydia could process what was happening.

"So," Ryann started, the heat from her body penetrating Lydia. "What's next?"

The hoarseness in Ryann's voice sent a wave of arousal through Lydia. She truly had no idea what was next, but she could hazard a guess.

Lydia lowered her eyes. She wanted nothing more than to kiss Ryann, but it couldn't possibly be the right move to make. "I don't know."

Ryann lifted her hand, placing it under Lydia's chin and lifting her head. Their eyes met, but Lydia didn't make the first move. She couldn't. Ryann's breath tickled her lips, sending a surge of emotions through her. All she could do was allow this to play out how she hoped it would.

"Tonight has really been something else," Ryann said, her eyes shining. "*You* have been something else."

"Ryann..."

"God, I want to kiss you." Ryann inched closer, her eyes dropping to Lydia's lips. "And I know I shouldn't. I know this couldn't possibly be a healthy relationship for either of us, but I need to feel your lips."

Lydia gasped, fisting her hand into Ryann's black shirt and pulling her close. She stumbled back against the counter, her back pressing against the granite, trapped by Ryann's slender but supple body. She could feel the energy between them, the heat as it tore through the miniscule gap where their breasts touched. She'd kissed a lot of women over the years, but before this one even happened, Lydia knew none could come close to Ryann.

Instead of thinking, Lydia leaned in and pressed her lips to Ryann's. Her lips were smooth, silky. She closed her eyes, never wanting this moment to end, but needing so much more than she was receiving. It would require a bed and some very messy sheets.

Lydia sunk into a world of only Ryann.

Locked.

Frozen in time.

Ryann's hands found Lydia's hair, frenzied but gentle. Soft, sweet, but urgent. With their bodies flush together, Lydia moaned into Ryann's mouth, appreciative when she didn't back away. This...it was pure fantasy. Lydia had dreamed of the perfect kiss with the perfect woman. At the age of thirty-three, it happened. God, it happened and then some.

Ryann's grip on Lydia's hair suddenly loosened, her lips slowing before she pulled away reluctantly. "Fuck." Ryann pressed her forehead to Lydia's, an instant regret in her once impeccable eyes. "I'm so sorry."

Sorry? No. That isn't the right reaction.

Ryann dropped her hands to her sides, taking a step back as Lydia's fingertips settled on her lips. Ryann appeared confused, but Lydia didn't know what could possibly be confusing about the situation.

"Lydia, I'm so sorry. It was the drink and you singing to me. The low-cut blouse. Everything, I just..." Ryann hung her head, seemingly defeated. "I fucked this up tonight."

"Ry—"

"I betrayed your trust as your friend." Ryann ran her fingers through her hair, exhaling a deep breath as her eyes widened. "Tonight was everything I've needed, but that...the kiss. It was a mistake."

"A mistake?" Lydia's heart tumbled into her stomach. This wasn't supposed to be how her night ended. She frowned. "Kissing me is a mistake?"

"You...you're so beautiful. Nothing about you is a mistake. But what *I* just did...it was the biggest mistake of my life."

Lydia fell silent. She had nothing to offer. A tear slid down her face as the emotion welled in her throat, but she couldn't come by any words. Ryann had just made her feel incredible yet worthless all at once. How did someone accomplish that in one fell swoop? Someone so beautiful. Someone who felt like the perfect fit against her body.

"Then you should go." Lydia's stomach lurched as she spoke those words. She couldn't deal with this right now, not when Ryann was still standing in front of her. *Sorry but no thanks* didn't really work for Lydia. She had just discovered that in the last few seconds. "Call a cab. You can wait in the porch."

"I'll walk." Ryann's shoulders sagged as she stepped away from Lydia and into the hall. She turned back when she reached the door, but Lydia struggled to meet her eyes. "I am sorry."

"Me, too." Lydia couldn't do this anymore. These feelings may have been new to her—apparently to Ryann, too—but she couldn't be kissed and then apologised to and called a mistake. This, whatever it was, stopped now. Friendship included. Lydia couldn't put herself through the torment of having Ryann within arm's reach, but never being able to touch her.

But Lydia also felt compelled to still be sure of Ryann's safety. "Hey…"

Ryann turned back, her cheeks wet with tears.

"Take care of yourself, okay?"

Ryann nodded, a weak smile working its way to her mouth. "Yeah, thanks."

"I hope everything works out for you. You deserve it."

"I, uh…I shouldn't call you again, should I?"

"Probably best if you don't." Lydia offered a small, pathetic smile. "But Ryann…"

"Yeah?" Ryann lifted her head, hope in her eyes.

"I am glad I was there that night. To stop you from doing something terrible."

"Yeah, and now I've hurt you."

Ryann disappeared through the door, closing it quietly behind her. Lydia could only cry for the woman she'd just kissed and for the way this night was ending. Relationships, once again, had proven to be a waste of time.

CHAPTER ELEVEN

Ryann dug the heels of her hands into her eyes in a desperate attempt to stem the flow of tears. She'd lain in bed awake all night, disappointed by her behaviour towards Lydia. Going back there after the bar last night was a mistake. She felt it as she agreed in those moments when she was caught between refusing and looking at Lydia the way she wished she really could look at her.

God, that kiss had blown her mind. It had also blown any chance of friendship with such a sweet, caring woman. But feeling those lips, Lydia's hand fisted in her shirt...absolute heaven. A dream. She should be walking around on air this morning. Instead, she was lying in bed with swollen eyes from an entire night of crying.

Ryann didn't know where to begin. She wanted to call Lydia. She wanted to show up on her knees. But what she wanted, she couldn't have. She'd known it from the moment their lips met. Yes, it felt incredibly satisfying having Lydia against her, her tongue slipping against Ryann's, but that didn't make it right. Nothing about last night could be considered right.

Ryann had basically ogled Lydia for the entire night, stupidly acting on her desires in a moment of weakness. She never thought

Lydia would understand, Ryann didn't understand it herself, but now she'd shattered any prospect of Lydia being in her life.

Ryann truly felt lost.

She picked up her phone and checked for any messages or calls. Nothing. She didn't deserve a message from Lydia, though. Lydia owed her nothing whatsoever. Ryann, this morning, had no right to anything concerning Lydia.

And then there was Sam. She was going to hit the roof when she found out what Ryann had done. Luciana too, probably. Neither of them had warned her of the potential heartache that came with last night, but at thirty-one, Ryann was capable of sensing it herself. She just chose not to. Instead of being reasonable, she chose lust. Instead of stepping back at the pub, Ryann went full steam ahead into something that could only end in tears. Literally.

A familiar dread settled in her stomach, one that usually came from a night out in the city. The hangover would come and go as the day progressed, but how she felt about Lydia would remain. This morning, Ryann felt as though it would never leave her. The sheer horror of her actions meant she hadn't closed her eyes last night, and it wouldn't improve any time soon. All Ryann could hope was that Lydia would realise she wasn't worth the time and attention, moving onto something and someone more fulfilling in life. Ryann certainly wasn't that person.

She lifted her phone and tapped a new message.

R: I'm truly sorry for any hurt I caused you last night. I ruined our friendship, something I know I'll never get back. You're really great. My leaving was nothing to do with you. I just make a mess of things and I dove in headfirst instead of thinking about the consequences. If I don't hear back from you by the end of the day, I'll remove your number from my phone. Thanks for being everything I need…at the wrong time. Ry x

Ryann threw her phone to the bed, her belly in turmoil as she thought about Lydia opening that message. Ryann didn't know whether to vomit or turn over and sleep the rest of the day away. Sleep seemed like the best option. If she was sleeping, the pain in her chest would surely subside. If she was sleeping, she couldn't get herself into any more trouble. If she was sleeping, nobody could call her out on her shitty behaviour towards an absolutely breathtaking woman.

Lydia turned off the grill, placing bacon onto her toast and sitting at the kitchen island. Her phone had pinged an hour or so ago, while she was still lying in bed and contemplating what happened last night, but she couldn't bring herself to read the message she knew was waiting for her. It would be from Ryann. It had to be. Soph wouldn't be awake yet; it was only nine a.m. Ryann was the only one who could be contacting her so early.

Had Ryann struggled with sleep like Lydia had? Unlikely, given the way in which she left. Was it all a part of her charm? Lure Lydia in, kiss her, and then disappear? Lydia had never imagined Ryann to be that kind of woman, but she couldn't draw any other conclusion.

Ryann had well and truly played her, for reasons unknown. Perhaps it was her way of getting Lydia back for saving her life. Maybe it was just who she was.

As Lydia sat in her kitchen that morning, she no longer cared. Her bacon sandwich looked too appealing to be tainted by thoughts of a woman who couldn't care any less for Lydia's feelings.

Her phone buzzed on the counter. A call was coming through. Lydia studied the screen; it was Sam. As much as she liked Sam, she didn't want to discuss any of this with her. If Ryann did feel bad, something Lydia strongly felt was unlikely, Lydia wouldn't listen to Sam begging her to give Ryann another chance.

The call cut out, her screen dimming. Lydia released a deep, long breath and then it started again. She considered answering the call, again deterred by her lack of desire to discuss Ryann. Once the call stopped, a message immediately came through.

S: Hi, Lydia. Sam here. Have you seen Ryann since last night?

Lydia's heart sunk deep. Sam couldn't contact Ryann. What did that mean? Her appetite suddenly diminished, thoughts now turning to Ryann floating in the river. She immediately picked up her phone and called Sam back. "Hello?"

"Hi. Do you know where Ryann is?"

"I assumed she was at home. Have you called her?"

"I have," Sam said, the sound of a small child laughing in the background. "Her phone is switched off."

"It is?"

"Seems to be, yeah. Just...I knew she was meeting with you last night. I was hoping she was with you, maybe."

"Why would she be with me?" Lydia hadn't meant to sound so cold towards Ryann's cousin, but that suggestion had caught her off guard. Ryann didn't spend the night at Lydia's.

"Sorry, I don't know. She doesn't usually turn off her phone, and I was calling to let her know that the shop is hers again."

"Well, that's great news." Lydia felt a brief respite from the curdling in her belly. "But she's not here with me. We kinda fell out last night."

"Oh."

"I don't think she will be coming around here anymore, Sam. I'm sorry I couldn't help."

"You don't think she's done something stupid, do you?" Sam's voice wavered.

"Well, I hadn't thought about it until you put the idea in my head," Lydia lied. "I'm sure she's just sleeping. She could do with having a long sleep and getting this day over with."

Sam sighed. "What happened?"

"Nothing important. I've helped her out and there is no more to it. We're not friends, Sam. I'm sure she has plenty of people around her."

"You are joking, right?"

"Do I sound like I'm joking?" Lydia pushed her breakfast away, climbing down from her stool and moving into the living room. "Really, I don't know where she is."

"You also don't sound as though you care where she is. So, something big must have happened."

"Maybe you should speak to your cousin. She can tell you all about it."

"Okay. I'm sorry for bothering you," Sam said. "And thanks again."

"Yeah, I'm kinda over the thanks and praise now, but you're welcome." Lydia ended the call, slumping back against the couch as she dropped down into the comfortable cushions.

She'd been a fool to believe that Ryann could have woken up here this morning. It sure felt possible when Ryann pinned her against the counter last night, her lips whispering everything she wanted and needed to hear. Emotion once again welled in Lydia's throat, tears building in her black, sunken eyes. She honestly couldn't bring herself to look in the mirror this morning, terrified for what she would find staring back at her.

This day. It could end right now.

Ryann groaned, the buzzer of her apartment repeatedly sounding with each second that passed. She'd heard it a few minutes ago and assumed she was dreaming, but it wasn't stopping, and she was now definitely awake.

Ryann rolled from her bed, her body covered by only a pair of boxers and a tank top. Quite frankly, she didn't care who was at the door. If they had the code to get into the building, they could manage seeing her half naked.

She pulled the door open, met with Sam's concerned eyes as she did. "Is there a particular reason why you're buzzing my door down on a Saturday morning?"

"A particular reason?" Sam scoffed. "I've been trying to call you all morning."

"Relax. It's what? 10 a.m.?"

"Try two in the afternoon." Sam pushed past Ryann, her heels pounding furiously against the floor. "I called Lydia."

"Because?"

"Because I thought maybe you would be there. You know, after last night."

"Oh, no." Ryann shook her head. Just the mention of Lydia's name hurt her heart. "That ship sailed, Sam. And now it's at the bottom of the ocean."

"Okay, I don't know what that means."

Ryann slumped against the nearest wall, tears threatening to spill over. "I just…"

"You just what, Ry?"

"I kissed her. Last night. I fucking told you and Luce I shouldn't have gone to that pub. And now look at me! I'm a fucking mess!"

"You kissed her? That's one hell of a development! This is good, though. I mean, Lydia seems wonderful."

"No, it's not. This isn't good…however *wonderful* she is." Ryann shook her head. How could any of this be good? "I'm not ready for a relationship. Certainly not one with Lydia. Ever."

"Because?"

"Because she was there when I was at rock bottom, Sam. She did her bit. Now I have to move on from my past life and figure out who I am. What I'm doing. Jen completely fucked me over and I have to figure out why. I mean, was it me? Am I just a really shitty girlfriend? Do people see me coming and run a mile in the opposite direction?"

"Did Lydia run a mile?"

"No, but you're not hearing me. Lydia is too good for me. Too pure and sweet. We have *nothing* in common," Ryann lied. "Just... it would never work."

"Yet you felt compelled to kiss her?" Sam's perfectly defined eyebrow rose. "Huh?"

"It just happened. We were at the pub and everything was going a little too well. She started singing to me on the karaoke and one thing just led to another. It was my fault. Completely. She didn't do anything wrong."

"And how did it feel when you kissed her?"

"I'm not doing this. I'm not going over something that is hurting me to even think about. I know what I did. I know what a bastard I am. I've accepted that and now I move on."

"Because that first time Luciana kissed me..." Sam paused and smiled. "I felt as though she was breathing life back into me. Like she saw nobody other than me in her world. And her lips...God, her lips were like coming home from one hell of a bad holiday."

Ryann sat down. Sam knew better than anyone how hard it was to restart your life. Especially a life that included love.

"Everything fell into place for me when she kissed me. I didn't feel bad, and I didn't feel guilty. I just relished the moment and allowed everything else to take its course. Because that's what life is, Ry. It's also what love is. It's about exploring what you want and who you are. It's about fucking it up but holding up your hands and admitting that you got something wrong. It's about doing the right thing for *you*."

"I have held up my hands and admitted that I got it wrong. The kiss...shouldn't have happened."

"You really believe that?" Sam crouched down in front of Ryann. "You really believe that kissing Lydia should result in this?

You feeling bad and her probably feeling like she's not good enough?"

"She's more than good enough."

"Did you tell her that?" Sam asked.

"Well, no." Ryann ran her hands down her thighs, blowing out a deep breath as the severity of her reaction sunk in. She'd walked out. Disappeared. Yes, Lydia had told her to leave, but Ryann didn't try to explain. She didn't apologise and then sit with Lydia. She kissed her and left.

"Come on, Ry. You're a better person than this. And this may be unexpected for you, maybe for Lydia too, but isn't the unexpected the best? Not knowing, figuring it out together. I didn't expect any of what I have now; you could have that, too."

"Oh, I think Luciana is a one-off, Sam."

"Jen really did a number on you, I understand that, but Lydia deserves more than this."

"Lydia is so great." Ryann's lips upturned, just the image of Lydia in her head warming her body. Settling her heart. "Last night was amazing. And I know we only sat in a pub, but we clicked so well."

"I know," Sam replied. "I can see it."

Ryann's brows drew together. "See what?"

"How much you wish you hadn't left last night. How much of an impact she's had on your life in such a short span of time."

"None of that matters anymore."

"It should. I know this is important to you, even if you tell me otherwise."

"She asked me not to call her again, Sam. I really hurt her last night."

"And what can you do to change that?" Sam climbed to her feet, but Ryann knew she wasn't leaving here without the correct answers. "You could show up there…"

Ryann laughed. "No. Not a chance. I've messed with her life

enough. I can't just keep showing up there and expecting her time. She has a life, a job. She has people other than *me* in her life."

"Then maybe give her some time." Sam nodded. "And to take your mind off it, I have something to tell you."

"Luce didn't give birth, did she?"

"No. At least, she hadn't before I left the house."

"Okay, then what?"

"The shop. I got it back."

Ryann shot to her feet, lunging at Sam and throwing her arms around her. Sam had really turned her life around; Ryann could never repay her. "Thank you!" She gripped Sam's face, kissing her hard on the cheek. "Thank you, so much."

"I know you won't let me down." Sam embraced her cousin. "You worked hard for that shop, to get to where you are. Just, don't let Jen get away with what she's done to you. That is *all* I ask."

"I won't. I'm simply biding my time."

"You and I are definitely related." Sam smirked as she pulled back. "I get the keys on Monday morning. You can either come to the office for them, or I can meet you there."

"Can I call you in the morning? I just...I have things to think about and decisions to make."

"I trust that you will make the right decision, so I'm going to leave and let you figure it out." Sam headed for the door of Ryann's apartment. She turned back to face Ryann at the door, offering her a full smile. "I'll see you soon, okay?"

"Sam..." Ryann's voice wavered. Her body couldn't handle any more emotion today. Everything was a whirlwind lately. "Thank you." It wasn't only the shop she was thanking Sam for. It was everything. Her advice. Her support. Her love.

"Anything for family, Ry."

CHAPTER TWELVE

One month later...

Ryann's mouth fell open, amazed as her eyes took in the newly decorated shop. Her shop. Her pride and joy. The last month had dragged on while she waited for this moment, but when she collected the keys from Sam, she decided there and then that she wanted to take her time before reopening. To give the place a new, fresh look. To wipe her past away and start anew.

It made sense. Nothing good had come from the last few years. Just a couple of months ago, she felt as though her life was over. Just a couple of months ago, Ryann didn't see a way out of her existence other than to end it all. Ryann could just as well not be standing here. A fresh start was for the best.

Ryann moved through the piercing area freshly painted by an artist Sam knew. The wall, originally a black pattern, was now an array of colours that replicated the pride flag in its own way. It wasn't obvious to anyone who walked in, but Ryann knew what it meant. It was her authentic self. Her happiness. Pride for who she was.

A smile curled on her lips, her shoulders sagging ever so slightly as her hands landed in the front pockets of her black, washed-out jeans. This month had been pretty easy going, providing she kept her mind off certain aspects of her life. Her love life, in particular.

Jen had called repeatedly, begging for Ryann to take her back now that her new squeeze had seen her for who she was. Ryann could only laugh and end the calls. But Jen and her pleading voice were the least of her concerns.

Now, if Lydia had called and begged Ryann for time, Ryann would have dropped everything to make it happen. But it hadn't happened. Lydia hadn't called once. Not even a text message. Nothing.

As much as Ryann wanted to show up at Lydia's place, she couldn't. It wouldn't be right, and it wouldn't be fair. Lydia's lack of contact meant that Ryann was no longer welcome in her life, and that was something she had to accept. It stung, but Ryann brought that decision on all by herself.

Lydia had contacted Sam some three weeks ago to check everything was okay with Ryann, but once Sam put Lydia's mind at rest, the call was disconnected and that was the end of all ties between them. Sam hadn't heard from Lydia since. Though Lydia was no longer a part of Ryann's life, she did appreciate that last call to Sam. It showed that even though they'd parted on bad terms, Lydia cared. That meant the world.

Ryann took a seat on one of the new couches she'd had delivered a couple of days ago, sinking into the soft leather and humming in appreciation as she did. Luciana had been her shopping partner, but a month on, Luciana was barely able to move around the house let alone anywhere else. She'd promised Ryann she would be here the day she walked into the shop once everything was completed, but Ryann understood that it wasn't as simple as that. Luciana was seven and a half months pregnant; a tattoo studio was surely the last thing on her mind. Kids and a wife came above all else. As it should.

Ryann checked her watch. Three in the afternoon. She knew she should go home and prepare for tomorrow's opening day, but a cold beer was what she craved. Alone, sitting quietly, with a pint in her hand. Life didn't get much better than that lately.

She stood and took her keys from the coffee table in front of her, the latest magazines scattered across the glass and ready to be opened by her first clients. Over the last few weeks, Ryann had been in touch with her regulars, and her other full-time artist, and all of them couldn't wait for Dark Angel to reopen. Now, she just had to be here in the morning, ready to get her life back into full swing. Ready to get things back to the way they were before *other* factors came into play and cast a darkness over her. Before women —before Jen—entered her life, Ryann was more than happy with how things were going.

She locked up the shop and slipped into the entrance of the pub next door. The usual smell of stagnant ale lifted as she walked across the dark, stained, red carpet, the bar her destination of choice. She ordered herself a pint and then took a seat towards the back.

The pub was small, roughly ten tables available and dotted around the part carpeted, part laminated space. It was far from classy, but it had real people in it. Everyone had a story. Everyone had a reason to unwind. Ryann appreciated that type of people more than any other kind – those who knew what it was like to sink into a cold pint at three in the afternoon.

Not everyone would get up and leave after the one drink they'd promised themselves, but other people's drinking habits weren't Ryann's business. She didn't know what the people in this room had been through.

Ryann sipped her pint, releasing a sigh as she set it back down and enjoyed the ice-cold liquid sliding down her throat. Her mind wandered. What would Lydia be doing right now? Had she called her old boss because her current one was sapping the life out of her? Or was she plodding along, taking the attitude from her boss, Bree?

Lydia didn't come across as the kind of person to take attitude from anyone, but Ryann knew how difficult it was to decide between her job and her sanity. She could only hope that Lydia had made the right decision for herself. Whatever that was.

Her phone buzzed. It was Luciana.

L: So sorry I wasn't there today. Having a terrible day. Hope everything is how you want it to look.

R: Don't be stupid. I didn't expect you to show up. The baby will be here before you two know it. My shop is last on the agenda.

L: I told you I'd be there, and I wasn't. Come for dinner this weekend?

R: Let's just see how things go. If you're both feeling up to it, I'll be there. Text me on Saturday.

L: I promise I will.

Ryann shoved her phone in her jacket pocket, once again relaxing back and watching the bubbles hit the surface of her pint. Her eyes wandered away, landing on the bar and the person standing at it. She could be wrong, but Ryann was almost certain Lydia was standing in front of her.

Dressed in jeans and a pair of Vans, her hair appeared longer than the last time they'd been in the same room. Yes, it was definitely her. Ryann knew that as Lydia turned, her beautiful profile showing.

If Ryann could move, she would head over there and say hello. But she couldn't. She found herself stuck to the seat, and it wasn't because of the dirty upholstery for a change. No, it was because she was worried about the reception she'd receive. Lydia had made it perfectly clear that she wanted no more to do with Ryann, so going over there was a waste of time, and potentially embarrassing.

Ryann gulped down more of her pint, almost wanting to leave it and head out the door. Why should she, though? Didn't she have every right to be in this establishment and enjoying a drink before she went home for the rest of the evening alone? Yes. Yes, she did.

Lydia turned around with her own pint, stopping dead when she realised Ryann was sitting in the spot she was heading towards. Her mouth fell open, clearly surprised to see Ryann enjoying a drink, but she continued to move towards her. Lydia looked as though she was cooking up some kind of comment, but Ryann was prepared for it. After all, she was the one who hurt Lydia.

Ryann smiled, trying to read the woman now standing in front of her and looking down at her. "Hey."

"You don't drink in here."

"Oh, I've been in and out over the last couple of weeks. Been busy at the shop so it was ideal if I wanted to unwind."

"Of all the pubs..."

Ryann lifted a shoulder. "This was the nearest."

"Right, well." Lydia ran her fingers through her hair, sighing. "See you. Bye."

Ryann opened her mouth to speak, instantly regretting her decision to do so. It wouldn't be well received, but she found herself about to talk anyway. "Did you want to sit here?"

"Oh, are you leaving?" Lydia asked, turning back.

"No, I meant...you can sit with me."

"No, thanks." Lydia walked away, leaving Ryann feeling disappointed.

Once again, her own fault.

She should leave. Lydia didn't need to finish work and be faced with the woman who kissed her and left. As much as Ryann had done nothing to warrant being run out of the pub—the place had become her regular in recent weeks—she knew it was best for everyone concerned if she did. She downed her pint and got to her feet, eyeing Lydia at a table on the other side of the room.

Ryann found her feet taking her exactly in that direction, even if she knew it was a mistake. "Hey. I'm just going to leave, okay?"

Lydia looked up from her phone and shrugged. "Do what you like. It's a pub, not my front living room."

"Right, yeah." Ryann nodded, biting her lip. "So, it was good to see you. You look great."

"I'm meeting someone," Lydia said.

"O...kay." Ryann found herself frowning. She didn't need to know who Lydia was meeting. It wasn't her business.

"I thought you should know before you turned on the charm and I had to let you down."

"Oh, I wasn't. I just...I was being friendly."

"Right. Well, bye then."

Ryann's heart sunk into her stomach. Lydia really did hate her. She knew she wouldn't be number one on her Christmas list, but she hadn't expected her to be so cold. So...uninterested.

She turned to leave before turning back again. One more thing had to be said. "I just...I am sorry."

Lydia stared. Her afternoon date hadn't stopped talking for the past thirty minutes, and she struggled to recall any of the conversation. The woman, Carly, was nice. A little too perky for Lydia, but she'd promised Soph she would get herself back in the game and that was what she was doing right now. Putting herself through unnecessary torture for her best friend.

Her date really did like the sound of her own voice. That was okay, though. Lydia had other things on her mind. Her only hope was that Carly wouldn't test her on their conversation so far.

She swirled the remainder of her pint in the glass, sighing when Carly finally fell silent. Could her date see the lack of interest in her eyes? It was probably that obvious this afternoon. Lydia had a good poker face when it was required, but she wasn't sure she had the energy today.

Ryann's fault.

That woman had truly thrown Lydia when she arrived here to find the tattooed beauty sitting in Lydia's favourite pub. It had been a month since they last had contact with one another, a month since they kissed...Lydia thought she was over the entire thing.

One glimpse proved she wasn't.

Ryann had invaded her every thought, her every waking moment.

Over the last few weeks, Lydia wondered if she'd made a mistake in shunning Ryann completely. She knew she was safe, knew her life was picking up again, but Lydia couldn't bring herself to call. Every text message from Ryann was deleted immediately, every attempt at communication dismissed.

Lydia thought that if she blocked Ryann from her life, her thoughts, she would move forward without issue. She had been wrong. Ryann wasn't a woman you simply forgot about. Especially not with the past they had. A short-lived past, yes, but a past, nonetheless.

Carly focused fully on Lydia, apparently waiting for a response. Lydia smiled. "Where did you say you were from?"

"South Liverpool," Carly explained. "Mum is from Sefton, but Dad is from the same street we live in now."

"You're close to them?"

"I guess so, yeah. So, what is it that you do?"

"I'm in marketing." Lydia chose not to offer much more than that. She wouldn't see this woman again, so Carly didn't need to know any more. "Look, I know we kinda planned to make an evening of this, but I can't stay much longer."

"Oh, is everything okay?"

"Yeah. I think I'm coming down with something. It's been

inching its way in for the last couple of days, and I'm not feeling great today."

"You should have called. We could rearrange?"

"Yeah, I guess we could." Lydia hated lying, leading someone on, but she didn't have the heart to tell this woman that she had Ryann on her mind and that she shouldn't expect a call. "Can I get in touch with you next time I have a few days off?"

"Of course, you can." Carly smiled, her green eyes smiling too. "I've enjoyed this, though. Just in case you were wondering."

"Me, too."

Carly eyed her phone, tapping the screen and checking the time. "Would you mind if I headed off? I can catch the next train if I leave now."

"No. Go and get your train." Lydia waved off Carly. "I'll call you, okay?"

"Looking forward to it." Carly stood, leaning in and pressing a kiss to Lydia's cheek. "See you, Lydia."

As soon as she was alone, Lydia relaxed back into her seat, contemplating one more drink before she left the pub. She might need the liquid courage for the apology she had to make. One that she hadn't expected to make today.

Ryann's face played over and over in her mind. A face filled with hurt as Lydia spoke to her with an attitude she didn't realise she had. Ryann may have caught Lydia off guard by being at the pub, but she didn't deserve to be spoken to like that. She had as much right to be in the pub as anyone else.

No drink. Stop putting it off.

Lydia lifted her bag from the floor, heading for the exit. As she stood outside, she glanced to her left to find Dark Angel partly lit. It certainly looked better than the last time she looked through that window. It looked…new.

Lydia peered through the window, smiling when she caught sight of the impressive work on the walls. Some kind of Pride mural sat on the wall to the left, equipment waiting and ready to be used. The place looked great.

"Can I help you?"

Ryann's voice shocked Lydia so much that she jerked forward and head-butted the window.

"You here to burn the place down?" Ryann cocked her head. Lydia knew the move would usually be coupled with a smile, but not today. It was clear in Ryann's eyes that Lydia was the last person she wanted to see. "At least let me grab my kit before you do."

"Hi," Lydia croaked.

"I tried pleasantries before."

"And now I'm here to apologise," Lydia paused. "Just...I didn't expect to see you in the pub."

"Don't worry; I'll find somewhere else to drink." Ryann stepped past Lydia, a brown paper bag in her hand. "You really don't owe me an apology. I guess I deserved it."

"No, you didn't." Lydia followed Ryann inside the shop, the smell of fresh paint and antiseptic evident in the air. "This place looks great."

"Thanks." Ryann continued to move through the open space, her back to Lydia at all times. "I was just having dinner before I got some more work done, so..."

Lydia knew Ryann wanted her to leave. She hardly expected to be welcome after her behaviour a short while ago. The problem was, Lydia didn't want to leave. Not right now. She truly did want to apologise to the woman who had kissed her and left her.

"I'll just say what I have to say, and then I'll go."

Ryann turned around, looking expectantly at Lydia. How had they come to this? Just a month ago, Lydia was thrilled to have Ryann in her life; Ryann seemingly feeling the same way. But now? They were strangers. Ryann looked good, though. She looked happy, just like the night they met in the pub. The night they kissed. The night it all turned to shit.

"How I spoke to you before..." Lydia started. "I'm really sorry. I had it in my head that I wouldn't see you again, so when I did...I didn't know what to do. What to say."

"Honestly, it's fi—"

Lydia held up her hand, cutting Ryann off. "No. It's not fine. Please, accept the apology."

"Sure, fine. Apology accepted." Ryann lifted her dinner from the brown bag, her eyes lifting and once again landing on Lydia. "Did you need something else?"

Lydia lowered her eyes, embarrassed by her behaviour. "No."

"Okay, well I only have a few hours left here, and I really need to eat and get on."

Lydia nodded, gripping the strap of her bag tight. The longer she watched Ryann, the more Lydia regretted cutting ties with her.

"Good luck with the reopening."

Ryann shoved a forkful of noodles into her mouth, smiling. "Thanks."

"And good luck with everything else."

"Yeah. You, too."

CHAPTER THIRTEEN

"I was awful to her, Soph." Lydia placed her head in her hands, holding back the emotion she felt bubbling in her throat. She had no right to cry. This was her own doing, and as Soph had so bluntly put it earlier on the phone, Lydia barely knew Ryann.

"I don't know why you're so upset. *She* pissed off without a second thought, not you."

"That's not the point."

"Then what *is* the point, because I'm really missing it here."

"It was the way I spoke to her," Lydia explained. "I'd had a bad morning at work, took the afternoon off before I wrung Bree's neck, and then Ryann got the brunt of it."

Soph shrugged. "She was in *your* local."

"It's a pub. She can go wherever she pleases."

"But it's a bit weird that she's taken to drinking there, don't you think?" Soph quirked an eyebrow.

Lydia couldn't say it was weird. Ryann had her studio back and the pub was next door. If she wanted to unwind with a pint, who was Lydia to question that?

"Not really, no."

"You're just hoping for something that's not there." Soph threw up her hands, climbing from the stool in the kitchen, and paced the floor. "She kissed you. She left. You're out of your mind if you even think about missing her."

"Actually, I kissed her."

"Does it really matter who kissed who?" Soph turned around, bracing herself against the counter and staring directly at Lydia. "The outcome was still the same, Lyds."

"It does matter, actually. I've been thinking about it. Ryann apologised for kissing me. She said she'd broken my trust as her friend. Yes, she may have instigated it, kinda, but I'm the one who flirted at the pub. I'm the one who invited her back here. *I'm* the one who *actually* kissed her.

"She left here believing that I hadn't wanted that kiss. At least, that's how I'm beginning to see it. I'm not sure she realises that I wanted it to happen, too. Okay, she may tell me that it was a mistake and that it shouldn't have happened because she's not into me, but if she thinks she's overstepped, she's very wrong. And I wouldn't know the answer to that because I ignored her calls. Then I spoke to her the way I did last night and the hurt in her eyes was awful. Horrible."

Soph cocked her head. "Maybe you should show up at her studio?"

"And say what? I already went there yesterday to apologise. She just said thanks and bye."

"Flowers? A posh bottle of something? I don't know…"

"Today was the re-opening," Lydia said with a sadness. "Kinda wish I could have been there to support her. She doesn't have many friends."

"I'm sure she had support."

"Maybe, but I was the one she came to when she needed advice about getting it back. I would have liked to be there to see the smile on her face when it opened its doors again."

"Sorry, Lyd."

Lydia wanted all of this to blow over. It wasn't possible, she wasn't that lucky, but Ryann not coming around anymore *had* left a hole in her life. A hole she didn't think could appear given the short length of time they'd known one another.

Truth be told, Lydia enjoyed Ryann's company far more than anyone else's. At one time, it worried her, but now she just wanted Ryann back in her life. Whatever way she could get. Friends, even acquaintances if it had to be that way. Just...something.

"Maybe I could send her a text?"

"Don't see why not."

Lydia took her phone from the kitchen counter, pulling up Ryann's number. She hadn't come across it for a couple of weeks, but it had always been there, sitting in her contacts and begging to be used.

L: Hope the opening went well...
R: Who is this?

Lydia's heart sunk. Ryann truly had deleted her number. She considered not replying, but quickly found her thumbs tapping the screen.

L: Lydia.

A bubble appeared, signalling that Ryann was replying, but then it disappeared. Lydia held her breath momentarily, but nothing came. No response. Zilch.

She threw her phone to the counter with a clatter. "Well, that was a waste of time."

"No response?"

"She asked who was texting and then chose not to reply when I told her who it was."

"Mm. Maybe she's just busy..."

Lydia sighed. "Maybe. Never mind."

Ryann groaned, falling back on the couch in the waiting area. Today was finally over, the studio's re-opening a huge success. The appointment book was full for the next month, only leaving Ryann with enough time to take one afternoon off a week, but it was hardly work when she loved doing it. An afternoon off would be manageable for now.

She didn't have any other priorities, Sam would have to be let down gently when she told her she couldn't quite look after Luca as much as she used to, but her cousin would understand. After all, it was Sam who took getting this place back into her own hands.

Ryann glanced around. Her other artist had cleared up before she left, so now Ryann just had to bring herself to stand up and take the ten-minute walk back to her apartment. Before she went home, she had something else she needed to do. The problem was, she wasn't sure she had the energy—mental or physical—to do it.

Lydia.

Taking her keys from the table in front of her, her phone too, Ryann climbed to her feet and stretched. Her back wasn't in the best form today; being hunched over for extended periods of time when she'd been out of it for a while wasn't the best idea she'd ever had. But the takings were higher than usual with plenty more to come. A glass back really was the least of her concerns.

The bell above the door jingled.

"Sorry, I'm about to close up," she called.

A familiar blonde stood in front of Ryann. "That's okay. I'm not here looking for a tattoo."

"Wait, I recognise you." Ryann tried to place the woman standing in front of her, coming up blank when tiredness set in. "How do I know you?"

"I'm Lydia's best friend," she said. "We've only met briefly."

"Ah. You're the one who outed her on the doorstep." Ryann nodded, taking her rucksack from the floor beside the couch. "What can I do for you?"

"Go and see her."

"Excuse me?" Ryann quirked an eyebrow. She had planned to head over to Lydia's this evening—that was the reason she hadn't responded to her message earlier—but she wouldn't allow someone to stand here and make demands of her.

"Please, go and see her."

"I'm not sure if she's told you, but she kinda doesn't want me in her life anymore."

Soph shook her head. "You're wrong."

"Believe me, I'm not. I appreciate you coming here, though I don't know why, but it's been a long day and I would love to go home and shower."

"Why did you walk out on her after you kissed her?"

Ryann frowned. "I'm not sure that's any of your business."

"She's my best friend. It's always my business."

"I don't even know your name; I'm not discussing my personal life with you." Ryann was sure Lydia had revealed her friend's name, but she continued to come up blank.

"And that's okay. Just...she wanted it to happen, okay?"

"Come again?"

"The kiss. Lydia *wanted* it to happen."

Ryann chose to store that information for another time. Lydia wanted it. Wow. "Did she tell you who I am? How we met?"

Soph nodded. "She did."

"Then I'm sure you can understand why us getting involved with one another is a bad idea."

"You're a dickhead for what you tried to do, but Lydia really likes you." Soph moved towards the door. "That night you two were meeting for drinks, I had to go around that afternoon and calm her down. She may not give a lot away, Ryann, but in her head...that night was a date."

Ryann stood speechless. Why hadn't Lydia given her a hint of that? *What more do you need? The woman sang to you and openly flirted.* "Then it looks as though I missed my chance." Ryann stared off at nothing. Resigning herself to the fact that she'd blown it with Lydia, her posture withered as her throat constricted.

This news should have elated Ryann; instead, it saddened her. "How do you figure that out?"

"She didn't look happy to see me yesterday, and she informed me that she was on a date."

"That was my fault." Lydia's friend held up her hand. "I encouraged her to date. But I know, *you* are who she wants to date."

Ryann scratched the back of her neck, confused by all of this. "I, uh…"

"I think you two need to get together and talk."

"Lydia is probably sick of talking to me. It's all we seemed to do."

"Play your cards right and talking will be the last thing you two are doing." She winked, disappearing out of the studio. The door closed gently behind her, a slight breeze travelling through the shop and directly down Ryann's spine.

Ryann swiftly dialled Sam's number, waiting for the call to connect.

"Hello, Superstar."

"Tell me I'm making a mistake…"

"Um, I'm not sure what you're talking about, Ry." Sam laughed. "If you mean the studio, that line of clients around lunch time should answer your question."

"About Lydia. Tell me it's a mistake to go over there."

Sam paused and then said, "I can't do that. If you want to visit her, do it."

I want to do more than visit her. "Her best friend has just been in. Asked me to go and see Lydia. Do you think I should?"

"You seem to be in a good place. Do what you *feel* is right, not what you think is right."

"Thanks. I gotta go."

"Thought so."

Ryann ended the call, noting the playfulness in Sam's voice as she did.

Sam was right. Nobody could make the decision for Ryann. Only she knew what she wanted and who she wanted in her life. It was Lydia, Ryann knew that from the moment she realised something more was happening between them. But Ryann would still keep her guard up as she visited tonight. Lydia may have apologised for yesterday, but their encounter had still happened. An encounter filled with uncertainty and mistrust.

Ryann knew what she wanted deep down. She felt it as she thought about Lydia. How her stomach rolled with anticipation. How her hands grew clammy as she learned of Lydia's desire to turn this into something more. A desire Ryann hadn't expected her to return.

Lydia blew her nose for the third time in minutes, sobbing into mid-air as she threw another tissue into the bin. Marley & Me would always get her square in the heart, the emotional state she was already in only making matters worse. Soph usually watched this film with her, both of them hugging it out at the end, but tonight it was airing on one of the satellite channels and Lydia couldn't resist. She was a sucker for a good cry.

Soph had called an hour ago to check in, but the call had been short and sweet. So long as Lydia didn't think about Ryann and how she'd spoken to her yesterday, she didn't feel so bad. But the more she heard Ryann's name, the more disappointed she felt. Even still, she'd kept her phone close by since she'd texted Ryann earlier—still nothing.

As the credits rolled, she plucked another Kleenex from the box beside her, powering off the TV and disappearing into the hallway. She needed a glass of wine and a year's worth of sleep. "God, I need to get a grip on my life."

The doorbell rang, frightening Lydia to within an inch of her life. Nobody could see her in this state, even if it would only be Soph. She pulled her hoodie around her tighter, dabbed her eyes with the tissue she was still holding, and opened the door.

"Hi."

Ryann stood before her, wearing a crisp white shirt and a beaming smile to match. Lydia wanted to say hi, but instead she found her eyes filling with tears, a sob escaping her mouth that she was unable to hold back.

"Whoa." Ryann stepped closer, catching Lydia before she could fall. "What's going on?"

Lydia remained silent, delighting in the sensation of Ryann's arms enveloping her as she cried into her chest.

"Lydia? Did something happen? Are you okay?"

"W-why are you here?"

"I wanted to see you. I didn't text earlier because I was busy, but mainly because I wanted to come over once I'd showered and had dinner."

"Will you stay for five minutes?"

"Come on," Ryann said. "Let's get you inside."

Ryann settled onto the couch beside Lydia, an uncertainty hanging in the air between them. Ryann hadn't expected Lydia's breakdown as she opened the door some twenty minutes ago, but Lydia had assured her that she was okay. Once Ryann got wind of the fact her all-time favourite film had been playing, she understood completely. Ryann couldn't watch it anymore either. It was too heartbreaking.

"I'm so sorry I was a wreck when you showed up."

"Don't apologise." Ryann waved off Lydia's apology. "I like a woman who is in touch with her emotional side."

Lydia lowered her eyes.

"I also love a woman who doesn't back down when someone has hurt her."

Lydia lifted her head, her bottom lip trembling.

"It wasn't ever my intention to hurt you."

"I kissed *you*, Ryann."

Ryann appreciated Lydia's honesty, but she still wasn't sure this was a good idea. Being here, sitting beside Lydia, only brought back the feelings she'd had the night they kissed. Feelings she thought had been buried in the weeks they'd avoided one another.

"And I kissed you because I wanted to." Lydia took Ryann's hand, her thumb grazing the black and grey rose tattoo covering the back of her hand. "I kissed you because it was all I'd thought about that day. God, I was a mess getting ready to meet you."

Ryann frowned. "Why?"

"Because I foolishly thought it could have meant more." Lydia shook her head. "This was all my fault, Ryann. Don't feel bad about it."

Ryann's heart thrummed, her pulse rushing in her ears. Today had brought a tonne of new information. A lot of things needed to be processed.

"So, if you've come here to apologise...don't."

"Lydia—"

"Please, let's not do this," Lydia replied. She appeared to be done with the conversation, but the same didn't apply to Ryann. "Did you want coffee while you're here?"

"You know, I'd love coffee."

Lydia's eyes brightened. "Yeah?"

"I've missed calling around here. Of course, I'd like coffee."

"Then I'll be right back."

Ryann relaxed into the soft material of Lydia's couch. Her home was huge—far too big for one person—but it was cosy. Homely. Weeks on, Ryann remained impressed by the dedication and maintenance Lydia had put into the place. Ryann would have given up long ago.

As the sound of the kettle boiling caught her attention, Ryann weighed up the pros and cons of how she felt about Lydia. She'd certainly found herself attracted to less-appealing women in the past; Lydia was a breath of fresh air. As much as Ryann didn't know what the future held, she felt conflicted about her present.

Over the last few weeks, Ryann hadn't done so well. Yes, she had the refurbishment of the studio to keep her busy and her mind off things, but a constant dullness in her chest had plagued her. The inability to sleep was also causing issues. Carrying a relentless heaviness around with her had been confusing, but as Lydia reappeared with their coffee, Ryann pinpointed exactly what it was. Regret. A deep regret not for kissing Lydia, but for walking out.

Ryann got to her feet, leaving Lydia with a confused look in her eyes and took the cup of coffee offered. She reached out, placed it on a coaster atop the mantelpiece, and turned back to face Lydia.

Lydia's brow drew together. "What?"

Ryann took Lydia's coffee too, set it down, then offered a small smile. One laced with apprehension, but genuine. Their hands found one another's. "Can we start again?"

"I'd like that." Lydia reddened.

"The way I acted...that's not me." If Ryann was ever going to move forward, to be happy, she had to be fully honest. "I panicked. My first thought was that I'd overstepped. I didn't have much to go on in terms of you being into me. And then I thought I'd ruined our friendship. I mean, the last thing I wanted was to lose you as a friend, Lydia. You've been amazing and I really didn't want to jeopardise that.

"That night after the pub, when you wanted more...well, I did, too." Ryann paused, the thought of staying here that night being something that had played on Ryann's mind often. What would have happened? If Ryann had known that Lydia wouldn't have turned her down, she never would have walked out. Even if she thought it was wrong at the time, her body felt it was right. "So, I'm sorry. For walking out. For not staying and discussing it with you. For just being a complete mess most of the time. Truly sorry."

"You know," Lydia started, "the tattoos and the leather jacket made me think you were some dangerous player. Someone who did as she pleased. But I was wrong about you. I knew I was wrong the moment the thought entered my mind. When I'm alone with you, it's perfect."

"Yeah?" Ryann tried to hide the smile twitching on her lips. "I'm not perfect, far from it, but I have a good heart. I just…"

"You just what?" Lydia visibly swallowed hard. "Ryann?"

"Are you sure you're into me? I mean, I don't really have much to give."

"That's what you think?" Lydia's eyes softened, her smile sympathetic. "I'm not sure I can recall the last time I was interested in another woman. Not like I am with you."

"You really are interested?" Ryann stepped closer to Lydia, her free hand settling on Lydia's waist. "Even after that night?"

"More so after that night," Lydia said. "You can't kiss a girl like that and expect her not to care."

Ryann's eyebrow rose. "Oh?"

Lydia smiled, the gap between them closing as her chest heaved. Ryann felt the same. She always did around this woman. Lydia tugged Ryann closer by the front of her jacket. "So, what now?"

"Oh, I couldn't possibly say." Ryann grinned, her eyes narrowing. "Anything you had in mind?"

"One or two things."

Neither of them interested in wasting another moment, their lips met. It took everything in Ryann not to throw Lydia down on the couch, touch her, and worship her the way she truly wanted to. It also took everything not to cry. Lydia brought out emotions Ryann didn't know she still had. But above all else, Lydia felt right. Against her, kissing her, whatever else came from this evening. It all felt right.

Ryann pressed her forehead against Lydia's, reluctantly ending their kiss. "Can I see you tomorrow?"

"O-oh, uh..."

"If you're not busy." Ryann wouldn't push this. She would wait until Lydia was available.

"I'm not busy, but it is kind of a big afternoon tomorrow."

Ryann frowned.

"The cup quarter-final," Lydia said. "My team is playing."

"Y-you're a blue?" Ryann almost fell to the floor; Lydia couldn't possibly support the London-based team they were playing. But whatever team she supported, Lydia was a football fan, so this could only be a match made in heaven. Jen couldn't have given a single moment of her time to football games, but Lydia? At this point with Lydia, Ryann should have expected to be surprised.

"Since I was in the womb."

"I'll be here. Kick-off is at four. Call me when you finish work and I'll be over. I'll bring everything we need."

"So, do you think...I mean, uh...is this an official date?"

"With a woman who loves football as much as me?" Ryann quirked an eyebrow. "Damn right it's a date. You're lucky it's not a proposal."

Lydia blushed, shaking her head. "You're something else, you know that?"

Ryann chose to lean back in, kissing Lydia with a little more than she offered before. Her tongue glided against Lydia's, a moan rumbling in Ryann's throat as she felt Lydia's hands slipping inside her jacket, sliding around and gripping her back. "Phew."

"Do you have to go?"

"I should," Ryann said, noting the sadness in Lydia's eyes. "But I could probably hang around for another hour."

"Good. I need your advice." Lydia shed Ryann's coat from her shoulders and pulled her down to the couch.

With Ryann's full attention on Lydia, her silver eyes shining,

Ryann wondered how she'd stayed away for a month. "What's up?"

"I'm meeting Jo tomorrow."

"Jo?"

Lydia cleared her throat. "My old boss."

CHAPTER FOURTEEN

Lydia turned her watch towards her. 11 a.m. Jo would be here any moment now, but Lydia wasn't holding out much hope. Jo hadn't once hinted that she had any positions available during their previous calls, but Lydia would ask. She couldn't do any more than that.

This morning, after another run-in with Bree, Lydia wished she'd left with Jo the day she walked. She wished she'd had the optimism to leave her position and see what Jo could build elsewhere. The need for security and stability had been what Lydia focused on, something she'd regretted ever since.

Now that she had Ryann in her life—only just—Lydia felt as though she had more support. Her parents had always been supportive, but that's not so easy to do when they lived all the way in Spain. Yes, she had Soph by her side, but Soph would tell Lydia whatever she believed she wanted to hear. Ryann, in Lydia's mind, would be truthful. She would discuss options and give her honest opinion but help Lydia through regardless. That was the kind of person Lydia perceived Ryann to be.

The bell above the coffee shop door jingled and Jo walked in. Lydia's first observation was just how well Jo looked. Her skin glowed, her eyes were bright—she looked fantastic. But Lydia felt an instant jealousy.

"Jo!" Lydia waved her old boss over. "I ordered you a latte."

"You're a bloody star." Jo sunk down into the seat across from Lydia. "Josh couldn't find his swimming trunks this morning and *Daddy* was too busy eating breakfast to get off his arse to look for them with him."

"Busy morning?"

"I walked straight into a meeting at nine. Saturday is supposed to be my day off. And then my assistant called in sick so that meant a painful ninety minutes without coffee." Jo spied the latte on the table, pulling it closer to her. "Even without you working for me, I can still rely on you."

The differences between Jo and Bree were stark. Lydia wondered how she'd ever coped without her old boss. She mentally patted herself on the back for doing so.

"How's tricks?"

Lydia's shoulders slumped.

"That bad?"

"I'm losing the plot, Jo."

Jo ran her fingers through her short, cropped silver hair. "I did warn you. I worked with Bree years ago. Spoilt brat is the only way to describe that woman."

"She threatened to fire me this morning." Lydia didn't know why she was surprised; Bree was forever threatening to let her go.

Jo frowned. "Why?"

"Her computer wouldn't turn on."

"You work for I.T. now, too?"

Lydia smiled, cradling her cappuccino in her hands. "Nope. But try telling Bree that. She always has an answer for everything. She's driving me insane."

"You are worth so much more than this, Lydia."

Lydia noted the sincerity in Jo's mocha eyes. Jo had never been the kind of woman to step all over her employees; it was what

Lydia admired more than anything else. Jo wasn't power hungry. She didn't talk down to anyone. She was a firm believer in her team being the most important aspect of her business. Without them, she couldn't survive. And she was right. It was a shame Bree didn't see life that way.

"Which is why I asked to meet with you."

Jo sighed, wrinkling her nose. "I thought as much."

"You don't have any positions available, do you." It wasn't a question. She was simply stating a fact.

"I do...kind of," Jo said. "I know how hard you work, Lydia. I know that without you, *Strive* never would have been what it is now. If you really want out of that place, I have a position for you."

"You do?" Lydia's eyes widened, a lump of emotion working its way to her throat. Lydia had come here this morning fully expecting Jo to turn her down, so to learn that she could move on, she was surprised. "I'll take it."

"Wait a moment," Jo laughed. "You may want to think about it for a little while. I don't want an answer from you right away, since the office won't be ready for another two months. I have the builders in at the moment."

"The builders? What office?"

"I'm expanding. And I want you to run the office."

All the breath left Lydia's lungs. How had she left *Strive* this morning in a mood only to walk in here and potentially have all her problems solved for her? Perhaps it was the universe repaying her for helping Ryann. Perhaps it was just Lydia's time to move on.

"Please, think about it," Jo said. "It wouldn't just be your average job. It would be *your* office."

"I can't believe you're offering me this, Jo."

Lydia didn't need to think about it. Jo was offering her the biggest opportunity of her life. To turn it down would be criminal.

"I want it. I *need* it."

"The office will be based in Leeds. It's in a lovely area."

Lydia froze.

Leeds?

"My plan once Leeds is complete is to look at London. I know I'll be a small fish with the amount of marketing companies already there, but it's really taken off for me. Walter certainly made sure I was the talk of the town before he passed away."

"Leeds..."

"Yep. Leeds."

"Oh." Lydia toyed with her cup, mulling over the idea of Leeds. Yes, this was one hell of an opportunity, but what about Ryann?

"I mean, you could commute, but running the office will mean late nights and early mornings. I have every faith that you can do it, that you can excel, but I do want you to think about it, Lydia."

Lydia smiled weakly. She knew it had been too good to be true. "Yeah. I should think about it."

"Everything okay?"

"You don't have anything in the Cheshire office?" Lydia looked up at Jo through hooded eyes. She knew the answer to her question, but she found herself asking it anyway. "Not even on reception or something? I'll take anything, Jo."

"You want to be a receptionist when I've just offered you your own office?" Jo's eyebrow rose; she was clearly surprised.

"Things have kinda changed for me recently."

"Things?"

"I'm...sort of seeing someone," Lydia said.

"Sort of." Jo nodded. "So, if this relationship you're talking about only qualifies as a 'sort of,' you should still consider your career. 'Sort of' isn't your style. We both know that."

"It's just very new."

"How new?"

"L-last night." Lydia realised how silly that sounded as the words left her mouth. Jo was clearly holding back laughter, but Lydia knew she couldn't possibly understand. "It's not like that. Ryann is great."

"And you know this just by meeting last night?"

"No, we've known each other for a couple of months...almost. She was going through some stuff, and I was there for her."

"And you've both finally come to your senses and realised you should be doing more than 'friends' stuff." Jo winked. "You know what, I get it. Take some time. Speak to your...partner. Just let me know when you've decided. Like I said, you have a while to think about it."

"I just...I don't know."

"I'd find you a place to live. But if you really did want the job and your other half couldn't commit to moving, the option to commute is still there. You'd be lucky to get an hour awake with one another by the time you got home, but this is your life. Your choice."

My other half. Lydia smiled.

Just hearing that made her heart expand in her chest. Would Ryann be her other half one day? Lydia certainly felt like it was a possibility. A strong possibility. But she also knew it wasn't that simple. They still had a lot to learn about one another. Anything could change in the coming weeks.

"I promise I'll let you know what I decide. But thanks, Jo." Lydia slid her hand across the table, settling it on Jo's forearm. "I do appreciate your offer."

"My company could definitely use your skills, Lydia."

Ryann emptied two bags of Doritos into a large bowl, various dips ready and waiting in Lydia's living room. She carried two beers in her arm, grabbed the bowl, and headed in the direction of the TV commentary.

Lydia was showering after returning from work later than she was supposed to. Ryann initially panicked when Lydia didn't contact her, expecting their first date to be cancelled. Ryann was working on that insecurity, though. At least, she was trying to. Lydia appeared perfectly happy last night when she was kissing Ryann, so Ryann knew her worries were unfounded. Unnecessary, too.

All day at the studio, Ryann had thought about that kiss. How Lydia looked directly into her eyes when their lips met. How Lydia's body relaxed yet reacted, the tension in her shoulders disappearing as Ryann confirmed her desire to move forward with Lydia. That kiss...it was perfect.

In those moments when Ryann chose to be bold, a confidence had surged through her. She didn't feel inadequate or unworthy of Lydia. No, she felt total calm and ease. But when her lips found Lydia's, Ryann's confidence was overtaken by certainty. That expanding sensation in Ryann's chest didn't feel unsettling or scary. She simply evened out her breathing, knowing it was a connectedness she felt.

Ryann could deny her feelings or look for excuses as to why Lydia deserved better, but deep down she knew it would be lies. Ryann wanted Lydia—that really was the end of it. A strong, mental focus was what she'd been lacking over the last few months, but now she had that back.

The last month could have been prevented if she'd discovered her need for Lydia the first time they kissed. In her heart, it was obvious. But in her head...a ridiculous idea she couldn't possibly entertain. If Ryann could just keep her mind and thoughts at bay, this would all be completely fine.

"How long do I have?"

Ryann twisted in her seat. Lydia was standing in the doorway, towel-drying her hair. Ryann couldn't help the grin that spread across her mouth. "You have a good half hour yet."

"Sorry I've left you sitting alone. Not exactly the best date."

Ryann took in Lydia's entire appearance. She hadn't had many opportunities to do that since they'd met. One or both of them usually had a dilemma, something preventing Ryann from clearing her mind and focusing fully on Lydia. But not tonight, and not ever again.

"It's the perfect date," Ryann said.

Lydia stepped further into the room, leaning down over the back of the couch. "Hi." With her eyes smiling, Lydia kissed Ryann slowly. "I'm really happy that you're here."

Ryann's eyes closed briefly, the sensation of Lydia's breath on her lips sending her heart rate that little bit higher. "Me too."

Lydia climbed over the back of the couch, settling down beside Ryann. The towel she once held lay discarded in the doorway, but Ryann wouldn't complain. Lydia's hand was now in hers.

"How was work?" Ryann asked, knowing Lydia probably hadn't had the greatest day.

"Well, someone from the office saw me with Jo."

"So?"

"So, Bree chose to discuss it with me as I was about to leave. She now thinks I'm feeding information to Jo."

"Then she doesn't know you at all." Ryann didn't like knowing that Lydia's boss effectively bullied her during the day. "Can't you do something about all of this?"

"She knows I wouldn't do that. She is just constantly looking for a reason to get on my back. I don't know how much longer I can take it."

Ryann gritted her teeth, angered for Lydia. "She's a bully."

"Agreed." Lydia shifted closer when Ryann held out her arm.

"What did Jo say? Anything available with her?"

Ryann immediately noticed the discomfort in Lydia's body language. "Can we talk about it later? I don't want to spoil tonight with talk of work."

"Sure," Ryann agreed. "I'm here to listen whenever you need an ear, okay?"

"Thank you."

Lydia sat on the edge of the couch, her knee bouncing up and down as the final minutes of the football match played out in front of her. She could hear Ryann's heavy breathing beside her. Their team was winning 2-1, but things had started to get a little close several minutes ago. With two missed goals from the opposing team in the last ninety seconds, Lydia wasn't sure she could watch the end of the game. If they won tonight, the Blues would be on their way to London to compete in the semi-final for the cup.

"Come on!" Ryann yelled. "Fucking hit it!"

Lydia held her breath as their striker flailed about on the edge of the box with the ball.

"COME ON!"

Lydia jumped up, her hands braced on the coffee table, her eyes glued to the screen.

Come on. Hit it. Just hit it.

The ball struck the back of the net in the top right corner, sending the goalkeeper diving in the opposite direction. Lydia threw herself over the coffee table, screaming and cheering as Ryann joined her. With the final whistle due to blow at any moment, this had to be it. Their team had to be on their way to London.

The sound of the referee blowing for full-time sent them both into a frenzy, Lydia and Ryann wrapping their arms around one another and jumping up and down. Chants of "come on you Blues" could be heard in the background as the crowd roared on the TV, but Lydia was too wrapped up in this moment *and* Ryann to join in.

Ryann held her face, smiling. "We're off to Wembley."

"It's been a long time," Lydia replied, her smile mirroring Ryann's.

"I already declare the semi-final to be another date with you."

Lydia's heart weighed heavy in her chest. She would love nothing more than to share another football day with Ryann; they'd been few and far between lately. But something in the back of her mind told Lydia that it wouldn't be as simple as just agreeing to another date with Ryann. Not until she had all the facts.

Lydia fell down into her seat, satisfied that her pulse would return to normal soon. Spending the evening with Ryann had been her only thought since last night when Ryann left, but after her meeting with Jo this morning, Lydia was torn.

She wanted Ryann here—more than ever—but they really should discuss Jo's offer. An offer that Ryann knew nothing about. Didn't she deserve to know? It was the least Lydia could do after Ryann came over here to work things out with her.

"That may be the best game I've ever watched." Ryann twisted in her seat, facing Lydia fully as she rested her head in the palm of her hand. "Without a doubt."

"Seriously?" Lydia had witnessed much better play from the team. "Nah."

"Because I got to watch it with you," Ryann said, scooting closer and taking Lydia's hand. "I'm not sure you realise how good it feels, dating a woman who is interested in sport."

Lydia offered a shy smile, lowering her eyes.

"Most people want to go out to be wined and dined, and maybe you do, I don't know that yet, but this was perfect to me."

"I'm glad you enjoyed it."

"Enjoyed it?" Ryann smirked. "Lydia, your company is more than enjoyable." Ryann leaned in, her breath washing over Lydia's mouth. "And I hope we can do this more often."

"Ryann..."

Ryann gently pressed her lips against Lydia's. As much as Lydia wanted to continue this, to spend the rest of the night curled up in Ryann's arms, she couldn't. Ryann deserved the opportunity to walk away now if she wanted to.

"I could spend all night kissing you."

Lydia pulled back, placing her hand against Ryann's chest. "Sorry, I can't."

Ryann frowned. "Did I do something?"

"What? No." Lydia's chest tightened, her head dropping. "No, you haven't done anything."

"I just...I thought when you kissed me earlier, you know? That it would be okay." Ryann backed off, taking the opposite end of the couch. "I'm sorry. I got carried away in the moment."

"Believe me, I want nothing more than to be kissing you, Ryann."

Ryann offered a weak smile.

"We need to talk," Lydia said. "And then, once I've finished saying what I need to say, you can stay, or you can leave."

"What's going on?"

"My meeting with Jo today," Lydia started. "She offered me a position."

"Lydia, that's great." Ryann grinned. She appeared to want to hug Lydia, but Lydia remained firmly planted in her spot. "Really great." Instead, Ryann reached out and squeezed her knee.

"She wants me to run her new office. Not work for her...but *with* her."

"I know this probably doesn't mean a thing to you, but I'm proud of you."

"Ryann...the offer is for her new office in Leeds."

Ryann adjusted herself in her seat, clearing her throat. "Okay."

"And I know neither of us are stupid."

"Oh, I don't know. I've been pretty stupid lately."

"It would mean late nights at the office. Probably stress too while I'm getting set up. And the commute...I'm not sure it would be possible. Not every day."

"Leeds isn't that far away," Ryann offered. "It's what? Seventy miles, give or take."

"Yes, but after working all day, I'm not sure I'd have the energy to drive home, only to drive back ridiculously early the next morning. It wouldn't be realistic."

Lydia loved the thought of coming home and spending her nights with Ryann, but how long could they keep that up? Plans would forever be ruined if Lydia had to work late. Dinner would sit on the table untouched because of last-minute changes to their evenings together. If Lydia knew it was possible, she wouldn't hesitate to do it. Ryann would be worth it, she knew that.

"That doesn't mean I couldn't come up to you after work each night. I'd get myself a train pass. Whatever. I could even learn to drive."

Lydia was enamoured by Ryann. She knew deep down that Ryann *would* make this work, even if that meant taking the train to Leeds at any given opportunity. Ryann wouldn't let her down. Still, it was no way to get to know each other. Not really.

"Ry—"

"No, don't end this because of a few miles, Lydia." Ryann did move closer this time, taking Lydia's hands and kissing her knuckles. "I know I messed you around and I know you probably don't think I'm worth the hassle but let me prove myself to you."

"I don't want you to prove yourself by sitting on a train every night, Ryann."

"No, I know." Ryann kissed Lydia's hand once more before sitting forward and placing her head in her hands. "But whatever you decide...I'm proud of you, okay?"

Lydia tilted her head and looked up at the ceiling. The urge to cry wasn't going to help matters tonight, so she would stem the flow of tears and deal with this like an adult.

"Only you know what you see in your future." Ryann climbed to her feet, taking the empty bowl and beer bottles from the coffee table. "I'll get this cleared up, okay?"

"No, leave it. I can do it later." Lydia attempted to stand, stopped by Ryann standing in front of her and in her way. "Ryann."

"I'm clearing up. You were kind enough to have me over, it's the least I can do."

"I don't want to see less of you." Lydia's voice broke, betraying her unexpectedly.

"I don't want that either. But this is an amazing opportunity for you, and I think you should grab it with both hands."

"But…" Lydia paused. "We're only just getting to know each other."

"And that's my fault." Ryann dropped her head, gripping the bottles in her hand against her stomach. "If I hadn't been stupid enough to walk away from you last month, we would know each other better."

"That would have only made it harder…"

"Made what harder?" Ryann asked, her forehead creased.

"Leaving here. Leaving *you*."

"I'm sure we can figure something out." Ryann offered a smile, but Lydia saw through the honesty of it, noting the apprehension immediately. "Right?"

Lydia chose to agree. Nothing was set in stone right now anyway. "Right."

"How about I clear up and then I'll stay a bit longer?"

"I'd like that." Lydia felt the urge to kiss Ryann. Climbing to her feet, their bodies collided. "Hey…"

"Mm?"

"I'm sorry I pulled away before. I just don't want you to think that you have to do this with me not knowing what I'll be doing in a couple of months."

"If I have to travel, I will. I'm honestly past caring at this point."

Ryann could only watch Lydia as she stood in front of her. Those silvery, grey eyes shone like the first night they kissed, but Ryann felt more connected to Lydia than she did that night over a month ago, despite the time they'd spent apart.

Perhaps it was the want she'd experienced as she sat at home alone, perhaps it was just Lydia as a person. Ryann wasn't sure she had ever felt so happy and at ease in another woman's company, but Lydia had provided that sense of comfort from the moment they met. Ryann should be worried since Lydia had just told her she could be leaving in a couple of months, but she found it hard to worry about something that wasn't final. In those short months, anything could happen.

Deep down, Ryann was terrified to lose this after only just gaining it, but she would make it work. She'd always wanted to learn to drive; life getting in the way prevented that. Now, this could be the perfect opportunity to do so. Ryann immediately erased the idea from her mind. With the hours she was currently working, it would take her forever to pass her test. Lydia didn't have forever; at least Ryann didn't believe so.

"R-Ryann..." Lydia spoke, her voice low.

Ryann focused fully on Lydia's beautiful features, thick, black hair flowing over one shoulder. "Yeah?"

"I do really want to make this work with you."

Ryann appreciated Lydia's honesty more than anything in the world. Jen had done nothing but lie through her teeth over the last year. Ryann had believed Jen's actions would make her wary about other women's intentions, but she didn't feel that with Lydia. Ryann knew without a shadow of a doubt that she could trust Lydia completely.

"Hey, I do, too." Ryann lowered the beer bottles and bowl back down to the coffee table, bringing her hand to Lydia's cheek and caressing the soft skin beneath her palm. "People manage long distance all the time."

"I don't want long distance." Lydia closed her eyes momentarily, her lips parting as Ryann's thumb feathered across her bottom lip. "I want to be here. With you."

"You have some time to think about it, right?"

Lydia nodded, her eyes still closed.

"Then don't worry about it tonight." Ryann's lips explored the skin of Lydia's neck, surprising them both. When a short, sharp gasp escaped Lydia, Ryann could only smile. "You smell good." Her lips moved higher, nibbling the shell of Lydia's ear. "And I know you're worried, I am too, but I'd really like to spend the rest of this evening with you...not thinking about it."

"Mm," was the only response Ryann received.

"Would that work for you?" The tip of Ryann's tongue worked its way across Lydia's jawline, finding her lips as Ryann's hand explored the soft skin of Lydia's hip.

"W-works for me really well."

Lydia's arms suddenly wrapped around Ryann's neck, and it was in that moment that Ryann chose to take matters into her own hands. Gripping the backs of Lydia's thighs, Ryann lifted her, wrapping Lydia's legs around her waist.

Their lips met fervently, their tongues dancing and exploring one another's mouths, but it was the moan that rumbled in Lydia's throat that had Ryann suddenly weak at the knees. So weak that the potential to drop Lydia was becoming greater with each beat of Ryann's heart.

Lydia drew back, her forehead pressing against Ryann's. "Hey, I wanted to ask you something..."

"Anything," Ryann said, breathlessly. "I'm all ears."

"Stay with—"

The doorbell interrupted their moment, Lydia groaning as Ryann set her down, her feet now back on the carpet.

"Damn it."

"You get the door, and I'll do what I was supposed to be doing before I got waylaid."

Every fibre in Ryann's being came alive, her body throbbing in all the right places. However annoyed she was by the person pressing the doorbell, it could only be a good thing. The thought of taking Lydia upstairs...it was far too soon.

Lydia's shoulders slumped as she nodded slightly. "Yeah, I'll get the door."

"You good?" Ryann curled her finger under Lydia's chin, observing the disappointment in her eyes.

"Guess so." Lydia straightened out her clothes.

Ryann smiled, beaming from ear to ear. "We have all the time in the world."

"Except I don't think we do," Lydia muttered, turning away from Ryann. "The universe is dead-set against us."

The doorbell rang out again, but Lydia needed a moment to gather herself and her thoughts. Whoever was calling unannounced had better have one hell of a reason for doing so. Nobody was due; this night was supposed to be dedicated to Ryann.

Lydia hadn't expected their actions to become so heated, but the moment Ryann lifted her, their lips attacking one another's, Lydia's entire body came alive. An arousal she couldn't be sure she'd ever experienced before rolled through her.

The letterbox opened. "Lyd?"

Shocked back into the room by a familiar voice, Lydia tugged the door open, scowling. "Soph, what the hell are you doing here?"

"Um, I just thought I'd drop by."

"I'm kinda busy," Lydia said, closing the door slightly behind her as she stepped outside. She had forgotten to update Soph on the Ryann situation. Her best friend had no idea tonight was a date.

"You look flustered, not busy."

So, take the hint. Lydia simply stared.

"O-oh." Soph's eyes widened, a grin spreading on her mouth. "You mean...she's here?"

"Yeah. I'm really sorry but I was hoping it would just be me and Ryann tonight."

Soph held up her hand. "Say no more. I'm going."

Lydia smiled as she nodded, silently thanking her best friend for understanding. Soph was never one to shy away from how she felt, so for her to not give an opinion right now, it meant a lot to Lydia.

"Call me tomorrow, okay? I really hope this all works out for you."

"Hey!" Lydia called Soph back, needing her friend to know just how much she wanted this to work with Ryann. "She's really great."

"I'm sure she is. You wouldn't be interested otherwise."

"But I need to talk to you tomorrow. I need…advice."

"On what?"

As Lydia was about to tell Soph the gist of her dilemma, the front door opened, and Ryann appeared behind her.

"Sorry, I was just leaving." Soph offered Ryann an apologetic smile. "She's all yours."

"No," Ryann argued, "come on in and drink beer with us." Ryann slung a tea towel over her shoulder, drying her hands on the edge.

Lydia frowned. Why would Ryann possibly want Soph sitting around the place? Hadn't they just been close to taking things to the bedroom? At least, that's how Lydia saw the rest of the night progressing. Now, she was bitterly disappointed *and* concerned.

"Oh, I don't want to intrude. I wasn't aware that you two were on a date."

"You're Lydia's best friend, yes?"

Soph smiled. "I am."

"Then you're not intruding." Ryann slipped back inside, leaving Lydia and Soph in the front garden.

Lydia wanted to argue her case and explain that Ryann really didn't want Soph here, but it was clear that Ryann *did* want exactly that. That issue was showing on Lydia's face judging by the way Soph was looking at her. "What?"

"You had other plans, didn't you?" Soph cocked her head, smiling weakly.

"Apparently not. Come in." Lydia fought the urge to slump her shoulders. She would instead savour the mind-blowing kiss she'd received just moments ago.

"I'll just stay for one." Soph reached out, squeezing Lydia's shoulder. "Or I could just tell Ryann I have other plans."

"No, don't lie to her." Lydia pulled Soph into the living room while Ryann clattered about in the kitchen. "I don't know what that was about, but if she needs you here to lessen the blow of rejection, that's her decision."

"Why would she reject you?"

"I might be moving to Leeds. I have a lot to think about, but I told her tonight and even though I thought things were moving along perfectly fine before you came here, she clearly doesn't want to be alone with me."

"You're moving to Leeds?" Soph's forehead creased. "But, why?"

"Jo offered me my own office. That's what I wanted to talk to you about tomorrow."

"Lyds, I really don't want you to move away."

"I can't stay at *Strive*, Soph. Bree is pulling me down further every single day."

"But you'll think about it before you decide? I mean, really think about it?"

Lydia nodded. "Of course. I don't want to leave either, but if it's going to further my career, and I think it will, I may have no choice."

"Ladies..." Ryann appeared beside them, frowning as she watched Lydia and Soph huddling in the corner. "Is everything okay?"

"Oh, yes," Soph said, slipping away from Lydia as she cleared her throat. "I only came by to tell Lydia something. I really can't stay."

"Oh, that's a shame."

"We should arrange a movie night or something." Soph moved

out into the hallway, glancing back at Lydia. "When you're both free, you know?"

"That would be nice." Lydia smiled, surprised when Ryann wrapped her arm around her waist. "I'll call you in the morning, okay?"

"Night, Lyd. Bye, Ryann."

"Yeah, see you." Ryann hugged Soph and smiled. "And thanks for yesterday…"

Lydia's eyes switched between Ryann and Soph.

What exactly had happened yesterday?

"You're welcome."

Something was going on. Soph didn't even look back as she scurried out of the house, the door slamming shut behind her. Ryann didn't appear to be in any sort of discomfort, though. That had to mean something.

Lydia cleared her throat. "Um, yesterday?"

"Oh, yeah. Soph came to the studio."

"Why?"

"Because she wanted me to come over and see you. Which I did."

"So, you only came here last night because she told you to?" Lydia didn't understand any of this. Ryann hadn't come here out of the goodness of her heart? "She left here and went to the studio…"

"I don't know where she'd been beforehand, but she showed up as I was closing last night."

"Right." Lydia scoffed.

"I was coming over anyway."

"If this is going to work out between us, I need you to be honest with me." Lydia calmed her emotions. She didn't want to come across as needy. So long as she was on the same page as Ryann, surely everything would be okay. "You showed up here after a month of us not speaking. You told me you wanted to be with me, but is Soph really the reason for you coming over? As much as I appreciate her having my back, I hoped you came here willingly. Not because my best friend guilt-tripped you into it."

But what Lydia really wanted to know, she was about to ask.

Just don't sound like a sex-deprived idiot.

"And why did you ask her to stay? Do you not want to be alone with me? I understand that Leeds has thrown things up into the air between us, but I didn't expect you to ask her to stay. I-I thought...I wanted...I was trying to ask you to stay the night. Doesn't that kinda speak for itself in how our night was supposed to go?"

Ryann laughed. "Have you finished?"

"It would appear so." Lydia flopped down onto the couch, shaking her head as she focused on the TV.

"Hey." Ryann paused, rounding the couch and joining Lydia. "I'm sorry if I upset you by asking Soph to stay. I just thought I was doing the right thing. She's your best friend and the last thing I want is for her to think that she can't come around if I'm here.

"I want nothing more than to be alone with you, Lydia, but I also want to take this slow. I'm glad Soph called in. Because if she hadn't, I would be in bed with you now and then it would have turned to shit. Like it always does for me. I need to do this right, okay?"

"Do it right?"

"I'm not looking for a one-night stand here, Lydia. No way. And I get the impression that you're not either."

"No, I'm not." Lydia ran her fingers through her dark hair, her eyes finally finding Ryann's. "But that doesn't explain you coming here last night."

"I was always coming over. Once you texted me, I knew I wanted to clear the air with you. In all honesty, I wanted you there for the opening. You'd been so good to me when I needed someone, and then you weren't there all because *I* was an asshole. But I was coming over. I promise you I was coming over."

"You didn't only show up here because of Soph?"

"No, and I was kinda pissed off with her at first. She came into the studio demanding that I see you. I'm really not into that. You know, being told what to do...especially by someone I don't even know."

"You still thanked her."

"Because in some way, she confirmed that I was doing the right thing in coming here." Ryann gripped Lydia's wrist, pulling her into her lap. "You're so gorgeous."

Lydia lowered her eyes, blushing.

"You are. Don't ever think that I'm using people to create a barrier between us. That's really not what was happening before."

"Sorry. I just...I got carried away before Soph came here," Lydia admitted. "Someone like you, kissing me...I wasn't prepared to wait any longer."

Ryann quirked an eyebrow. "Someone like me?"

"Nothing." Lydia chewed her bottom lip, her cheeks reddening.

Ryann lifted Lydia's head, every ounce of attention firmly on Lydia. "Do tell."

"Just...the tattoos and stuff."

"What about them?" Ryann frowned, glancing down at her exposed chest above her tank top. "I mean, I can't really change them. They're on me forever."

"Oh, I wouldn't want you to change them." Lydia shifted in Ryann's lap, fully aware that she would have to restrain herself from going any further than kissing this evening. "I've never been with a woman who looks so...badass."

It was Ryann's turn to blush.

Lydia leaned in, peppering kisses along Ryann's jawline and towards her ear. "Just..."

Ryann moaned softly. "Tell me. Please, don't hold back."

Lydia unintentionally ground down in Ryann's lap, Ryann's hands now finding her thighs. Everything about this woman had Lydia's attention, but when they were alone like this, Lydia felt as though she couldn't control herself. Since the moment they'd first kissed, however awful it may have ended, Lydia had found herself daydreaming about Ryann. Her nights involved thinking about nothing else. Lydia didn't know how to respond to that. She'd never felt this way before.

"I-I shouldn't." Lydia pressed her forehead to Ryann's, inspecting those beautiful eyes as their lips brushed.

"Hey..." Ryann caught Lydia's bottom lip, taking it between her teeth as her hands slid beneath Lydia's T-shirt. "You should always tell me how you feel. It's important to me."

"Trust me," Lydia said, breathlessly. "Y-you don't want to know right now."

"Lydia, you're grinding in my lap. Believe me, I want to know what's got you that way."

"All of this. All of you," Lydia paused, her eyes closing momentarily when Ryann slipped her hand around her lower back. "It's the biggest turn on."

Ryann moaned, capturing Lydia's lips, sliding their tongues against one another's. "Good to know." She grinned against Lydia's mouth. "Really good to know."

Lydia ground down once more before pulling back. "But you want to take this slow and I respect that." She climbed from Ryann's lap, clearing her throat. "Because I really want this to work."

"F-fuck." Ryann's head fell back against the couch, her hands finding her face.

Lydia knew how she felt; the wetness between her legs couldn't only be one-sided in all of this. But Ryann wanted time, she wanted it slow, so that was what she would get.

"Stay a bit longer?" Lydia asked as Ryann's eyes found hers. Dark with desire and arousal.

"I'm not going anywhere. Not yet."

CHAPTER FIFTEEN

Ryann twirled her phone through her fingers, her mouth dry as she contemplated calling Lydia. Last night when she arrived home, a tremendous guilt continued to plague her. Instead of feeling elated that she'd spent the evening with Lydia, she felt awful as she drifted off to sleep. Long distance had never been something she envisaged, so why had she readily agreed at the drop of a hat?

Because I'm so into her that it's ridiculous.

Ryann bounced her leg up and down, glancing at Luca as he took a mid-morning nap. Sam's place was quiet, only the sound of Sunday dinner being prepared from the kitchen disturbing the peace. The silence meant one thing: time to think. Too much time, actually. Ryann, this morning, would have preferred Luca's screaming and laughing.

"Have you called her?" Sam asked quietly, stepping up behind Ryann where she sat on the couch.

"No, not yet."

"Just phone her. If she's busy, I'm sure she will tell you."

Ryann stood up and turned around. "Just...I have some stuff on my mind."

"What stuff?" Sam's hands found their way to her waist as she sighed. "I thought you told her you wanted to be with her?"

"I did. I *do*."

"So, call the woman and ask her to join us for dinner. If you don't, I will."

Ryann gritted her teeth. She really didn't have the mental capacity for this today. She knew what Lydia had to do, but explaining that to anyone, Sam included, seemed to be an issue. "Sam..."

Sam stared.

"Fine, I'll call her."

Ryann moved out onto the decking, bringing up Lydia's number and calling it before she could change her mind. She'd love to spend the afternoon with Lydia—even if her heart was telling her to slow down and think about all of this.

"Hello?"

"H-hi," Ryann paused. "I'm having Sunday dinner with Sam and Luce. I was wondering if you wanted to come over."

"For dinner?"

"Well, yeah. But if you're busy, don't worry."

"I'm standing with my head in the fridge right now. I've spent twenty minutes trying to decide what I can throw together for dinner. I haven't had the chance to shop this weekend."

"Oh, well..." Ryann cleared her throat. "That's my fault, I'm sorry."

"Your fault?"

"Taking up all your time."

Lydia laughed. "Trust me when I tell you that I'd rather spend my time with you than worry about the weekly food shop."

"So, I called at the right time then?" Ryann teased.

It felt good hearing Lydia's voice, however short-lived it was going to be. They could talk on the phone while Lydia was living in Leeds, but it wouldn't be the same. Ryann also wouldn't expect

Lydia to pine after her when there was an entire city of women she could date.

"Dinner would be really great. If Sam and her wife don't mind?"

"They suggested it."

"That's really nice. Send me the address and I'll be over whatever time you want me there."

"Okay, well you can come over whenever you want. I mean, you don't have to—I'm sure you don't want to listen to a screaming kid all afternoon—but you're welcome here any time."

"Ryann, is everything okay?" Ryann heard the concern in Lydia's voice; it was the same concern Ryann felt. "Hello?"

"Yeah, everything is fine. Just tired and not ready to face Monday tomorrow." Ryann hated lying to Lydia. That wasn't the type of relationship she wanted. "I'll send you the address now, okay? And I'll see you soon."

"Okay. See you."

Ryann ended the call, staring down at the screen for a moment longer. She knew Sam was watching her from the kitchen. As beautiful as the huge floor-to-ceiling windows in Sam's house were, they only provided less privacy when it was needed.

"So, am I setting another place at the table?" Sam's voice penetrated Ryann's thoughts.

Ryann spun around, her best fake smile plastered on her mouth. "Yep. Extra place. She will be here soon-ish."

"Fantastic." Sam grinned, rushing into the kitchen to finish preparing dinner. "And if you're not busy, I could use a hand in here."

"Be right there."

Lydia followed the long path towards Sam's home, her excitement building as she thought about spending the afternoon with Ryann and her family. It wasn't often she had the pleasure of meeting someone whose family was welcoming, and Lydia appreciated it. Her only issue was that Ryann was growing on her quicker than she would have liked. With Leeds firmly on her mind, all of this with Ryann was more than Lydia could handle.

Lydia wished her time spent with Ryann wasn't tinged with uncertainty, but it always would be. Could she truly leave Liverpool—her home—as well as the woman she was fonder of than any other in the past? Such little time spent together shouldn't result in this desperate need to be with Ryann, but that only showed Lydia how much she wanted Ryann in her life.

Her car slowed as she stopped outside an impressive home. It didn't surprise Lydia how beautiful Sam's house was, but she still gasped slightly when her eyes landed on the lake the house had been built off.

She took a moment to gather her thoughts—her feelings—before cutting the engine on her Jaguar and stepping out of the car. She'd decided on casual today; Ryann wouldn't mind. But as she stood outside the gigantic glass-fronted, bungalow-style house, Lydia wondered if she should have worn her best Chanel dress. She could do expensive when the occasion required it, and right now appeared to be one of those times.

Ryann appeared on the decking, her usual black, ripped skinny jeans hugging her thighs in all the right ways. Lydia swallowed hard. It was becoming more difficult to keep her eyes and hands where they should be when Ryann was around. Lydia wasn't one for holding back if she found another woman attractive, but she didn't quite know where she stood with Ryann. More so now that Leeds had been brought into the picture.

She slowly walked towards Ryann, Sam's home towering over them both as the distance shortened between them. "Hi. Gorgeous place."

"You found it okay?"

"Well, I was hoping I wouldn't break down as I drove off the main road. You know, murderer waiting in the bushes kinda feeling?"

"Ah. I've had that before at night in a cab. It didn't help that the driver looked like something from an episode of *Criminal Minds*."

"Exactly." Lydia smiled, hesitating as she leaned in towards Ryann. "Anyway, it's good to see you." Avoiding the lips she desperately wanted to kiss, Lydia opted for Ryann's soft cheek. "And thank you for inviting me over here. It means a lot."

"Sam suggested it." Ryann winced as those words hung in the air between them. "T-that doesn't mean that I don't want you here, though. I do."

Lydia's eyebrow rose. "You're sure about that?"

"Of course."

"Ryann, do you think maybe we could talk tonight?" Lydia needed Ryann to agree. Whatever was going to happen over the next couple of months, she needed for it to not come between them. "If you're not busy?"

"I don't know what my plans are yet," Ryann said, chewing her lip. "But if Sam doesn't need me to have Luca for a few hours, yeah."

Ryann didn't look as though she wanted to talk. In fact, Lydia wasn't sure she was even welcome here. She may have been told otherwise, but Ryann appeared a little standoffish. "You know, it doesn't matter. It wasn't anything important."

"Okay, well, did you want to come inside?"

Lydia shoved her hands in the pockets of her jeans, her messenger bag slung diagonally across her body. "Guess so."

The excitement she'd felt as she drove here was quickly disappearing, and now Lydia was left with a sinking in her stomach. The same feeling she'd had the night they kissed, and Ryann left. It wasn't pleasant, it also wasn't ideal, but Lydia was in somebody else's house so whatever she had to say to Ryann could wait. She wouldn't ruin the atmosphere by calling Ryann out on her lack of interest this afternoon.

But then Ryann unexpectedly took her hand, leaning in and pressing a kiss below Lydia's ear. "I'm glad you're here, okay?"

"O-okay."

"Lydia, hi." Sam rushed across the kitchen, pulling Lydia into her arms. "Really glad you could make it."

"Thanks for inviting me over."

Sam pulled back, smiling as her eyes shifted towards Ryann. "Are you kidding? This one's had a face on her since I picked her up."

Lydia glanced Ryann's way, narrowing her eyes. "Really?"

"Pay no attention to her," Ryann said. "She gets like this when she has people over."

Sam walked away, shaking her head. "Lies. She's been thinking about calling you all morning."

Lydia caught Ryann rolling her eyes. It wasn't followed by a smile or a laugh, though. No, it was followed by a look of annoyance. What the hell was going on with Ryann today?

Lydia wanted to believe that perhaps Ryann *was* just tired, but it felt like something more. Something that could possibly relate to their discussion last night. She understood, though. Lydia hated the idea of leaving, so Ryann likely felt the same way. Or maybe not; she couldn't read Ryann very well. As intriguing as that was, it was also frustrating.

"Take a seat both of you," Sam called out from the kitchen, motioning towards the living room. "Luce will be down with Luca in a few."

Lydia followed Ryann and her slumped shoulders into the living room, removing her bag and setting it on the floor beside her. This home really was something to admire. Lydia prayed she could do that someday, because right now, all she could think about was the uninviting way in which Ryann greeted her.

"So," Ryann started.

"You know, I think I should probably just meet Sam's wife and kid and then let the four of you get on with your day."

"What? Why?"

"Let's be honest, Ryann, you really don't seem like you want me here."

"I do. It's just...our Sam gets ahead of herself."

"Why? Because she told me in a roundabout way that you wanted to see me?"

Ryann lowered her head, blowing out a deep breath.

"There's nothing wrong with missing someone. I know the feeling."

"But when you leave for Leeds..." Ryann shook her head, choosing to not finish her sentence.

"I haven't decided yet."

"It's a no-brainer, Lydia. Why the hell would you stay here in a job you hate when someone is offering you an amazing opportunity? You're obviously very good at your job if Jo is giving you your own office."

"Because it's not as simple as just packing up my life here and moving away."

"Seems pretty simple to me," Ryann countered. "I'm sure you can find someone to rent the house. Someone you can trust."

"None of this is about the house. Trust me." Lydia tugged at her fingers. Was Ryann really that stupid to believe it was merely about living arrangements? "I have decisions to make and I'd like you to be around while I make those decisions." Lydia slid her hand to Ryann's. "If you want to?"

"You know I do. But I don't get a good feeling and Lydia, I don't know if I can handle losing anything else."

"You said we could figure it out." Aware that they weren't the only people in the house, Lydia lowered her voice. "Last night, you told me we could work it out."

"And you told me you didn't want me travelling to you."

"Please, can we talk tonight?" Lydia knew she was pleading,

her voice holding a desperation she hadn't heard before. "If you're able to, I'd really like to talk about it."

"I know what you need to do. I know you're going to Leeds. Me being here couldn't stop that." Ryann sat back against the couch, removing her hand from Lydia's grip. "As much as I want to be around for you, to be *with* you, I'm not stupid. There are a million other women out there suited much better to you than I could ever be. But for as long as you wanted something with me… I'd travel."

Lydia could only stare.

Ryann thought she could find something better? No. That didn't sound right. Ryann was amazing, sweet, honest. That was all Lydia could hope for in a woman, and she had it in front of her. Ryann Harris was quickly becoming someone Lydia knew she could fall deeply in love with. The connection, the spark, it was there in bucket loads.

"I *know* we wouldn't last. You'll meet someone gorgeous who will sweep you off your feet, and I'll be here, going through it all again. But you know what, that's okay. We can enjoy what time we do have together, and when the time comes…I'll always be your friend. I couldn't ever not be your friend."

"Ryann, I don—"

"RYNAN! RYNAN!" Luca came rushing towards the couch, helped up by Ryann into her lap. His little arms flung around her neck, his face buried there as one tiny eye peered at Lydia suspiciously.

"Hey, bud." Ryann wrapped him up in her arms, her smile beaming and almost stealing Lydia's breath. "Have you met my friend, Lydia?"

Luca shook his head, scowling. He clearly had no intentions of giving away his best friend.

"Isn't she pretty?"

His dark eyes brightened as he sat up in Ryann's lap and inspected Lydia.

"Hi, Luca." Lydia offered her best smile; this kid was adorable.

Thick, dark hair sat combed over on one side of his head, with dimples in both cheeks telling Lydia that Sam was the one who'd given birth to him. He was a mirror image, meaning he also had a resemblance to Ryann.

"DINNER!" Sam bellowed from the kitchen, frightening the life out of Lydia. Not only did she have one terrifying glare, Sam also had an impressive set of lungs on her.

Luca scrambled from Ryann's lap, almost losing his footing as his tiny legs attempted to find their balance. Ryann held a protective arm behind his back, giving him the opportunity to find his way himself. She had a lot of love for Luca, that much was clear. Lydia could watch their interaction all day long.

As they both got to their feet, a blonde, heavily pregnant woman appeared. With the bluest of eyes and one hell of a smile, Lydia wondered if this entire family were drop dead gorgeous. "Hi." Luciana held out her hand. "It's great to *finally* meet you." She shot a glare at Ryann; one she'd obviously picked up from her wife. "I've heard a lot about you."

"H-hey," Lydia stammered, suddenly feeling inadequate in this house full of models.

Here she was in her casual jeans and an old T-shirt, while Luciana looked immaculate in yoga maternity pants.

"Come on, you two. Sam will have an aneurysm if we don't shift our arses."

Lydia swallowed hard, remaining in her spot as Ryann followed Luciana. When she turned around, her expressive eyes smiling back at Lydia, Ryann suddenly frowned. "You coming?"

"Only if you promise to come home with me when we leave here later."

Ryann nodded, her shoulders relaxing. "I promise."

CHAPTER SIXTEEN

Lydia watched the lake, ripples on the water from the gentle breeze taking her mind off everything else in life. The grounds of Sam and Luciana's home really were beautiful, but Lydia couldn't quite enjoy it completely. How could she when she didn't know if she'd ever see this place again? How could she possibly lap up the enormous lawn and its surroundings when she didn't know if Ryann would ever want to be exclusive with her?

She was a fool to believe it could happen now that she had a future to think about, but for just a brief second, when she *had* thought about it, it felt incredibly fulfilling. To call Ryann her girlfriend. Her other half. The woman she would one day love. Just for those small seconds when she'd considered it, she was happy. But she wasn't stupid, nor would she expect Ryann to give her what she wanted in terms of a relationship and falling in love.

It had broken her heart earlier as Ryann said the things that were clearly on her mind, but Luca had appeared, and Lydia hadn't been given the chance to respond. She wanted to, she wanted to tell Ryann that how she felt was completely off the mark, but Sam's home wasn't the place to discuss such important matters anyway. Lydia had known that from the get-go, but Ryann had blurted it all out regardless.

Dinner had been beautiful, Sam and Luciana's company everything Lydia expected it would be. Though Sam was a very wealthy woman, she didn't flaunt it. Okay, her house gave it away from the moment Lydia approached on the gravel path, but as a person, Sam was very much down to earth and not interested in her wealth. Luciana was exactly the same. Neither made Lydia feel less than, included her in every discussion they had over a roast beef dinner, and actively invited Lydia to talk about anything she wanted to. Luca had even taken a shine to her by the time dessert was cleared away and everyone was back in the living room.

But Ryann remained quieter than Lydia would have liked.

Last night when Ryann was leaving Lydia's house, she didn't appear to be in any kind of distress about the Leeds conversation, but by the time she'd gotten home, something had definitely changed for her. What that was, Lydia couldn't hazard a guess, but she really did want to discuss it all with Ryann before this day was over.

Ryann was headstrong, some may say stubborn, but Lydia would do whatever she could to make her listen. This—whatever they could call it—meant too much to Lydia for her to see it end without any kind of communication. Ryann, from the moment they'd met, had impacted Lydia's life hugely. In what way, she couldn't quite say, but everything felt different. Even at the office when Bree was breathing down Lydia's neck…it didn't feel so daunting.

Tomorrow was the beginning of a fresh week, a new day, and Lydia actually felt positive about going to work. She didn't expect any change from Bree Stevens, life didn't work out that way, but she didn't feel stuck anymore. Jo had thrown her a lifeline, one hell of an opportunity, so if Lydia chose to stand up and leave tomorrow, it wouldn't matter. What it all came down to was the fact that Lydia had choices. Options. A chance if it all ended at *Strive*. That was the difference, and that was what she would focus on tomorrow morning.

"Everything okay?" Sam appeared beside Lydia, holding out a cup of coffee. "Ryann won't be much longer. Luca is almost finished with his bath."

"Oh, that's okay. I was just enjoying the peace and quiet out here." Lydia offered a thankful smile as she took the coffee from Sam.

"Did you want me to leave you alone?"

"No. Join me, please."

Sam sat down at the outdoor furniture, relaxing back with her own cup of coffee. Lydia felt Sam's eyes on her, but she wasn't sure she wanted to make it known. Sam seemed to have the ability to read the room; she could tell when something was wrong.

"Everything okay with Ryann?"

Lydia faced Sam fully. "I don't know what you mean."

"She's been very quiet. She was worried about calling you this morning. I don't know, but something isn't right with her."

Lydia smiled weakly. "I think that's my fault. I'm sorry."

"O...kay."

"I've been having a bad time at my job with the new boss. My old boss has offered me my own office."

"That's amazing." Sam beamed.

"But it's in Leeds. I told Ryann about it last night and she's been a little off today."

"Ah." Sam set her coffee down, crossing her legs as she clasped her hands on the table in front of her. "So, Ryann is having a moment?"

"I think so, but you'd honestly have to ask her. I'm not sure she even wants me here."

"She does." Sam held up her hand. "Whatever is going on inside that head of hers, she *does* want you here. I know she does."

"Mm, I'm not so sure," Lydia admitted. "And I want to discuss it all with her tonight, but I know she's going to blow me off. I just get a feeling she won't be available."

Sam frowned. "Why wouldn't she be available tonight?"

"Oh, she wasn't sure if she would be here with Luca or not."

Sam dropped her gaze, nodding slowly. "And now she's using my child as an excuse to not face her worries."

Lydia panicked. She'd completely put her foot in it. "No, I mean…I just assumed she may have been here. Sorry, my bad."

"Don't lie for her. It doesn't suit you, Lydia." Sam climbed to her feet. "Let me have a word with her. A swift kick up the arse should do the trick."

"No, Sam, it's really okay. If Ryann doesn't want to talk, I'm not going to force her to discuss something she has no interest in."

"Lydia—"

"She thinks she's not good enough." Lydia's lips clamped shut, and she smacked her hand over her mouth. She shook her head, her eyes closing momentarily. "You know what, I'm just making a mess of this." Lydia got to her feet, taking her bag from the spare seat beside her. "Please could you tell Ryann I had a great day, and thank you to you and Luciana too, but I'm going to head off home."

"Stay, please."

"I can't," Lydia explained. "Ryann is uncomfortable enough already with me being here. Tell her to call me if she wants to, okay?"

"She's falling in love with you, Lydia."

A laugh escaped Lydia's mouth. She'd never heard anything so ridiculous. "Okay, as much as I love you getting involved, I think it's time you took a step back."

Sam's eyebrow rose. "Excuse me?"

This was it. This was the moment Sam murdered Lydia. Whether that would be with her stare or an expensive pair of heels was anyone's guess. "Sorry, I just don't want Ryann to know what you've just said. It couldn't be further from the truth."

"Sure about that?"

"How could she be falling in love with me? We've had two dates, Sam. If today can be called a date, that is."

"You think this attraction only started since you reconnected?" Sam asked. "Because it really didn't. Ryann has been into you since the day you met."

"Sure." Lydia laughed, shaking her head. "Thanks for dinner but I'm going to leave now. Bye, Sam."

Lydia rushed down the decking, throwing herself into her car as quickly as she could. Ryann appeared beside Sam, frowning as Lydia met her eyes and backed away from her parking spot. Ryann looked hurt and confused, but Sam could explain it if she really needed to. It was one thing to worry about her future, but to hear that Ryann was falling for her changed everything…if it was true.

"I just don't know why she left," Ryann said through gritted teeth, tapping her foot against the floor of Sam's Range Rover. "I mean, did I do something? I must have. She doesn't need this."

"Why do you assume you did something, Ry?" Sam sideglanced her cousin. "You seem to think you're this big fuck up, but I can assure you, you're not."

"I own the mess I am, I've always been this way, but Lydia has enough going on in her life." Ryann chewed her lip. "You know what, just drop me off at home. If she wants to see me again, I'm sure she'll call."

Sam cleared her throat. "She told me about Leeds."

"She did?" Ryann nodded, lowering her eyes as she toyed with the edge of the drawing Luca had given to her. It was sweet. A jumbled mess of colours that, according to Luciana, resembled Ryann and Lydia. "So, she's made her decision?"

"Not that I know of," Sam said. "What do you think she should do?"

"I think she should take the job. She'd be a fool not to."

Sam slowed the car, pulling over at the side of the road. "And what about you?"

"What about me?" Ryann twisted in her seat. "I have nothing to do with her decision, Sam."

"If that's true, why didn't she accept the offer there and then? Why is she taking time to think about it if you don't matter?"

"Uh, because she has a life here in Liverpool. She has friends and a home and—"

"And she has you."

Ryann frowned. What was Sam trying to say? "She doesn't have me. I mean, she does…but once she finds her feet in Leeds, she will meet someone else. She's gorgeous and has *everything* going for her. That woman is going to be someone's wife one day." Ryann turned away from Sam, her eyes blurring as emotion lodged in her throat. She focused on the street outside the window, praying her tears would remain at bay. "She's really great. Just…beautiful."

"Tell her, Ryann."

Sam's hand suddenly pressed against Ryann's shoulder, comforting her. "Tell her what?"

"That you want her to stay. That you want a relationship with her. I know it may all be too soon, but if you put it out there, tell her how you feel, maybe it could be the deciding factor when it comes down to it."

"You mean…she'd stay for me?"

"Mmhmm."

"You're out of your mind." Ryann laughed, a tear escaping her eye and sliding down her cheek. "I know you like everyone to have that happy ending, Sam. I know you want to think of the world as one big happy bubble, but it's not really working out that way for me. Just…"

"You think she's too good for you? That you wouldn't be worth the trouble of her staying? That she deserves more?"

"Basically, yeah."

"Biggest load of shit I've ever heard." Sam pressed the accelerator, driving away from the side of the road.

Ryann could only stare at her cousin. Why was everyone so intent on telling Ryann how to live her life and who she should have in it? Why couldn't she be left alone to deal with her own issues herself? *Because you do silly things when you're left alone to figure it out.* Ryann sighed, giving herself a moment to think about what she wanted to say.

"Look," Ryann started. "I know how I feel about Lydia. I know that given half the chance, I'd never let her out of my arms, but it isn't that simple, Sam. I've offered to commute to see her and I told her we could make this work, but could it really? I mean, you've seen her. I'd be an idiot to think that she could move away and not fall in love with someone else. You must surely understand that?"

"I don't understand it. And maybe you need to slow down, give yourself time to think, but at least tell her how you feel. You're pushing her away without realising it, and I know that deep down you're falling for her, Ry. I can see it in the way you look at her when you think nobody is paying attention. I see it all."

"I am falling for her," Ryann confessed. "But I won't tell her that. It's not fair to her, Sam. If I go in there telling her things she doesn't want to hear, it'll only confuse her more when she's deciding whether she can leave or not. I don't want to be the deciding factor. I don't want to be the one who keeps her here while she stays in her shitty job with her shitty boss. I want Lydia to do the right thing for her. Not for anyone else. She deserves the chance to be incredible."

Sam eyed Ryann. "You know, that's really big of you."

"I'm doing this because it's the right thing to do. We barely know each other, Sam. We've spent one evening together and that was marred with talk of Leeds anyway. I haven't had the chance to take her out to dinner or even show her the apartment yet. And to be honest, I'm kinda glad about that. She'll probably forget about me once she's busy with work."

"You think she'll forget about you?"

Ryann laughed, nervously. She didn't want to think about the possibility, she couldn't; it would only eat her up inside. But Ryann knew the truth. Of course, Lydia would forget about her. "Probably. Maybe. I don't know."

"You really should stop thinking so little of yourself. I don't think you realise just how much people love you. Lydia included."

"Don't." Ryann held up her hand. "Don't say stupid things, Sam. It only makes everything worse."

"Well, we're here," Sam said. "What are you going to do?"

Ryann swallowed, the light flickering in the living room window of Lydia's home. She wanted to knock on the door and stay a while, but Lydia had left unexpectedly earlier, and Ryann didn't believe it was her place to question that. Perhaps she had done something wrong, perhaps Lydia did want answers, but Ryann couldn't deal with the confrontation.

"I don't know. Did she tell you why she was leaving?"

"She thought you were uncomfortable with her being at dinner," Sam said, her eyes focusing on the road ahead of her. That only told Ryann that it wasn't the entire story. Sam had said something to Lydia.

"What did you do?" Ryann asked, her voice calm and level. "Before I knock on that door and make a fool of myself, I need to know what you said to her out on that decking."

"I'm sorry, Ryann. I thought I was helping."

"Sam?"

Sam held her head in her hands, groaning. "She told me that you didn't think you were good enough. I offered to talk to you before you left for the night, but she asked me not to."

"Okay."

"And then...I said that you could maybe be falling for her."

"Y-you what?" Ryann's heart slammed in her chest. Harder

than ever before. How could Sam have been so stupid? "Please tell me you didn't..."

"I'm sorry, Ry."

"I can't believe you did that," Ryann said, her anger rising. "Thanks a lot, Sam. Really. Thanks for really fucking this all up for me. I owe you one!"

Ryann shot out of Sam's car, slamming the door and taking the steps to Lydia's home faster than she thought possible. Whatever the outcome of this evening, Ryann had to tell Lydia to pay no attention to Sam and her stupid comments. Whether they were true or not, Ryann would lie if it meant Lydia didn't get completely scared off by Sam. This...it was impossible. As Ryann hammered on the door, she thought it always would be.

"Whoa. What's going on?" Lydia stared, wide-eyed. "Why are you banging my door down?"

"Please, can I come in?" Ryann clutched either side of her head, breathing deeply through her nose.

"Of course, you can. Just...calm down."

Ryann nodded, aware that she was behaving a little crazy. "Sorry. I didn't expect you to open the door to me."

Lydia stepped aside, closing the door again once Ryann was safely inside. "How did you get here?"

"Sam."

"Oh." Lydia walked slowly into the kitchen. "Is everything okay?"

"You left. I'd like to know why."

"I needed some space," Lydia explained. "I'd had a lovely afternoon, but things don't feel right between us, Ryann."

Ryann's forehead creased. "So, what now? I mean—"

"Ryann..."

"I know what Sam said to you. I'm sorry if she scared you off."

"You really don't have to explain. I told her she was *way* off the mark."

Ryann closed the distance between them, offering the smallest of smiles. "I don't know what I feel for you. This all happened so quickly but in the wrong way at the same time. But I know that I want to be with you. I want to be by your side. Last night I went home and worried that it couldn't work, but it can. I know it can.

"I just...this is all really unexpected for me. Some days I don't know if I'm coming or going. You just appeared in front of me and changed everything. While I love that, it does kinda scare me. It wasn't supposed to be this way. I was supposed to be single while I figured out the mess that is my life. And as much as I don't want to see you leaving for Leeds..." Ryann paused. She would be by Lydia's side whatever she chose to do. That was her final decision. If it hurt down the line, so be it. But if it didn't, if things *did* work out, it could be amazing. "You should. You have to. We will figure it out along the way. This feels too good for it to fizzle out."

"I called Jo when I got home."

Ryann offered a half-hearted smile. "Yeah? You did? That's great. This is going to be amazing for you." Just when she thought she could finally have Lydia, to be something more with her, Ryann felt as though the weight of a thousand bricks had landed on her chest. "Well, I think so anyway. I'm really happy for you. Your boss is going to hit the roof, but you deserve this, Lydia." Ryann lifted Lydia's hand, aware that she was rambling, and kissed her knuckles. "Leeds is great. I've never been myself, but I've heard good things about it."

"I turned down her offer."

"No," Ryann said, confusion whirring around her head. "Why would you decline?"

"Because I want to be here. In the house I grew up in. With some gorgeous woman in my life."

Ryann couldn't be sure, but she believed Lydia could be referring to her.

"And I know I hate my job, but surely there are other options. I don't want to move away from the city I love. I don't want to move away from you, Ryann. Not when I'm only just learning about you. When we're only just getting started."

"But—"

Lydia held up her hand, cutting Ryann off. "Stop looking for excuses, Ryann. I have one question for you and then this is the end of the discussion about Leeds."

Ryann nodded slowly, unsure as to why Lydia had chosen her over Leeds. "Okay."

"Do you want to be with me?" Lydia asked. "I'm not asking if you want to spend the rest of your life with me, but is it going to be worth my while staying around here?"

"Y-yes." Ryann gripped Lydia's face, tears threatening to spill. "Yes, it'll totally be worth your while."

"Then Leeds is done. Dead and buried. I don't want to discuss it anymore."

"Was Jo upset that you didn't take the offer?" Ryann dropped her hands, guiding Lydia towards a stool at the breakfast bar.

"Actually, no. She said she knew I wouldn't take it because I hadn't accepted the offer there and then."

"Sam said something like that to me on the way over here."

"It seems as though everyone around us knows what we should be doing but us." Lydia smiled shyly, picking at a non-existent spot on the counter. "Wouldn't you agree?"

"I would, yes."

Lydia's decision to stay meant a lot to Ryann, but now it was time to date one another exactly the way they should have...from the moment when they realised they wanted one another. It couldn't be that hard, especially since Ryann felt as though she was in a place where she *could* give Lydia her all.

Her studio was back up and running, she had a place to live, and Jen was completely out of the picture. For the time being, at least. Ryann still had the small matter of contacting the police about Jen, but she didn't want to worry about that tonight. Lydia had chosen her...the first woman to ever do something like that, so that would be where her attention would lie tonight. Solely on Lydia.

"Can I stay for a while?"

"Only if I can snuggle up against you on the couch while shitty TV plays in the background."

"Snuggle. Shitty TV. Got it."

CHAPTER SEVENTEEN

Lydia rose from the chair at her desk. She needed a closer look at the river this morning. She'd woken feeling bright-eyed and very much ready to work hard, and, thankfully, Bree had left her alone this morning. So far, anyway. She knew her boss wasn't having the best morning, so to lessen the stress, Lydia had sent one of the assistants out for Bree's favourite coffee before their meeting. She was due in Bree's office in the next ten minutes, the assistant nowhere in sight.

Don't let me down now, Janine.

Lydia leant against the frame of the window, the darkened glass providing a screen from the beaming sun high in the sky this morning. She and Ryann had talked at length last night about Lydia's unexpected decision to remain in her hometown, and they both felt better for it. Judging by the way in which Ryann kissed her before she left for the night, Ryann *certainly* felt better.

They'd spoken briefly this morning, Ryann explaining that she had a full schedule at the studio today. Lydia had suggested lunch, but Ryann couldn't fit it in. It would be a quick sandwich at the studio before she was back at it until closing. Lydia had considered showing up and surprising Ryann with lunch, but she didn't quite know her own schedule yet, and she couldn't be sure Ryann would be available at the time she'd arrive.

"Miss Nelson?"

Lydia turned, her smile wide as she thought about Ryann. "Yes?"

Bree, as usual, held her defensive stance. "Are you ready to begin?"

Lydia checked her watch. It was earlier than the meeting had been planned for, but she would be lying if she said she didn't want to move this along. Janine must have been held up at the coffee shop. "If you are, yes."

"Well, I'm standing here waiting for you, so?"

And there it was. The familiar attitude Lydia had come to loathe. "Works for me."

Lydia grabbed her files from the desk, glancing up as the sound of heels pounding the corridor floor caught her attention. "I'm so sorry. I got caught up at the shop and then I bumped into someone in the lift."

"Don't worry," Lydia said, taking the coffees from Janine. "She's just called me in. You're just in time."

"Oh, thank God." Janine placed her hand over her chest. "Well, good luck."

Lydia disappeared into Bree's office, her folder under her arm as she manoeuvred the door closed holding two coffees. "I picked you up a toffee nut latte. Oat milk." She placed it on Bree's desk before stepping back and taking a seat of her own. "Extra shot."

"T-thanks." Bree frowned, clearly not expecting Lydia's kind gesture.

"Okay, so..."

"Before we begin, I'd like to ask you about Jo Carmichael."

Lydia sighed. They'd been through this already. "Bree, I haven't told Jo anything about the company. She didn't even ask. We'd arranged to meet for other reasons."

"And what were those other reasons?" Bree sat back, crossing her legs and retrieving a pen from her desk. She always had a pen in her hand; it was just a shame she rarely used one. Everything was done by the staff around the office while Bree sat back and watched it all play out through her glass-walled office. "As your boss, I believe I have a right to know."

"It was...personal."

"You're going to Jo Carmichael with personal issues? I'm sure she has better things to do than listen to you, Lydia. Don't let it happen again. I don't want her calling and complaining that you're hounding her over pointless bother."

Lydia frowned. "Jo is my friend. Not my ex-boss or ex-colleague."

"She's only your friend so she can get inside gossip from this place. Do you think I was born yesterday?"

Lydia wasn't doing this. Bree *wouldn't* bring down her mood. "Could you just tell me what this meeting is about?"

"I'll tell you when I'm good and ready. If I find out you're meeting with Jo anymore, this new contract we could *potentially* have today will be out of your hands so fast—"

A knock on the door interrupted Bree. Lydia was thankful for whoever it was.

"Come in!" Bree climbed to her feet as the door opened. "Ah, Mrs Foster."

Lydia's eyes remained on Bree, the disgust she held for the woman bubbling away under the desire she had for Ryann right now. If Ryann was here, she would put Bree in her place in a matter of seconds. She was kinda cool like that.

"Looks like I'm right on time."

Lydia frowned. She recognised that voice. Her nose was also familiar with the expensive perfume wafting towards her. She turned in her seat and stared up at Sam.

"O-oh, hi." Lydia shot up, pushing her chair aside. Sam eyed her, giving her a look that told Lydia to go along with whatever Sam had up her sleeve. "Mrs Foster?"

"You must be Lydia Nelson," Sam said, extending her hand. "I'm looking forward to working with you."

"W-with me?" Lydia realised she was stuttering. Why? She knew Sam.

"Sit down, Lydia." Bree tutted. "How are you, Sam?"

"Great, thanks. Planning to get this project signed off once I have my marketing team in place."

"You usually use freelance…"

"I do, but I've seen a lot of Lydia's work and I have to say, I'm sorry I didn't snap her up sooner."

"Well, she has a few other projects on right now, don't you, Lydia?" Bree gave Lydia one of her stone cold stares, but Lydia wouldn't fall for it. Not this time.

"No. I've actually finished everything I was working on. I wanted this Monday to be the start of something new I could sink my teeth into."

"Great. So, you can join me for lunch down at the dock, Lydia? Say…eleven?"

"I have nothing in my schedule right now. Eleven should be fine."

Bree cleared her throat, offering Sam a seat beside Lydia. "Perhaps we could all just hold on for a moment while we discuss what it is that you need, Sam."

"You know what I need. I told you on the phone this morning. And I want Lydia overseeing it all."

"You haven't seen the work of my other staff yet…"

"I don't need to. I've spent the entire weekend meticulously going over Lydia's work. She is the one I want working with my company."

"Well," Bree paused. "I'll have to check wi—"

"Who will you have to check with, Bree? You own this company. And I know your father was very fond of Miss Nelson. He spoke about her often."

"He did?" Lydia interrupted. "I miss Walter."

"Lydia, you can go now." Bree's gaze switched between Lydia and Sam. "And since you have nothing to do, you can go and get me a fresh coffee. This one isn't good enough."

Sam laughed. "You're sending your best staff out for coffee?"

"She claims she has nothing to do." Bree rolled her eyes, relaxing back in her seat once again. "Well, chop chop."

Lydia held her nerve. She could blow like she'd wished to do so many times since Bree took over the company, or she could rise above it and walk away. She chose the latter. Sam wanted her to work on her company's marketing; she wouldn't allow anything to get in the way of that.

Bree was intent on making a fool of Lydia, so she would step out of the office while she could and take a moment to breathe. Fresh air would do her a world of good, even though a kick to Bree's shins would likely feel so much more therapeutic.

"Sam, it was lovely to meet you." Lydia got to her feet. "And I hope that I'll be working with you soon."

"You will," Sam said, straightening her back. "Because if Bree doesn't agree to it, I'll be taking my business elsewhere."

Lydia chose not to respond, instead walking out of the office and leaving the door open as it had been since their meeting started. It took everything within her not to fall to the floor laughing; she had to remain professional. Seeing Bree being taken down several notches was something Lydia hadn't anticipated, but something she could certainly watch again.

She took her suit jacket from the back of her chair, lingering around the coffee machine so she could hear the conversation going on inside Bree's office.

"I'm not entirely sure where you get off on speaking to your staff like that, but I would consider toning it down a little. Nobody likes a bitchy boss."

"Show me the figures, Sam."

"I think you forget who you're speaking to," Sam snarled. "I may have pulled you out of the red six months ago because nobody wanted to work with you, but I won't do it again. Piss me off and you'll be looking for a job in the local supermarket."

"Why do you want Lydia?"

"Because she's the best here. And yes, that includes you."

Bree laughed. "If she's so good, why doesn't she have her own company?"

"I don't know. You'd have to discuss that with Miss Nelson. But make no mistake that I have no issues in replacing *you* with *her*."

Lydia's mouth fell open. What was Sam talking about? How could she replace Bree? It was Bree's company.

"Actually," Sam continued, "I think it's about time we had a serious discussion, Bree. Things here aren't quite working out the way I hoped they would be."

Realising that she'd stood around for too long, Lydia slid out of the door and into the hallway that led to *Strive*. She would ask Sam what this all meant during lunch, but until then, she would continue her daydreaming about Ryann.

The tattoo gun in Ryann's hand buzzed, vibrating through her skin and directly into her bones. She really did have a lot on today but concentrating on the task at hand meant that she could focus her mind on Lydia. If she had something positive floating around her head, her work wouldn't suffer.

Small talk came and went during tattoo sittings, some clients choosing to grit their teeth and get it over with, others wanting to discuss their entire life. She didn't mind which way it swung, but she was coming to the end of her current design, a mandala covering a regular client's elbow. His silence told Ryann everything she needed to know. Pain. The inability to discuss *anything* with her.

"Almost there, Paul. Focus on your breathing."

Ryann remained hunched forward, applying the last touches to the design, taking a little more ink onto the end of the needle from the small plastic pot to the right of her. Everything she did came from her right-hand side. It was a routine she'd become accustomed to over the years. When she was working, everything had to be perfect.

"You seeing the kids this weekend?" Ryann asked, small talk seeming like a good idea right now.

"No. Claire is taking them away to see her parents. I get them for the next two weeks to make up for it, though."

"That'll be nice. Any plans with them?"

"Shay wants to do the safari park, and Amelie wants to do the zoo."

"Good thing you have them for the next two weekends then." Ryann laughed.

"Mm," Paul paused. "Now I just have to decide which one we do first. That's going to cause trouble in itself."

"Rather you than me, mate." Ryann removed the needle from Paul's skin, powering it off and setting it on the film-covered table. "All done. Give me a minute to get it cleaned up and you can take a look."

"Perfect. Thanks, Ry."

The shop phone rang, Ryann's other artist picking up the receiver while she reeled off the aftercare required to one of her most regular customers. He didn't need to know, but she made it a habit to recite it to every customer whether it was their first piece of work, or their hundredth. It still mattered.

"Ry?" Shona, her artist, caught Ryann's attention. "Call for you."

"Okay, I'll be right there." Ryann finished up with Paul with the promise that he would be back in for additions to his sleeve once he had the funds to do so.

Crossing the open plan space, she picked up the receiver. "Ryann speaking."

"Hi, it's me."

"Lydia?" Ryann frowned. "Why are you calling the studio?"

"I didn't want to disturb you by calling your mobile. Are you okay to talk for a minute?"

"Sure, what's up?"

"Do you have any idea why Sam is at the office where I work?"

"Um, nope," Ryann answered. "But she's a businesswoman so I'm assuming she's doing business things."

"She's planning to work with me. I don't know what the hell is going on."

"Honestly, babe, I don't know. I promise you."

Babe? Christ, Ry. Get a grip.

"S-sorry."

"It's okay. I'm meeting her for lunch at eleven to go over the contract. I suppose I'll find out more then."

"Okay, well…I hope it's a good day for you."

Ryann was secretly thrilled that Lydia hadn't rebuked her use of the word *babe*. It was a slip of the tongue, nothing more.

"It's actually been a really good day for me."

"Good. That's what I like to hear." Ryann smiled fully. If Lydia was happy, so was she. "Hope it continues."

"So, while I have you here, I was wondering when I'm going to get a view of your place."

"Oh, uh…" Ryann chewed her lip. "Whenever you like. I don't know what time I'm going to be home tonight; Monday is a late close for us."

"At some point through the week, maybe?" Lydia offered.

"Sounds like a date."

"And should I bring an overnight bag with me?" Lydia's voice held an element of teasing, but it still caught Ryann off guard.

"O-oh, I mean…if you want. That should be okay. If that's what you want."

"You're blushing, aren't you?"

Ryann was, in fact, blushing. She was blushing a lot. "No."

"Liar. I'll speak to you soon, okay?"

"Okay. And Lydia?"

"Mm?"

"It was really nice hearing your voice." Ryann rested her ass on the edge of the desk in the office, her eyes closing as she listened to Lydia's soft breathing. "Really good."

"I know the feeling. I'll text you tonight. Bye, Ryann."

"Bye, Lydia."

CHAPTER EIGHTEEN

Lydia tapped her manicured fingernails against the table. Sam had texted her an hour ago telling her where they would be meeting. Bree hadn't called; she hadn't shown any interest in the marketing deal Lydia had unknowingly brought in for the company, but she couldn't say she cared. She was used to the lack of appreciation for her work from her boss, so this wasn't any different. The less Bree was in Lydia's life, the better.

That left Lydia wondering why Sam had come to the office today. It also led her to contemplate how Sam even knew Lydia worked at *Strive*. Sam had a lot of explaining to do, and Lydia would appreciate that explanation before they got down to any kind of business.

The door to the coffee shop opened and Sam walked in, her usual air of confidence hitting everyone in the face as she did. In her tailored grey suit, she looked better than the entire establishment put together. She waved Lydia's way, motioning towards the counter.

Lydia stood, waving Sam over. She'd taken the liberty of ordering two cappuccinos, hoping that Sam would settle for that. "Hi. I ordered us coffee."

"You did? Thank God." Sam slumped into the seat facing Lydia. "It's been a long morning."

"Mm, I agree."

"And before we start, I want to say I'm really happy you and Ryann worked everything out."

"She really tells you everything, doesn't she?" Lydia smiled, cocking her head slightly.

"No, I dragged it out of her. She wouldn't tell me anything otherwise."

"So, did she also tell you where I worked? Because I don't recall *actually* telling her."

"No, she didn't," Sam confessed. "I've known *Strive* for a long time. Me and Walter Quinn go way back. He was actually responsible for the marketing on Bryant Tower. Long before you joined the company."

"Right, okay."

"Your old boss, Jo—"

"You know Jo?"

"I do. We had many drunken nights going over marketing plans many years ago. She holidayed with me and Lucia in the south of France once or twice...before she settled down and got married."

"Okay, why don't I know any of this? And who is Lucia?"

"My late-wife. Ex-wife," Sam said, wrinkling her nose. "She was my wife before she died, and I met Luciana."

Lydia offered Sam a sympathetic smile. "I'm sorry."

Sam shook her head. "Anyway, when Jo left *Strive*, Bree took over. That woman is the bane of my fucking life, I swear. I knew it would only be a matter of time before she cocked it all up and *Strive* started to struggle. But she did that in record time. Bad agreements with companies, a poor attitude which meant nobody wanted to work or be associated with her, she just...I don't know what Walter was thinking when he handed everything down to her. He was a good man, but she had him wrapped around her little finger.

"Six months ago, I was having dinner with Bree and consulting with her on a potential new project of mine. I'd heard that the business was struggling but getting information from her is impossible. We had several bottles of wine, and her tongue started to loosen. She blurted out everything. She was close to losing the building, the business, everything Walter, Jo, and *you* had worked hard for. He always complimented your work and he always talked about you when we met for lunch. His figures and his portfolio skyrocketed when you joined the team, Lydia. I know that, because *I* now have full control of *Strive*."

"What?" This was all too much for Lydia to comprehend. Lydia's mind blanked, her brain momentarily shutting down. And then her thoughts started to swirl, and she couldn't focus.

She was truly stunned.

"I offered to buy the business off Bree but leave her at the top so word didn't get around. I didn't want everything Walter had built to crumble because of her incompetence, so I bought her out. That company is mine. I also didn't have the time to work at it myself, so it was easier for me to watch on from behind the scenes. Bree knew I was watching, and things picked up again."

So, the rumours had been true. *Strive* had struggled like Bree had suggested several times to the staff, but not because of their lack of work. Because of Bree, herself.

"Oh."

"So, really...you work for me."

"Okay, look..." Lydia lowered her voice and leaned in, beckoning Sam closer. "Does this mean I have permission to tell Bree where to shove it the next time she speaks to me like something she's just stepped in?"

"Won't be necessary." Sam shook her head. "Bree is...getting a change of scenery."

"I don't follow."

"You *officially* work for me now. You'll be taking over at *Strive*. I was going to put you in my office at Phillips & Priestly, but Bree has had her chance."

Lydia froze. Sam hadn't just really told her she was taking over. Surely not.

If Lydia had been standing, she would have fallen to the floor. Even sitting on the comfortable chair that she was, her knees felt weak. Her body, too. Sam had just lifted a huge weight from her shoulders, and Lydia didn't know what to say.

Sam waved her hand in front of Lydia's face, frowning. "You with me?"

"*You're* Phillips & Priestly?" Why was that the only sentence to come from Lydia's mouth? Wouldn't *thank you* be more appropriate?

"Well, I'm Foster now. But to save things getting complicated, Luciana and I agreed that the company name should remain the same."

"Okay, I need more than coffee." Lydia blew out a deep breath. How had everything turned itself around so that now she was *actually* working for someone she was extremely fond of? "Whew."

"I know this is a lot to take in, and I know it's probably none of my business...but Ryann said you were staying. That Leeds was off the table."

"It is. I don't want to move away. I love Liverpool, it's my home. And I want to be around for Ryann."

"Then the least I can do after you considering Ryann in your decision to stay here is to give you the job that should have been yours a while ago. You've worked your arse off for *Strive*, and you deserve the opportunity to show everyone what you're capable of."

"But what about Bree?"

Sam nodded, clearing her throat. "Bree has been offered a lower position at the office but is unable to accept it. She will be leaving the company in seven days."

Lydia's brow drew together. "Oh. Right."

"You deserve this more than anyone at that company, Lydia. Please, don't decline my offer."

"Oh, I'm not." Lydia grunted. "I may feel slightly sad for Bree, but not *that* sad."

"To be honest, it's been a long time coming. Maybe I should have overhauled the place some months ago, but I haven't had the time. You know…"

"I can't believe this is happening." Lydia would spend the foreseeable future pinching herself. That or she would wake up to discover it was all a dream. "I didn't expect this at all."

Sam winked. "Well, I'm full of surprises."

"You used to terrify me," Lydia admitted, lifting her coffee cup and staring at Sam over the rim. "That first time you came to mine, I was absolutely terrified."

"Thanks." Sam snorted.

"No, I mean it. You just have this unwavering confidence and I didn't know whether to shake your hand or kneel before you."

"Yeah, I'm not into that kneeling malarkey. Just a handshake is perfectly fine." Sam added a little sugar to her cappuccino.

"But now I feel like we're friends."

Sam nodded. "We *are* friends, Lydia. I told you if you needed anything you only had to ask. Having said that, I understand that you didn't know I actually owned *Strive*. If I'd known it was you Ryann was dating, that you were the Lydia Nelson that Walter always spoke about, I'd have done this sooner."

A wave of emotion washed over Lydia unexpectedly. Sam really was an angel. First, she'd done everything imaginable for Ryann, and now it was Lydia's turn. She hadn't anticipated it, nor would she ever dream that Sam would put her in this position, but she would be forever grateful.

Lydia's voice broke when she finally said, "Thank you, Sam."

"You saved my cousin's life. Now it's time to give you the career you really want. It's the least I can do."

"So, I really am going it alone?"

"Jo wouldn't have offered you the Leeds office if she didn't think you were capable. But don't worry, we won't let you go this completely alone. Not until you're ready."

"Wow."

"Now, should we get some lunch and then get out of here for the day? I have a wife at home who is becoming more and more needy as the hours pass."

"I have to get back to the office."

"For?" Sam smirked. "I don't believe I need you for the rest of the day. Actually, take the week off. Recuperate. Visit Ryann. Do whatever you want, but stay away from that building. Bree needs a little time to calm down. She won't be in the best mood."

Lydia felt a headache approaching. She didn't know what day it was now that Sam had pumped her full of information. "Right. Okay."

"Take the week. Monday is a fresh start. For you *and* the company."

"Okay. Got it."

Lydia and Sam climbed to their feet, Lydia's legs still a little weaker than she would have liked them to be. Sam rounded the table, holding out her hand, but Lydia chose to pull her into a bone-crushing hug.

"This means so much, Sam. Seriously. Thank you."

"I have a good feeling about this, Lydia."

Lydia could only nod in response. The first thing she needed to do was see Ryann. And then she could think about the changes she was about to make in her life. Lydia had never been the kind of person to allow someone to walk all over her, but fear of the unknown in terms of her career had made it possible for Bree to do exactly that.

The constant complaints from Bree, the unnecessary ranting around the office…Lydia had tried to take it all in her stride. To rise above, as many would say. But that was easier said than done.

And then Bree eventually homed in on Lydia, picking at every little thing she did. Lydia knew she could be twice the boss Bree could ever dream of, and now Lydia was ready and fully prepared to take charge of her own life. She wouldn't answer to Bree Stevens ever again. Not in this lifetime.

"Walk out with me?" Sam asked, linking her arm through Lydia's. "I still hate coming here."

"Coming where?"

"The docks."

Lydia faced Sam as they made it outside. "Why? This place is gorgeous."

"The bistro explosion a few years ago," Sam explained. "I was caught up in it."

"Shit. That was you?"

"It was." Sam sighed, glancing over to the other side of the dock where the new bistro sat. "One of the most terrifying times of my life, but I made it through."

"I'm so thankful that you did."

Lydia caught the emotion in Sam's eyes. An emotion people didn't often see. Sam had always been a pillar of strength whenever Lydia was in her company, but that mask had slipped ever so slightly this morning. Sam may not even be aware of it, but Lydia enjoyed seeing a softer side to Sam. Lydia was very fond of both sides.

"You and Ry have plans tonight?"

"No. It's a late close at the studio and she has a lot on, so I'll just wait and see her when things settle down at work."

"You sound disappointed," Sam said, her heels clicking against the cobbled sidewalk. "Why don't you surprise her?"

"How?"

"Go over there tonight when she's home. I'm sure she'd love to see you."

"I don't even know her address." Lydia shrugged, looking down at her feet when they reached the end of the dock.

"Well, isn't it a good thing I'm here?" Sam nudged Lydia's

shoulder, a more playful side to the older woman creeping through that tough exterior. "I'll text you the address. You'll have automatic access to the gate. And I'll also give you the code for the main door. Just…don't give it to anyone."

"No, I wouldn't."

"I know, but the residents at Bryant don't take too kindly to random people walking the corridors of their complex. So, keep the code safe, okay?"

"I promise."

"Okay, well I should get home. I wasn't supposed to be working today."

"Oh, I'm sorry."

"Don't be. Luciana told me to pick up pickles while I was out. I think I'm off the hook as long as I show up at home with them."

"You two love each other a lot," Lydia said. "It's so beautiful."

"Well, Luciana was *my* Lydia."

"I-I don't…" Lydia frowned.

"She saved my life."

CHAPTER NINETEEN

Lydia stepped out of the lift, the doors quietly closing behind her as the carriage whooshed back to life and descended the many floors it had brought her up. Tonight, everything felt different for her. Tonight, life felt incredible. She'd always prided herself on working her way to the top of her career—without a helping hand from anyone else—but this didn't feel like a helping hand. It didn't feel like Sam had offered her the world for the sake of it. Sam was taking a chance on Lydia, and she wouldn't let her down.

Lydia had walked around town for most of the afternoon, stopping occasionally to do a little shopping. She'd bought a gift for Ryann, one of the reasons she was here, and treated herself to a few new items for her wardrobe. Nothing too expensive—Lydia wasn't frivolous when it came to money—but it did feel nice to splash out a little. It felt as though she deserved it.

With a brown paper bag in her left hand, Lydia slowly approached the first apartment door on the left of Ryann's floor. Knowing Ryann was behind it—or at least that's what she hoped —sent her heart rate higher than normal.

On the way here she'd wondered if Ryann would be okay with

her showing up unannounced, but after the day she'd had, Lydia no longer cared. She wanted to see Ryann, to kiss those soft, gentle lips. Anything else that came with it would be a bonus.

Deciding she could no longer wait, Lydia curled her hand into a fist and knocked gently on the door in front of her. Her palms became clammy, her mouth a little dry, but once she saw Ryann, she knew the slight panic she felt would be worth it. It wasn't anxiety on Lydia's part, though; it was a nervous excitement.

The lock clicked and the door slowly opened. Ryann looked worn out, her gorgeous eyes tired, but Lydia's heart stopped momentarily in her chest. Ryann stood before her wearing nothing but a tank top and a pair of boxers. With her long, tattooed legs exposed, and the lack of a bra evident, Lydia didn't know whether to step closer or run away. Ryann, her body...Lydia had no words.

Her legs were adorned with some familiar, common tattoos. The sugar skulls, the dreamcatcher, birds, more roses, scripture, and a whole array of other designs. But it was the way in which they merged together, and the impressive shading that drew the eye. A simple word would look incredible tattooed on Ryann's lithe, handsome body though.

"Lydia, how did you get in here?"

"I, uh..." Lydia shook her head, taking a moment to breathe slowly. "I brought you a gift. I saw it in town today and I thought it would be perfect for you."

"Oh, you didn't have to do that."

Lydia caught the blush creeping up Ryann's neck, settling on her cheeks, but the image of a naked Ryann on top of her was overpowering everything else.

"Nobody has ever done something like this for me before." Ryann stepped aside, opening the door wider. "Please, come in."

Lydia hesitated. Was it the right thing to do? As she glanced down Ryann's body once more, her dark brown hair pulled up high on her head in a messy bun, her undercut on display, Lydia knew her answer. She didn't care if she threw herself at Ryann tonight; she would face any consequences as they came.

"Thanks." Lydia stepped past Ryann, their bodies brushing as Ryann immediately leaned in and kissed Lydia.

"So, you didn't say how you got in here..."

"Sam gave me the code and your address."

"She tried to call me earlier, but I'm still mad at her for what she did at dinner yesterday." Ryann closed the door, applying the lock before joining Lydia in the kitchen.

"You really shouldn't be mad at her." Lydia smiled fully, handing over the bag in her hand. "She's amazing."

"That may be true, but I don't appreciate her getting involved in my business. I can handle this, you, myself."

Lydia arched an eyebrow. "You can handle me, huh?"

"Not what I meant. I'm sorry." Ryann smiled, glancing down into the bag. "Oh, wow." She pulled out a leather jacket, dropping the paper bag to the floor. "This is for me? You bought me this?"

"I did. Just a gift. I couldn't resist it."

"That's really sweet, Lydia." Ryann tried it on for size; it fit perfectly. As Ryann's slender fingers zipped the jacket up, Lydia swallowed hard. Her mouth had never been so dry. Ryann in boxers and a leather jacket was something to be admired.

"Wow."

Ryann lifted her head. "Does it look okay? I've been wanting a new one but hadn't seen anything I liked."

"Yeah," Lydia said as she chewed the inside of her mouth. Ryann was inspecting the jacket, but Lydia was very much inspecting Ryann. "Looks nice."

Ryann stepped closer, her own eyes following the plunge neckline of Lydia's blouse. Lydia knew she had a good cleavage, it was one of her best features, but seeing Ryann ogling while she was half dressed didn't help the wetness between her thighs.

"Thank you." Ryann kissed her softly, slowly. Her lips lingered, demanding something more, and Lydia obliged.

Lydia had kissed Ryann now on multiple occasions, but never while feeling like this. Ryann felt closer than she'd ever been, mentally and physically. Lydia's lips danced across Ryann's; she needed so much more than this. Given half the chance, she would devour Ryann here and now. Their tongues collided, sliding and dancing against one another's, as Lydia fisted her hand in the front of Ryann's leather jacket.

Lydia trembled, her knees loosening as her skin flushed. The heat had nothing to do with the temperature in the room. It was all down to Ryann and the desire Lydia felt for her. A desire that flooded her body with warmth.

Lydia's fingers tingled, aching to touch Ryann, and as Ryann moaned into Lydia's mouth, she instinctively pushed Ryann back against the kitchen island. Lydia's body craved to be touched by Ryann, her heartbeat pounding in her ears as Lydia became lightheaded. Ryann was kissing her like she meant the world and more.

"F-fuck," Ryann breathlessly pulled back, her eyes black. "I wasn't expecting that."

"Ry—"

Ryann placed her index finger against Lydia's lips, smiling as she shook her head.

"You look absolutely incredible tonight."

Lydia didn't want this moment to end, but she didn't look *that* good. "I've only been to work."

"Then I should really get a job at your place." Ryann took her bottom lip between her teeth, her eyes travelling to Lydia's cleavage once again. "Because, shit...I feel like I can't keep my hands off you."

"Then don't." Lydia pressed her body against Ryann's. "Don't keep your hands off me. Don't stop this tonight."

Ryann lifted her head, her deep, dark eyes finding Lydia's. She knew that look. It was a look she hadn't seen too often from Ryann. A look that told Lydia she was about to be touched *everywhere*.

"You've no idea how much I want you." Ryann turned Lydia in her arms, pulling her back against her body. She wrapped her arms around Lydia's waist from behind, kneading her breast through her blouse. "How much I've wanted to touch you. Taste you." Ryann spoke low in Lydia's ear, her tongue travelling down Lydia's neck. "I don't know where to begin with you..."

Lydia trembled, her head falling back on Ryann's shoulder. "I'm all yours, Ryann."

Ryann released a deep, steady breath. "Fuck, yes, you are."

Surprised, Lydia found Ryann popping the buttons on her blouse, her suit jacket hanging open off her shoulders. She stepped forward, slipping whatever she could from her body. Now standing in her bra and skirt, Lydia closed her eyes as the zipper on the back of her skirt lowered. Ryann's hands felt incredibly good on her body; she couldn't begin to imagine how they would feel against her bare skin. Touching her. Inside her. Taking her perfectly.

"Ryann..." Lydia's head lolled forward as Ryann placed slow, sloppy kisses up the back of her neck, Lydia's hair falling over her right shoulder. "Oh, God."

Gently biting down on Lydia's shoulder, Ryann smiled against her tattooed skin, sliding her skirt over the curve of her ass. Stepping out of it once it had fallen to the floor, Lydia turned around. She needed to see Ryann. To kiss her. To hold her. Frozen in her place as she focused fully on Ryann, Lydia tried to understand what was going through Ryann's mind.

Ryann's jaw slackened momentarily. "I-I don't know how this happened."

"Which part?" Lydia frowned. "Me getting naked?"

"Me, being lucky enough to have you in my life."

"Oh, I'm the lucky one." Lydia stepped closer, unzipping the leather jacket Ryann still wore. If she was naked, Ryann needed to be, too.

"Lydia, I just need another moment to look at you." Ryann

followed Lydia's hands as they released the zipper at the bottom of her jacket.

Lydia created a little space between them, no longer worried as to how this night would end. Ryann was close to drooling, that much was clear. It could be the fact that Lydia was standing before her, lingerie covering her body. It could also be the garter belt and suspenders Ryann couldn't take her eyes off. Whatever was going through Ryann's mind, Lydia felt incredibly wanted.

"Y-you dress like this for work every day?"

Lydia shrugged, the palm of her hand now splayed against her naked stomach. "Not always…"

"And what kind of occasion would require you to dress like this?" Ryann asked, her chest heaving as her eyes travelled the expanse of Lydia's almost naked body.

"When I know I'm coming to see you."

"You did this all for me?" Ryann closed her eyes, breathing deep through her nose. "R-really?"

"Maybe," Lydia said, stepping forward and taking Ryann's hand. "And I could be way off the mark coming here dressed like this, but I don't think I am."

"No. You're not." Ryann pulled Lydia flush against her, her lips tasting the skin of Lydia's chest. "You're really not."

With Ryann's hot breath on her skin, Lydia ground down against the thigh that had somehow ended up between her legs. Every sensation Ryann created felt overwhelming, but incredibly satisfying, too. Her smooth skin pressed against Lydia's, her tattooed thigh providing just the right pressure for the moment. Ryann's tongue expertly rolled over the nipple now between her lips, Lydia's bra shed and on the floor.

"O-oh," Lydia gasped, gripping the back of Ryann's head, her fingertips grazing the undercut she had come to adore. "T-that feels…" Lydia trailed off her own words, unable to form a coherent sentence.

Ryann moved lower, her tongue lapping at Lydia's skin…hot

and wet. Her fingers curled around the waistband of Lydia's underwear, dark eyes staring up at Lydia and silently seeking permission. Lydia took her bottom lip between her teeth, a slight smirk on her mouth as she nodded slowly. Ryann's eyes lit up, bright and eager. Lydia heard the groan as black lace slid down her thighs, her arousal growing with each breath of Ryann's against her skin.

She'd imagined this moment. She'd dreamt about it. But now that it was happening, Lydia realised she couldn't possibly have come close to knowing what this would feel like. Her world was spinning, her heart racing, and then Ryann was sitting back on her knees, slender fingers ghosting up the backs of Lydia's thighs. All those daydreams didn't come close to this moment. They never could.

Ryann looked up into Lydia's eyes. Of all the women she'd dated, every woman she thought she was into, this was the one. The one that would remain burnt into her memory, on her skin.

With each movement Ryann made, Lydia trembled. Excitement rose inside Ryann, a slight flutter in her chest reminding her just how much she wanted this to work. In this moment, she never wanted to let Lydia go. And as Ryann climbed to her feet, her hand gently steadying her against Lydia's hip, she knew she would never be able to.

Lydia meant more than Ryann knew...and more than Ryann had been willing to admit to herself. This wasn't just sex, it wasn't just "getting to know one another." No, it was that intimacy Ryann had craved since she first started dating many years ago. That moment when you realise the woman before you meant more than life itself—that was exactly the mindset Ryann was in.

Lydia's eyes glistened, her hand working its way across Ryann's stomach, lowering slowly. Ryann held her breath; she wasn't sure she could ever have comprehended how it would feel to be touched by Lydia.

As Lydia's hand travelled south, Ryann's blood quickly followed. The moment Lydia touched her, Ryann was sure she would explode.

Lydia took her bottom lip between her teeth, pressing herself against Ryann as she cupped her through her boxer shorts. "I think we should take this to the bedroom."

Ryann's eyes closed, and she nodded. "Yes."

Expecting Lydia to create a space between them, Ryann gasped when her hand disappeared beneath the elasticated waistband of her boxers. Lydia's fingers probed, gathering Ryann's wetness as she slipped one between her swollen lips.

"F-fuck." Ryann gripped the edge of the kitchen counter, determined to remain upright.

No sooner had she felt Lydia's fingertips exactly where she wanted them, they were gone.

Ryann opened her eyes to find Lydia running the flat of her tongue up her index finger. Sweet Lydia, the woman who always appeared so mature and put together, so...unlike this, was tasting Ryann off her fingers. The world had gone crazy this evening.

Ryann instantly bent, wrapping her hands around the backs of Lydia's thighs, and lifted her. Slickness coated Ryann's stomach where Lydia rested, her tank top riding up as she manoeuvred them both through the open space of her apartment.

The sound of Lydia's heels falling from her feet and hitting the floor only pushed Ryann further towards the edge. The edge of some pent-up frustration between them, but also the orgasm of a lifetime. Ryann knew exactly what was happening here. Worlds would be rocked tonight.

Almost falling through her bedroom door, Ryann wasted no time in getting down to business. She'd held Lydia at arm's length for long enough; it was time to really let go. To make this woman feel wanted, special, adored.

Lydia sunk down into the soft mattress, shuddering as Ryann's lips trailed up the side of her leg, reaching her inner thigh. The arousal she felt could be considered earth-shattering, but Ryann wanted to focus her attention on Lydia, not herself or her own needs. Ryann would have the opportunity to let go before the night was done, she was certain of that.

Slowly kissing her way towards the slickness that had coated her stomach only moments ago, Ryann suddenly pulled back, removing her tank top and her boxers. She didn't have time to waste—she'd done more than enough of that over the last couple of months. Now that she had Lydia in her bed, beneath her, Ryann was going to make the most of it. After all, she had no idea what tomorrow would bring.

"R-Ryann..." Lydia murmured, her head buried deep into the pillow.

Braced on her arms above Lydia, Ryann smiled. "You okay, babe?"

Lydia pulled Ryann flush against her, the skin on skin contact leaving a trail of goosebumps all over Ryann's body. When Lydia's thigh slipped between Ryann's legs, she almost lost it. All sense of time and where she currently was went right out of the window, the wetness she felt as she pressed against Lydia the only thing keeping her grounded. Grounded, yet flying higher than ever before.

Hands wandered, tongues danced against one another, but it was the way in which Lydia's chest heaved indicated to Ryann that she needed something more.

Ryann slid her hand between their bodies, pressing two fingers against Lydia's soaked lips. Stunned when she found a piercing, Ryann could only grin harder.

"O-oh." Lydia arched her back, her mouth hanging open. "Y-yes. More..."

Ryann smiled into another kiss. "More, huh?"

"So much more."

"You're so fucking gorgeous."

Watching Lydia's soft features, her eyes never leaving Lydia's face, Ryann pushed inside her. Deep. Warm and wet. Pulsing. Ryann wasn't sure she'd ever wanted someone as much as she wanted Lydia.

With long, raven hair splayed across the pillow, Ryann braced her free hand against the wall and dipped her head, taking Lydia's nipple between her teeth. With the moans and the gasps, Ryann was on top of the world. Rolling her tongue as she picked up her pace, the expensive bed slammed against the wall, Lydia's sex throbbing around Ryann's fingers.

"H-harder," Lydia begged, wrapping her arms around Ryann's neck and pulling her into another deep, fervent kiss. "P-please."

Ryann obliged, a sheen of sweat covering her naked body as she gave Lydia exactly what she wanted. What they both needed. Pressing her thumb to Lydia's clit, her walls clenched, making it harder for Ryann to move inside Lydia.

"Hey..." The tip of Ryann's tongue slowly ghosted up Lydia's neck before Ryann's gaze landed on intense, grey eyes. "You wanna come?"

"Fuck, yes." Lydia's nails dug into Ryann's back, dragging up her skin and eliciting a moan Ryann hadn't thought she could muster up. This side of Lydia was new. New but so *very* welcome.

Keeping a steady rhythm, Ryann worked the skin of Lydia's neck, never wanting this moment to end. When Lydia tightened around her fingers again, Ryann lifted her head, drawing Lydia's eyes towards her own.

"I want to see you," Ryann whispered against soft, swollen lips. "I want to watch you come for me, Lydia."

Lydia gripped Ryann's face, cradling it in both hands. "I'm so lost in you, Ryann."

With one final thrust, a guttural moan ripped from Lydia's throat, her entire body convulsing.

Ryann slowed her movements, coaxing out every last wave of

Lydia's orgasm before she built her up to the next one. She could only watch the woman below her, a bottom lip firmly between her teeth. Lydia coming undone was something Ryann planned to watch for a long time; nothing was as beautiful.

Ryann's arm gave out, sending her crashing on top of Lydia. She didn't appear to mind, strong arms wrapping around Ryann, holding her close. Pressing a kiss to Lydia's chest, Ryann sighed with contentment.

"I'm lost in you, too."

CHAPTER TWENTY

Ryann woke to bright sunlight beaming through the window. In her sex-filled haze last night, she'd forgotten to close the blinds. As she glanced to her left, Ryann realised she didn't care. She wasn't sure she'd care about anything else ever again. Lydia was lying beside her, soft breathing soothing Ryann, her bare skin delectable. Ryann wanted to reach out, wanted to touch Lydia until the end of time, but she shouldn't. Lydia had to work today, as did she, so another hour's sleep for the astounding woman beside her was the least she could do.

Ryann, on the other hand, had no chance of sleeping any longer. Now that she was awake, watching Lydia, sleep was the last thing on her mind. Last night had truly rocked Ryann's world. Lydia was something else. Ryann couldn't say she'd ever felt so content with another woman in her bed. As of this morning, Jen never existed.

When Lydia appeared at her door last night, a gift in her hand, Ryann had been blown away. Of course, Lydia came across as the kind of woman who would treat her other half when she wanted to, but Ryann hadn't expected it. She'd spent so long in her last relationship doing everything to keep Jen happy that she hadn't realised how little she'd gained from it.

Jen never showed up with flowers, offered to cook dinner for them, or spent the evening wrapped up in Ryann's arms. She was always too busy working out, taking a course online to better her personal training certificate, or out with friends. That hadn't bothered Ryann in the slightest, not until this morning. Being here with Lydia's scent still very much all over her, Ryann was seething.

She wouldn't show that, though. The last thing Lydia needed was an angry Ryann who only now realised what a complete bitch her ex was. She supposed she always knew deep down, but it really didn't matter anymore. Nothing relating to Jen would matter ever again. Ryann had what she needed, even if just a couple of months ago she'd had nothing.

One day, when she could truly repay those who'd been there for her, she would.

Slowly and quietly rolling out of bed, a chill hit Ryann's naked body. She could only smile, thinking of last night. Lydia had shaken her world last night, true, but Ryan had returned the favour. Multiple times. Over and over again.

Ryann grinned, creeping out of the bedroom and into the open-plan space she now called home. Sam had really turned her life around, but it was all down to Lydia in the first place. Without Lydia, her kind words, and the promise that everything would be okay, Ryann wouldn't be here. That knowledge hit her harder than it ever had.

She'd been stupid to think that ending her life would solve her problems. In many ways it would have, but those she loved and appreciated would have been left to deal with the aftermath. If she'd stepped off that ledge and into the river those months ago, Ryann wouldn't be waking up to the woman she was falling for.

It stung. It hurt deep in her belly. But it wasn't relevant anymore. Lydia had pulled her out of a dark place she never imagined she'd find herself in...and life was how it should be.

Taking a bottle of water from the fridge, Ryann glanced down at the floor. Her new leather jacket lay beside Lydia's entire outfit, but even that looked good together. Silk and leather. Class and badass. Ryann liked the images it was conjuring up in her mind—images she wasn't sure would ever fade.

Lydia straddling her. Ryann rolling her tongue over beautiful pink nipples. Lydia deep inside, taking Ryann better than anyone else ever had. A shudder rolled down Ryann's spine, Lydia's moans repeating in her head like a blockbuster movie. How her lips parted, and her mouth fell open as Ryann brought her to the most intense orgasm either of them had experienced. Everything about Lydia Nelson was exactly what Ryann needed. She would never complain about life again.

Ryann contemplated coffee, deciding to give it a little while longer before her caffeine relief kicked in. She was enjoying this feeling of floating, of not having a single care in the world. She grabbed her tank top from the floor, followed by her underwear, and slipped them on. As much as she wanted to see Lydia's sweet face, Ryann would wait and retrieve fresh clothes once Lydia was in the land of the living.

She flopped down onto the window seat, looking out at the early morning tide. The weather didn't appear too windy, only a slight breeze evident in the trees below Bryant Tower. The sun was detaching from the sea as it rose higher in the sky. Ryann knew it was going to be a good day. How could it not?

"You're one lucky, lucky bastard, Ryann Harris." Her head fell back against the wall, eyes closing as Ryann gave herself a moment to think, to feel. Her body ached in all the right places; her muscles tight as she stretched her legs out across the seat. But the sensation she focused on more than anything else was her heart beating perfectly in her chest. "God, I have one hell of a woman in my life."

"Will I ever get to meet her?" Lydia's sleep-filled voice penetrated Ryann, sending her head upright. "Good morning."

"Mornin', gorgeous." Ryann felt her face start to hurt from

smiling so big. "Can I make you some coffee? Get you some juice? Water?"

"Coffee would be amazing." Lydia yawned, stretching out her body.

It was then that Ryann realised Lydia had found the wardrobe. Wearing a pair of grey sweats and a thin T-shirt of Ryann's, Lydia still looked an absolute vision.

"Sorry. I wasn't sure if it was okay to walk around here with my arse out."

"That will always be more than fine." Ryann climbed to her feet, stepping up to Lydia. "Don't ever forget that, okay?"

Lydia smiled lazily, her eyelids fluttering closed as Ryann planted a kiss firmly on her lips. "Okay."

"I didn't want to wake you."

"Once you got up, I couldn't sleep," Lydia said, wrapping her arms around herself as she moved into the kitchen and settled on a stool. Ryann watched her every move, Lydia's eyes trailing to the clothes on the floor. "Sorry. I'll get everything picked up."

"Stay where you are." Ryann powered up the coffee machine. Lydia really had no reason to worry, even if her eyes told a different story. "There's no rush here, okay?"

Lydia's cheeks reddened, her eyes lowering as she smiled faintly. "Sure, yeah."

"How do you like your coffee?" Ryann felt terrible. She'd just spent the entire night wrapped up in Lydia, but she didn't know how she preferred her morning coffee. How embarrassing. "I'll remember for next time."

"Next time?" Lydia's eyebrow rose. Ryann couldn't quite read the room this morning. It was far too early.

"Well, I mean..." Ryann busied herself in the kitchen, turning her back on Lydia and closing her eyes momentarily. Had she just assumed that this would be a common occurrence? Yes, she had. "If you ever wanted to stay over again."

Ryann felt a presence behind her, arms wrapping around her

waist. "I'm joking. Last night," Lydia said low, her lips grazing Ryann's ear, "was amazing."

Ryann's entire body shuddered as Lydia's breasts pressed against her back. This really was one of the best mornings she could recall.

"And I really wish you didn't have to work today."

"You have to work, too."

"I have the day off."

Ryann turned in Lydia's arms, frowning. She didn't quite know Lydia's work schedule, but she assumed she would be at the office all day. She usually was during the week. "Oh?"

"I'll explain everything later. My job is the last thing on my mind right now."

"Okay."

"Can I come by the studio? I'd love to watch you work."

Ryann grinned. "You would?"

"I would." Leaning in, Lydia's lips gently pressed against Ryann's. Mornings could quickly become Ryann's favourite time of day, especially if she had this woman wrapped around her body.

Ryann moaned when Lydia took her bottom lip between her teeth, releasing it slowly. "You really have to stop kissing me like that. I can't concentrate when you do."

"What exactly do you need to concentrate on?"

"God, I don't know." Ryann puffed her cheeks and breathed out slowly. She really didn't know what she needed to concentrate on, but if Lydia continued to kiss her, to tease her, she also wouldn't be going to work today. And, unfortunately, she really needed to. "Can I make us some breakfast?"

"Yep. I'm starving."

Lydia climbed from her car, the widest smile she could possibly sport spreading across her face. She couldn't recall getting from

Ryann's to her own home, but she made it unscathed. As much as she didn't want to leave Ryann some thirty minutes ago, Lydia knew it was for the best. Things were quickly heating up for them again, and Ryann had little time to shower and leave for work.

Living in the city meant she didn't have to travel as far, but forty-five minutes to shower, dress, and get out of the apartment wasn't very long for anyone. Lydia had considered showering with Ryann, but quickly chose against it, instead showering in the main bathroom while Ryann took the en suite. They would have many other mornings together.

Slow and steady, Lydia.

"What time do you call this?"

Lydia looked up to find Soph sitting on the step outside her front door.

"Um...early?"

"Been somewhere nice?" Soph enquired, her eyes narrowing as she watched Lydia take her keys from her bag. "I mean, you look like you've just come home from work."

"I've been with Ryann."

Soph arched an eyebrow. "Oh?"

"Get inside and I'll tell you all about it." Lydia swatted her best friend's shoulder, rolling her eyes. "I don't need the neighbours hearing about my wild night with the world's hottest tattoo artist."

"Wild night..." Soph trailed off. "Interesting."

"Oh, it was." Lydia couldn't stop the smirk forming on her mouth. "It was very interesting."

Her heels clicked across the parquet flooring in the hallway, her bag dropping to the floor with a thud. Lydia felt the intrigue seeping from Soph. Her best friend never did hold back on waiting for someone to discuss in their own time.

"Well?"

"OH, MY GOD!" Lydia exploded, facing Soph. "Soph, you've no idea. Of all the sex I've had, Ryann was just..." Lydia paused, trying to find the right words to describe the woman she fell asleep beside last night. "I can't even describe it."

"Well, you're going to have to try."

"Mind-blowing. Thrilling. Oh, I don't know. Everything I never imagined I'd *ever* experience."

"That good, huh?"

Lydia needed more coffee. She needed a long nap too, but Ryann continued to steal every ounce of attention she had. Pressing the kettle, she collected two cups from the cupboard and motioned for Soph to sit down.

"She told me you went to the studio, by the way."

With the whirlwind few days Lydia had been subjected to, she'd completely forgotten to discuss Soph's decision to show up at Ryann's studio. She wasn't angry anymore, but she did want an explanation.

"Oh. I was hoping she wouldn't."

"Ryann really isn't the type to keep things from me."

Soph smiled weakly. "You know her that well already?"

"Well, no. But I know the kind of person she is. I know she wouldn't keep anything from me that could hurt our relationship."

"Me going to visit her would hurt your relationship?" Soph asked. "I mean, you're actually together now?"

"We haven't talked about it. We didn't have time this morning. But we will," Lydia said, her voice cheery to match her mood. "Everything has happened so fast since she showed up last week. Neither of us have really had time to sit and breathe."

"Then maybe you need to slow down."

"Nah, I'm done with slow. I wasted a month ignoring her, Soph. A month when I could have been doing much more exciting things."

"You ignored her for a reason."

The spoon in Lydia's hand clattered to the counter. "Do you not want me to be happy?"

235

"You know I do," Soph said, rounding the island and taking Lydia's hand. "All I want is for you to be happy. But please, slow down."

"Why? What's the point? I want Ryann. She wants me. There really is nothing more to say about it."

"Fine." Soph shrugged, dropping Lydia's hand. "When it all goes tits up, don't come crying to me."

"You sound like my mother," Lydia deadpanned.

"Maybe you could ask her what she thinks about all of this."

"Maybe you could just be happy for me and let me get on with my life, Soph. If you didn't want me to be with Ryann, why did you go to the studio and tell her to come here?"

"I do want you to be with Ryann. Anyone who looks at you can see how much you're into her. But I don't want you to go headfirst into this. I'll be the one you cry to when it falls apart. I'll be the one you lash out at. I'll be the one who has to see her best friend heartbroken."

"Ryann wouldn't hurt me." Lydia's heart fluttered in her chest at the mention of Ryann's name. That's how she knew this was going to work out. Lydia was no stranger to relationships and dating, but nobody had ever remained on her mind like Ryann. The reason they met wasn't the first thing Lydia thought about anymore. No, it was everything that Ryann was that sat firmly at the front of her mind. "I know she wouldn't."

"Great. Well, now that we've cleared that up, you can explain why you have the day off."

"You wouldn't believe me if I told you." Lydia sighed, handing Soph a cup of coffee. "Trust me."

"Try me."

"Let me get comfortable." Lydia ushered Soph through into the living room, removing her phone from her bag on the way through. She fully expected a call from Bree, yelling about how much she hated Lydia, but it was Ryann she was hoping to hear from.

"Right, so—"

Lydia's phone started to ring in her hand, her eyes lighting up immediately when she saw Ryann's name on the screen. "Hi."

"Hey. I made it to the studio just in time."

Lydia smiled, Soph's eyes burned through her. "That's good. Now I don't have to worry about you stopping my visits at night."

"Not sure I could ever do that."

"No?" Lydia felt herself blush, Ryann's voice melting her.

"No," Ryann replied. "So, did you really want to come here today?"

"If that would be okay…"

"More than okay. Call me when you're headed over."

"No problem. I have a few things to do here, and then I'll change and head over."

"Perfect." Lydia knew Ryann was smiling. "And Lydia?"

"Mm?"

"Last night was great."

Lydia blushed again. If Soph didn't have her eyes on her, Lydia would tell Ryann just how great last night had been. "It was. I'll see you in a while, okay?"

"Bye, babe."

Lydia's heart leapt. "B-bye." She lowered the phone from her ear, staring at the screen until it dimmed. Ryann was…everything.

"Okay, now that you've finished phone sex, can we get back to your story?"

Lydia furrowed her brow. She couldn't remember what she should have been discussing with Soph. "Story?"

"About why you're not working."

Lydia's eyes widened. "Oh, right. Well, you know Sam, Ryann's cousin?"

"I've heard about her, yes."

"You won't believe what she's done for me…"

CHAPTER TWENTY-ONE

Lydia stopped at the end of the road, glancing up the side street on which Ryann's studio sat. This morning had flown by in a blur; Lydia wasn't sure she'd even brushed her hair since she returned home earlier. At least it didn't look a mess as she peeked at herself in the window of the deli she was standing outside of.

Everything felt nerve-wracking as she parked her car in the multi-storey down the road, but Lydia couldn't put her finger on why. Ryann had been more than accommodating last night and this morning, so why did Lydia feel as though she was meeting this woman for the first time today?

Lydia wanted to seem cool and calm, but inside she was a complete wreck. She was about to spend time with Ryann outside of their homes, and she wasn't sure Ryann would be all that impressed with what she found. Lydia was plain. She was sure some would describe her as dull. She didn't really have any major interests or hobbies. But Ryann, she was an artist. A very good artist. Lydia could only imagine how impressive her work was inside the studio, human canvases coming and going as the day progressed.

She bit her lip, slowly walking towards the Dark Angel sign.

Just be you. You've always lived by that.

Lydia cleared her throat, smiled at one of the regulars smoking outside the pub next door, and approached the studio. The buzz of a tattoo gun could be heard as she opened the door, a little bell jingling as she did, but Ryann was nowhere to be seen.

Another artist stood at the reception, flicking through what Lydia assumed was an appointment book, nobody else around.

"Hi, excuse me?"

The artist's eyes rose from the appointment book. "Hiya, love."

Lydia was taken aback. The woman with blonde dreadlocks dragged high up on her head had purple eyes. It wasn't what Lydia expected, but she smiled fully, nonetheless.

"Is Ryann around?"

"She's finishing up with a client. Take a seat and I'll have her over to you as soon as possible."

"Okay, thanks."

"Do you have an appointment or is this just a consultation?"

"Oh, I'm just here to see Ryann," Lydia explained, picking up a magazine from the glass table in front of her.

The artist's eyes widened. "So, you're the one she hasn't stopped talking about all morning?"

"I am?" Lydia suppressed a ridiculous grin, her eyebrows raising instead.

"Lydia, right?"

Lydia nodded, her insides warming at the thought of Ryann telling her staff about her. "That's me."

"Lovely to meet you. I'm Shona." Shona rounded the desk, offering her hand to Lydia.

"Hi." Lydia held out her own hand, the buzz of the tattoo gun coming to a halt.

"Sounds like you're right on time," Shona said, every possible place on her face pierced. "Can I get you something to drink? Coffee, water, beer?"

"You have beer here?" Lydia asked.

"Not supposed to, but out back, yeah. Sometimes Ryann works late on inventory and invoices. She likes to have a beer to hand."

"You know, I think I'll go for a coffee, if that's okay?"

"I'll get that for you."

Ryann cleaned up her room, checking her watch and praying that Lydia would soon be here. She'd sent her client outside to Shona for aftercare instructions, and her next client had cancelled. Usually she wouldn't take well to a client cancelling—it confused her routine when they did—but today she was thankful for it. It meant she had the next two hours with Lydia to do whatever they wanted.

Applying fresh wrapping to the bed, Ryann cleared her gun away, preparing it for her next client this afternoon. She would grab herself some coffee once she headed back out into the main area of the studio, and then she would wait patiently.

She lifted her phone from the top shelf above the ink choices, in some way relieved to find no messages from Lydia. If she hadn't text or left a voicemail, she hadn't cancelled. That didn't mean there wasn't still time for another cancellation in her day, though. Ryann just hoped she would show.

Leaving her room, she removed a protein bar from her back pocket, tearing it open with her teeth. Ryann lifted her head and her heart stuttered when she spotted Lydia in the waiting area, engrossed in a magazine. She quickly rushed into the bathroom at the studio, checking herself over in the mirror. She could be in any state by now after tattooing for the last two hours.

Satisfied that she looked good enough, Ryann smoothed the creases from her black, drop-sleeve tank top, and pushed the strands of hair out of her face. Running her fingertips over her eyebrows, she neared the mirror and gave her face a once over. Okay, she couldn't do any more than that.

With her shoulders pulled back, her heavy Dr. Marten boots pounding the laminate wood floor, Ryann put on her biggest smile and headed for Lydia.

"Hi," Ryann said, pushing through the swinging, hip-height door, and stopped in front of Lydia. "Really happy you could make it."

"Oh, hi." Lydia shot to her feet, a shy smile on her face. "Are you finished with your client? I can just sit around here until whenever you have some time."

"Lucky for you, my next client had to cancel. I don't have anything on for the next two hours."

"Really?" Ryann wouldn't ever tire of the huge smile Lydia sported around her. "That's amazing."

"It is?"

Lydia stepped closer to Ryann. "I've been thinking about you all morning."

"Mm, same here." Ryann lowered her head, smirking as Lydia's fingertips brushed her own. "Did you want to come through to the back and I'll get you some coffee?"

"Shona already brought me some."

"Okay, well bring it through. We can sit back there."

Lydia followed Ryann, offering her a grateful smile as Ryann held the swing door open for her. Shona winked in Ryann's direction, giving her boss a nod of the head and a thumbs up when Lydia's back was turned.

This was all new for her. Jen never showed up at the studio; nobody usually showed up for Ryann. At one time, her staff joked about whether her girlfriend even existed. But now, Lydia was here and very much real.

"How was your morning?" Ryann shoved her hands in the pockets of her jeans, slowing her pace as Lydia flopped down onto the couch in the back room. It wasn't quite a staff room, more of a place where Ryann would kick back when she didn't have anything on. Just a couple of months ago, it was where she was sleeping. "Anything exciting happen so far today?"

"Other than waking up with you? Nope."

"Mm," Ryann agreed, inserting a coffee pod into the machine and allowing it to work its caffeine magic. "You know, it felt really good having you at my place this morning."

"I enjoyed being there," Lydia said. "Maybe it could happen again sometime..."

Ryann's smile widened. "I'd like that."

Lydia took in the small room they'd commandeered while Ryann took in Lydia's appearance. Skin-tight jeans covered her legs, a pair of worn Vans working well with her ripped T-shirt. It was hard to believe that the same woman had been at Ryann's last night in suspenders and an expensive suit. Still, Ryann liked that Lydia could pull off any look she wanted to.

"So, you said you'd tell me why you have the day off work."

"Actually..." Lydia paused, sitting forward and clasping her hands together. Ryann leaned back against the counter, admiring her eyes. "I have the whole week off. I mean, I'm sure Sam is going to want to see me at some point, but I don't have to be at the office until Monday."

"Huh? Sam?" Ryann was confused. *Why would Sam have anything to do with Lydia's job?*

Lydia explained everything about her meeting with Sam yesterday, dropping bomb after bomb. Ryann couldn't believe what had unfolded. Lydia had been beside herself with hate for that job, or the boss at least, and now Sam had handed over the reins to Lydia. Incredible.

"So, I don't have to work until next Monday."

"Wow. And you work for our Sam now?"

"Guess so," Lydia laughed. "Jo is involved, too. I don't think either of them will be too involved once I find my feet, but for now, at least I won't be alone. Turns out Sam and Jo are good friends."

"Why doesn't that surprise me?" Ryann ran her hand over her face, shaking her head. "Sam knows everyone."

"Apparently so."

"And you're okay with all of this? Sam getting involved and whatever else?"

"More than okay with it. I think Sam gave Bree her chance. Maybe she knows something about the figures that I don't. Maybe Sam was waiting for the perfect opportunity to fire Bree, I don't know. But she believes I can excel, and I won't let her down. This is what I've been working towards for so many years, Ry."

Ryann loved Lydia's enthusiasm. It was something beautiful. "You will be amazing, babe." Ryann crouched down in front of Lydia, caressing her cheek with the pad of her thumb. "I know you will."

"Isn't it crazy how everything's happened?"

Ryann laughed from deep within her belly. "Outrageous."

"But it feels good, doesn't it?" Lydia's eyes fluttered closed as Ryann moved closer. "With us? How life is kinda coming together for us..."

"Feels incredible, Lydia."

Their lips met, but Ryann kept her wits about her. The door was wide open, anyone could walk in, and as much as she loved being against Lydia, neither her staff nor anyone else needed to see such displays of affection in a workplace. Ryann would keep it professional in here. If she didn't, God only knows the state they'd both be in by the time they'd had *coffee*.

Lydia pulled back, a questioning but apprehensive look in her eyes. "Hey, will you do something for me?"

"Sure. Anything."

"Pierce me."

"Um, why?" Ryann sat back on her knees, the coffee machine beeping to signal her brew was ready. "I mean, you *actually* want a piercing? I know you already have one, but is this one just for the sake of it, or...?"

"Mmhmm. I definitely want one."

Ryann narrowed her eyes. "Because you don't look very convinced."

"Please, Ryann? I want you to do it."

"Okay, fine." Ryann got to her feet, taking her coffee from the machine. "Let me finish this, and then I'll take you into the other room. Did you have something in mind?"

Ryann's mind drifted back to last night, surprised when she found Lydia's clit pierced. Yes, Lydia had mentioned that she had a piercing, and Ryann kinda guessed as to where it could possibly be, but it had completely left her mind. She was both shocked and aroused that someone like Lydia, so proper, would have such a piercing.

"My nipple."

"Wow. Okay. You're sure about this?"

"I'm sure." Lydia nodded, climbing to her feet and closing the distance between them. "Seeing yours last night...it only made me want one more."

"You've thought about getting it done? This isn't just a spur of the moment kinda thing?"

"No, I've thought about it. I was just never sure. But seeing yours and your reaction to being touched...yeah, I want one."

Ryann felt the temperature in the room suddenly rise. Lydia really was too much.

Lydia steadied her breathing, following Ryann into the back room where more intimate piercings took place. She trusted Ryann, of course, but the idea of a piercing today hadn't really been on the agenda. Was she trying to impress Ryann? Lydia didn't believe so. She had other ways of impressing her, none of which involved pain or the possibility of crying in front of a potential girlfriend.

Lydia had a high pain threshold, but something told her this wouldn't be smooth sailing. Nobody's nipple appreciated a needle through it; she was sure her own would feel the same way. Something told Lydia she was going to hold her breath until it was all over, before passing out in Ryann's strong, tattooed arms. That wouldn't be the worst scenario, Ryann would always catch her if she fell, but it *would* be embarrassing.

"Okay, hop up onto the bed." Ryann closed the door behind her, flicking the lock to show that the room was engaged. "Give me a minute to get set-up and it'll be over in no time."

"Phew. Okay." Lydia slowly climbed onto the bed, rubbing her hands up and down her thighs as she got comfortable. Ryann was gloving up. "Can I sit up for a moment or do you want me lying down now?"

"No, you can sit for a minute." Ryann glanced over her shoulder, smiling Lydia's way as she took what she needed from the drawers. "You feelin' okay?"

"Me? Yeah."

Ryann turned, stopping beside the drawers. "Why exactly have you decided to have a piercing?"

Lydia shrugged, her eyes darting around the room. "Feeling rebellious, I guess. I don't know."

"But you're sure you want this?" Ryann held up the sterile packed equipment in her hand. "I mean, if you're unsure, I don't want to do this. I *wouldn't* usually do this."

"Ryann, I'm fine. I just get nervous before a piercing. I'm sure most people do."

"Where did you have your last one done?" Ryann asked, Lydia knew she was making small talk to keep her mind off what was happening.

"A place in London when I went away on a girl's weekend with Soph."

"Painful?"

Lydia smiled. "Actually, no. Not really."

Before Lydia could think properly, Ryann was beside her with a tray of instruments. She chose not to look; she'd never been fond of needles. Inspecting one now would only have her on her back and passed out.

"Did you have any jewellery in mind? Bar, ring…"

"What would you suggest?"

"Well, I'd say the barbell. They don't snag as easily on your clothing. And when I tell you that you really need to be careful with it, I mean it. It may look all hot and pretty once it's healed, but the slightest knock during the healing process and you'll know about it."

"Okay. Be careful. Got it." Lydia nodded. "And the bar sounds good to me."

Lydia kept her eyes on the wall ahead of her, Ryann's certificates of hygiene, awards, and anything else that required a certificate pinned to it. The sound of instruments being removed from packaging had Lydia's heart rate up a little, but she focused on Ryann's soft perfume instead. She really shouldn't be worried; she was in the safest hands possible.

"Okay, top off."

Lydia did what was asked of her, unclasping her bra as she placed her T-shirt on her lap.

"I'm going to give it a clean, and I should warn you, unfortunately, no lace bras for the foreseeable. Devastating, *for me*, but still."

"You like lace, huh?"

"On you? Very much so."

Although Ryann was talking freely with Lydia, she was also fully concentrated on the task at hand. Her eyes hadn't once found Lydia's since the set-up of the procedure had begun; Ryann was completely professional.

"Okay, do you want to check the marking of it?"

Lydia shook her head. "No, I trust you."

"Okay, you ready?"

Lydia released a slow, steady breath. "As ready as I'll ever be."

Ryann leaned in, pressing a kiss to Lydia's lips. "One minute and it will all be over. Lie down for me."

"Okay." Lydia got into position, no longer willing to talk her way through this. Her mouth was dry, and her hands were clammy.

Ryann secured the clamp around Lydia's nipple. "Take a few deep breaths, babe. You're okay. You'll feel a sudden sharp sensation and then it'll all—"

Lydia held her breath. Ryann hadn't even finished her sentence before piercing through Lydia's nipple. The pain was manageable, but she was thankful she was only having one done. She felt a slight tugging at her nipple, and Ryann was inserting the barbell through the hollow needle Lydia hadn't realised Ryann had since put in.

"Be over," Ryann finished, standing back and admiring both her work and how Lydia's chest now looked. "Gorgeous."

"That's it? It's done?" Lydia sat up on her elbows, glancing down at the jewellery. "Wow. Looks great."

Ryann took a bandage from the sterile area, applying pressure to Lydia's breast before taping it down. "Yep. That's it."

"That was quick." Lydia sat up, giving herself a moment to breathe. She felt a slight light-headedness, but nothing she would worry about.

"Did you want to discuss aftercare in here or over a bottle of water outside?"

"I could really use a bottle of water. Mouth is kinda dry."

Ryann shrugged. "That's normal. As humans, we prepare ourselves for the worst and get ourselves wound up."

"Thank you for taking such good care of me," Lydia said, climbing down from the bed. "How much do I owe you?"

"Nothing. That one was on me."

"No, Ryann—"

Ryann held up her hand. "It was on me. That's the end of it."

Lydia drew Ryann closer, kissing below her ear. "Thank you."

"Can I take you out for lunch?" Ryann checked her watch, appearing satisfied that she had time. "Or even just to the deli for a salad and sandwich, and then I'll cook for you this weekend?"

"Lunch would be great."

"And the weekend?" Ryann looked expectantly at Lydia.

"The weekend sounds perfect."

Ryann had somehow ended up back at Lydia's place, the fire flickering in front of them, the living room door closed tight as they snuggled into one another. Calm. Centred. Cared for. That's what Ryann's body told her as she pulled Lydia closer, her arm wrapped around her shoulder.

She could count on one hand the number of times she'd done this with Jen. Relaxing at the end of the day wasn't ever really on her ex-girlfriend's agenda. No, Jen preferred to meet up with friends, drink wine, and then show up long after Ryann had climbed into bed. It became normal.

Before she met Jen in Australia, Ryann had spent her days perfecting the studio. Love was the last thing on her mind, only her career spurring her on most days. She still lived with her mum, but Ryann didn't see it as an issue. They'd always had a strong bond, a sisterly relationship.

Once she returned from Australia—the supposed love of her life in tow—Ryann knew it was time to focus on what really mattered. Love. Happiness. Her career would always be there, the studio too, but she wanted to give Jen her undivided attention whenever possible. Seeing her girlfriend happy meant a lot to Ryann.

"The last time I did this," Lydia said, her voice hoarse from lack of conversation, "was when I was still with Niamh."

"You don't really talk about past relationships much."

Lydia glanced up at Ryann. "I hadn't been in a relationship for about two years before I met you. I couldn't really commit to anything serious because of work, but I also never found anyone I *wanted* to be serious with."

"I bet everyone wanted to date you growing up." Ryann smirked; she knew she was right. Lydia was gorgeous, every woman's—and man's—dream. "I'm just glad you managed to fend them all off. I wouldn't be here now if you'd settled down years ago."

"I wasn't the skinny kid in school. I mean, I wasn't overweight, but I carried a little bit more than the popular girls. And I had braces. Trust me, I was fending *nobody* off when I was growing up." Lydia sighed. "And then as I got older, I may have had nice teeth but the rest of me was still grim."

Ryann loved Lydia's curves, and the double D's that went with them.

"In history class, the lads called me 'Hideous Lydious.' That lasted until I went on to do my A-levels, but by that point, I couldn't care what they were calling me. I was excelling with all of my grades, and the girls who'd managed to scrape their way through their GCSE's—and picked on me for five years—wanted to know me...because they realised it would require *actual* work to pass."

"Bunch of dickheads!"

"Eh. I'd say I came out of it all on top." Lydia slid her hand up and under Ryann's tank top, her fingers splayed against her abdomen. "Most of them are now stuck in relationships with boys they were shagging in school. They hate them, but they're set in their ways. God forbid should they be seen to be single."

"Sounds like they got their karma."

"And I got mine," Lydia said, leaning up and kissing Ryann hard.

"Careful of your boo—"

Lydia pulled back, her face draining of all colour.

"Boob."

"Shit, fuck!" Lydia winced, unravelling herself from Ryann and sitting forward, breathing deeply.

Ryann shot out of the living room, taking her rucksack from the floor and heading for the kitchen. She soaked a compress from her bag with cold water and rushed back into Lydia.

"Here, let me help you." Ryann got to her knees in front of Lydia, unbuttoning her shirt and thankfully finding no bra present.

"Fuck, that hurts."

Ryann removed the bandage she'd applied earlier, replacing it with the cold, wet compress in her hand. Gently, she held it in place, watching Lydia's face change as it slowly soothed the ache and sting she was likely feeling.

"Better?" Ryann asked, her eyebrow arched.

Lydia nodded, her eyes closed. "Yes. Thank you."

"Good job I'm here to look after you. It's only the first day and you've almost ripped your tit off." Ryann allowed Lydia to hold the compress in place, leaning up and kissing Lydia's forehead before removing a fresh bandage and tape from her rucksack.

She placed them on the coffee table, leaving the bandage in its sterile pack, and sat back down beside Lydia. "Why don't you give it some air for a while?"

"Yeah, could do."

Ryann got comfortable on the couch, motioning for Lydia to lie between her legs.

Okay, this feels ridiculously good.

"You want to stay the night?" Lydia asked, her shirt hanging open as she lay back against Ryann. "Not sure what you have on tomorrow."

"I'm packed busy tomorrow, but there's no reason why I can't stay over."

"I'll run you back to your place for whatever you need," Lydia said, her tone light. "We could grab some food on the way back."

Ryann leaned forward, kissing Lydia's hair. She would give up every night alone for this. Because quite frankly, Lydia meant the world to her. "Works for me."

CHAPTER TWENTY-TWO

Ryann tapped her trimmed fingernails against the wooden table in front of her. Jen was weaving through the crowd; she couldn't mistake her ex-girlfriend. With hair holding that much volume, it was hard not to stand out in a crowd of people.

Ryann watched Jen approach, her stomach in turmoil for what her ex could possibly have to say to her. Jen had tried and failed over the last six weeks to contact Ryann, so why was Ryann sitting here willingly meeting with her? One final conversation, perhaps. The last goodbye. Closure.

Ryann relaxed back in her chair, folding her arms across her chest. She could think of many things she would rather be doing than sitting in a coffee shop, number one on her list being with Lydia. They hadn't spoken much since earlier in the week, but Ryann understood. Lydia had a lot of work to do now that she'd met with Sam. With just one night together since Lydia came by the studio, Ryann was certainly missing her.

Ryann hated Sam meddling in business that didn't concern her, but this time it had worked out for the best. They were now on speaking terms again after their run-in, and Ryann was appreciative of the fact that Sam had intervened, ultimately getting Lydia out of the office she hated. She should have been surprised to find out that Sam owned *Strive*, but she wasn't. Sam had her hand in all kinds of businesses.

Jen flopped down in the seat facing Ryann. "Hi."

"Let's just keep this short, okay?"

Jen rolled her eyes, huffing as she dropped her bag to the floor. "Ryann, I really want to work things out with you."

"I'm not here to listen to your grovelling. You said you had something you needed to tell me, so here I am. If you lied to get me here, I can be on my way. It's no trouble."

"No, I didn't lie." Jen sat forward, her features softening as she rested her head in the palm of her hand. "You look great, by the way."

"Thanks."

"Did you contact the police?" Jen asked, chewing her bottom lip. "I know what I did was unforgivable, but I'm willing to overpay on the repayments to get it cleared quicker."

"Overpay?" Ryann laughed. "That's going to take you one hell of a long time to clear the debt, Jen."

"I know, but that's my own fault. I'm the one who took out the loans, and I'm the one who will repay them."

"You knew what you were doing, didn't you?" Ryann leaned forward. The vein in the side of her head pulsed, but she would keep her anger in check. Jen wasn't worth the fury. "You knew that if you repaid the minimum amount each month, I couldn't do anything about it."

"I don't know what you're talking about."

"I called the debt advice centre. I can't claim it was fraud because you didn't take the money and run. They can't prove I didn't know about it, and since you made payments each month, it doesn't look dodgy on their end."

"O-oh." As much as Ryann believed Jen was clued up on this, her ex *did* look genuinely surprised.

"I could call a lawyer, go through pointless paperwork and

whatever else comes with it, but that's going to cost me...and you've already cost me enough."

"Ryann, I am sorry." Jen slid her hand across the table, settling it over Ryann's balled fist. "Babe, please."

"Don't you dare 'babe' me." Ryann lowered her voice as she removed her hand, seething that this woman could have the audacity to behave like this. "The sooner you realise we're over, the quicker you can move on."

"I don't want us to be over. I made a mistake."

"Which mistake was that? Taking out thousands in my name or fucking another woman?"

Jen lowered her eyes, a sob escaping her.

Ryann couldn't deal with this right now. For the first time in weeks, she was happy. Happy that her and Lydia were starting over. Happy that she had a home and a job. Happy to have Jen out of her life. "I need to leave. I have plans."

"What plans?"

"I have a date tonight." Ryann cleared her throat, studying Jen's face. "I don't think you realise just how much you ruined my life, Jen."

"I'll repay it. I swear."

"It's not even about the repayments," Ryann said, her teeth gritting. "Two months ago, I took a walk down by the river. You know, the week after I left the house for you and what's-her-face?"

Jen remained silent, tears in her eyes. Something about her appeared different, but Ryann couldn't put her finger on what it was. It didn't matter.

"I climbed over the railings that night...planning to end my life."

Jen's eyes widened. "W-what?"

"I thought we were happy, Jen. I thought I was going to marry you and have a beautiful life with you. I know you cheated in the past, but I overlooked that. Foolishly, I know that now, but I loved you so much that I was willing to forgive you and try again. We were supposed to marry and have kids. Our kids would be best friends with Sam and Luciana's kids. Life was supposed to be great."

Ryann's stomach rolled. The thought of Jen sleeping with someone else still sent her disgust through the roof.

"And then I walked in to find you with *her* again. Not just text messages, but in our bed. Do you have any idea how much that hurt? I mean, do you even care? Not only did you take me for everything I had, the studio included, but you had to insult me one more time by fucking another woman in *our* bed."

"Ryann, I had no idea…"

"No idea about what?"

"T-the river." Jen's voice cracked.

"Why would you? You were too busy setting up home with that fucking woman."

"Come home with me," Jen pleaded, squeezing Ryann's hand. "Please. Come home and we will start again."

"I'm seeing someone else, Jen." Just the thought of Lydia settled every ounce of anger Ryann held inside of her. Once this meeting with Jen was over, Ryann could be on her way and spend the evening with Lydia. Life, today, was perfect.

"Ry—"

"I don't want to hear it." Ryann cut Jen off, holding up her hand. "We'll figure out a repayment plan and you stay out of my life. It can't be that hard for you to work out. You're not as stupid as you look."

Ryann stood, the chair screeching back against the concrete floor. She could only stare Jen down; she had nothing else to say to the woman who had ruined her life. "Bye, Jen."

"I'm pregnant."

The words hung in the air, Ryann's mouth slackening as she took them in. Light-headed and shocked to the core, Ryann blinked rapidly. She couldn't have heard Jen right.

"Ry?"

"D-did you just—?" Ryann shook her head. No. She couldn't have heard that right.

"Yes. I'm pregnant."

"H-how? I mean...who?" As much as Ryann wanted to leave, she found herself returning to her seat. She needed answers. "Did you have a one-night stand?" Ryann *needed* that to be the answer to all of this.

Jen smiled weakly, her eyes lowering. "No."

"Sorry, what?"

"I said no. I didn't have a one-night stand."

Ryann suddenly felt numb all over.

"Ryann," Jen started, "I know this isn't ideal, but it was supposed to be a surprise for us."

"A surprise!" Ryann shot to her feet again, her eyes widening. "Are you telling me what I think you're telling me?"

"T-this baby. It's ours."

No. Ryann couldn't raise a child with this woman. Not in a million years. Jen had pulled some stunts lately, but this was something else. This, she couldn't comprehend.

"I went to the clinic a week before you left. I just...I knew the cheating was wrong, and I wanted out of it. I didn't know what to do, and I knew once you found out you would leave, so I went there. I had the insemination. I hoped it would bring us back together."

Ryann remained silent for a moment. At one time, the decision to have kids with Jen was a big thing. Ryann loved kids, she dreamed of a big family, and Jen was privy to that. For her to use a child as a way of keeping Ryann cut deep. It pained her to know that Jen would do something so drastic when it was supposed to be something so sacred. Something made out of love. A child was not a weapon. It was not a means of entrapment.

Even if Ryann did want this with Jen, she couldn't stand by her. Because then she would be giving into the actions of one hell of a cruel, spiteful woman. And Ryann couldn't be that person.

She couldn't love this child fully, knowing why it had been conceived. Because of lies and deceit. Because its mother needed something to keep Ryann in her life.

A deep laugh rumbled in Ryann's throat. This was absurd. "You're out of your fucking mind."

And then it dawned on her.

Lydia.

How the hell was she supposed to explain any of this to the woman she was dating? Lydia, who was the only person Ryann could see in her future. Yes, it was early days, but the thought of Lydia being unable to understand this was painful. This news was going to put one hell of a spanner in the works. A spanner that could shatter everything they were slowly building with one another.

"I can't do this with you, Jen."

"You want kids, Ry. Now's your chance."

"I don't want a kid with *you*. Especially when I've been trapped into doing so. Because *that* is exactly what this is. You, trapping me."

"We picked this donor together. We sat through endless nights looking for the right person. This baby was supposed to be our future."

"And you can thank yourself for fucking it all up." Ryann leaned forward, placing her palms on the table for support. "I wish you well but fuck me...you've got some nerve."

Ryann lit the final candle on the table, her heart in her throat at the thought of Lydia's imminent arrival. She'd spent the last two hours preparing dinner, but she couldn't recall how she got to the point of finishing everything and setting the table. This evening, so far, had gone by in a blur.

The bomb she had to drop was really going to disrupt her relationship with Lydia. Ryann felt it as she slid her key into the lock some three hours ago. Today was supposed to be a day off from the studio, giving her all the time in the world to prepare for their date. While Ryann still wanted Lydia in her life as much as she did this morning, she knew the information she'd received today could change that. Lydia wouldn't be to blame; this was just another part of Ryann's messed-up life. If it wasn't one thing, it was another.

Ryann checked over the table, satisfied that everything was where it should be. She hoped Lydia would appreciate it. She also hoped Lydia didn't see it as an apology for the fact that Ryann—in some way—had a kid on the way.

This cannot be happening.

She slumped down into the window seat overlooking the river. Up here, thirty-plus floors from ground level, nothing mattered. Jen and her problems didn't exist. The bustle of the city was irrelevant. Ryann's life felt complete.

But then everything came flooding back. Ryann thought she was rid of Jen and the trouble she brought into her life, but it seemed that wasn't quite true. Her only hope this evening was that Lydia wouldn't stand up and walk out.

Ryann rested her head back against the wall, her heartbeat racing. Everything in her mind was moving too quickly for her to process. How the hell had her life come to this? She clutched her arms to her chest, squeezing her eyes shut. The last thing Ryann needed was red, puffy eyes when Lydia arrived.

The buzzer sounded.

As much as Ryann felt filled with dread, she had to get this over with.

Her legs moved until she reached the receiver on the wall. "Hello?"

"Is this the home of the gorgeous woman I'm having dinner with?"

Ryann smiled instantly. "Apparently so."

"Are you ready for me?"

"Of course." Ryann couldn't stall any longer. She released the lock on the main door, and with a sigh said, "Come on up."

Ryann stood frozen at the door. In an ideal world, the fact that she had even agreed to meet with Jen today wouldn't matter. This wasn't an ideal world, though. It was a messed-up parallel universe that Ryann no longer wanted to be a part of.

Not only did she have to explain her conversation with Jen to Lydia, she also had to tell Lydia they'd met at all. She hadn't thought it was worth bringing up, Lydia didn't need to concern herself with ex-girlfriends, but now that everything was up in the air, Ryann was beginning to wish she'd told Lydia this morning. Even just a simple text message would have sufficed.

A light knock on the door jolted Ryann. Her heart fell into her stomach.

The door opened. "Hi. Good to see you."

"Wow, you don't look so great." Lydia frowned, leaning in and pressing her palm to Ryann's forehead. "Are you feeling unwell? Temperature?"

"No, I'm okay." Ryann closed the door, ushering Lydia further into the apartment. "Can I get you something to drink?"

Lydia slid her long coat from her shoulders, Ryann momentarily taken aback by Lydia's choice of clothing. "I'll have whatever you're having."

Lydia was wearing one of her expensive work suits again. Ryann would never not be attracted to it. "Well, I opened a beer, but you're not dressed for beer."

"Huh?" Lydia frowned, her eyes following Ryann's and down her body.

"You look...wow."

Lydia always looked wow. Ryann shouldn't be surprised.

Lydia waved off Ryann's ogling. "I thought maybe we would be going out but then you texted and said you wanted me to come over here."

"Did you want to go out?"

"No. Here is so much better." Ryann lost Lydia's gaze to the interior design of her apartment. She could understand, though. Bryant Tower was impressive. Lydia may have been here before—woken up here—but she'd never really had time to look around or take in the entire apartment. She'd been busy *under* Ryann last time.

"Well..." Ryann stretched out her arms. "Knock yourself out. Make yourself comfortable." While the small matter of Jen and her pregnancy was on Ryann's mind, she would wait it out and give Lydia some time to unwind after work. She was likely to lose this woman once she opened her mouth and bared all anyway, so why not give it a little more time?

Lydia reached forward, refilling her wine glass as Ryann stepped up to the table with an impressive beef wellington on a serving platter. Dressed in her best, most expensive skirt-suit, Lydia felt a little awkward sitting down to dinner with Ryann. If she'd known, had time, she would have gone home first and put on something more comfortable. Too late now; dinner was ready.

"Wow, that looks impressive."

Ryann set down the dish. "It's been a while since I made it, so go easy on the criticism when you taste it."

"I doubt it tastes bad," Lydia said, leaning forward and inspecting it. "But I do have one question..."

"Shoot." Ryann sat down, swigging her beer.

"What mushroom did you use for the filling?"

"Porcini."

Lydia grinned; Ryann knew how to cook. "Perfect."

"I've used chestnut before today, but I prefer porcini." Seeing Ryann in this environment, comfortable and not second-guessing herself, really appealed to Lydia. "How do you prefer your beef?" Ryann carved the food in front of them, glancing up at Lydia. She could only stare, taken aback by Ryann's eyes in this moment. Soft, gentle, caring.

"Medium, thanks."

Lydia sat back while Ryann got to work on plating up dinner, fresh vegetables, and the homemade dauphinoise potatoes already in front of her. She appeared to be less agitated than when Lydia arrived, so perhaps Ryann was just nervous about their dinner date. It had been a funny week, one Lydia was glad to see the back of.

"Good day?" Lydia asked.

"S-sure, yeah. Kinda."

With dinner now in front of them, Lydia tucked in, desperate to taste the succulent beef. "Oh, wow." She placed her hand over her mouth, closing her eyes and savouring the taste of the prosciutto ham woven through the dish. "This…Ryann, this is amazing."

"It's nice to have dinner with someone who appreciates it."

Lydia noted the half-smile Ryann was sporting. "Hey, are you okay?"

Ryann was visibly worried, her eyes flitting around the room instead of her attention being on Lydia.

"Ryann?"

"Sorry, I just have some things on my mind," Ryann said, lowering her eyes and repeatedly turning over the fork in her right hand. Lydia instantly grew worried; she didn't like seeing Ryann in this state. "I-I can talk to you, right? I can be honest with you without us falling out?"

"I'd like to think so, yeah." Lydia set her cutlery down, giving Ryann her full attention. "What is it?"

"I met with Jen today."

A wave of uncertainty hit Lydia like a tsunami.

Why would she possibly want to meet with her? Thankfully, Lydia wasn't the type of person to hit the roof without all of the information first. So, she simply nodded and listened.

"I don't like to discuss that side of me with you; it's not your problem. Jen is my ex, and I'm sure you have a million other things you would rather be doing than listening to me talking about her."

Lydia reached her hand across the table, taking Ryann's. "You know I'll listen."

"She's been calling since before you and I reconnected," Ryann explained. "Asking me to take her back. Apologising. You know, the usual stuff. But I've spent the last month or so ignoring her."

"Okay..."

"She left me a voicemail a few days ago telling me she had something important to discuss. That she really needed to talk." Ryann sat back in her seat, seemingly exhausted by it all, but her hand remained in Lydia's. "It was the same day I called the debt advice centre about what she'd done. I know Sam offered to help, but I really don't want any more help from her. She's done far too much as it is. They explained that it wouldn't be as simple as just having her arrested for fraud. That in some way, it was my word against hers."

"What? That's total crap!"

"She was making payments on the loans. Minimum, but still."

"So, what? She gets away with it?"

"Well, she's going to now, yes." Ryann exhaled a deep breath. "I was considering calling the police anyway, a lawyer and whatever else I needed to make sure she didn't get away with it."

"And you've decided not to?" Lydia arched an eyebrow.

How could Ryann let this woman get away with almost ruining her life? This didn't make sense, but it also wasn't Lydia's business. Not really.

Ryann shook her head. "I can't."

Lydia's thumb caressed the back of Ryann's hand. It was the only way she could show her support at the moment. In Lydia's eyes, Jen was a criminal. Why didn't Ryann see that, too?

"She's pregnant."

Lydia's eyebrows rose in surprise. This ex of Ryann's really was something else. "Wow. So, she's just been sleeping her way around the place, huh?"

"Not quite." Ryann cleared her throat, her eyes finally finding Lydia's. As beautiful as they were, something in them told Lydia she wouldn't like the rest of this conversation. "Last year, we went to the clinic and went through the process of looking into having a baby. I'd caught Jen cheating a month or so before that, and we agreed to try again. I told her we would pick the donor and if in a year's time she still loved me, still wanted to be with me, we would get the ball rolling."

Lydia's hand fell away from Ryann's. Her heart slowly but surely sunk, emotion balling in her throat.

"I don't know how far along she is, but she went to the clinic a week before I left. A week before I caught her cheating again. I don't know *what* possessed her to get pregnant while she was in bed with someone else, but she is. Jen is pregnant."

"R-right."

"So, I'm just a bit off this evening. I'm sorry." Ryann squared her shoulders, blowing out a deep breath. "But, you're here and I don't want to spoil your night. So, let's eat."

Spoil Lydia's night? Oh, it had been spoiled the moment Jen and her pregnancy landed on the table. Lydia was no longer hungry.

They weren't exclusive, but Lydia had hoped it would happen one day soon. Now, not only would they *not* be exclusive, but Ryann was about to become a mother.

Lydia stood up, placing her napkin down. "Can I use your bathroom?"

"Of course. You know where it is."

"T-thanks."

Lydia rushed across the open space as quickly as her heels would allow, the walls closing in on her as the air grew thick with fear. This was one almighty blow. One she hadn't expected at all.

She quietly glided the lock across the bathroom door, her back connecting with the expensive wood as she slowly slid down it, bringing her knees up to her chest. This wasn't the night she had in mind on the way over here. Sitting on the bathroom floor of a flashy apartment in her best suit while the woman she was falling for unknowingly ripped her heart from her chest. No, this wasn't what she had in mind at all.

But perhaps it was best that they discovered Jen's pregnancy now. At least this way they could slowly drift apart with less heartbreak than if they found out months down the line. This was for the best, Lydia knew that, and if Ryann was happy about becoming a parent...Lydia would be, too. Ryann deserved happiness after the terrible time she'd had. Lydia just wished it was with her and not some ex-girlfriend who caused nothing but trouble.

Ryann hadn't openly expressed her desire to go back to Jen, but having a child in the picture changed everything. Ryann had taken her ex back once before, and with a baby on the way, it was surely a no-brainer that she would do it again. As much as Lydia was loving this dating stage with Ryann, she wasn't hers to keep.

Wow, this hurts more than I thought it would.

Lydia wiped away the tears that had fallen down her face, dropping to her silk blouse and leaving mascara stains as they did. This night was turning out to be one huge mess. Not only did she have to go back out there and act as nonchalant as she possibly could, Lydia would now have to do it with her blazer buttoned up. Ryann would know something was wrong.

Just don't be angry with her. She has enough going on.

Lydia climbed to her feet and made herself look as presentable as she possibly could. It was a waste of time, her eyes were bloodshot, but maybe Ryann wouldn't notice. She cleared her throat and left the bathroom.

"Hey, wasn't sure if you'd got lost." Ryann's smile widened, only hurting Lydia's heart that little bit more. "I cut you a fresh piece. The other was going cold."

Lydia couldn't do this. Ryann was possibly the sweetest

woman she'd ever met—would ever meet—but she couldn't finish dinner here. If she did, it probably wouldn't stay down long enough. She felt sick to the stomach at the thought of this soon being over.

"Ryann, I don't feel so good." Lydia didn't like lying, but she had nothing else to offer right now. "Would you mind if I headed home?"

Ryann shot to her feet. "Oh, God. Did my food make you sick?"

"No, it was beautiful," Lydia said. "All of this. The candles and the soft music. It's all been really lovely."

"Damn, I never even got to play you my Bon Jovi vinyl." Ryann sighed, shaking her head. "Next time?"

"Maybe, yeah."

Ryann narrowed her eyes, stepping closer to Lydia. "Maybe? Like, maybe you don't want to do this anymore, or maybe you're not as into them as I thought you were?"

"Ryann..."

"Ah, I get it." Ryann backed away, nodding slowly. "You *are* into them, but you're *not* into me. I thought you would walk when I told you about Jen. I just...I guess I hoped it could have been different." Ryann offered Lydia a weak, heartbreaking smile.

Lydia's heart ached in her chest. "God, I'm *so* into you, Ryann."

Ryann stared.

"But you have decisions to make and a child to raise. And while you do that, whether it's with Jen or not, I should probably vanish into the background."

Ryann barked a laugh. "W-what?"

"This isn't funny, Ry."

"No, it is. It's fucking hilarious." Ryann approached Lydia, slowly unbuttoning her blazer. Her eyes landed on Lydia's blouse. "Have you been crying in the bathroom?"

Lydia chewed her lip, closing her eyes briefly.

Ryann's hand found Lydia's chin, her fingers soft as she tilted Lydia's head to meet her eyes. "Hey, look at me." Ryann dipped her head, her sweet smile waiting for Lydia as their eyes met. "I don't *ever* want to find out that I made you cry in a bathroom again. Talk to me, tell me how you're feeling."

"This, Ryann. You've just told me that Jen is pregnant. How did you think I would react?"

"Lydia, Jen is not my business anymore."

"She's having your kid!"

"Is she?" Ryann asked. "She's having the kid of some dude whose sperm I helped her pick."

"But you were still involved in that process."

"I wasn't there when she made the decision, and I wasn't there when she had the insemination. Forgive me if I don't feel as though I should be there to support her." Ryann took Lydia's hand, guiding her towards the huge corner couch in the living room. The lights remained low, the moon high up in the sky providing a little more natural lighting around the space they shared. "Lydia, did you think I was going to break this off with you?"

"Mm."

"No way. There is no way that's going to happen." Ryann leaned in, kissing Lydia slowly, softly.

Lydia would spend her entire life kissing this woman if it was possible, but Jen did niggle at the back of her mind. Would Ryann always feel this way, or would Jen worm her way back in? Ryann was strong, independent, but Lydia knew how much she loved being around kids. In this moment, she didn't believe it was as cut and dry as Ryann believed it to be. Ryann pulled back, her thumb tracing Lydia's bottom lip. "I'm so sorry I upset you."

"I just..." Lydia shook her head.

"You what?"

"I know I probably sound stupid, but the thought of losing you—"

Ryann drew Lydia in, kissing her bottom lip, the tip of her nose, her forehead. "You won't lose me. Since I met you, you're all I think about. Jen is my past and she will stay there."

"She's not going to just disappear, Ryann."

"She can do as she pleases. You are who I want in my life, Lydia. This week, barely seeing you, it's been hard. And I know it hasn't been long, but I'm so looking forward to summer with you. Autumn. Winter, snuggled together. That's how far ahead I'm thinking, and I don't care if I'm foolish for doing that."

"I've thought about that, too."

"Good." Ryann stood up, pulling Lydia up with her. "Can we just enjoy dinner together and go from there? I've really been looking forward to this with you."

"You're sure about this?"

"When I came home today, I panicked that you'd run out on me when I told you I'd met with Jen. I should have told you this morning when we talked on the phone. For that, I'm sorry. But then I realised that you wouldn't just walk away without discussing it first, and now we've done that, I'm not worried about anything else."

"I can't believe she's going to get away with what she's done to you."

"I can't have a pregnant woman arrested, Lydia. I know exactly what she's done, but I couldn't do it. I'd never forgive myself."

"No, I know." Lydia wrapped her arms around Ryann, holding her close. "Thank you for being honest with me. Now I know what's happening, I won't get a shock when she turns up in several months with a kid in her arms."

"She doesn't know where I live, don't worry."

"That doesn't mean anything, but I'll be by your side when that time comes. Okay?"

"You know, I really appreciate that." Ryann guided Lydia back towards the dining table. "Did you maybe want to stay the night?"

"I'm meeting Sam at midday tomorrow, but I have nowhere to be before that, so I'd love to stay."

"I, uh..." Ryann turned back to face Lydia. "You know I don't want anyone else, don't you?"

Lydia shrugged. "I'm surprised I was ever lucky enough to get you. It wouldn't be a shock to me if I lost you to someone else."

"Babe..." Ryann smiled, her head cocked slightly. "I'm all yours. If you'll have me?"

Lydia squeezed Ryann's hand. "You know I will."

"So..." Ryann paused momentarily. "Exclusive?"

Lydia's heart jumped in her chest, her evening ending better than she thought it would. "I'd love that."

Ryann crossed the room, taking her Bon Jovi vinyl from the sleeve and placing it on the turntable. With the needle precisely in place, the sound of an electric guitar played out around the apartment, sending a rush of affection through Lydia's entire body. She wouldn't ever forget the night she sang to Ryann. Never.

Ryann turned around, holding out her hand to Lydia. "Dance with me?"

Lydia approached and Ryann took her in her arms. "I'd dance with you every second of the day."

CHAPTER TWENTY-THREE

This truly was the life. For Ryann, at least. As she lay flat out on the couch, the sound of her shower down the hallway powering off, Ryann could only imagine what she would be feeling if she had chosen to take Jen back. It wouldn't be this unbridled happiness, she was sure of that.

As the weeks passed, Jen continued to seek Ryann out. Usually at the studio, occasionally at the local deli, even hounding Sam for Ryann's new address. Sam had threatened her with legal action—she was smart that way—and Jen had slowly retreated. Ryann didn't expect that to be the end of it, but whatever came, she would face it head-on.

While life was good, Ryann spent her days and nights wrapped up in Lydia. It was hard not to when she had such a beautiful woman in her life. Lydia's beauty wasn't only external though, like most women Ryann had come across. No, beauty was laced throughout Lydia. It was pumping through her veins. If Ryann could bottle up how Lydia made her feel, she would never have to worry about a single thing again.

The sound of humming down the hallway caught Ryann's attention. She smiled as Lydia came strolling barefoot into the open space. Over the last three weeks, Ryann couldn't stop the smile she wore. At times her face hurt, but it was all worth it.

"What are you smirking at?" Lydia narrowed her eyes as she reached the kitchen, her hand on her hip.

"You. Because you're gorgeous."

"That's all you ever say."

Ryann sat up on her elbows and shrugged. "Because it's true."

"Mm. Sometimes I wonder if you're just trying to get in my pants when you tell me how gorgeous I am."

"I don't need to do that to get into your pants." Climbing from the couch, Ryann stalked towards Lydia and held out her hand. "And you know it."

"No, you're right." Lydia drew Ryann in, curling her finger under her chin and kissing her slowly. "But I really don't think I have the energy for you and your incredibly artistic body tonight." Lydia ran her palms down Ryann's bare arms, smiling. "So pretty."

"Like the woman in my life." Ryann winked, dragging Lydia towards the couch. "Did you have another late lunch today?"

"No. Sam showed up with Chinese. It was only a flying visit. I think Luce is beginning to struggle."

"Yeah, not long to go now."

"You know, when the time comes…I'd be happy to come and look after Luca with you. Or bring him here, whatever. Or to my place."

"That's sweet." Lydia flopped down beside Ryann, pulling her legs up and into Ryann's lap. Ryann's hands instinctively found Lydia's calves, massaging them like she did most evenings. "You feel a bit tense tonight, babe."

"A lot of standing 'round."

"You work in an office. At a computer. What are you standing around for?"

"Sam had me head my own presentation this morning to some investors of hers."

"Interesting," Ryann said.

"And, I nailed it."

"Of course you did, babe." Ryann kneaded a little deeper, rolling her eyes playfully when Lydia moaned. "So, you're settling in okay with Sam?"

"She's been amazing, Ry. Really. She's given me free reign over everything, and she loves the ideas I've given her so far for this new build she has coming up."

"She was supposed to be dropping her hours."

"She was only there for a couple of hours today. She didn't even stay for the lunch she brought me. But I suppose when you've been so focused on business for so long, it's hard to settle down and forget about it all."

"No, I know," Ryann agreed. "And don't say anything to Sam, but I overheard Luciana on a call the other day. I don't know if she's thinking about going back to the brigade."

"Beats going back to the escort agency."

Ryann trusted Lydia with her family's stories, and she'd told her everything. From Sam losing Lucia. To Janet, Luciana's ex-client, and everything in between. Janet hadn't been common knowledge until Luciana told Ryann about it one night over drinks when Sam was working. Ryann couldn't believe what Janet had put her through, the abuse and the suspended sentence, but that woman was well and truly out of their lives now. The prison stretch finally put the fear of God in her. But if she ever did show up in the city again, Ryann would be there, waiting for her own shot at the bitch who destroyed Luciana in many ways.

"I lost you there for a moment..."

"Sorry, I was just thinking about Luce."

"Everything okay?" Lydia scooted closer, almost sitting in Ryann's lap.

"Yeah. Just the thought of her going back to that agency. I know she wouldn't, she doesn't need to, but just the thought of it makes the hairs stand on the back of my neck."

"I can imagine."

"And as for the brigade," Ryann started. "I'm not sure how Sam will feel about that either."

"You said it had been a problem for them in the past..."

"Kinda. Yeah."

"Maybe you just overheard the conversation wrong. It happens."

"I hope so," Ryann said, exhaling a deep breath. "But tonight is about us." Ryann wrapped her arms around Lydia, making them both comfortable on the couch. Lasagne was in the oven, both were home from work, and it was Wednesday evening. "And I'm going to snuggle the shit out of you."

"Mm, sounds like the perfect kind of night." Lydia curled her body towards Ryann, nuzzling her face in her chest. "Did you have a good day?"

"Busy, but good."

"Heard anything from Jen?"

Ryann shifted slightly. Her ex's name coming from her girlfriend's mouth always left her feeling uncomfortable. "Just once today."

"That's something, I guess."

"I'd rather she wasn't calling at all," Ryann said, twisting and facing Lydia better. "And I don't want to talk about her anymore. She infuriates me."

"I'm sorry."

"Don't be." Ryann's lips gently caressed Lydia's, her hand gliding up and down Lydia's thigh. "You're by my side and that's what counts."

Lydia stacked the last of the plates into the dishwasher, her stomach full to bursting from the dinner Ryann had cooked. In all honesty, she would have eaten more if there was any left; Ryann really did have a knack for cooking up the most delicious food. Simple, but very satisfying.

Ryann had made one or two comments over the last few weeks about how this was all new for her, but it was for Lydia, too. It had been so long since she'd been in a committed relationship that she wasn't sure she could be somebody's everything again. Of course, Ryann instantly settled that, explaining that they would work it out together, but Lydia had never felt so at ease around anyone else. Gone were the days of spending her nights alone; now she had Ryann to keep her warm…wrapped up safely in her embrace pretty much every night.

Everything changed after Ryann told Lydia about Jen and her pregnancy. Sure, Lydia didn't like knowing that Ryann had an ex lingering in the background just ready and waiting to pounce, but Lydia believed that they felt enough for one another to overcome Jen and the child she was carrying.

Ryann had made it clear that the child in question had nothing to do with her. Lydia first thought that Ryann was in denial, but the more she thought about it, the more it made complete sense. The decision to not go any further with Jen's pregnancy was down to Ryann, and whatever Ryann chose, Lydia would stand by that.

Jen had really hurt Ryann with everything that happened between them, but to trap her through insemination was something Lydia couldn't quite understand. Did Jen really believe Ryann was stupid enough to go back to her? Evidently, she did. Ryann had promised Lydia she would be completely open and honest about how she felt regarding Jen and the pregnancy—Lydia couldn't ask for more than that.

"You need a hand here?" Ryann asked, stepping up behind Lydia and wrapping her arms around her waist. Ryann's lips found Lydia's neck, the sensation something Lydia was becoming accustomed to. "Or we could go and have wild, mind-numbing sex and clear the rest away later."

"You know I like to have everything cleared away before we settle down for the night."

"I know," Ryann whispered, "but I've been thinking about you all day."

"I thought you had work to do. A design for your client."

Ryann nipped at Lydia's neck. "All done."

Lydia turned in Ryann's arms, resting her arms over her shoulders. "Hey, can I ask you something?"

"You know you can."

"My first meeting with Sam…she said you didn't have anyone else."

"Works for me." Ryann shrugged, a defensiveness in her tone kicking in. "I've never really needed anyone."

"And that's fine. But do you really have no one other than Sam?"

Ryann frowned. "I have my mum."

"Oh." This was new information to Lydia. Ryann never spoke about her mum. "Well, uh…"

"She's living in Crete." Ryann unravelled from Lydia's body, heading for the couch.

"That's nice."

"For her, yeah." Ryann snorted. "I'm sure she's living her best life while I'm stuck here."

Lydia chose her next response very carefully. While she felt a little offended by Ryann's comment, she was sure Ryann didn't mean it. She was also sure Ryann had a perfectly good explanation for why she didn't talk about her mum. Actually, either of her parents.

"You want to be in Crete?" Lydia chewed her cheek, wiping her hands on a towel before joining Ryann in the living room. "With your mum?"

"I was never invited."

"Okay, I don't know what that means."

"She went out there for a holiday around eight months ago. I offered to go with her, but she said she wanted to go alone. That she'd like to explore and spend some time by herself. I thought that was kinda brave of her. You know, going alone?"

Lydia nodded, getting comfortable beside Ryann.

"A month later, she called me. Told me she was staying there and that she'd met some ex-pat."

"That's the cutest story."

Ryann laughed as she shook her head. "No, it's not."

"Oh, come on. You must have been happy for her." Lydia didn't understand Ryann's lack of support for her mother.

Ryann stared at Lydia, confusion in her eyes. "Why would I be happy for her? She fucked off and decided to tell me she wasn't coming back. It had been her plan all along. They'd been talking online for almost a year. She was just waiting for the right time to leave."

"Oh."

"Yeah, oh."

"So, you don't speak anymore?" Lydia felt sad for Ryann. As much as she wished to be in Spain with her own parents, and as much as she held that small hint of jealousy, Lydia would never fall out with them over it. The difference here was that Lydia *had* been invited to move to Spain with her mum and dad. Ryann hadn't.

"I email her once a month. You know, exchange pleasantries and tell her I hope she's well. I usually get a short response with the latest picture of them together. I'm not really interested, to be honest. She didn't once tell me what she was going to do and I'm not sure I can forgive her for that. It was always just me and her."

"Does she know about the river?"

"Nope. And she'll never know. She doesn't *need* to know."

Lydia chose not to push Ryann. She was in a good place now. "Your dad?"

"Never met him," Ryann said, shrugging. "Mum claims she doesn't know who he is either."

"You don't believe her?"

"I suppose I do." Ryann sat forward, running her fingers through her hair. "I did try to look for him, but he wasn't on my birth certificate, so I don't have anything to go on."

"Sorry, Ry."

"I can't miss something I've never had. I can't have a connection to someone I don't know exists. I mean, obviously he does exist, but in my world...not so much."

Lydia didn't realise just how little Ryann had in her life in terms of family. Now that they were much better acquainted, Lydia believed she had a place to ask. She no longer felt as though she would be intruding if she questioned any of Ryann's past. A past she really didn't discuss.

"Is this why you're kind of a loner?"

"Wow, you're just reeling off the questions tonight. Am I going to need a therapist by the end of it all?" Ryann laughed, but Lydia recognised it to be nerves. Was she wrong for enquiring?

"Hey, I'm just trying to get a little insight into your life. I don't care what did or didn't happen, I just want to know everything there is to know about you."

"I'm a loner because during my late teens, I was attacked on the street. Twice." Ryann's body language changed, her shoulders curling inward as though she was protecting herself. Telling Lydia this...it had to be painful.

"W-what?" Lydia shot forward, her hand settling on Ryann's back. "Attacked?"

"I guess I just had that look about me. People assumed they knew me, knew I was gay, and chose to attack me for it. Once was outside the studio while I was still an apprentice. In broad daylight, too. The other happened at night when I was coming out of a gay bar. The friends I was with that night didn't stay around for me. I was left alone with a broken nose after being pushed face first into the floor.

"But that was okay. By losing them, I learned I didn't need them in my life. I didn't want friends who wouldn't have my back.

It's much easier to close myself off from people who only want me around when they need something than to appease people and pretend I like their company. But yeah, there's nothing like a homophobic attack to show you who really is in your corner. Turns out...nobody."

"Oh, Ry."

"So, I'm not a loner because I'm a weirdo who doesn't like people. I just find it hard to trust people. If I don't know what they're truly about, I keep them at arm's length. And for the last several years of my life, living by that has worked out pretty well for me."

"Completely understandable."

"And I've just never really been much of a people person. Our Sam is the same. She has a very small group of friends."

"But Ryann, I've never seen you with *any* friends. You don't talk about anyone."

Ryann glanced at Lydia over her shoulder, offering a small smile. "Because I'm quite happy with my life the way it is."

"Of course. Yeah."

Lydia slumped back against the couch. It was no surprise Ryann ended up at the river that night. She had nowhere to turn. Her mum had in some way abandoned her, and she had no friends to speak of. Lydia couldn't imagine going through an episode of cheating *and* a debt crisis with no support.

Lydia had told Ryann that she needed a new circle of friends the night they met, but she hadn't anticipated this. Ryann didn't need a *new* circle of friends, she just needed...friends.

Lydia chewed her lip. She needed to ask Ryann another question. One she believed was necessary. "Ryann?"

"Yeah?"

"Do you think you *should* see a therapist?" Lydia knew what was coming, but she still asked regardless. "I mean, I know you're feeling a lot better, and that's amazing, but with everything that's happened over the years, it could be a good idea."

Ryann shrugged. "I've managed before."

"I really don't want you to *manage* though," Lydia explained. "I want you to be happy, with friends, and whatever else you're missing in your life."

"Trust me," Ryann side-glanced at Lydia, "I'm not missing a single thing in my life. I have you. I have Sam, Luce, and their family."

"I know, it's just..."

Ryann held up a hand, shaking her head. "I really don't need therapy. If I *ever* feel like I did the other month, I promise I'll tell you."

"Have you had more than one episode of feeling that way?"

"No. That was the first time."

"Well..." Lydia paused. "We have each other now. And I couldn't be happier about that." She could beg Ryann to seek therapy until she was blue in the face, but it wouldn't necessarily make her sit up and listen.

Only Ryann could make that decision for herself. Lydia wasn't qualified, nor was Sam, to make any kind of assessment—mental health wise or other. Lydia could only pray that Ryann was being truthful when she told her she didn't need therapy. Lydia still thought it was a good idea regardless of the fact that Ryann was well at the moment. "I'm really happy."

"Me too, babe." Ryann fell back beside Lydia and into her arms. "Me too."

CHAPTER TWENTY-FOUR

"Hi, Mum." Lydia flopped down onto her bed, her laundry strewn across it. "I've been trying to contact you."

"Sorry, love. We've had a storm the last few days. The WiFi was iffy so I couldn't email you back."

"But you and Dad are okay?"

"We are, love. And you?"

"Mum, I'm so good." Lydia grinned, her body relaxing into her bed. She had so much to tell her parents, her mum especially. They'd always had a great relationship, more of a sister bond than mother and daughter.

"Oh?" Julia's voice held a questioning tone.

"You remember I emailed you a few months ago to tell you about the woman I met at the river?"

"I do. I'm still very proud of you for what you did. That poor girl must have been going out of her mind to end up in a position like that."

"Well...she's my girlfriend now."

"S-she's what?" Lydia's mum asked. "Did you just say she's your girlfriend?"

"I did, Mum. And you will *absolutely* love her. She's just... God, she's perfect."

"Well, that's some story to tell your kids," Julia said. "And she's okay now? She's worked through her issues? Therapy, I assume?"

"It wasn't quite like that, no. Ryann didn't go to therapy. I suggested it to her, but her cousin stepped in to help. She was having money troubles, through no fault of her own."

"O...kay."

"Her ex-girlfriend. She just...she wasn't great. Ran up a lot of debt in Ryann's name that Ryann didn't know about. She lost her business and stuff and felt she had no way out of it."

"Oh, love. That's awful."

"But she has her business back. And her cousin, Sam...well, she's just amazing."

"She certainly sounds it."

"She got me a new job," Lydia explained, the sound of waves crashing in the background. "Mum, are you at the beach?"

"We are. Dad was meeting with a friend here, so I thought I'd have myself a glass of wine."

"Did you want me to call you later?"

"No, I want to hear all about this new job! You know, the one I didn't know you were looking for."

"I wasn't looking, not really. But you know how much I don't like Bree."

"Mm, I know." Julia's voice changed. Lydia had a very honest relationship with her mother. There were no secrets. Usually, before Ryann, Julia was the one Lydia turned to. Even though an ocean separated them, Julia was still on hand to be there for her daughter.

"Well, Sam got me out of *Strive*. She gave me an office in her building. You know the developers, Phillips & Priestly?"

"Oh, those fancy developers?"

"Yes, well, it's Sam's company."

Lydia reeled off everything that had happened in the last few weeks.

"Well, it sounds like you've landed on your feet, Lydia. It would seem to me that you were supposed to meet Ryann when you did."

"You think?"

Julia had always been a firm believer in the universe playing a part in people's lives. Lydia believed it too to some extent. But meeting Ryann...she never saw that coming.

"Oh, yes. And I want to know all there is to know about Ryann. You said she has a business?"

"She does, but Mum? Can we discuss it another time? I got out of the office early today, so I was planning to surprise Ryann. She's been working all week."

"Of course. Go and spend the weekend with your Ryann."

Lydia sighed, smiling wider. "My Ryann."

"Well, that's what she is, no?"

"She is, Mum," Lydia agreed. "She really is."

Lydia pushed through the door of Dark Angel, excitement bubbling away in her belly. Knowing her mum was happy for her made a world of difference, but it wouldn't have changed anything if she hadn't been happy or given her blessing. Lydia would struggle to accept anyone's opinion when it came to her relationships and love.

Because that's what this was.

Love.

Lydia wasn't a fool, she knew Ryann couldn't possibly feel the same way, but that didn't matter. She could love Ryann without it being returned right now. Ryann probably had far too much on her plate to have the chance to fall for Lydia.

A month on since they finally gave in and decided to try out a relationship, Lydia was falling faster than she knew she should. She wasn't worried, though—Ryann would never hurt her. This, and everything they had to come, would happen when it happened. Lydia could tell Ryann how she felt and hope that it didn't scare her off, or she could wait until the time was right. She chose the latter as she took a seat in the waiting area.

We have forever. There's no need to rush.

Lydia had thought about discussing her feelings with Soph, but she wasn't sure it required a discussion. Lydia had fallen in love; what needed to be discussed? No reason in the world could stop her feelings for Ryann, nothing ever would.

Shona came from the back of the studio, a strange smile on her mouth. "H-hi, uh...Ryann is just busy a minute."

"That's fine. She wasn't expecting me."

Shona nodded, clearing her throat. "You know, you should really call before you show up. If she's working on a big design, you'd be sitting here for hours."

"Well," Lydia shrugged, "I don't have anywhere to be, so I don't mind waiting."

"Right. Okay."

Shona chewed her lip, flicking through the appointment book. Lydia watched her body language change. She appeared to be uncomfortable. After a moment, she lifted her head. "Why don't you go out and grab you and Ryann some lunch? She's been working a lot today and I know she'd appreciate it if you showed up here with a sandwich or something for her."

"She hasn't had the chance to eat?" Lydia turned her watch towards her. "It's almost three."

Shona shrugged. "The life of a tattoo artist."

Lydia sat for a moment longer. She contemplated ordering a delivery, not wanting to miss Ryann once she was available. "I'll give it another ten minutes."

Ryann rocked back in her office chair; her hands clasped behind her head. Jen had somehow managed to catch her at the studio while she was available and now she was refusing to leave until they'd talked.

"I really don't know why you're here," Ryann said, glancing down at Jen's pregnant belly.

Jen followed Ryann's eyes. "I'm showing kinda early. I didn't think I would be yet."

"That's none of my business." Ryann's eyes shot up, aware that she'd been staring too long. "Why can't you just get on with your life and leave me to mine, Jen?"

"I've been trying to get you for five minutes for weeks now. I have something for you." Jen dipped her hand inside her bag, pulling out a white envelope. "We're even now, okay?"

"What?" Ryann frowned, taking the envelope from Jen. "What is this?"

"It's every penny I owe you. I paid ten off myself a few weeks ago. This is the rest of it. It's a cheque. Should only take a few days to clear."

"How did you find this kind of money?"

"Mum," Jen said. "And I'm leaving. I'm moving down to Bristol with her. She's going to give me a hand with this one. I have a job interview next week."

"Your mum? Why did you take it all out in the first place if your mum already had this kind of money, Jen?"

"Honestly?" Jen sighed, running her fingers through her hair. "I don't know. Because I saw the extra zeros in my bank account. Because I was getting away with it. The plan was always to pay it back before you even noticed, but then you found the letters."

"Wow." This woman really had some nerve. If Jen had been in debt, Ryann would have helped her out. But to know that she did this purely because she could—because she was getting away with it—Ryann didn't know whether to let it go and move on or punch the nearest wall.

She chose to remain calm. Her life had been that way recently, Jen wasn't about to come in and disrupt it all once again.

"But, Ryann...this is everything I owe you."

"Well." Ryann nodded slowly. "Thanks, I guess."

"I am sorry, Ry." Jen leaned forward, squeezing Ryann's knee. "I've made a lot of mistakes in the past, but what I did to you was the worst. Losing you...I've been so stupid."

Ryann glanced up at Jen. For the first time in many months, she seemed sincere. "T-this doesn't change anything, you know."

"I know. I lost you."

"But I do wish you well. I hope you can rebuild things in Bristol. Living with your mum...it could be good for you."

"When the time comes...do you want me to let you know?" Jen placed her hand on her belly, a faint smile on her lips. "Maybe send you a picture or something?"

A sadness settled in Ryann. One she hadn't expected to feel. Jen had almost sent Ryann over the edge, but in the beginning, it had been good. It had been exactly what Ryann wanted. Still, she knew she should distance herself. Lydia was by her side now. Ryann wouldn't make her feel uncomfortable by staying in touch with Jen.

"I think it's probably best if you don't."

"Right." Jen lowered her eyes. "Well, I should go. Let you get back to doing what you do best."

"Yeah. I need to eat and then get home." Ryann stood, showing Jen to the door. "I have two more appointments and then I'm out of here."

Lydia scrolled through the delivery options on the app on her phone. She wasn't sure what Ryann would feel like, but Chinese was usually a good option. At least, it sounded better than the boring sandwich Ryann had most days for lunch. Lydia had offered—on multiple occasions—to prepare a lunch for Ryann for the following day, but Ryann had yet to take up that offer, explaining that she didn't want to put Lydia out.

"Okay, Shona...Chinese or that new Mexican down the road?"

"The Chinese is nearer. Won't take you long to get there and back," Shona said, her eyes drifting towards Ryann's closed office door.

"I was planning on having it delivered so it doesn't really matter."

"Right."

Lydia narrowed her eyes. "Is something going on that I don't know about?"

"What?" Shona's brow creased. "No. Don't be stupid."

"Because it seems like you're trying to get me out of here and—"

Ryann's office door opened slowly, the sound of more than one voice reaching Lydia's ears. Lydia remained in her seat, watching as Ryann left her office, a blonde woman following behind her. Lydia didn't know who she was, until her eyes travelled lower to find a slight bump.

Everything within Lydia shuddered, Ryann's hand now resting on the bump as she smiled. What the hell was going on? Lydia tried to remain positive, she had to, but then she watched Jen lift both hands to Ryann's face and lean in. Their lips met. It was a slow, single kiss, but it was a kiss, nonetheless.

Lydia wanted the expensive leather couch to swallow her whole.

Ryann lowered her eyes as Jen stepped back and walked away, but Lydia couldn't move from her seat. Ryann wasn't even aware that Lydia was in the waiting area. She felt Shona's eyes on her, but Lydia's world was beginning to slow as Jen approached her.

Their eyes met, Jen smiled sweetly, and then she left the studio.

"I, uh..." Lydia got to her feet, shaking her head as Ryann's eyes landed on her. They were wide. Very wide. "I've just remembered that I had something I needed to do," she said, throwing her thumb over her shoulder as Ryann opened her mouth to speak.

Lydia returned her focus to Shona. She looked as though she was about to break down for Lydia. That wouldn't be necessary, though; Lydia could manage breaking down all by herself. Once she left the studio.

"R-Ryann is finished now," Shona said, offering the weakest of smiles. She looked like a deer caught in headlights. "Go through."

"No, thank you." Lydia just needed to keep her voice level for a few more moments. "Thanks for keeping me company, but now I know why."

"No, Lydia. It wasn't like that." Shona switched to Ryann; clearly she needed help here. "Lydia's here, Ry," Shona said, her voice upping an octave.

"Ryann knows I'm here." Lydia's stomach flipped, the idea that Ryann was going back to Jen playing on her mind. "See you, Ryann."

Lydia backed up and took her messenger bag from the floor beside the couch. She didn't know where she was going or what her plan was, but she needed air and some space. The more she stared at Ryann, the more she felt dread searing through her. This feeling wasn't what she expected today.

Lydia turned and walked out the door, the fresh air hitting her cheeks at the same time her tears did. If she just kept walking, this would all be over in no time. If she just kept her head down and her mind focused on something other than Ryann, she would be okay.

But then her vision blurred as the tears came faster. She stopped for a moment, leaning back against the wall next to the deli, praying Ryann wouldn't come out after her. Lydia's chest felt tight, her breathing faster than she would have liked it to be. She placed her palms flat against the wall; she needed to feel grounded.

"Lydia!" Ryann rushed towards her, sheer panic in her eyes. "Please come back inside the studio."

"I have to go." Lydia threw her thumb over her shoulder, turning to leave.

"Wait, babe. Please?" Ryann's hand settled on Lydia's wrist, her grip remaining when Lydia didn't turn around. "What you've just seen back there...it really wasn't what you think it is."

"You just stood there." Lydia turned around to face Ryann; her forehead creased. Of all the situations in the world, this wasn't the one she thought she would find herself in today. Everything hurt. Her joints, her stomach, her head. "She kissed you, and you just stood there and took it."

"It wasn—"

"While you caressed her bump," Lydia said, her voice barely audible.

Ryann dropped her head and Lydia's wrist. "Fuck."

"Yeah. Fuck." Lydia turned on her heel and left Ryann standing in the street.

She didn't look back, she didn't slow, she simply powered down the main road and towards her car. The best she could do right now was work. After all, nobody could hurt her while she was locked away in her office. Ryann...she couldn't hurt her.

CHAPTER TWENTY-FIVE

The sun beamed through Lydia's office window, her mood not lifting from the grim churning in her stomach. She'd come to work, locked the office door, and remained still behind her desk. She hadn't even bothered to turn on her computer; she had no energy for work today.

Lydia could have gone home, she could have called Soph, but she just wanted to be alone. Home was a no-go anyway; Ryann would head there before anywhere else. As much as she wanted to believe that kiss meant nothing, she was struggling with the image. If Ryann hadn't wanted Jen to kiss her, she wouldn't have lingered. If Ryann felt nothing for her ex, she wouldn't have been alone with her in her office.

Ryann promised to be transparent with Lydia when it came to Jen. She had to be—the woman was carrying a child that should have been Ryann's. But that promise had been broken. As far as Lydia knew, Ryann had been avoiding Jen for many weeks. Maybe Lydia had been stupid to believe that, Ryann wasn't exactly hard to find. Jen only had to show up at the studio and she would find Ryann working away.

A knock on the door pulled Lydia from the hurt. She chose to ignore it. Nobody knew she was here; it was her afternoon off.

Another knock.

"Lydia? You in?" Sam's voice crept through the door. "Lydia?"

"Just a minute." Lydia wiped her eyes, checking the small mirror in her top drawer for mascara stains. She'd learned from last time—waterproof was her only option.

Lydia opened the door to find Sam smiling back at her. "I saw your car out front. Why are you still here?"

"Just thought I'd work through the afternoon."

"You'd already left to meet Ryann when I was leaving at lunch."

"And now I'm back," Lydia said, offering Sam a fake smile. "Did you need something, or…?"

"No, I guess not." Sam sighed, eyeing Lydia. "So, I was thinking of doing dinner tomorrow. You and Ryann joining us?"

"Oh, I have plans." Lydia moved back into her office, leaving Sam to decide if she was joining her or not. "I haven't seen much of Soph over the last few weeks. I thought I'd better make plans with her before she starts complaining that I'm not being a good enough friend."

"Oh, okay."

Lydia dug her nails into her palms, she needed to keep her composure until Sam left. Just the mention of Ryann's name hurt her heart. Perhaps things would work out okay, Lydia didn't know, but in this moment…she felt as though she'd just lost Ryann. Honestly, it shouldn't hurt like it did.

"Well, I'm assuming Ryann will be with you then…"

Lydia moved towards the huge window in her office, wrapping her arms around herself as she watched the boats bobbing up and down on the river. "Not that I'm aware of."

"Lydia, you seem a little distant today. Is everything okay?"

"Sure. Tired, you know?"

"You should go home. Relax and unwind. Call Ryann and have her come over to run you a bath."

Lydia closed her eyes, tears threatening to fall once again. "Ryann's busy."

"After work."

"Sam..."

Sam closed the door, the sound of her heels slowly crossing the distance between them. She placed her hand on Lydia's shoulder. "What's going on?"

"Nothing, don't worry." Lydia wiped her cheeks as she shook her head. "Everything will be fine."

"Did something happen?"

"From where I was standing, yeah."

"Sit down. You look like you're about to fall down."

Lydia took a seat at her desk, surprised when Sam crouched down in front of her.

"Just...I went to the studio. Ryann came out of her office with Jen."

Sam looked up to the ceiling, exhaling a deep breath. "Why do some women insist on interfering with my fucking family!"

"Sam, it's okay. Ryann didn't seem bothered that she was there. Maybe they're on good terms now or something, I don't know."

"Ryann wouldn't be friends with her. Not after what she put her through."

"Right," Lydia snorted. "The kiss mustn't have happened then."

"K-kiss?" Sam's eyebrow rose as she gripped Lydia's knees. "What kiss?"

"Ryann didn't realise I was there; I'd gone there to surprise her. She was very hands on with Jen's baby bump...and then Jen kissed her."

Sam shook her head. "Ryann wouldn't have wanted that kiss."

"Perhaps not, but she didn't pull away either."

"You know, she fucking infuriates me at times." Sam breathed deep through her nose, climbing to her feet. "You want me to speak to her?"

"No. I don't want you to do anything, Sam. Please, this is between me and Ryann."

Sam held up her hands. "Okay."

Lydia took her phone from her desk and picked up her bag. "I'm just going to head home, okay? If Ryann calls or shows up here…you haven't seen me."

"Lydia."

"I just need some space, Sam. A night to myself."

"Okay, fair enough."

Lydia leaned in and hugged Sam. "But thank you for offering to be a shoulder."

"I'll call you tonight, okay?"

Lydia sighed. She wasn't sure she would be in the mood for talking later. "Sure. Okay."

Ryann rocked back and forth, sitting on Lydia's front step with her head in her hands. That kiss from Jen meant nothing at all. It wasn't even a kiss that could be considered to mean something. At least, not to Ryann. It was more of a goodbye, an apology, than anything else. Jen was leaving, and Ryann was happy about that. Well, she was supposed to be happy. Instead she felt filled with dread.

She could understand Lydia's reaction; she herself hadn't expected Jen to show up. But Ryann needed the opportunity to explain. Lydia had to give her that before deciding to walk away. Usually, Ryann would sit back and allow her life to fall apart, but not this time. Lydia meant far too much to her.

This last month had been incredible in every way imaginable for Ryann. She'd slowly learned what Lydia liked and what she didn't. She knew that the spot on her lower back towards her right hip was her biggest erogenous zone. The reaction Ryann received when she ventured there was enough to stop her heart momentarily. She knew that she would never have the opportunity to watch a horror movie with Lydia—the terror Lydia expressed just at the mention was enough to explain that. She knew that when Lydia was seven, she was caught stealing a Mars Bar from the local shop. As terrible as theft was, Ryann couldn't help but smile at the image it conjured up, Lydia terrified as she peered over the counter and handed it back.

She knew that Lydia wanted to travel over the next year or two before settling down to have kids. That Thailand was her destination of choice before anywhere else. The thought of Ryann experiencing that with Lydia sent her heart rate soaring.

And then there were the little things. How Lydia preferred her coffee at particular times of the day. Morning usually meant a strong coffee, little milk with two sugars. Throughout the day she would swap to a smaller cup, but still drink just as much—Lydia claimed she wasn't drinking the same amount, though. And then at night she preferred a chai tea, perhaps a glass of wine if it had been a long day.

All of this probably meant nothing to some people. Just standard knowledge of the woman you're dating. But to Ryann, this was important. She couldn't even recall how Jen took her coffee and they'd been together much longer than Ryann had been with Lydia. It was also important because it reassured Ryann in her own mind that Lydia was the one for her.

Over the years, dating had dwindled. She believed she'd got lucky with Jen, but really it was the fantasy and magical life she lived in Australia. Ryann had met Jen during surfing lessons—Jen being her teacher. At a time when Ryann didn't have a care in the world, her studio doing more than well, Ryann went full steam ahead into the relationship, declaring her love for Jen before she even knew what she truly felt.

But Lydia was different. Ryann knew this was the real deal. Lydia hadn't once demanded anything from her other than her time and attention. She didn't throw hints at Ryann about a new pair of shoes she'd come across in town. She didn't discuss finances like Jen had. Lydia was every woman's ideal woman. Ryann couldn't exactly put her finger on why or how, but it was true.

Lydia Nelson had become Ryann's everything.

An engine cut out, the radio blasting through the closed windows and providing a dull thump. Ryann knew it was Lydia when the hairs on her arms stood on end the moment the door opened. As much as Ryann wanted to rush out the gate and take Lydia in her arms, she remained still and silent. Whatever came next would be on Lydia's terms.

"Oh." Lydia froze at the gate, staring down at Ryann. "I thought you'd still be at the studio."

"You really thought I'd finish work without looking for you?"

"Ryann, I don't really want to do this right now. My head is throbbing, and I just want to get inside and spend some time alone."

"Okay." Ryann got to her feet, brushing non-existent dust from the back of her jeans. "I'll let you be."

"Thank you," Lydia said quietly, squeezing past Ryann and moving towards the front door.

The sound of the key grinding in the lock sent a torrent of sadness through Ryann. She had to at least apologise before Lydia disappeared inside.

She cleared her throat. "Lydia?"

"Yeah?" Lydia spun around; her long, black hair tousled over her shoulder.

"Can I just say what I came here to say before I leave?"

Lydia nodded slowly; Ryann noticed she'd been crying.

"Thanks, uh…" Ryann scuffed her foot across the concrete, her hands falling into her back pockets, the leather jacket Lydia bought her hanging off her shoulders. "I made a mistake today.

One I'm pretty sure is about to shape my future. But, I just...I need you to know how sorry I am. It wasn't supposed to happen. I didn't *want* it to happen. Jen caught me off guard, and I know it's no excuse, but I'm not really used to this kind of thing."

Lydia frowned. "What thing?"

"Having women fighting over me."

"I'm not fighting over you," Lydia said, her tone level. "I don't have the energy or the desire to fight over anyone. That's not the type of relationship I want."

"No, I know that. I just mean that I'm not used to having *anyone* interested in me, let alone two people," Ryann explained. "I'm not worth the fight, I can assure you of that, but when you go inside your place now, I need you to believe that I never wanted Jen to kiss me. I never wanted her in the studio at all. She just...she showed up. She told me she really needed to see me.

"And maybe I was stupid to give her a second of my time, but it worked out in the end...kind of. She came to tell me she'd cleared the debt and that she was leaving for Bristol. She'd come to say goodbye. And that's all the kiss was. It wasn't anything other than her saying goodbye."

Ryann wasn't sure she was making any sense, her excuse feeble, but she had no idea why Jen had kissed her so that was the best she could come up with.

Lydia continued to stare, showing no interest in what Ryann was saying.

"I'm not sure who you think I am, Lydia, but I can safely say that I'm *not* some womaniser. I don't have a long list of women I've had in my bed. Christ, I've been in three relationships and that's all. I've never cheated, and I never would. I know how cruel it is and how hard it is to deal with. I'd never do anything to hurt you, Lydia. Not intentionally. You mean far too much to me. After everything you've done for me, I just...I couldn't ever do anything to hurt you."

"Are you only saying all of this...I mean, are you with me...b-because you feel obligated?"

"No." Ryann lowered her eyes. "No. Never."

Ryann wanted to reach out and pull Lydia into her arms. She wanted to kiss her until the sun began to rise. God, she wanted to do so much. But she couldn't. The distance between them felt greater than it had when Ryann kissed her and walked away. This... Ryann wasn't sure she was coming back from it.

So, she stepped forward, took two steps up to reach Lydia, and kissed her softly on the cheek. "If you think you can forgive me, call me." Ryann took a step back, staring directly into Lydia's pained eyes. "Because I'm in love with you, Lydia. And I don't want a meaningless kiss to ruin this. *Us.*" Lydia remained silent; her expression emotionless. "I am sorry. Have a nice weekend."

Ryann turned and left Lydia's garden path as quickly as she could. Just three months ago, she didn't think she would ever utter the words "I love you" again. She didn't believe it to be possible. But Lydia showed up at a time when she didn't know which way was up, didn't know whether she could keep fighting day in day out. Lydia showed up and Ryann fell. Hard.

CHAPTER TWENTY-SIX

Lydia stood in the motionless lift, wary of the fact that she had just effectively broken into Bryant Tower. Yes, Sam gave her the code some time ago, but she hadn't used it since. Whenever Lydia visited Ryann, she'd buzzed her way in. Now, standing with puffy red eyes and a lack of sleep evident in her appearance, Lydia started to panic.

It wasn't about the code; it was the fact that she was about to see Ryann for the first time since Friday. Lydia had been a coward —and a bitch—when Ryann had waited for her on the doorstep. And then Ryann uttered those words, the words Lydia didn't believe she would hear any time in the near future, but Lydia allowed Ryann to leave anyway.

For two days, Lydia had replayed that moment in her mind. As she lay in bed, when she showered. While sinking a bottle of wine that night she had toyed with the idea of calling. During breakfast the following morning, Lydia's desperation only grew. Yet here she was, Sunday afternoon, with no idea what was about to happen. In an ideal world, Ryann would forgive her for not showing sooner, but this wasn't an ideal world. This was a world in which Lydia felt tiny. Like she'd gone unnoticed this entire weekend.

That wasn't necessarily a bad thing, not at all, but Ryann didn't deserve to wait an entire two days before Lydia could bring herself to communicate. The fact that she needed to process wasn't Ryann's problem; Lydia shouldn't have made it that. She knew Ryann would be wondering what was happening—she too had wondered the same thing over the last forty-eight hours—but Lydia had finally taken the step to show up. Now she had to pray Ryann would accept her.

She pressed the button for the floor she required, her belly whooshing as the lift carriage did the same thing. She really didn't feel so good right now. But Lydia knew—whatever the outcome—that just seeing Ryann would put her at ease. She knew that the moment the front door opened, everything would fall into place. It had to. This couldn't be it for them.

The bell signalled Lydia's arrival and her blood ran cold. So cold that she shivered as she stepped out into the corridor. Ryann's front door was just a few feet away from her, so close she could almost touch it. Lydia just needed to move her legs and she could be on her way to doing exactly that.

Lydia paused for a moment, flexing her fingers as she rolled her head on her shoulders. She'd felt tense since the moment she stood up in Ryann's studio; she really needed it to budge. She pressed her back against the wall, allowing her head to fall back as she stared up at the bright spotlight above her.

She couldn't recall a time when she'd felt such anxiety, but she'd brought it on herself. All weekend she'd worried, panicked, that Ryann would close the door in her face. Instead of thinking positive and believing that they could talk through this, she'd thought up the worst-case scenario and gone with it.

The sound of a lock turning caught her attention, Lydia's forehead creased as she tried to determine which door it had come from.

And then Ryann's door opened.

Ryann rushed out, locking the door quickly. As she turned, her eyes landed on Lydia.

"Hi." Lydia smiled weakly, toying with the car key in her hand.

"Hi, uh...I'm sorry, but I can't talk right now. I have to get to Sam's. Luciana went into labour."

"Oh. That's great," Lydia said. "Well, wish her good luck from me, yeah?"

Ryann ran her fingers through her hair, her eyes circled with dark rings. "I will, yeah."

Ryann bounced on the balls of her feet as she pressed the call button on the lift. Lydia stood beside her, aware that there was one hell of an atmosphere between them, but their discussion could wait. A woman in labour was far more important than Lydia's feelings today.

They both took the same carriage, the doors slamming closed as they descended Bryant Tower.

Lydia opened her mouth to speak, falling short of any words.

She sighed, closing her eyes as she shook her head. Ryann's focus remained fully on the metal doors; this didn't feel very positive.

The bell once again sounded out, the doors opening.

"Ryann?" Lydia followed Ryann out to the front of the building, desperately needing some kind of communication with her. "I know you have a lot going on and I'm last on that list, but would it be okay if I called you? Maybe this evening or something?"

Lydia was clutching at straws. She was holding onto whatever she could.

"I'm sure you don't have the time, what with taking care of Luca and waiting on news from Sam, but—"

A taxi pulled up next to Ryann.

"You know, never mind. I hope everything goes well for Sam and Luciana. I just...I'll see you around."

"I'm sorry, I really have to go." Ryann's shoulders sagged as she exhaled a deep breath. "But, yeah. Call me later."

Lydia's entire body relaxed hearing those words. "Did you want me to drive you to Sam's?"

"No, thank you. The taxi is already here."

Lydia nodded, lowering her eyes. "Okay."

"I really have to go," Ryann said, hesitating as she stepped towards Lydia. "Bye." Ryann leaned in, pressing a kiss to Lydia's cheek. "I'll speak to you tonight."

Ryann lightly kissed Luca's head, fixing his blanket how he liked it before stepping out of his room, a dim light shining in the corner. Luca didn't understand what was going on, or why his parents were rushing around a few hours ago, but Ryann was satisfied that he was settled and would likely remain asleep for most of the night. It didn't matter; she would snuggle with her little man any time she could.

Sam had called, explaining that Luciana had been admitted to the maternity ward, and now they all just had to wait. It could be a couple of hours, it could be tomorrow. Ryann had already called Shona and explained that she wouldn't be at the studio this week; she wanted to be here for her family after everything Sam had done for her. Shona had called one of the freelance artists, and he would be taking one of the rooms for any walk-ins they had. Ryann had kept her schedule light over the last week, knowing that Luciana could go into labour at any moment. Sam had told her not to worry, that she would send Luca to her parents, but Ryann wanted to help out.

She crept down the spiral staircase, the quiet of the house not really what Ryann needed this evening. She didn't want to be alone with her thoughts—or alone at all—but here she was. Alone, as usual. She should be used to the loneliness by now; it was becoming a common theme in her life, but she hated it.

Since meeting Lydia, Ryann had felt completely consumed by

happiness and friendship. Once their relationship blossomed, she felt a tremendous amount of love. Not necessarily an *in love* kind of love, but just love. Now, she wasn't sure what she felt. Other than loneliness this weekend, Ryann couldn't put her finger on her true feelings.

She loved Lydia, she meant it when she told her that on Friday, but she would be lying if she said she expected anything back from that declaration. She understood Lydia's need to process—she'd still witnessed Ryann kissing another woman however meaningless it was—but even a text message explaining that she needed space would have sufficed.

That lack of contact really wasn't what Ryann expected.

She took her phone from the island in the kitchen, surprised to find a message from Lydia.

L: Any news on Luce?

Ryann smiled; Lydia was fond of Sam and Luciana.

R: No, not yet. Sam said she would call if things changed.

L: Would you keep me updated? I know you have no reason to do that, but I really would appreciate it.

Ryann chewed her lip. Lydia hadn't actually done anything wrong. A lack of communication didn't mean she didn't want her around. And she *more* than wanted Lydia around.

R: You could come over and wait to hear anything here with me...

L: You wouldn't mind?

Ryann paused for a moment. She needed Lydia to understand that she wasn't blowing her off earlier. She really had to get to Sam's place for Luca.

R: I miss you.

A little bubble appeared. Ryann suddenly froze. Would Lydia feel the same way?

L: I miss you, too.

R: So, come over?

L: I'm on my way.

Ryann smiled as she locked her phone, moving towards the window and focusing on the twinkly lights on the decking. Luca was sound asleep, his monitor on the table, and now she just needed Lydia here so they could finally clear the air.

Headlights suddenly lit the gravel path leading towards the house. Ryann frowned; Sam couldn't possibly be coming home for the night. She'd never leave Luciana alone at the hospital. And then Ryann realised it wasn't Sam's car. No, it was Lydia's.

Was she already on her way here when she texted?

Ryann quietly opened the front door, stepping out onto the decking. Lydia cut the engine, climbing from her car, stopping when she found Ryann waiting for her.

"You coming in?"

"I don't want to creep you out, but I was kinda already at the end of the path."

Ryann smiled. "You were?"

"Just...I hoped you wouldn't ask me to leave if I showed up, so I thought I'd test the water first with a message."

"Then you should come in so I can lock up for the night."

"The night?"

"I mean, if you wanted to stay over..."

"I don't have my things with me," Lydia said, taking the steps up the decking. "I could go home and grab a bag..."

Ryann held out her hand, pulling Lydia against her. "Are we okay?" she asked. "I mean, do you believe that I never meant to hurt you?"

"I do. I wouldn't be here if I didn't believe you."

"Then you don't need to go home for a bag. I'll have something spare in the stuff I brought here a few days ago. You know, Sam wanted me to be prepared."

Ryann turned to head back inside, stopped by Lydia's hand wrapping around her wrist. When Ryann turned back to her, Lydia's eyes held that look they once had for Ryann.

"I'm sorry I didn't call you. I needed the night to think things over, and then I panicked. There's no excuse, but I do know that I overreacted when Jen kissed you."

"Come inside with me?" Ryann asked, angling her head towards the door. "It's getting cold out here."

"Of course."

Ryann closed the door, flicking the lock before following Lydia into the living room.

"I meant what I said to you, Lydia."

"I know. Jen doesn't mean anything to you. I should have known that and not ran out…"

"That's not what I'm talking about," Ryann said, shifting from left to right. Her gaze fell to the floor; she didn't know why she felt so nervous. "I meant—"

Lydia took Ryann's hands, holding them close to her as she drew Ryann into her body. Lydia dipped her head, finding Ryann's eyes. "Ryann…"

"I don't expect you to say it back."

Lydia lifted Ryann's hands, kissing her knuckles as she smiled against her skin. "This was never supposed to happen, Ryann. Falling in love was so far from my plans, my future. I didn't think I'd ever find anyone I'd love. I didn't think anyone would ever love *me*. I mean, I'm just me. I'm not exciting, I live for my job, and I allow the world to pass me by without taking chances.

"But you came into my life unexpectedly and then I didn't know what I was doing most days. I was thinking about you when I knew I shouldn't be. I promised to distance myself, but I couldn't. You may think that this is all one-sided, Ryann, but I can honestly tell you that it's not.

"Friday was a strange day for me; I didn't expect Jen to walk out of that room. But you wondered who I thought you were, and I *know* without a shadow of a doubt, that you're the woman I love. I know that you wouldn't do anything to hurt me—you don't have a bad bone in your body."

"You're going to make me cry," Ryann confessed, her voice breaking.

"I love you too, Ryann."

Ryann gripped Lydia's jacket, pulling her close as Ryann perched herself on the back of the couch. With Lydia standing between her legs, Ryann could only study her face. Her eyes were honest; there was no mistaking it. How they glistened...not a flicker of uncertainty. The love Lydia claimed to have for Ryann was pulsing through her, electrifying as Lydia's hands found their way to Ryann's shoulders.

"You've changed my entire outlook on life..."

Lydia stared, unshed tears gleaming in her eyes.

"But it's not just what you did for me, how you saved me. It's *everything* that I love about you, Lydia. Being with you, watching you sleep beside me...I never imagined I would find someone who cared about me the way they care about themselves. I didn't think I would find a relationship that was equal and trustworthy and pure bliss. But that's what I feel with you."

"I feel the same way," Lydia said, bringing her hands up to Ryann's face, caressing the skin across her jaw. "My life was work. Now, it's you."

"I just want you to be happy, babe. If that's with me, you know I'll never let you down."

Lydia silenced Ryann, kissing her hard.

Ryann melted into Lydia's touch, her lips caressing and removing every doubt between them. Jen had left, Lydia was here, and life was good again. It may not have been overly great since Jen kissed Ryann, but in reality, life had been significantly better since the moment Lydia and Ryann met.

The ache that settled deep in Ryann's bones told her everything she needed to know. Lydia was here and not leaving. Tonight, Ryann would worship every inch of Lydia. They loved one another...did anything else really matter?

Ryann pulled back breathlessly when her phone started to ring in her pocket.

"You should get that," Lydia said, her pupils dilated.

Ryann shook her head, leaning back in to capture Lydia's lips. "It can wait. It won't be anything important."

"It could be Sam."

"No, not yet." Ryann continued on her quest to make love to Lydia. "No chance."

The call cut out, giving Ryann the opportunity to pull Lydia flush against her body.

It didn't matter if neither were in their own beds, this was happening here and now. Luca was safely asleep upstairs, and Ryann had nothing to worry about.

Lydia pulled back. "Please, check who it was..."

"Fine," Ryann exhaled, her chest heaving with anticipation.

And then her phone started to ring again.

It was Sam.

"H-hello?"

"Only me," Sam said. "Just thought I'd let you know that baby girl Foster entered the world some thirty-seven minutes ago."

"What?" Ryann's eyes widened, happiness bursting inside of her. "Sam, that's amazing. Congratulations."

"Rhian cannot wait to meet you."

"D-did you just—?" Ryann allowed her question to trail off.

Sam cleared her throat, emotion evident. "You do so much for us, Ryann. Luca is besotted with you...Rhian will be, too."

"Wow. Kinda feels like you named her after me."

"Because we did," Sam whispered. "And she really suits it."

Lydia caressed Ryann's cheek as a tear slid down it. "Ry, what's wrong?"

"Is someone there with you?" Sam asked.

"Just...Lydia. Is that okay?"

"She showed? I'm so happy for you, Ryann."

Ryann shrugged, a blush creeping up her neck. "She showed."

"Well, I have a wife and child to get back to. Is Lydia staying over? Do you have enough food in?"

"Lydia is staying over." Ryann's voice dropped an octave as she focused on Lydia's darkening eyes. "M-more food won't be necessary, there's plenty here."

"Fab." The cheeriness in Sam's voice warmed Ryann's heart. Everyone was happy; that meant so much to Ryann. "Oh, and Ryann?"

"Y-yeah?" Ryann swallowed; Lydia's hand was slipping down the front of her jeans.

"Not on the couch, please."

Ryann reddened. *How does Sam know what's going on?*

"Or the kitchen worktop. I have to feed my child from it."

"Sam, I wouldn't."

Lydia's lips trailed Ryann's neck, her pulse throbbing with every breath against her skin.

"Mm, I'm sure you wouldn't."

Ryann had nothing.

"There's a perfectly good rug in front of the fire. Light it and woo Lydia."

"Bye, Sam."

Ryann threw her phone to the couch, dragging Lydia further into the open-plan living room. She guided Lydia down onto the rug, grabbing the control that sat at the side of the fireplace. The fire came to life, flames dancing high within seconds and lighting up Lydia's eyes. Ryann could spend forever like this, knelt between Lydia's spread legs, a tremendous amount of love almost bursting from her chest.

Ryann leaned down, her lips hovering above Lydia's. "I'm so happy you came over."

With her hands fisted and tangled in Ryann's shirt, Lydia nodded. "Me too."

Lydia suddenly flipped Ryann, her back now firmly against the rug. Every inch of her body begged for more, Lydia's hand popping the button on her jeans only leaving Ryann in a heightened state of arousal. This was common now, feeling how she did just from a single word Lydia spoke, the slightest action, but tonight was different. Perhaps it was the makeup sex they were about to have, or the fact that Ryann was truly going to make love to Lydia. She didn't know, she also wasn't going to overthink it. However this night progressed, it would be with them both naked and sweaty.

"These last two days…" Lydia paused, slowly lowering Ryann's zip. "I've felt so alone. So…lost without you."

Ryann's heart swelled.

This woman was unbelievable.

"And I know that was my own fault, but from this moment on, I never want to be without you again."

Ryann fought back tears, her back arching when Lydia lowered her mouth to the waistband of her boxers. Her hot breath teased Ryann's sensitive skin, her tongue dancing slowly, gently, across her hip.

"All I want to do is devour you, Ryann."

"Be my guest." Ryann gripped the rug beneath her as Lydia was lowering her waistband.

"To touch you all night long."

"Fuck." Ryann gritted her teeth. Lydia moved off Ryann's thighs, removing her jeans and boxers in one swift move.

When Lydia stilled, Ryann lifted her head. She knew Lydia appreciated her body art, it was impressive after all, but as Lydia's fingertips followed the outline of the sugar skull towards her inner thigh, Ryann almost lost her mind.

"I just need to know one thing, Ry."

"A-anything."

"Do I still make you wet?"

Ryann's entire world crumbled. The home she was in closed in around her. All she could feel was Lydia's touch; nothing else mattered.

"Because knowing you're wet," Lydia explained, her fingertips tracing Ryann's slick lips, "makes me soaked."

"Babe, please…"

Lydia disappeared lower, spreading Ryann's legs as she settled on her stomach between her thighs. Each breath from Lydia further teased Ryann, every word having the potential to send her over the edge.

"Mm." Lydia separated Ryann's lips, the tip of her tongue teasing her clit. Every nerve ending lit up, a heat tearing through Ryann's body as Lydia applied more pressure.

"Holy shit!" Ryann's mouth clamped shut, her hands found her face. As much as she wanted to writhe and moan, Ryann had to remember that they weren't alone in the house. "Babe…"

Lydia sunk her fingers inside Ryann, slowly, deeply. This was excruciating, Ryann knew that, but she loved every second that Lydia's hands were on her body. Inside her. All over her skin.

"I've missed you." Lydia suddenly sucked Ryann's clit between her lips, her tongue rolling over the hardened bud.

Ryann could only tangle her fingers in Lydia's hair, forcing her face against her soaked, throbbing sex. Ryann bucked and moaned, gasping when Lydia added another finger. It took everything within her not to cry out; Ryann needed this to last a little longer.

Having Lydia here, inside her and fucking her like she meant the world, Ryann's emotions became overwhelming. Just two days ago when Jen left the studio, Ryann thought her happiness was over. She thought Lydia wouldn't ever give her the time of day again, but she'd been wrong. Lydia was very much in her life. And, in love with her.

"I-I need…" Ryann loosened her grip on the back of Lydia's head, her hand eventually falling away and gripping the rug once again. "Shit, I need you to fuck me harder."

Lydia looked up through hooded eyes, a smirk forming on her mouth. She climbed up Ryann's body, crashing her lips against Ryann's, and sunk deeper. "Whatever you need, I'm your girl."

Ryann's world turned black; every limb tingled. Lydia really was her girl. In every sense of the word. But it was how Lydia felt against her that shattered everything Ryann felt. The good, the bad, the uncertain. Lydia was everything Ryann wanted in life, and she refused to lose her.

"You feel so good," Lydia whispered, her thumb pressing against Ryann's swollen clit. "And I really need you to come for me so we can take this elsewhere. I want to fuck you all night long." Lydia kissed Ryann, their foreheads pressed together. "I know you want to. You're so tight."

Ryann gave into her arousal; Lydia deserved that.

As Lydia's body rocked above Ryann, the sound of sex the only sign of life around the house, Ryann gripped Lydia against her, biting down on her shoulder as she came undone beneath her.

Hard and intense.

Ryann pulled back, gasping. "Don't stop. Fuck don't stop."

Lydia pushed Ryann's orgasm to its limits. "I want every piece of you."

"S-still coming." Ryann shuddered, her body convulsing as wave after wave of pleasure tore through her. "O-oh."

Lydia slowed, but Ryann knew that wouldn't be where their night ended. Lydia had a look in her eyes that confirmed exactly that. A look that Ryann was more than prepared to enjoy for the foreseeable future.

"You...are just..." Ryann trailed off, exhaling a long breath, her chest heaving.

Lydia quirked an eyebrow. "All yours?"

Ryann bit her lip when Lydia eased her fingers out of her, sucking them into her mouth. "All mine."

CHAPTER TWENTY-SEVEN

Three months later...
Lydia shoved the last of her belongings into her suitcase, her aviators sitting atop her head in anticipation for the sun that would soon touch her skin. Her sun lotion sat wedged into her shoes, her perfumes wrapped up in her clothes, her bikinis just waiting to be removed from her luggage.

Holidaying together was considered the make or break of a relationship, but Lydia wasn't worried. Not in the slightest. Spending time with Ryann in a hotter climate was going to strengthen them. Sangria on the beach, late dinners sitting at the water's edge. Lydia had been waiting for this moment since the night they booked their flights together.

Lately, *everything* was done together.

When Lydia wasn't working late or away from home consulting with companies, Ryann was at her place. Breakfast, lunch, and dinner were rarely eaten alone anymore. Their relationship hadn't slowed, it hadn't faltered. Since the night Lydia declared her love for Ryann, nothing had been the same.

She dropped down onto the edge of her bed, smiling as her

eyes landed on Ryann's leather jacket hanging off the top of the door. That item of clothing had become a part of the fixtures around Lydia's home, a permanent reminder of their relationship. The first time they touched one another.

Her body shuddered.

"Babe, you almost ready?"

Lydia cleared her throat. "Yeah. Just zipping up. I'll be down in a few."

"Okay, well give me a shout when you're ready to bring your luggage down. I'll grab it for you."

That was sweet. But it was also Ryann. She couldn't do enough for Lydia, always being chivalrous. Just perfect in every sense of the word.

"It's okay, I can manage."

Ryann suddenly bounded up the stairs, clearly taking them two at a time to reach Lydia quickly. "I said I've got it." Ryann leaned against the doorframe of the bedroom, her eyes bright and excited. "Can't wait to get away with you."

"You've been like a child on Christmas morning since last week."

"What can I say?" Ryann lifted a shoulder. "I'm going to be living it up in the sun with the most beautiful woman in the world."

Lydia held out her hand, ushering Ryann closer. "Come here..."

Ryann approached, straddling Lydia's lap.

"You're everything to me, you know." Lydia's hands fell to Ryann's ass, holding her securely in place.

"Hard to believe." Ryann blew out a deep breath, shaking her head as a blush crept onto her cheeks. "But this break away, meeting your parents...I'm super excited."

"They're going to love you."

Lydia had no doubt in her mind that her parents would

welcome Ryann with open arms. She just had that vibe about her. Every parent's dream. The one woman every mother wanted to welcome into her family.

"And Crete?"

The plan was to spend two weeks in Spain with Lydia's parents, before flying on to Crete for two weeks with Ryann's mum and partner. Lydia knew Ryann wasn't overjoyed with the idea, but she couldn't avoid her mum forever.

"Crete is...I don't know," Ryann paused, running her hands down her face. "I'm feeling a little apprehensive."

"You know your mum can't wait to see you."

"I know, but I don't know *him*. I'm also not sure I want to know him."

"Beautiful..." Lydia paused, searching Ryann's eyes. "I know you don't trust easily, it's actually one of the things I love about you most, but your mum is happy and in love."

"I know. It just still stings, you know?"

"Completely understandable. But, if we arrive there and you see how happy he makes her, can you welcome him into your life?"

Ryann remained silent for a moment, clearly pondering that thought. "I guess so."

"Then all I ask is that you try." Lydia leaned up, capturing Ryann's lips. "It's all you can do."

"But first, we have two weeks in Spain." Ryann grinned, climbing from Lydia's lap. "And that's about to start any moment now."

Lydia stood, forcing her suitcase closed and lying across it. "I'll crush, you zip."

"I crushed a long time ago, babe." Ryann winked, sending Lydia into a fit of laughter. This easy-going lifestyle they'd become accustomed to was really working for Lydia. "Did I ever tell you how much I love your laugh?"

"Once or twice."

"Well, I'm telling you again." Ryann secured the zip, shaking her head when Lydia started to go red in the face. "What exactly do you have in this case? It looks like you have your entire wardrobe."

"Not much. Just enough to see me over. My perfume..."

Ryann shot out of the room, poking her head around the door of the bathroom. "Um...how much perfume have you packed? I only see one bottle on your stand."

"E-eleven."

Ryann's eyes widened. "Who the hell needs eleven bottles of perfume?"

Lydia huffed, climbing from her luggage and shrugging. "I like to smell good."

"Woman, you're crazy."

Ryann looked out across the river, leant back against the bonnet of Lydia's car. The wind blustered around them, the water wilder than it should have been for the time of year. Spring had come to an end, summer was in full swing, but the weather down on the promenade today told a different story. Climate change really was happening.

Lydia leant against her car beside Ryann, her legs crossed at the ankles while their hands intertwined. Lydia had asked Ryann if they could stop at the river before heading to the airport, and Ryann willingly agreed. For the first time since they'd met, Ryann was standing in the very place she'd contemplated ending it all.

"You okay?" Lydia squeezed Ryann's hand.

Ryann smiled weakly. "Yeah. I'm okay."

"How does it feel being back here?"

Ryann thought hard about her response. She couldn't say she felt a particular way about it, other than disbelief at the position she'd once put herself in. Her chin started to tremble, a tingling in her face becoming apparent as heat crept through her entire body.

"Feels okay, but *I* feel like a dickhead."

Lydia pushed off her car, shaking her head. "Maybe we shouldn't have come here."

"No, it's fine. I promise. Just...I can't believe I got to that point. Instead of speaking to someone, instead of asking for help, I climbed over that fucking railing."

Ryann felt her own anger bubbling away under the surface. Anger for what she'd not only put herself through, but Lydia, too.

"You were in a bad place, Ry."

Ryann scoffed. "Not so bad that I had to think about ending my life."

Ryann was right. She knew she was. There were people out there in much worse positions than she'd been in. People who'd become disconnected from their family. People who used drink and drugs as a means of getting by because life was too much to handle. People who didn't have a single soul they could turn to. Ryann wasn't in that position—she never had been—so coming here and doing what she'd planned to do only made her hate herself more than she originally had.

"You know, even though Jen did what she did...even though I lost a lot, climbing over those railings has to be the single most stupid, pathetic thing I've ever done. And I know I was at a low point, I know anyone can find themselves in that position, but imagine if I'd gone through with it. Imagine if I'd thrown myself into that water..."

"I don't want to imagine it," Lydia said, her voice breaking.

"The thought of you not showing up when you did...I don't know." Ryann ran her fingers through her hair, the fresh undercut tickling her fingertips. "I was in such a stubborn mood, there was no reasoning with myself."

"Do you truly believe you would have jumped?" Lydia asked, standing in front of Ryann. "Whether I'd been here or not, can you honestly say you would have done it?"

"No," Ryann confessed. "I'm not sure I have the balls—the

strength—to do something like that. And I know, I know it makes me sound stupid, but something would have held me back in those final moments. Whether that would have been Luca, my mum, you…I don't know. But I don't believe I could have gone through with it."

"It was a cry for help."

Ryann nodded, chewing her bottom lip as she lowered her eyes to the floor. Could Lydia see the embarrassment coursing through Ryann? The shame she felt. Could everyone around see it, too? That's certainly how it felt as her eyes flickered around the open space. People judging, laughing internally at just how ridiculous Ryann had once been.

Ryann angled her body away from the eyes of the strangers she felt penetrating her, bearing witness to her shame. Her eyes were wet with tears, but she didn't need this. Inside, deep down, Ryann was happier than she'd ever been.

"Well, I'm certainly happy that you chose to climb back over. That you trusted me enough to be the one to listen."

Ryann lifted her hand, settling it against the side of Lydia's face. "Thank you. Seriously."

"You're welcome."

"I never meant to frighten you that night, Lydia. I never meant to put you in a position where you felt you had to approach me. But I am glad that you did. Just…seeing your smile, your eyes, it gave me some hope. It told me that I could be okay if someone like you had taken the time to stop and talk to me. You saw all the people here; nobody else came close."

"Some people don't like to get involved."

Ryann smiled. "No, and I don't blame them. Who has time for other people's crap?"

"It wasn't crap. It was you needing a friend. Someone who would listen to what you were going through."

"You told me I needed new friends…but I didn't really have any to begin with."

"I know." Lydia's smile was faint, but it was there. "If I'd known, I wouldn't have let you leave that night."

"You'd done more than enough for me. I'll always be grateful for that."

"So, what's next?" Lydia asked, pulling Ryann away from the car. "Some friends?"

"Nah, I have exactly who I need in my life." Ryann's arms wrapped around Lydia's waist, her lips pressing against the tip of her nose.

As she pulled back, staring deeply into Lydia's eyes, Ryann's entire being lit up with gratitude, admiration, and love. Every morning when she woke with Lydia, Ryann felt an undeniable sense of love, but standing here now, at the place they first met, she was overwhelmed by how much had happened in such a small space of time.

Some five months ago, Ryann would have fallen to her knees for a woman like Lydia. She would have given up the entire world to feel just an ounce of what she felt right now. Though at one time she believed she couldn't possibly be good enough for this woman, standing here had proven that she was. That she always would be.

She felt safe and whole with Lydia. She felt a constant euphoria from the simplest of touches, words. As Lydia stood before Ryann, a genuine love and honesty beaming from her eyes, Ryann could only drink in the moment. She wanted to remember this feeling forever.

Lydia cocked her head. "You left me for a second."

"I was just thinking."

"About?"

Ryann held Lydia close, her head dipping as she placed a chaste kiss to Lydia's lips. "You. How much I love you. How beautiful you are...inside and out. I could go on."

"Don't. You'll make me all emotional and I don't want mascara running down my face on the way to the airport."

"Then I believe it's time to hit the road and catch a flight."
"You excited?"
"To lounge around with you in a bikini? Always…"

Sign up to my mailing list to be the first to hear about new releases, and to be in with a chance of winning books!

www.melissaterezeauthor.com

DID YOU ENJOY IT?

Thank you for purchasing Before You Go.

I hope you enjoyed it. Please consider leaving a review on your preferred site. As an independent author, reviews help to promote our work. One line or two really does make the difference.

Thank you, truly.

Love,
Melissa x

ABOUT THE AUTHOR

Oh, hi! It's nice to see you!

I'm Melissa Tereze, author of The Arrangement, Mrs Middleton, and other bestsellers. Born, raised, and living in Liverpool, UK, I spend my time writing angsty romance about complex, real-life, women who love women. My heart lies within the age-gap trope, but you'll also find a wide range of different characters and stories to sink your teeth into.

SOCIAL MEDIA

You can contact me through my social media or my website. I'm mostly active on Twitter.

Twitter: @MelissaTereze
Facebook: www.facebook.com/Author.MelissaTereze
Instagram: @melissatereze_author
Find out more at: www.melissaterezeauthor.com
Contact: info@melissaterezeauthor.com

Also by Melissa Tereze

Another Love Series
The Arrangement (Book One)
The Call (Book Two)

The Ashforth Series
Playing For Her Heart (Book One)
Holding Her Heart (Book Two)

Other Novels
At First Glance
Always Allie
Mrs Middleton
Breaking Routine
In Her Arms
Forever Yours
The Heat of Summer
Forget Me Not
More Than A Feeling
Where We Belong: Love Returns
Naked

Co-Writes
Teach Me (With Jourdyn Kelly)

Titles under L.M Croft (Erotica)

Pieces of Me

Printed in Great Britain
by Amazon